BURNING
SECRETS

BURNING SECRETS

Book Two in
the Scottish Mysteries

CLIO GRAY

urbanepublications.com

First published in Great Britain in 2017
by Urbane Publications Ltd
Suite 3, Brown Europe House, 33/34 Gleaming Wood Drive,
Chatham, Kent ME5 8RZ
Copyright ©Clio Gray, 2017

A CIP catalogue record for this book is available
from the British Library.

ISBN 978-1-911331-29-2
EPUB 978-1-911331-30-8
MOBI 978-1-911331-31-5

Design and Typeset by Michelle Morgan

Cover by Michelle Morgan

Printed and bound by CPI Group (UK) Ltd, Croydon, CR0 4YY

urbanepublications.com

THE SCOTTISH MYSTERIES SERIES

BOOK 1 – DEADLY PROSPECTS

BOOK 2 – BURNING SECRETS

BOOK 3 – HIDDEN PASTS

'Clio is that rarest of finds, a natural writer...'
Jan Rutherford, Scottish Booktrust

'Gray is a writer you can rely on not to write quite like anyone else... ...more Mervyn Peake and Gormenghast than Jane Austen and Sense and Sensibility...'
Lesley McDowell & Colin Waters, Scottish Sunday Herald

'Clio has an incredible flair for atmosphere, imagery, setting and description...There is a strangeness and originality about her work that absorbed me...'
Alan Bissett, author

BURNING SECRETS

CONTENTS

1   Beginnings

2   Light Beyond the Sea

3   Horse Thieves and Flag Breakers

4   Ockle, and the Other Side of Things

5   A Swan amongst Islands

6   Simmy, and the Recompense of the Dead

7   Getting There, Even if it's Not Where You Want to Go

8   Missing Minerals, Missing Men

9   Burned Down Bothies, Ripped Down Flags

10 Wicker Coffins, Floating Chapels

11 Consecrated Boards on Unconsecrated Waters

12 Inside the Snail

13 Strangers and Sundials

14 Being Strong, Being Weak

15 Everyone Going Whichways

16 Broken Eggs, Broken Men

17 Tapping a Way Back to Life

18 The Lion Flexes its Claws

19 And Now the Riddle

20 The Misdeeds of the Dying

21 Like Fleas on a Dog

22	The Blind and the Not-So-Dumb
23	God Forgets His Duties, but Oswald Does Not
24	The Briars that Bind
25	Talking, and Towers that Might Not Be So Impregnable
26	Perfect Days, Not-So-Perfect Problems
27	Loyalty, and Living Up to It
28	Bad Discoveries, Better Plans
29	Respect and Retribution
30	From the Ends of the Earth
31	Dead Men Alive, and Live Men Rowing
32	Limbs From Limbs, Skin From Bone
33	Well, That's One Way to Learn
34	Black Slugs, White Clover
35	Sleeping Vials and Venom
36	The Builders Go On Forever
37	The Nocturnal and the Night
38	Sheep and Lambs
39	Hands that Need to Be Washed
40	And So He Cries
41	Tiger Taiga
42	And Everything Changes, Once Again
43	Another Shift in the Equation
44	The Bad Dying of the Almost Dead
45	As Always, Another Bloody Book
46	Revelation, Disappointment, and Generosity
47	Decisions
48	Narrow Tracks, Wide Worlds
49	Hands that Need to Be Washed

Historical Note

Map of Scotland showing location of
Ardnamurchan Peninsula and locale of *Burning Secrets*

CHAPTER 1

BEGINNINGS

Strontian, Ardnamurchan Peninsula, December 1869

The brief respite of Advent Sunday had come and gone, and back to work went the men of Ardnamurchan Peninsula to the lead-mines that kept them solvent. Hard labour and long hours, but a better livelihood than many had along this crooked shore, other villages bled dry as the youngsters left for Glasgow – girls to the factories, boys to the shipyards on the Clyde – leaving them husks without animation, old men and women ageing on in their small black houses, starved of news, work and food.

Not so for Strontian, and Matthias McQuat took pleasure in the patterns the frost had scrawled across the heather and moss as he climbed the hill, in the thin plates of ice the night had scratched over the burns that ran down the brae, the plink and plash of water running beneath them reminding him of the overheated glass old Bob Farrow used to make in the village before he'd died and the glassworks gone with him. Matthias took the same path every morning start of work-week, the same path up the hill to scan for signs of stress in the workings below; hollows in the earth that could be indicators of a pit-corridor's imminent collapse; patches of dying vegetation, or grass uncommonly lush, that might mean the leaching up from the lead of some other mineral they could put to their advantage, maybe one they'd not come across previously, as had happened before. It was the Age of Industry, after all, a time when knowledge was currency to be swapped and shared, and Matthias McQuat couldn't get enough of it. He'd been born with curiosity and had the aptitude to exploit it, earning him a scholarship at the monks' school over the water from Corran. Seven years studying there, learning more about mathematics, geology and engineering than all several generations of peninsular men stacked end to end, the monks unfolding the world out at his feet, Matthias paying them back ever since with tithes from the mine-profits, a due written into his contract and neither stinted nor begrudged.

Matthias looked down from the hill and saw his labourers threading their way up the frost-bitten track from their strung-out homes, the meeting and greeting between them and the foremen whose pocketbooks were already out, pencils licked, divvying up the duties that needed doing, which workings needed shoring or extending, who was to be chopping and shaping wood for pit-props, paring it into timbers to be carried down the ever-extending labyrinth of tunnels being burrowed out beneath the hill. He saw a straggler running up the track behind them, pushing a black curl of hair impatiently to one side as something caught his attention and down he went on one knee, shoving his fingers straight through a sheet of ice and plucking a stone from the freezing water below, holding it up, looking at it this way and that. This time-lagger, had he been anyone else, would have been severely ticked off, a black smudge put on his time-card, for Matthias had the notion of each day's passing - and the need to use it wisely - ingrained into his body. Every hour of every day of the seven years spent under the monks' tutelage had been marked out by a bell, or stratified by hour candles. Primitive techniques but precise and honed, training the men within the monastery to become accurate instruments, acquiring the rhythm of bell and candle, as Matthias's body had, still adhered to thirty eight years later. He should have felt anger, then, at this straggly lad with his hand just pulled from a freezing pool but instead he regarded with interest the boy with the rook-black hair holding up the stone he'd secured from the water, watching as he gazed at it with the same intent others reserved for rubies and gold. This lad was no ordinary worker from the village. This was Jed Thornbrough, who'd appeared out of nowhere a couple of months before, landing on Matthias's doorstep with the astonishing news that the latest mineral sample Matthias had sent off to Edinburgh was of such great interest it had been sent on to London, to one of the country's most eminent geologists. And more astonishing still, this geologist had announced the sample virtually unique and of a type seen only once before, the previous specimen coming also from Strontian – delivered and catalogued half a century before by this same geologist's father – but then misplaced, existing now only in his father's sketches and notes. And so important was this discovery that the geologist had straightaway called for a volunteer to go and investigate and up popped Jed Thornbrough, the only person keen enough to set off on its trail from one end of the kingdom to the other, from London to the Highlands of Scotland, to the peninsula of Ardnamurchan, one of the most westerly corners of that wild and inhospitable country.

It took Jed the best part of two months to get there, taking a boat from London to Aberdeen, the railway from there to Glasgow, travelling the rest of the way on foot since he'd run out of money and had no way to take one of the steamers that regularly plied their way up Loch Linnhe into Fort William. Jed was unconcerned for the hardships and dangers as he tramped alone along the paths and tracks many would have thought impassable. He blew into the village of Strontian like a westerly gale comes in from the Atlantic, unexpected and unpredictable, with an edge to him sharp as flint and a gaze that took in everything about him, from the eagles soaring over the mountains to the otters, seals and seaweeds that pushed at the sea loch's edge.

From the very first moment Matthias opened his door to this small seeker of the new his life had been irreversibly altered, not that he'd known it straightaway. The lad had been tired to the point of exhaustion, clothes torn and shredded by the brambles, bogs and bushes he'd toiled through. He'd only one bag which, once unpacked, Matthias saw contained nothing more than several pairs of socks all worn out at their heels, none in pairs, all stinking like a midden trodden over by pigs; a few dirty undergarments; several books – all well-handled, miniscule notes marked in their margins; a dozen pencils and a well-made knife for those pencils' sharpening; several notebooks jotted through with drawings of the plants, animals and minerals he'd seen on his way. His pack also contained a microscope – expensive, hand-made, with five interchangeable lenses, and with the microscope Jed also produced slides – all clean and tightly regimented within a custom-made, velvet-lined case, complete with a packet of silk squares for the cleaning of their glass.

That microscope was the most perfect thing Matthias had ever seen, apart from Jed himself, who threw himself into his work with a fervour rarely seen in this neck of the woods. His given task was to map out the mines, take detailed notes of the various minerals associated with the lead-workings: where they were found, in what capacity they were linked with the ore; in particular he was looking for further examples of the mineral Matthias had sent to Edinburgh, the indirect cause of Jed coming here in the first place. This last task was hampered by Matthias not having specific note of where it had been found – a hard ask in a working mine. Jed didn't take issue, just set to straightaway with string and pegs, dividing into squares the vague area Matthias had pointed at, one of which he methodically searched through every day, no matter the weather.

But there was so much more to Jed Thornbrough than that, as Matthias soon discovered. He was a constant whirlwind, never seeming to stop unless he was actually asleep, a task he went at as he did every other: something that needed doing and doing well, always going to his bed at the same time each evening, always waking and dressing precisely seven hours later. Which was exactly what Matthias did himself, giving him the oddest feeling that Jed was a younger echo of himself who had been existing unknown in the outer world all this time and finally returned home.

The weeks following the arrival of Jed Thornbrough were for Matthias a strange and exciting time, at least until all that business started over on Havengore when it felt like a sinkhole had opened up beneath him ready to swallow him whole.

CHAPTER 2

LIGHT BEYOND THE SEA

Advent Sunday came and went for Matthias, and for others too. For Sholto McKay it started as he rounded Cape Wrath at the very tip of Scotland. Where he came from – Trondheim in Norway – Advent Sunday was considered the first day of the ecclesiastical calendar, celebrated with wreaths, hymns and candles. Sholto was not religious in any specific way but he keenly missed the old traditions that had brightened the streets during the darkest month of the year, the loss of colour and light they brought to every household window. All that surrounded him now was sea, the day dimmed and brightened at the same time by the snow that squalled and fell, settling lightly on the water for a few moments before being subsumed by salt and wave. Sholto was miserable within his damp socks that squelched with every step he took in his even damper boots. He lurched across the deck of the ancient boat endeavouring to take them on the final leg of their journey and peered into the gloom, trying to get a glimpse of land, spy a chink of light from some faraway homestead, some candle in some obscure window; but all he saw was snow and sea and the darkness of the day that would soon be done in completely. He was frustrated they'd been so long on the water given the relatively short distance they needed to travel, the crew diverting every time they spotted the water boiling with fish and chucking out their nets, waiting a few hours before pulling them in again. It had been almost a week since he and Brogar Finn departed Helmsdale harbour, together with their new helpmeets Gilligan and Hugh, acquired after he and Brogar had investigated the incidents connected to the Kildonan Gold Rush, a Gold Rush Sholto knew would officially end at midnight on the 31st of December, several weeks from now. And thank God for it, he thought. It had been his first foray in the employ of the Pan-European Mining Company of Lundt and McCleery's and he'd been completely unprepared for the violent events that had happened in its wake. That he now understood the whys and wherefores of the entire event did not decrease his sadness for the loss of life engendered. Neither he nor Brogar had been pleased when the Company deemed it expedient to keep them in Scotland rather than recall them back to Scandinavia, nor had either heard previously of their present destination: the Ardnamurchan Peninsula and the Galena Ore mines of Strontian.

Ardnamurchan was an odd sounding name, but Sholto was a linguist and had no difficulty getting his tongue around the syllables or what it meant: *High Place of the Sea Hounds* being its literal translation from the Gaelic, a language Sholto had become passably familiar with in Kildonan; Sea Hounds were perhaps the otters, or maybe the seals he'd spotted not long back, their whiskered faces popping out of the water by the bow the closer the boat got to land. Despite previous misgivings he was intrigued by the place they were going to, though had not perked up nearly as much as Brogar on this journey, proving himself once more to be the man Sholto was not – supremely comfortable on the sea and in the company of sea-going men.

Earlier that day, as they wiped their lips from yet another breakfast of fish – which also comprised every other meal they'd been given on board – he'd brought the subject up. Sholto liked fish, and had enjoyed the variety of both its kind and cooking whilst on this boat, but was beginning to hanker for food that was green and crisp, or sweet and baked.

'I don't suppose you realise, Brogar, but it's Advent Sunday,' Sholto said, 'and I can't tell you how much I would pay right this minute for a slice of Advent Cake.'

Brogar laughed out loud and swept his arm out to encompass the broad horizon of the sea.

'But my God, Sholto, where do you think men like this are going to conjure up something like that?'

To which Sholto, of course, had no answer.

'You'd not even mention it,' Brogar went on, 'if you'd had to shovel down your neck half the things I've done on my travels just to stay alive.'

The rebuke was timely and true, for Brogar had ventured more widely for the Company, and far longer, than Sholto ever would or could. He'd shuddered with the rest of the crew the night before when Brogar entertained them all with a few tales of those times, including a graphic description of having to butcher and eat the raw flesh of a frozen pack-dog when he'd been stranded somewhere in the middle of the Siberian tundra. It illustrated to Sholto just how different he and Brogar were temperamentally, and experientially. But they'd rubbed along fine together during the Kildonan incident, proving themselves to be two complementary halves of a well-functioning whole, and Sholto was as proud as he was glad to have a man like Brogar at his side.

You have to look on everything we do as an adventure and a challenge. That's what Brogar had told him, and that was what

Sholto tried to do now as he looked out into the drawing down of this Advent night. At least he wasn't stuck in that God-awful subterranean office in Trondheim, his working environment until a couple of months before, and a place Sholto never wanted to go back to. He forgot about his cold, wet feet, concentrating instead on the remarkable fact that he, Sholto McKay, was heading off for new and unknown adventures, just as Brogar had said they would. As if on cue the snow chose that moment to cease, the sun still a couple of fingers above the horizon, and Sholto breathed in sharply. The coast they were approaching was fractured into a thousand inlets, reminding him strongly of the Norwegian fjords, and to his right rose the dark humps of the Outer Hebrides, wallowing like a pod of beached whales out across the Minch. A few moments later, the boat passed between the Isle of Skye and the mainland, and there were the jutting triangular heads of the snow-covered Cuillin mountains, shining like New Year beacons, suddenly flooded a deep dark red as the sun went down, as if they'd been poured over with blood.

New beginnings, Sholto thought, the boat slewing away to the south-east and bringing them within sight of the Ardnamurchan Peninsula. *And thank God I'm here, and nowhere else.*

CHAPTER 3

HORSE THIEVES AND FLAG BREAKERS

Archie Louden was picking over his horse's nether right hoof, his back cricked into the shape of a crescent moon as he bent down low, squinting to see what might be caught between horn and hoop. His anxiety made his sight all the poorer and he fidgeted in his pocket, hoiking out the precious pair of spectacles stored there in their leather case. He released them, thrusting the glasses onto the bridge of his nose, feeling their metal frame pinch and stay. With his glasses on it didn't take long to see the ridge of splinter that had jammed itself into the gaping shoe. He cursed, for he had only an hour since picked this horse up at Kilchoan, having had the great stroke of fortune to find a boat in Oban coming over to the peninsula this afternoon, saving him a long and tedious overland journey. But now he was being slowed up all over again. It was obvious the shoe had been newly shod though not well, for one of the nails had already loosened and was sticking out where it should have been flat, hence enabling this little skelf of thorn the animal must have trodden on to get caught beneath. He took its shaft between his pincers, braced his shoulder against the piebald's shank, and yanked it free. The horse shied briefly against the nick of pain, then snuffled and whinnied, glad of the relief, and Archie hoped to God the nail would hold fast the last few miles home and that the entire shoe would not be cast because of it.

It had been a hard haul this trip, and Archie Louden swore again as he caught his thumb in the stirrup strap which made him drop the pincers in the mud. He was up to his wrist in it before he managed to retrieve them, and sighed as he brushed his hand against the rough burlap of his leggings before replacing the pincers in his pack-bag. They would have to remain mucky until he got back to the island and had time to clean them properly. He brushed his hand against the grass to wipe it as best he could on the swags of bent-over reeds and then removed his spectacles, replacing them gently into their case, and the case back into his pocket. As he did so he reflected on how bad, how blurred and flat, his world became without them, appalled at his dependence on a couple of pieces of glass held inside a wire frame, and sent up a quick prayer for the man who had created them, the same man he was on his way to now.

He stroked the rough mane of the mare, saddened that her owner had allowed it to get into such a tangle, knotted with hardened mud that he tried to loosen, though without much success. The truth of it was that he was exhausted from all the travelling and might have done better to stop the night in Oban as originally planned. Still, there it was; he was almost home now. He smiled to think on the sparse, rock-lined shores that single word evoked, and of Gustav Wengler, his employer, the creator of his spectacles, and how truly extraordinary that man was. Louden's mother always said that people were like clocks, some keeping to their proper hours, others going slow or fast, the rare few showing one time but choosing to strike out another. These last, she said, were the ones who made mankind stride forward to do the best that men could do. And if such an analogy held true then it was undoubtedly applicable to Gustav Wengler, who had more sides to his intelligence than a clock has minutes in its day; a man who had a way of thinking so peculiar it passed most folk by, including Archie, who was no slouch in the knowledge department and had several advanced degrees from well-thought-of universities, and not only in Scotland. Archie shook his head, keen to get back to Havengore and Wengler, as he always was when he was away. It was the one part of his job he disliked – these sporadic leavings, being sent away to England or abroad to fetch whatever Gustav needed to test out one theory or another. Such journeys gave him opportunities other scholars could only dream of, but all Archie ever wanted was to be allowed to stay on Havengore permanently, be a proper part of whatever new thesis Wengler was working on. And the more he thought on it, the more he longed to be back. He was no fool; knew that Wengler cared less for Archie's assistance than he did for his many books. Every time Archie reappeared – even after several months' absence – Wengler would greet him as he always did, glancing up from his work for a moment to cast a critical glance over Archie's dishevelment, shrivelling his nose at the smells brought in by his travelling before turning back to doing whatever it was he'd been doing all the while Archie had been away; but it made no difference to Archie. He knew how privileged he was to be working in whatever capacity for Gustav Wengler, the famous mathematician, the even more famous recluse. But this time he knew his homecoming would be different and that Wengler would be counting down the days until Archie returned, because this time he was bringing with him something Gustav had been trying to locate for almost as many years as Archie had been with Wengler, which was almost a decade to the day. And so close was Archie now that he could see the shallow saltings on the other side of the strait and the pale outlines of the massive stone buildings rising up from the flatlands of the island like a fabulous raft of swans, their white walls glistening in the light of the fast-dying sun. It made Archie's blood pulse all the faster just to see them and know he was one of the few privy to their purpose. He was almost within reach, and all that separated him from the island was the boat needed to take him across the water, and so he spurred his piebald on.

A quarter hour later he reached the point at Ardslingnish that poked out into the sea like the nose of an inquisitive fox, and straightaway he jumped down and went to raise the flag to alert the ferryman that someone wanted crossing to one of the islands out in the Sound. He was dismayed to find the flag ripped from its ropes, sagged to a limp shroud in the mud at the flag-pole's foot. Archie clicked his nails nervously, wondering if this meant smugglers were abroad. The light was dimming fast, the sea a dull roll of grey untroubled by any breakers this far inland, unruffled by the wind – a good night for bringing in contraband from the Continental boats that could be lying out there unseen in deep waters. Archie supposed he could ride on, get to the next ferry point, but by then it would certainly be too dark to cross and he'd have to stop the night on this side of the Sound anyway. Instead he plucked at the ruined flag, wondering if he could get it working, get its bright white square lifted so it could be seen by Hesketh Wood the ferryman, who spent his days rowing up and down the coast, checking the ferry posts with his telescope. He got his glasses out again and examined the flag a little closer only to find that such a quick mend would not be possible, and he would have to spend some time to fold and stitch a new running line to take the rope through the banner's edge. He swore at the storm or the smugglers that had brought it down and although he had the means to set it all straight, get it up again, he knew it would take far longer than the last half hour of light there was left to the evening. He sighed again, gazing across the water towards Havengore.

Nearly is only almost – some old proverb from way back when, whose words sounded unbidden in his head as he led his horse back to the pile of straw bales and peat blocks that had been fashioned into a hut. He knew he was defeated and would get no further that night. Best thing was to snug himself up, get a lamp lit, light a fire, rest up. Come dawn he would mend the flag as best he could and get it flying. Over to the island soon afterwards. He was frustrated to be so close and yet so far, but had no other option, so he hitched his horse up to the iron spike that had been rammed into the earth beside the hut and left her snorting and at ease, plucking spasmodically at the straw stalks protruding in abundant mouthfuls from its makeshift walls.

When he came to the front of the bothy he was both surprised and pleased to see a light already glowing through a crack in the bales that had been plugged into the doorway to keep out the cold, glad he had someone else to pass the night with, someone with whom to swap tales and maybe a little food and drink, someone who had got here before him and already built up a fire against the night. He was a little irked this person hadn't bothered to wash out the ruined ferry flag as he would have had done, nor tried to mend it himself; but maybe, Archie thought, whoever was inside was not wise to the ways of travelling about these parts, or maybe had not the means to mend it as Archie had. Either way, he would be company at least, and nothing bad about that.

He was not a suspicious man but had enough traveller's nous to go back the few paces to his horse and pat down his saddlebags, removing a small package and placing it carefully inside a pocket of his jerkin from where it could not easily be stolen. He took another flatter object out and slipped it into his shoulder bag, removing his outer coat before slinging the bag over his neck again to keep it close before re-donning his coat. He knew he was probably being overcautious but these parts were rife with men who valued commodities over life, who daily played the odds with the excise men scouring every bank and bay for those bringing in contraband from France and beyond. The last thing Archie did before entering the bothy was to give the blanket he kept beneath his saddle a quick shake to rid it of excess mud then rolled it up, placed it like a scarf about his neck so as to leave his hands free to remove the hay bales that were barring entrance into the hut.

As he approached the bothy he heard a noise behind him and had only halfway turned when a truncheon hit a wicked blow to the side of his head that felled him before he'd time to take another step. The man who'd wielded the truncheon called out to his companion inside the hut, who now burled through the ragged layers of hay-bales as if they'd been made of feathers, and within a few seconds they'd dragged the unconscious Archie inside.

'Not very clever,' the first man puffed, as he started rifling through Archie's pockets.

'Not 'alf at all,' said the other. 'Did ye see where he put them?'

'Aye,' replied the first. 'Jerkin. Left side. And something else inside the bag.'

'Hope they're worth summat,' commented his partner, as he tugged Archie's coat open, uncovered his satchel, began to undo the buckles. 'What about the horse?' he added hopefully, hearing her still chomping contentedly at the wall at the back of the hut.

'Piebald mare, maybe four years old, not tall but sturdy. Can think of plenty be glad to have another added to their plough.'

They were disturbed in their occupations by Archie Louden's sudden and unwelcome flutter back into consciousness, not having reckoned on the truncheon's blow being partially deflected by the roll of the blanket around Archie's neck, nor his fight to protect his life and what he was carrying.

'Look lively!' the nearest man shouted as he saw Archie's eyes flickering open, though was not fast enough to dodge the blow from Archie's fist punching out at him, catching him on his jaw, sending him rocking back on his heels.

'Shite, boy… 'e's seen us,' the other man grunted. He'd just had time to get his hand inside Archie's hidden pocket to retrieve his prize and now snatched it out, tearing the paper it was wrapped in, seeing the corner of something glinting finely just within.

'What'll we do? What'll we do?' his partner-in-crime was gasping, trying to right himself, rubbing at his jaw where Archie's fist had caught him. He wasn't hurt badly, only surprised, and now very frightened.

'Wheesht yur squealing,' said the other as he adjusted his stance, got to his knees, thrust one of them hard down onto Archie Louden's shoulder as he took up his heavy stick of oak, his prisoner writhing beneath him, unable to focus on the man above, only on the dark abyss beyond.

'Oh God, no, no!' Archie shouted, seeing the lifted truncheon swinging down towards him, but it came down anyway and this time with such vicious force there was no word for the pain it caused him when it hit, the wood smashing deep into his nose, driving the bones and cartilage right through his buccal palate and deep into his throat, stopping his breath, blurring his life like a flicker-book he'd once seen of a boy jumping a dyke – as slow or quick as your thumb could make him go – and felt such agony in his chest a saw might have been having at it. He could distinguish nothing outside of himself at all, only the obscure observation that he felt rain falling on his face, the warmest and gentlest kind of rain he'd ever felt, unaware that it was composed entirely of his own blood.

The two men who'd started the simple act of robbing Archie Louden looked on his prostrate body and then went outside, unhooked Archie's horse from its tethering, the piebald mare bucking once or twice, not recognising who was taking her from her pasture, calming the moment she was given a handful of wild cabbage by one of them, who'd thought to pull it up from the ground nearby.

'You didnae need to have done that,' the cabbage-pulling man was whining, sniffing back snot with every breath, choking on it, wiping a hand across his eyes.

'Not nearly,' his companion replied. 'Seen our faces, didn't he? And besides, look at this stuff. Might be worth a bloody fortune.'

He held out the small package he'd retrieved from Archie's jacket and put his thumb through the tear, ripping it wider, showing the edges of two gold-set brooches and the large jewels held within their mountings. 'Gotta be worth a pretty penny have these,' he added, 'if we can find the right handler.'

'But what about him?' the other asked, leading the piebald a few yards away to better feeding, his legs shaking with the violence of the encounter, not having expected anything like this.

'I've got it,' the older man replied. 'Didn't I always say you'd no need to get your lily-whites dirty, that I'd look after this end of things?'

The man leading the horse away could not stop his sniffling, had begun to sweat badly, had imagined in his head – when they'd heard the horse coming – some kind of sneaky, almost heroic encounter, the poor from the rich and all that, but felt an icy grip in his stomach at what might happen next.

'I'll just take the horse on a little, then?' Harald said, eager to be away, wishing that Dunstan would take the hint and do the same.

'You do that,' Dunstan's voice was gruff, maybe angry, and Harald skidded off from the hut towards the sea loch, pulling the piebald on behind him, the rising panic urging him to run and fly instead of keeping a steady pace so's the horse would follow easy and not begin to buck and fight against him.

'Should we stay for the job?' Harald asked shakily, glancing nervously out to sea, getting a mere grunt in reply.

'So, meet you where?' Harald tried to sound loud and positive, but his voice came out like the squall and pipe of a wing-shot bird.

'Meet you bloody nowhere,' Dunstan replied. 'You'll get shot of that mare over top of Corran, quick as you can. Kip with it night over if you have to, an' I'll do the tidy up here.'

The tidy up, Harald thought, and didn't like the words nor what they implied but wasn't the man to stand against Dunstan, as not many would. And when Harald was almost a quarter mile distant he heard a stuttering sort of whoosh and turned his head, looked back, saw a spraint of embers leaping high as spring-maddened larks into the darkened sky and knew the flag-hut had been set to flame and felt a lump in his throat as if the noose was already tightening about it.

Oh God, he thought, *oh God*, and crossed himself with a clumsy, shaking hand, clutching hard at the horse's reins with the other and could not stop himself, began to jog along the rough and muddy track away from Dunstan and the hut, the stolen horse protesting, whinnying, the whites of her eyes shining brightly in the falling night.

CHAPTER 4

OCKLE, AND THE OTHER SIDE OF THINGS

The cribble rasped with the rough rub of corn being passed over it, the separated flour tappering out through the mesh and against the sides of the funnel before falling with a soft *ploof* into the bowl below. Simmy looked at the meagre results of her labour with dispassion, elbows sore from going at it for too long, neck cricking as she tried to stop the dust from her eyes, blinking at the grit that had nonetheless gathered in their corners, caught at the back of her throat and mouth. She looked up and away towards the stream that wound down to the loch, and back along the narrow track that led up to the village, at the tops of the lime-and-holly hedge that ran from the village to the lych-gate of the chapel on the small knoll above. She was thinking of the rough wooden box deposited in it earlier that morning, just past dawn, and of the man it held within who had been stowed in a sack in the village ice-house for the past while, until today. At least they supposed it to be a man, going on what was left of him: the large boots and bones dragged out of the creek near the laundry pool a few weeks back.

There'd not been a flake of flesh nor hair upon him, and only a few tangles of cloth wrapped about those dark, peat-stained bones; nothing to tell who he was or where he'd come from nor how long he'd been in the water, although that he'd been in the water a long time was not in doubt. All they knew of this person was that Simmy's brother's fishing gear had caught on some of the burlap the man had maybe employed as a cloak, and brought him in. They'd assumed, given where he'd been found, that he'd possibly got himself snarled in a trawl-net, illegally going after the salmon and sea-trout that were so abundant in the sea loch at certain times of the year – fine to fish in the sea but not the sea loch which was in the purview of the estate; either that or they were the remnants of one of those outside men who used this coast as their own, who never considered the likes of Simmy and Harald, who brought in Christ knew what from the Continent to sell on in Glasgow despite the excise men sweeping through their village every now and then, disrupting everything, stamping their horses through grass and paddock, eating their food, drinking their drink, or what little of either the villagers had to spare. This last seemed most likely, since no one had come looking for him, not in all the time he must have been lodged down there below the water, caught up in the bottom reeds or stuck beneath a sunken tree-bole, or however he'd been kept down before Simmy's brother Harald had brought him up.

Simmy thought of her brother now and where he might be. She straightened her back from cribble and quern and scanned the yard for him, the surrounding fields that marked out their croft, but couldn't see him anywhere. She put her hand to the pocket of her smock and felt the small lump of her folded handkerchief and the other thing her brother had found when he'd brought that long dead man in. He'd kept it hidden from everyone these past few weeks, confessing it only to Simmy that very morning. He'd been acting a bit odd these last few days had Harald, no doubt from keeping such a secret, which was something he'd never been good at, and at last he'd blurted it out.

'Everything was such a tangle,' he stuttered. 'I didn't even see it at first, what with all the mud and that. And ayething was pretty much black.'

He sniffed, rubbed his nose against his sleeve, eventually producing the tiny glimpse of gold from out his pocket, laying it down neat and round on the grass between them. 'It was all caught up in yon bits of net by its chain,' he'd gone on, trying to argue his corner. 'Stuck in all that muck I left on the bank after I picked out the bones. Didn't find it till ages after...'

Simmy had only seen proper gold once before, when the bishop came to mark the last New Year gone, the whole congregation kneeling after service, kissing his ring as he blessed them one by one. But she knew what it was the moment Harald unscrewed the ring from a corner of his handkerchief, releasing the perfect circle of it back out into the world. Simmy looked closely at it, noting how small it was, thinking probably it had once belonged to a woman or maybe a child, which perhaps explained why it was on a chain, though a cheap one, slimy-linked, that must have once hung about the dead man's neck.

Simmy turned back towards her brother and slapped him sharply across the face, no matter that he was already far taller and brawnier than she would ever be, and quite a few years older.

'You've kept it all this time and said nothing?' she demanded of him, and he smarted at the slap, flexed his jaw, face fixed with the look of defiance that had always marked his days, and would probably shorten them.

'I was jus' gonna give it to Aileen,' he countered. 'On her feast day, so's, well, you know. Just in case.'

Simmy sighed and understood. Aileen was their cousin, though she looked more like Harald than the rest of the family put together. Ever since old Bob Farrow had finally kicked the bucket a decade past and Aileen's family had moved in from the next glen over and taken over his place in the glass-working shed, if not the glass-working itself, Aileen and Harald had spent most of their free time together. Always him and Aileen and nobody else, as if they lived and breathed a different kind of air to the rest of them, talking quietly for hours upon hours about who knew what, spending every moment not working in the fields or on the croft or animals, in a compact kind of kinship that excluded everyone else. The two of them reminded Simmy of the warblers that ran tittle-tattling amongst the reeds, loud as fishwives until you closed on them, when suddenly they went silent and disappeared.

Aileen's birth-date was the 13th of December, feast day of Saint Lucy, the Light-Giver of Syracuse, who'd nonetheless seen fit to give Aileen none of her advantages, for Aileen came out of the womb with eyes like a boiled fish. She looked pretty enough when she was sleeping, though not at any other time, except to Harald. And because of this, and because she understood, Simmy lowered her slap-tingled fingers from Harald's face and looped them instead beneath the chain that held the ring. It broke immediately, falling straightaway to the ground in pieces. The ring, though, was shiny, as if it had just been forged, polished into perfection from the several weeks bumping about deep inside her brother's pocket. She picked it up. Its inner surface was rough, felt grooved, probably damaged, and on the upper surface were squiggles, some miniscule words she couldn't understand but had the feeling she'd seen something like them before. The huge, stone-blocked sundial in the corner of the churchyard came to mind and how in summer she lay upon its surface gazing up at the clouds and sky, the metal warm beneath her body like a second sun radiating out its heat; she went there in winter too, brushing the snow from off of its wide-brimmed face, releasing the gnomon that was shaped like a sail standing proud from its centre. And she wondered now if Aileen and her brother did the same, lying side by side, dreaming of better days when they were free to be properly together, namely when Simmy and Harald's da died – which surely couldn't be long now. He was no longer as strong in his arms or as free with his fists as he used to be, had developed a choke in his chest this last winter, a crusting over of his breath that failed a little more every time the wind blew cold and hard.

And that made the quandary of what to do with the ring even more complicated. Ever since Harald had turned it over to Simmy she, like her brother, was finding it hard to let go. She knew the dutiful thing to do would be to hand it over to the minister, let him make of it what he would. It might even help identify those bones. She tried to imagine that random assemblage as a person who'd once walked and breathed, loving the woman or child whose ring he'd strung about his neck. But it seemed a thing given to them when nothing else was theirs: not the house they lived in, nor the land they worked – both belonging to the Big Estate – and certainly not the waters around the coast in which they fished that seemed more under the purview of pirates and smugglers than anyone else these days.

So what to do, Simmy thought. Perhaps the ring could be considered fair game – finders, keepers, and all that. Certainly that's how everyone considered the sundial – spotted at an especially low tide by a single brown timber edging through the water, all that was left of a boat that had grounded on a sandbank. They'd had to wait until the tide fully dropped before the men of the village walked out along the broomway to haul what was left of the boat from the silt, and with it the broad face of the sundial that had shone up at them from just below the water's surface, begging for release from the tatters of sacking that clung to its edges. They'd managed to drag it back to proper land, with breaking backs and slippery ropes, and set it up in the churchyard where it had been ever since. Harald had been greatly instrumental in its recovery, for although he'd only been twelve or thirteen at the time he'd been an ox of a boy, growing stronger with every year, and for months afterwards he'd gone back out at every low tide, going on and on about what might still be buried out there: some other salvage, some lucky find that would see them right.

'Take you away from da and his thumpings,' Harald said in explanation. 'Then it'd be just you and me, Simmy, just you and me.'

It might have been true at the time, but not now. Now it would be Harald and fish-eyed Aileen, and where would Simmy be then? Left behind was what, not wanted except to be the eyes Aileen didn't have and to do the jobs Aileen couldn't do. And that was not a good enough life for Simmy, and because of it she kept hold of the ring, kept it within her pocket and her private ken. She had a guilt at keeping it so, but not enough to be worth confessing.

CHAPTER 5

A SWAN AMONGST ISLANDS

Havengore Island, just off the Ardnamurchan Peninsula
Between the peninsulas of Morvern and Knoydart runs the Sunart
sea loch, sleek and blue, edges ragged by rocks and bays, small
beaches excavated out between piles of boulders; and up those
beaches run lines of ropes with boats strung out along them from
their anchors in the sea. Several islands rise like turtle-backs from
the waters of the loch: Oronsay and Colonsay being the largest;
unremarkable lumps of granite, though with fine grass growing
between their rounded stones: good for the sheep and cattle who
are swum out to them on low spring tides for summer grazing.
Another of these islands, small and previously undistinguished,
had been renamed Havengore by its latest owner, bought lock,
stock and spume-sprayed barrel seventeen years before. It still
possessed the same grey-pocked surfaces, sea-splashed, shell-
scattered shores, as its neighbours, but it was now a place of
wonder, called by the locals The Island of the White Cathedral on
account of the huge buildings erected there: tall and slender walls
and arches nobody had seen close-to except the specialist workers
brought in to build them, and Archie Louden, and of course

Gustav Wengler who'd commissioned them and lived amongst them unperturbed ever since.

Wengler was the titular owner of the Galena Ore Mines over on the mainland, inherited from his father – a Danish engineer who studied mineralogy in Edinburgh and bought the mines near Strontian on a whim and a lifetime's savings, going there filled with excitement and plans and never leaving, as his son had never left his little island since his first footfall there, content to be confined with his White Cathedral; able, but unwilling, to leave.

He was there now, though found he couldn't concentrate, couldn't work, couldn't do anything but tap his fingers again and again upon the window sill, unable to stop counting out the numbers of his desperate drumming. He was up to nine hundred and ninety one of nine hundred and ninety seven – the last prime number before reaching that most ordinary, though perfectly rounded, figure of one thousand.

His life had been completely knocked out of kilter, all rhythm drained away, all order destroyed, leaving a chaos he couldn't cope with, and all because his assistant hadn't had the grace to turn up at the time his letter from the previous week stated that he would. Two nights had passed since that appointed time, two nights and one full day, and Gustav Wengler believed he'd been remarkably self-controlled to have gone so long past the given deadline without adequate explanation. When Archie hadn't shown up Wengler had been at first perturbed and then angry; but he was nothing if not rational, and reminded himself that the world outside his island was just that: outside, and therefore – as much as he despised it – outside his control. Horses, after all, could drop shoes, and weather could intervene with unforeseen ferocity, tides swing against their habit, storms blow up dependent on the mores of winds engendered a hundred, two hundred miles from these shores. These were all things Wengler knew and understood, especially concerning the tides, for he'd accustomed himself to their engagement with Havengore the very first year he'd spent here, studying them for one calendar year exactly, right down to the hour, right down to the minute. He could even conjure up other scenarios that might have stopped Archie in his tracks – the sudden onset of illness perhaps, or maybe a freak and heavy snowfall in Oban where he was to have landed, although this latter seemed unlikely as not a flutter of snow, nor even a brief show of hail, had fallen here in Havengore.

Yet despite all his rationalisations Gustav Wengler was profoundly disturbed by Archie's continued non-appearance, so much so that eventually he'd done what he'd never done before and gone down to the tiny pier that stood at the neck of the creek separating his island from the mainland, setting up the flag to tell the ferryman he was needed and needed fast, the one that signalled Disaster! and nothing less. Even so, it seemed an age before Hesketh Wood finally rowed his boat across, Wengler fretting all the while from his lookout tower, counting out nine hundred and ninety seven three more times upon its window sill before he saw Hesketh creaking in his oars, when Wengler left his lookout and went down to the shore to meet the man at the pier, stuttering out a few short questions:

Had anyone heard of Archie Louden yet?

Had the man arrived in Strontian?

Was he sick? Was there a snow-storm? Was there an obstacle on the road from there to here?

If Hesketh Wood had truly been expecting the disaster the flag signalled he gave no hint of it, merely answered *no, no,* and *no* again to all Wengler's questions before pocketing the letter Wengler gave him and the several coins that were worth more than his monthly wage, at which point he became as animated as a cricket when the sun begins to shine and agreed straightaway to get over to the mines and hand Wengler's letter to the manager there.

Θ

Matthias McQuat was much surprised by the appearance of Hesketh and his letter.

'You said Gustav Wengler gave you this?' he asked, after he had scanned the few words scratched out, apparently with some haste, upon the page.

'Nunudder,' Hesketh gave back to him. 'Said that like as not you'd 'ave a little summat for me, for the bother and the like, and for taking you back over?'

Hesketh knew he was chancing his arm with this ask, but times were hard. Most of his trade these days was local, transporting people and assorted livestock up and down the waters slicking the peninsula or over to the other side when landslides or snow blocked the thin track leading over to Ockle. It didn't pay well, and on top of that his croft was not thriving, his cattle going under with blue tongue, black foot and Lord knew what else. So when Matthias took out a few coins from his pocket and handed them over, Hesketh took them with alacrity, agreeing to return to his ferry post and wait for them while Matthias rounded up his young helpmeet.

It took the boy Matthias had sent almost half an hour to locate young Jed Thornbrough and bring him back down from the mines, but Matthias was keen for the lad to accompany him. Wengler's letter could not have been plainer – *Get to Havengore soonest, urgent matters to discuss* – though what those urgent matters were Matthias had no idea. He'd known the older Gustav well, Matthias being almost a replacement son given that his own was as buttoned up in his own head as a cockle within its shell. It was a terrible day for Matthias when the old man slipped down a flooded mineshaft and snapped his neck, and he'd grieved far more than had Gustav's actual son who, since inheriting his father's estate, had never once left his island – not even for the funeral or to visit the mines. Instead, Matthias received bare instructions from Wengler's lawyers to carry on as he'd always done, and every year Matthias dutifully sent off copies of the mine's accounts to the lawyers, receiving pre-signed consents and pro-forma orders in return.

It seemed likely this urgent summons related to Archie being away on one of the extended trips Wengler sometimes sent the younger man on, that probably he was running low on supplies, although such an oversight had never occurred before. There was also the faint possibility Wengler had come up with some invention to aid the workings of the mines, which he'd done twice before. No one knew exactly what he got up to on Havengore, but everyone knew there was more than a hint of the mad scientist about him. The White Cathedral was evidence of that. But there was one, far more sinister reason Matthias could imagine for the summons, a niggling fear he'd had for years: that Wengler had chosen to divest himself of his father's mines completely, sell the land to the highest bidder to do with it whatever they chose. Possible disaster then for Strontian, and Matthias had mixed feelings as he looked towards Havengore, eager for the chance to see the soaring white walls of the buildings there at first hand and also to meet the man himself, find out how he functioned in his self-imposed isolation, and what he did with all his days.

Jed appeared suddenly over a hillock, running fast, face red with exertion and anticipation, hardly stopping once he'd reached

Matthias, wasting no time with trivial greetings but throwing himself into the trap that was ready and waiting to take them to Hesketh's pier.

'Are we really going over to Havengore?' Jed asked, evidently excited, voice high and a little strangled, eyes bright, cheeks shining. Matthias smiled. He was not surprised. Lord knew what tales the mineworkers had told Jed in the past couple of months about the reclusive Wengler. Jed had often asked Matthias about Wengler and Matthias had told him all he knew, which wasn't much, though it struck him that Jed always spoke the man's name like a monk speaking of a saint.

'I can't believe we're actually going there!' Jed said as Matthias joined him in the trap, and they were off. The ride was too jumpy and bumpy for either to say another word, and it was a quarter hour later before they left the main track and diverted onto a muddy lane that ended up, fifty yards down, onto a small sandy beach almost directly opposite Havengore. Hesketh was ready, boat partway shoved out from the shore, ropes slackly bound to a post buried waist-down in the sand, Jed and Matthias spilling from trap to boat and straightway out into the Sound. It was only once they'd shoved off, and Hesketh was hard at his oars, that Matthias had the space and breath to speak.

'So what is it you know about Gustav Wengler that I don't?' he asked with a hint of merriment, noting Jed's gaze fixed straight ahead, eyes unwilling to shift from Havengore, like a starving man heading for a feast.

'Well some, since I've been here,' Jed answered, a little abstractedly, 'and what you've told me. But mostly from before.'

'Before?' Matthias answered, greatly surprised. This was the first he'd heard of it. And how was that even possible? Matthias was about to ask Jed about this unexpected development when

Hesketh steered them into the bore of the incoming tide which caught them broadsides, slewing the boat badly to one side and spinning them almost in a circle. Hesketh had been expecting this and lifted his oars from the water, allowing the current to pull them along a way before dipping in his oars again, bringing the boat out of the current. Hesketh drew a well-earned breath and said what Matthias had feared he would, having witnessed the state of the tide.

'If you're stopping any time out here,' he managed between pulls, 'then you'll be out here the night.'

No use protesting. Matthias knew the way of the water and how swift and strong it could run, especially when the tug of the moon was on the tide's side, as it was now. Hesketh could land them easily enough but would need to take his way back straightaway if he was not to be swept several miles up-shore on the incoming tide, which was getting stronger by the minute.

'Right enough,' Matthias agreed, nodding at Hesketh and Hesketh dipped his chin in return, bent his back to his task, legs braced against the running boards, oars creaking in their rollocks, and minutes later the boat was scraping up the shingle of the small bay by the pier and out scrambled Matthias and Jed. Hesketh didn't wait longer than it took for Matthias to tell him to be back by eight the following morning, when the tide would be on the slack.

The sun was low in the sky, giving out the kind of light that deepens colours, softens edges, lengthens shadows, lends depth and warmth to everything it touches, from the rounded pebbles on the beach to the wet seaweed draped over the rocks that lined the shores of Havengore. Far more impressive was the way the sun caught the tops of the monuments that were tall enough to be seen above the grassy clutch of rocks beneath which they had landed. Matthias caught his breath to see how smooth and graceful were the curves of those white walls, the sight of them so much more astonishing than they'd ever appeared in the eyeglass he'd often trained on them from the shore.

'Havengore,' Jed whispered, and Matthias didn't need to look at the lad to know he was smiling, felt a small wisp of laughter in his own throat at the sheer beauty and incongruity of what they were looking at: those beautiful arches and pillars that might have been sculpted from silk.

'Havengore indeed,' Matthias echoed, and both stood there side by side, sun-lengthened shadows almost touching, jutting out from their boots along the ground and up the rocks towards the scrub of gorse and bramble at its top. The moment was broken by the sudden materialisation of a man from behind that small hump, that made the two of them jump. He was tall and thin, almost to the point of emaciation, the sparse points of his cropped, spiky hair caught by the light of the setting sun into a nimbus about his head, making the neck that was connecting his head to the rest of his body look too slender and frail for the task, with an Adam's apple so prominent it seemed as if he'd swallowed a plum and got it stuck.

'Mr Wengler?' Matthias asked, and the man closed his eyes, nodding vigorously, before moving swiftly back up the path he'd come from, motioning them to follow. Jed and Matthias exchanged glances but didn't need telling twice and up from the beach they went, following the skinny man as he ran back the length of the path that tethered the beach and the pier to his home as if a hive of hornets was at his back.

CHAPTER 6

SIMMY, AND THE RECOMPENSE OF THE DEAD

Sunday morning, chapel-time, and Simmy was dawdling in the yard. Hens were fed, goats milked, eggs scrabbled out of the chooks' laying places beneath the hedges and in the roost, and Simmy was now raking out the pen they kept their two cows in. The church bells were sounding out their last warning that mass was about to begin but she couldn't go there, not today, not with that small gold ring hidden away inside the pocket of her smock, sewn shut the night before to keep it safe while she was at her chores.

For the first time in her life she didn't know what to do. Of her and Harald it was always Simmy who was the thinker, but she wasn't sure she could think her way through this. Part of her told her she must go up to the minister and give the ring up; another part – small but vociferous – said no, don't do that, not yet, because it was theirs now, and what harm in hanging on to it for a while? And what if Harald was right about giving it to St Lucy, her feast day only a short while away? Simmy wasn't sure saints had any need of gold in heaven nor even if she believed in saints, or heaven for that matter; but if by some freak chance they did exist then who was she to say that the flash of a piece of gold might not persuade one of their multitude to intercede on Aileen's behalf?

Either way, Simmy couldn't go to chapel and take part in mass with the ring burning a hole in her conscience. She knew the minister – Oswald Harlow – would come pay them a visit during the next few days to find out why she'd not been at service, if maybe her da was worse, if she or Harald or any of the animals were sick. She could make up some excuse for a couple of weeks but after that it was going to get really difficult. But after that St Lucy's day would have come and gone, at which point she would have to come clean anyway, exchange the ring for the minister making prayers on Aileen's behalf. In her wilder moments Simmy wondered if she could sell it. She knew gold was worth money – and Lord knew they could always do with that – but she'd no idea how much it was worth nor where she could hawk it. Worse, she wouldn't be able to face Harald if she did. He might be a rough lad with nothing much between his ears except the wind, but he had a childlike faith that not even she could shake, and if she didn't produce the ring come the 13th of December there was no knowing what he would do. Only that Harald would never speak to her again, and then Simmy would be all alone with their cantankerous, unpredictable father who was not dying as fast as either of them would have liked. Another sin – to be wishing him dead like she did – and another she could never tell the minister about, no matter how much she liked and respected the man. Reverend Harlow had always been on Simmy's side, standing up against her father and insisting Simmy come to class at least until she could be taught to read and write. And Christ knew, she valued that above all else.

'Because she's aptitude, Mr McRailty,' Reverend Harlow said, 'she has aptitude, sir, and determination, and such qualities are not to be squandered. Certainly not in one so young.'

Aptitude and determination: strong words, good words, ones she was proud of, but no use to her now. There were just too many possible actions and outcomes, and so for the moment Simmy pushed them out of her head, carried on with her daily tasks: grind, grind, grinding at the quern-stone, looking up every now and then towards the chapel as the hymn-singers' songs seeped out of its walls towards her, sure of only one thing: that she wouldn't be able to keep the secret of the ring much longer.

Θ

Gustav Wengler was not a man of many words, nor did he take fools gladly. He expected others to keep up with whatever was going on in his head without his having to explain. The moment Jed and Matthias caught up with him and were in his house he slammed the door shut behind them.

'I don't like to be outside too long,' Wengler said. A statement, no apology. No offers either of food or drink, Wengler not tarrying in the kitchen they'd landed in longer than it took him to cross the floor and sprint up the spiral staircase at its opposite end. The three emerged at its top into a thin corridor, Wengler leading them straightaway into a cavernous room with bookcases on two walls, large blackboards covering the surface of another, and a desk parallel to the last. Every scribble on the blackboards was neat and precise, and every book and paper on shelf and table neatly regimented, like soldiers awaiting inspection. Wengler was more at ease now he was back in familiar territory, his body relaxing as if he'd been a fish stranded upon the sand but now felt the sudden pulse of life-giving saltwater in his gills.

Despite this brief reanimation it was obvious to Matthias that Wengler was nervous, distraught even. The man couldn't keep still, fingers tapping at every surface he could reach. At the exact centre of the room was a wooden stool, the only seat apart from another at the desk, and Wengler subsided onto this central stool, fingers going methodically to its lower edge, head bowed, eyelids fluttering as if he was trying to keep them closed, or maybe open, but unable to make the final decision to do either. Matthias was about to speak but Wengler got in first, his voice thin and reedy, jittery with a panic bordering on hysteria.

'Archie's not back,' Wengler bleated from his stool, fingers clutched about the edges of the wood. 'Archie's not back,' he said again. 'He was due back three days ago. He sent a message up from Oban. But he's not back. Archie's not back.'

So, Matthias thought, mildly disappointed to find there was no emergency after all but just as he'd supposed: the assistant sent away had been delayed for one of a hundred reasons, and Wengler found the deviation intolerable. Huge relief too for Matthias that he wasn't about to sell off the mines, and a modicum of pity as the man sat glued to his stool as if it was the one thing in the world he could rely on, remembering what the father had once said about the son:

'He's a little odd, Matthias. He's a mind can roam the universe like you or I roam the hills. He sees patterns in places the rest of us would never even think to look.'

It was about as much as Old Man Wengler ever said about his only child over the years: that he was special, had no choice but to live differently, that he gathered numbers and theories like a dog after sheep. Matthias had never really understood until now, when it seemed an understatement.

'Are you in need of supplies?' Matthias asked mildly. 'Any foodstuffs we can provide you with will be…'

'No, no,' Wengler was up off his stool, flitting around the room, touching each board, each book, as he passed it by before subsiding once again onto his seat, fingers tapping rhythmically at its base. 'No,' he repeated softly. 'That is not what I want. What I want is for you to find Archie Louden and bring him back. I cannot function adequately without him. He must be here. He has things with him from Denmark that I need. And he told me he would be back three days ago.'

Wengler slumped, head going down, small spare shoulders going with it, exaggerating the pitifully prominent lines of his clavicles as they went, such an awful sound emanating from his throat that Matthias feared the man was crying, a fear augmented by the two fat wet blotches that fell onto the boards by Wengler's feet like unexpected rain.

'We'll find him, Mr Wengler,' came the bright voice of Jed Thornbrough. 'Please don't despair, sir. That's exactly why we've come here, and we'll find Archie, wherever he is.'

Matthias frowned, both at the interruption and the unfounded expectation of delivery Jed was promising.

'Can I see the missive Archie sent you about when he would be back?' Matthias asked. Wengler took it from his pocket and handed it over.

Have landed in Oban, Matthias read out loud. *This letter will probably reach you faster than I will myself, but I will be back on Havengore by the start of Advent week. Hold fast, sir, for I have with me what I was sent for.*

'But that's just it,' Gustav Wengler muttered miserably once Matthias finished reading. 'He's not back, and no more what he went to fetch. So tell me, where is Archie Louden?'

Matthias noted that Wengler seemed more concerned by the late arrival of whatever it was Archie was transporting than Archie himself, but he said nothing.

'It's just not like him,' Wengler whispered. 'He's always back when he says. It's just not like him.'

Θ

Jed and Matthias were cold and uncomfortable in the room Wengler had roused himself enough to point out to them. The room was Archie's own: one bed, one desk, one chest of drawers. Everything smelled of damp and neglect, but Jed soon got a fire going in the grate, and another in the kitchen downstairs where they made a paltry meal with what they could find in the cupboards: a soupy stew, a bowl of which Jed took up to Wengler who had strayed from his stool, and was now standing absently at one of the large windows whose vista led across the Sound.

'We'll find him, sir,' Jed said softly. 'Never fear that we won't.'

Wengler didn't move. He was up to nine hundred and sixty three and couldn't stop his count. Jed left him to it, went back down the spiral staircase to the kitchen where Matthias was hunched about the fire with a damp blanket over his back.

'I can't believe anyone would choose to live like this,' Matthias said, teeth chattering slightly with the cold. The wind had come up with the falling down of the sun and brought the rain with it, both blowing off the sea and tappering against the walls and windows of Wengler's dwelling; nothing to be seen outside but darkness, no twinkling lights of other villagers, no sense of anyone being nearby; only the lapping of the waves upon the shores of the tiny island as if it knew it had them surrounded and they had nowhere else to go.

'I think it's grand,' Jed answered with an enthusiasm that should have surprised Matthias, but didn't. He'd already sensed some kind of connection between the two when they'd been upstairs with

Wengler, had the feeling that it was as much as Jed could do not to go running up to every bookshelf and board and table to take his look.

'Fancy living out here and spending every day reading books, having ideas and testing them out,' Jed went on. 'I'm telling you, Mr McQuat, I'd be here in half a second if I had the chance, and so would this Archie fellow. He'd not have given this up, not if he'd any choice in the matter.'

'But he's been living here for ten years,' Matthias countered. 'Surely that would be enough for anyone.'

'Not for me,' Jed answered blithely. 'I'd spend every second of every day here with a man like Wengler, if I could.'

Matthias shuddered inside his blanket and leaned closer towards the fire. He'd always known Jed was a different kind of lad the moment he'd set eyes on him, but he'd not expected this.

'You seem to know a lot more about him than you've said previously,' Matthias said, a little curtly. 'So how is that?'

Jed came over to join Matthias by the fire, bringing a couple of glasses and a bottle of wine he'd found somewhere that looked older than Jed himself. It would have been brought here by Old Man Wengler, Matthias knew, who always liked a touch of the luxurious no matter he was living in the sticks. He must have kept a stash here for his occasional visits, probably getting it from one of the smuggling runs, and who could blame him? Not Matthias, and he took the glass Jed handed him with appreciation, knowing it would be good.

'I know he's as unlike you or me as pepper is from salt,' Jed began, spilling out more in the next couple of minutes than he had the whole time he'd been in Strontian. 'He wrote this brilliant paper once about the Ancient Egyptian system of multiplication and how it could adapted to use quadratic equations in a new way.

Here look,' Jed went on, bringing out his notebook and quickly creating a table of numbers.

'So, here's the basics of the system: say you want to work out what thirteen times fourteen is. The first column is made by doubling the number before, so one, two, four, eight, which equals thirteen. Then they start a second doubling column with the next sequential number, which of course is fourteen: so fourteen, twenty eight, fifty six, one hundred and twelve. Now that's done they have a kind of shortcut. See here?' Jed pointed. 'By adding in a multiple of the first row by ten, like this, they've abbreviated the whole sum. It's really similar to the old Russian way of multiplication by doubling, which no one had realised before. And see if you do this and this with a set of equations...'

Matthias looked from Jed to his notebook and raised his eyebrows at the elegance of the solution, which was quite stunning. But Jed wasn't finished.

'He wrote another paper called the Hedgehog Theorem that posited that if you thought of the earth as a rolled up hedgehog and tried to make all the spines go in one direction you could never succeed. You'd always end up with a sticking up tuft at one pole or another and you should have seen the formula he used to work that out! Almost three pages long!'

Matthias took a sip of the deep, dark burgundy in his glass and considered. This insight of Jed's knowledge of Gustav Wengler was a revelation.

'How many other of his papers have you read?' he asked, Jed replying immediately and with enthusiasm.

'Everything I could find. He's a genius, Matthias. No other word for it. He's worked on all sorts of famous problems – Goldbach's Conjecture, Fermat's Last Theorem... One of his best was adapting Tartaglia's Three Jug Puzzle into shifting not water but time, mass and energy to prove that the three are integral to pretty much everything. Tartaglia was really interesting. His actual name was Niccolo Fontana, called The Stammerer because he got his lips and tongue sliced through when he was twelve, during the French massacre on his home town of Brescia. And going back to Fermat's Last Theorem, Wengler has given the closest solution yet to that proof…'

Matthias ceased listening. So here was the real reason Jed had come here and why he'd stayed so long; not because of any rare mineral, nor Matthias's company, but solely in the hope of meeting Gustav Wengler. Jed prattled on oblivious.

'And then there's this place called the Tower of Brahma, a monastery in the Himalayas where they've spent the last few hundred years shifting golden discs around on jewelled spikes. The idea is to get all sixty four discs onto the second spike, but they can't just pile them on. They can only move one disc at a time and can't put a bigger one on a smaller one. It's a bit like an extended version of that puzzle with the fox, the cabbage and the rabbit. Anyway, point is that it will take them forever to complete the task, which is just as well because they believe that when they do man's work will be done and the world will come to an end. Wengler pointed out that if they got a fourth spike and worked to a complicated formula he provided, then they could get the whole thing done in about three weeks!'

The end of the world. Not quite, but Matthias put down his glass, couldn't drink any more, felt sick and betrayed, like a dog who gets up quietly in the night and elects to sleep as far away from his master as he can get.

CHAPTER 7

GETTING THERE,
EVEN IF IT'S NOT WHERE YOU WANT TO GO

Sholto and Brogar were dropped off the following morning at one of the small peninsulas sticking out into the Sunart, told to go up a short distance where they would find a bothy and a flag they could raise to alert the ferryman they were wanting taking further down the loch. The boat that brought them in was already sailing off into the distance when they discovered there was no flag to be seen, only a pole standing stark and bare-armed into the sky, and a blackened circle set back some way where the bothy must once have stood but was no more. Brogar and Sholto stamped their feet upon the frosty shingle, sending Gilligan and Hugh off into the hinterland to try and find someone who might know where they should go from here. Sholto was alarmed that the Company had sent them to such a remote and apparently uninhabited place with no firm plans, but Brogar reassured him. He'd spent a lot of time in Finnmark and Siberia and compared to places like that, he told Sholto, this was nothing.

'You've to learn to bide your time,' Brogar said. 'It's something you'll need to get used to. Use it to look at what's about you, try to get a general idea of the outlay of the land, what lies here and what might lie there.'

Brogar was right. Just by scuffing their boots through the pebbles on the foreshore they'd already uncovered a few interesting specimens – rough agate and serpentine, a few fossils – and were still examining their finds when the boys returned a couple of hours later. They arrived by boat, a man named Hesketh Wood at the helm, Gilligan and Hugh having located the next ferry post down the peninsula and an intact flag already hoisted by someone wanting Hesketh to take a load of eggs into Strontian.

It didn't take long to load themselves and their paltry gear onto Hesketh's boat, Sholto having left his precious books in Kildonan from where they could be sent on either to here, if it looked likely they'd be staying for some time, or back home to Trondheim if not.

'Gotta fetch a cupla others on the way,' Hesketh informed them. 'But if your boys is right then it's the same man you're wanting to see anywise. Had to leave him over on Havengore last night.'

Sholto started at the name for it was one he knew, though obviously not from here. Havengore, or Hven as it was more properly named, was hundreds of miles away in the Sound of Denmark, an island that was the site of Tycho Brahe's famous observatory of Uraniborg, the Castle of the Heavens, after Urania – the muse of the stars. He would have asked about such a coincidental nomenclature but Hesketh was already pushing off and in a moment they were zooming down a thin thread of current, Gilligan and Hugh laughing and shouting as they splashed their hands in the freezing water, catching up bits of seaweed, exhilarated by this new adventure, as if leaving their home for the first time in their lives, and rounding the treacherous seas of Cape Wrath and down through the Minches past Skye, had not been enough.

Sholto smiled to watch them, for he too was feeling innervated. It had been such a slog getting over from Kildonan, and he'd maybe not enjoyed the sea journey as much as Brogar had, but everything here on this west coast looked different to the east, far less bleak, far greener despite the winter – everything smaller and cosier somehow – and no snow, which was a relief. His blood was pulsing through his veins, giving him a keen sense of being alive and happier than he'd been for years. He'd survived his first challenge working in the field with Brogar Finn and gained that man's respect by doing so. He'd encountered – and solved – several brutal murders, and almost been murdered himself for the trouble, but by God, it had ensured he would not be consigned back to his underground office at home. Sholto breathed deeply, wondering what new adventures this posting would bring.

The boat was going fast down the skinny bore, Hesketh skilfully plying both rudder and oars, Gilligan and Hugh laughing loudly, leaning dangerously low over the sides of the boat, so much so that Sholto was about to chide them until he saw in the distance the strangest of sights. He squinted into the morning and raised a hand to his brow to see the better. They'd sighted several small and unremarkable islands up and down the Sound already but straight ahead lay another one, and he had no doubt at all that it must be Havengore, and not just because Hesketh was steering the boat deftly, if indirectly, towards the one small opening that lay between the forbidding granite boulders that scattered its shores, but because of what was rising up from its core. He wished he had his binoculars to hand to study the smooth white walls that grew to their heights from the grey and green foundations of the island like some giant flower. The sight of them was so incongruous and unexpected that Sholto gasped. It was just like witnessing the real Havengore, if on a smaller scale.

'The buildings?' he asked. 'What are they?'

Hesketh didn't need to turn to know what Sholto was talking about.

'Some sun shite,' he answered succinctly. 'And if you think them're queer, wait 'til you meets the man what built 'em.'

He might have said more, but they were close enough to Havengore for Hesketh to have to lock the rudder and pull hard at the oars to steer the boat in towards the small pier. 'Anywise,' Hesketh continued, allowing the boat to glide in under its own momentum to the shallows, 'you can ask Mr McQuat about'm. He's yon loon yous both is looking for and it's him I'm to be picking up, so it's kinda two for one, if you ken what I mean.'

Sholto had no idea what Hesketh meant, for he wasn't listening. *Some sun shite*, Hesketh had said and Sholto smiled, for the man was right. That's exactly what they were, or at least what the original buildings had been designed for over on that other island in the Danish Sound. How such simulacrums had ended up here was anyone's guess, but just then they grounded and Hesketh was jumping into thigh-high water, Gilligan and Hugh following suit, the three of them dragging the boat in alongside and securing it to a mooring rope dangling loose from the jetty, pulling both boat and passengers to land.

Θ

Matthias slept well in spite of himself. The vague malevolence he'd imagined when he'd been listening to the sea the night before had lulled him to sleep almost the moment he lay down on Archie's surprisingly comfortable bed. Jed had elected to curl himself up in a few blankets by the kitchen fire but was nowhere to be seen when Matthias got down there not long past dawn. He fed the fire from the stock of logs left for the purpose just outside the door, discovered when he went outside to relieve himself. And by Christ it was a beautiful morning, crisp and clear, his breath lingering softly in the air above him, almost enough to dissolve the disappointment about Jed he'd felt last night. Almost, but not quite. He went back inside with his logs, hung a kettle from the hook in the inglenook to heat some water, gathered what he could from the cupboards: an almost empty caddy, just enough scrapings to make a pot of tea, a bowl of sugar cubes that were disintegrating in the damp, the cups they'd used the previous evening. And then from up above came the small murmur of Jed's voice and a couple of footsteps on the boards and he knew the lad was with Wengler. He wondered briefly if the man had gone to bed, if he actually had one at all, had maybe slept on the hard floor of that room at the top of his spiral staircase. Either way, Matthias had better things to be thinking about, like how his foremen at the mines were doing without him being there. Fine enough would be the answer to that, because he'd briefed them thoroughly before leaving for Havengore. They'd been as worried as he at the summons, all assuming the worst and nothing any of them could do about it. Matthias wanted to tell them soon as he could that this wasn't so, but for the while he was stranded on the island and Jed was up top with Wengler talking about God knew what, and no better time for him to take a quick peek at those pale buildings that had intrigued him for so long.

Θ

'Oh but this is extraordinary!' Jed was saying, looking at the neat lines of notes written out on Wengler's blackboards. 'Surely this is part of the *Steganographia*, Book Three. But I didn't think anyone had managed to decode it…'

Wengler waved an arm, shrugged a shoulder.

'Just something to occupy me,' he said. 'I shall probably rub it all out tomorrow.'

Jed was aghast. His hard trek to Ardnamurchan had paid off at last, in as much as he'd finally got to meet Gustav Wengler and was not only standing in his study but looking at his work, talking to him about it, thinking that most probably Wengler had rubbed out more amazing ideas from his blackboards than folk like Jed would ever come up with in a lifetime. He gazed at the boards with intense concentration. He didn't want to get out his notebook and copy it all down for that would have been tantamount to plagiarism; but it didn't bear contemplating that all this could be wiped out with one uncaring sweep of Wengler's arm. He was certain he was looking at Wengler's take on Trithemius's fifteenth century work on cryptography – the *Steganographia* – one of the most famous puzzles in the mathematical world. It was one Jed was well acquainted with for he'd had the temerity to tackle it himself – along with every other hopeful trying to make his name in the field. But the *Steganographia* was not just any old treatise. It had been written in code and took an entire century from its initial publication to discover its key – called the *Clavis* – enabling people to decipher the first two books. The third book, however, remained a mystery, differently encrypted and no key yet found. Until Wengler. For here on his blackboards were all his workings out, and Jed was agog. Not that Wengler was taking any mind of it. He had begun counting out his numbers again, counting them over and over the whole night through. He'd not gone to his bed, just as Matthias had suspected, but stayed sitting at his window sill looking out onto the black night, hoping Archie would miraculously appear, though of course he did not. The chances of him turning up in the middle of the night were absolutely zero, the wind too strong, and no way for him to cross from the mainland to the island even if he'd managed to get to the peninsula. But still he found himself unable to desist from his vigil, his mind carrying on turning and churning like the waters about his island, and nothing the rest of his body could do to make it stop. He needed Archie back. He felt as if he was on one side of an equation, impotently waiting for the other half to come along and give him purpose. His life was governed by logic and reasonable expectation, the rigorous testing of hypotheses and results, but this pattern had been thrown out of the window when Archie had not only failed to reappear at his stated time, but still hadn't appeared three days later, and Wengler was afraid. The only person who had offered some approximation of balance was this newcomer moving slowly around his room. He couldn't remember the boy's name but recognised he had a passable understanding of his work, which lent credence to his assurance to Wengler that all would be right, that Archie would be located by hook or by crook. And so Gustav Wengler did something completely out of character: he embraced the irrational, and had hope.

Θ

Matthias went out into the morning, going first down to the jetty to raise the flag on the unlikely off-chance Hesketh had forgotten he and Jed needed picking up, in case the few coins he'd given the man the day before had sent him off on some kind of bender. He didn't think it would be so, but it was always best to be sure. Afterwards, he took his way back up beyond the house, going towards all those strange monuments Wengler had caused to be built upon his island. Up close they were so much more astonishing and perplexing than they'd seemed from the other side of the water.

There was a massive column sunk into an underground chamber, and from the column, at ground level, radiated out maybe twenty or thirty spokes just wide enough to take a man daredevil enough to walk upon them, each supported from below by several arches, the column rising another several metres up above his head. And then there was an extraordinary wedge-shaped structure like a side of cheese, with two concentric in-built circles slanted upon its surface, staircases threading between their walls so you could ascend to the highest level of the wedge from either side, and then walk back down to the bottom via the straight stone steps that bisected them both. There were markings, Matthias saw, made at regular intervals around these circles, though he could discern nothing of their meaning, and a circle of archways around it as if to focus the sun during each quarter season. It was the last building that gave him a clue as to the purpose of all these monuments, for it was something more down to earth, literally, consisting of several rings of stone laid out flat upon the ground. These too had markings, and these he recognised, for they clearly represented the hours of the day – right down to the minute – on the inner ring, the months of the year on the intermediary, and glyphs of constellations on the third. The centre, however, was empty but for the short tussocks of grass and thrift that were growing there, giving it the unsettling appearance of being incomplete, of missing a vital part. Matthias got no further in his explorations, for he was interrupted by an angry yelling coming from the direction of the house and he looked up to see Gustav Wengler's pale face and narrow body teetering dangerously on the sill of one of the upper windows.

'Hi there! Get off that!' Wengler sounded apoplectic. 'You've no right to be there. No right at all, and I demand you remove yourself!'

Matthias did and speedily, not only because Wengler was shouting at him but because he saw Hesketh arriving in his boat, apparently already laden with several passengers and as intrigued as he was by these buildings he was keener still to get off the island and back to the mines.

Θ

'I've a couple of fellers in me boat as have come to see you,' Hesketh said as Matthias intercepted him coming up the path towards the house. 'Left 'em down by the shore so as not to upset yon mannie at the hoose.'

Matthias nodded with approval. You didn't lock yourself up on an island for nigh on twenty years if you had a yen for company, and now Matthias had actually met Gustav Wengler he was more certain of this fact than ever. Wengler already seemed on the edge of a nervous breakdown because his assistant was missing, and Matthias worried for the man's sanity if they added more trauma to his already disrupted days.

'I've just to fetch Jed,' Matthias replied, 'and sort out a few more things with Mr Wengler. Can you give me maybe half an hour?'

'Surely can,' Hesketh replied easily.

'And for Heaven's sake,' Matthias added, 'don't let anyone start wandering about on the island. Keep them by the boat. The man almost had a fit just now when he saw me out by those...' he was momentarily stuck for a word, wanted to say instruments, for it struck him that was exactly what those very odd buildings of circles, stairs and arches reminded him of. 'Just keep them away,' he said. 'Keep them down on the shore and out of sight if you can.'

'Righto,' Hesketh said and went back down the path, catching two lively looking lads with his arms as they came bowling up the small path. 'Back down yonder, you two,' Hesketh said, though without aggression. 'This here's private property and you can't just be gallivanting over it like it was your own.'

Nicely put, Matthias thought, wishing he'd had the wit to heed such words himself, hoping he hadn't done irreparable damage to his relationship with Wengler who, after all, was his employer and could sack him any time he chose.

When he got back to the house he found Jed in the kitchen slurping down a cup of cold tea he'd poured from the pot. His face was animated, cheeks flushed, and there were a couple of books lying on the table beside him.

'You didn't just take them…' Matthias started to say as he looked pointedly towards the two leather-bound volumes.

Jed didn't bother to look affronted, just tucked the books into his bag and smiled.

'He's given me the loan of them,' Jed said with excitement, 'on the promise that we'll go take a look for this missing man of his.'

Matthias sighed. 'But where are we to start? We don't know the first thing about what his plans were, apart from that he should already be here.'

'Ah, but we know more than that,' Jed said, adding, with absolute conviction, 'and I'm telling you, Mr McQuat, this Archie fellow wouldn't have just absconded, not from all this. I think Mr Wengler is right to be worried. And that letter he has from Archie? Well, it was sent just after he landed at Oban coming in from Denmark, and sent on the up and up and paid over the mark so it would reach Havengore a couple of days before he did himself. Mr Wengler said his assistant always did so, precisely so Mr Wengler wouldn't have to fret about when he'd be arriving.'

Matthias had to admit these didn't sound like the actions of a man about to run off and leave his employ.

'But he's only, what? Three days late?' Matthias said. 'Maybe he got sick, maybe the boat bringing him grounded on a sandbank, got stuck in fog.'

Jed shook his head. 'I don't think so. Mr Wengler kept every letter Archie ever sent him when he was off on his excursions. Every one. All dated and in order. He showed them to me this morning and this is the first time Archie has ever been late. In fact he always seems to have built in a safety net for just such accidental hindrances, and has always got back at least twenty four hours before his given deadline. Always,' Jed emphasised, 'apart from this one time.'

'So he built in a bit of leeway and got it wrong,' Matthias countered. 'I can understand that.' And so he could. He'd have done the same in Archie's shoes, now he'd met their joint employer. Never upset the cart would have been the first rule; never step out of place, always do what was expected of you, and never, ever be late.

Jed was nodding. 'I know that,' he said, 'but you've got to understand that working for the likes of Gustav Wengler is a privilege.'

Matthias felt that stab of betrayal again, invoking anger this time and not regret. There were beetles that not only looked like bees but generated the right smell, all so they could sneak into a hive and get to the honey source without being noticed. And that was how Jed had treated him. He wanted to snort in derision, but Jed was talking again.

'And we did say we'd look. I promised him...'

This time Matthias did snort, but Jed was twitching, looking so distraught that Matthias's finer side came to the fore.

'Of course we'll look, Jed,' he said. 'But no matter what you've told your Mr Wengler I can't promise what we'll find. Come on,' he said more gently. 'Hesketh's waiting. Best we were gone.'

They cleared away their tea things, putting everything back into the cupboards exactly as found, doused the meagre fire in the grate. Matthias didn't understand the weird totality that was Gustav Wengler quite as Jed appeared to do, but he grasped enough to know that Wengler had an underlying order to his universe and that the non-appearance of Archie Louden was undermining every stick, every brick of it, uplifting every last kellick, leaving him a man adrift. And the last thing Matthias wanted was for Wengler to go completely off the rails. He had a whole village to think of, a village dependent on the mines for its livelihood, for lifting it out of the desperate poverty so many of their neighbouring villages had already sunk into.

Keep him sweet, Matthias thought. *I've got to keep him sweet.*

And with that in mind he made a last foray up the spiral staircase to tell Gustav Wengler he would do everything in his power to locate the missing man.

'I can't promise we'll find him,' Matthias said to Wengler, just as he'd said to Jed. Wengler had moved from his window sill and was sitting once again upon his stool in the middle of the floor, fingers twined and still, like a cat's cradle halfway done upon his lap. And it was not anger or jealousy Matthias felt to look on him then but compassion that his life really had been undone by so simple a disruption as his assistant not coming home to Havengore when he'd said he would. He cast a proper look about the room in which Wengler spent his days, at all the books, at the table with its neat stacks of papers and folders all spaced with care and deliberation like tiles upon a roof; he looked at the huge blackboards filled with neat lines of chalk-written words and equations he couldn't understand the beginning of, let alone the end, despite all his training in mathematics and engineering. And he understood that Jed and Wengler's father had been right. This man really didn't think along the same lines as the rest of them, and he understood also that if you worked for Gustav Wengler in the capacity Archie Louden did then you really would do your damndest to get back to Havengore on time, if not before.

'We'll find him,' Matthias said softly. 'I'll search high and low for him, all the way from Oban to Ardnamurchan if I have to.'

Gustav Wengler turned his face slowly towards Matthias, though did not catch his eye. To Matthias's great relief there was no outburst about him having been spotted crawling over Wengler's monuments, and instead the man began to rock gently back and forth upon the wood.

'I hope you do,' Wengler whispered, his fingers starting out their tap, tap, tapping again upon the stool's base. 'For if you don't, then I fear everything is lost.'

CHAPTER 8

MISSING MINERALS, MISSING MEN

Matthias left the dismal wraith that was Gustav Wengler and went back down the spiral staircase, swearing he really would do all he could to locate Archie Louden, though with little idea how to go about it. He followed Jed to the landing stage to be greeted by the sight of two strangers poking about upon the shingle, lifting up one stone after another before dropping them down again. Alongside were the two boys Hesketh had earlier stopped from running up and over Wengler's island. Matthias could have done without any more complications to his day, was already thinking on how he might be able to locate the missing man – send folk down to Oban, have them track his journey from there to here, how far he'd got; send others to Corran ferry, if anyone remembered him crossing; send yet more men out to the villages strung along the shore-line up and down the coast for any sightings, asking at ostlers' and coach stops. The last thing Matthias needed was another dimension to these problems but he was undoubtedly intrigued by the two men waiting for him down on the shore. The dark haired one had a vicious scar running from eye to chin, and shoulders that could have given an unruly bullock a run for its money; the other looked like a priest who has lost his flock, with a prominent streak of white running through his otherwise dark hair.

'I'm sorry,' Matthias said as he approached the two unknowns. 'But who are you exactly? Hesketh says you have business with me.'

The larger man looked up straightaway from the shingle, kicking away the stone he had just been studying.

'We're from Lundt and McCleery's Pan-European Mining Company,' Brogar explained, 'and I gather from our many sources that you've uncovered some kind of new mineral and we, my friend, are here to investigate it.'

Θ

Matthias took Brogar and Sholto to his home. He made only one quick stop at Reverend Harlow's house, knowing he'd buried the remains of the bag of bones - found a while back at Ockle - earlier that morning.

'I'm sorry I couldn't be there,' Matthias said, but Oswald merely shook his head.

'More important things going on, I suspect,' he said, and Matthias nodded his agreement. How important those things were they were neither of them yet fully cognisant, but burying a body was also important, even when no one knew who he was.

There wasn't enough space at Matthias's home to billet his four visitors comfortably, but there was his barn out back, and although he and Jed argued long and hard that the Company men take their own beds in the house both Brogar and Sholto assured them they'd be happier in the barn, and Gilligan and Hugh happy in the stables. All were starving, tucking eagerly into the meal Matthias's housekeeper had left the previous evening. The woman was past her best, as both she and Matthias knew, and in truth he only kept her on – and she only stayed – because they were in the habit of it and there was no one else to take her place. She'd made a simple but belly-filling meal of hare, potato and turnip stew, mopped up with a quick batch of skillet scones, and all tucked in with vigour.

They had much to talk about, and Jed hardly allowed Brogar and Sholto to get their boots off before quizzing them about the mineral that had brought them all to Ardnamurchan.

'I've been looking for another sample ever since I got here,' he said, 'but so far have come up empty handed. I'd be happy to show you my notes and where I've already searched.'

Matthias coughed, Jed glancing over quizzically, unaware he might have said too much, that Matthias had never heard of this Lundt and McCleery's, let alone where their interests lay.

'Can you tell me a little about your employers?' Matthias asked, before Jed could say any more. 'I've not heard of them before and know no reason they should be interested in our mines.'

'Apart from the fact that the mineral you recently sent to London is entirely new to science?' Brogar replied jovially. 'And that it's been found nowhere else in the whole of the world but here?'

'As far as we know,' Sholto cut in with a note of caution. 'But a most extraordinary find, nonetheless. The company we work for has offices in many cities and contacts in many more, and none of their researchers have ever come across anything like it.'

'And your company does what, exactly?' Matthias persisted. He'd good reason to be concerned. The Galena Ore Mines mined lead ore, as its name implied, and lead was good money; but if more could be made from it then that might give him an ace up his sleeve if they never did find Archie Louden and Wengler reacted as badly to that scenario as he suspected and went into meltdown.

He eyed his visitors with less suspicion than before, reassessing them as potential allies who might be able to buy up the Galena Mines if push came to shove.

'Obviously you've questions, Mr McQuat,' Sholto said.

'Matthias, please,' said Matthias, and Sholto nodded affably and went on.

'Matthias, then,' he said. 'So let me try to explain. Lundt and McCleery's is obviously concerned with mining, but also casts a wider net.'

Matthias nodded, for this much wasn't hard to guess.

'Here in Ardnamurchan you mine for lead ore,' Sholto went on, Matthias impressed he'd got the pronunciation of Ardnamurchan right. He'd an odd accent, this Sholto – not exactly Highland, and certainly not English, but slightly clipped – as if he knew all the words but hadn't spoken them for a long while. 'So here's the rub,' Sholto went on. 'Occasionally mining for one thing will throw up something unexpected, and when something new comes along we get sent to take a look at it. Provide resources for research that might not otherwise be done.'

'And you try to figure out whether it can make you any money,' Matthias stated, and saw Sholto and Brogar exchange glances, and this time it was Brogar's turn to speak.

'That's it exactly,' he said. 'That's precisely what we do. And let me tell you I've been from Scandinavia to the Carpathians doing exactly that for the past twenty years; but the Company will only act upon whatever report we give them, and what report we give them is entirely up to you.'

Sholto looked over at Brogar with admiration. He knew what Brogar had done over in Brora, supporting Solveig McCleery's entirely unsanctioned re-opening of the coal mines there, and understood that Brogar would never allow the Company to ride rough-shod over any place that was not willing to take them. It seemed he was not the only one convinced.

'There's been only one previous finding of the mineral,' Jed piped up, looking at Matthias, who nodded. He knew what the lad was going to say, for they'd spoken about it often, about Jed's researches into the sample that had gone missing years before.

'The initial find,' Jed went on, 'was turned up by French POWs sent here as workers during the Peninsular Wars, long before Mr McQuat took over.'

Long, long before, Matthias wanted to put in, but did not, letting Jed carry on.

'It ended up in a geological collection in St Thomas' in London. That's a medical place,' Jed added for Brogar and Sholto's benefit, 'and it was one of the physicians there – an amateur geologist – who spotted it, an Irish man who...'

'His name was Adair Crawford,' Sholto interrupted to Jed and Matthias's immense surprise, though not so Brogar who was well enough acquainted with Sholto to know he was nothing if not a brainbox filled to the ginnels with every small and insignificant report that had ever crossed his subterranean desk in Trondheim, before he'd been sent out into the field a few months back.

'I read a paper that mentioned him years ago,' Sholto continued, 'disseminated through the Linnaean Society. He was the one who christened it Strontianite, after here, and brought it to the attention of your great Humphrey Davy...'

'Exactly!' Jed put in excitedly. 'I was just going to mention him! He did some fantastic experiments. I've tried to recreate some of them but, well, they weren't quite as successful as his were.'

Matthias smiled, as did Sholto, both knowing how Humphrey Davy had risen – against all odds – to become one of England's foremost chemists, most famous for the theatrical demonstrations he carried out during his public lectures at the Royal Institution; a woodcarver's son from Penzance who became a household name and a Sir, changing the face of science for his own generation and those who followed his death forty years previously in 1829. One of Jed's heroes, and quite rightly so.

'So I gather,' Sholto said mildly. 'But I also gather that after some initial enthusiasm Davy lost interest, moved on to other things. And that's why we're here, to put that right, to put the name of Strontian on the map once and for all.'

'And you really think it's worth pursuing?' Jed said, gazing at Sholto with shining eyes.

'I do,' Sholto agreed, 'and so do Lundt and McCleery's, especially now that Crawford's Strontianite has been officially deemed a new element, renamed Strontium, incidentally, after the one place – this place – where it has been found.'

He was gratified by a short silence as everyone – including Jed – took in this news, a silence broken only by Brogar Finn scraping out the last of the stew from pot to bowl.

'So what might this do for us?' Matthias asked bluntly, speaking in his capacity as mine overseer, village protector, the man on whose shoulders rested the fate of all the men and women of Strontian and indirectly of the whole of Ardnamurchan.

'That will depend entirely on you,' Sholto said. 'Allow us free rein. Let us take our look, see if we can locate what young Jed here has been unable to, see if we can find more of this mineral and discover what use it might be to science, and therefore to the Company.'

'And afterwards?' Matthias persisted. 'What will happen then, if you do find anything?'

Sholto shrugged and held up his hands.

'I don't know, Matthias. Let's just see if we can find it first.'

'My colleague is being reticent,' Brogar said, smiling broadly as he placed his empty bowl on the table. 'If we find enough of the stuff to make it more than a flash in the pan then you'll be batting off geologists with a stick. Mark my words, Matthias, we're only the vanguard. It's not every day you stumble across a new element, and with new elements come new properties, new experiments and new discoveries that can lead to who knows where.'

Sholto grimaced. It was too early to let Matthias believe this could be the case. He chose to change the subject, and there was one completely unrelated circumstance he was curious enough about to do just that.

'I meant to ask,' Sholto said, 'that island, the one we picked you up from. Who is it lives there?'

'That's Gustav Wengler,' Jed replied, before Matthias could open his mouth. 'And... oh my God!' Jed went the colour of the inside of a cucumber. 'I forgot! How could I do that?'

'It's all right, Jed,' Matthias said, patting Jed's shoulder, rather pleased the lad had forgotten Wengler since they'd had visitors, new stimuli for his imagination. 'No need to panic. I've already thought about how we should go about it. We'll close the mines tomorrow for a couple of days, get the men on his trail. And it will have the added benefit of giving our guests a chance to look around undisturbed.'

'Something going on we should know about?' asked Brogar, never one to ignore the obvious.

Matthias shook his head. 'It's nothing really. A man missing who should have returned here a while back. Wengler's assistant, out on the island. He was coming back from a collecting mission in Denmark, got as far as Oban but hasn't been seen since, at least not around here.'

'And he just wouldn't do that!' Jed added with a fervour that had Matthias closing his eyes briefly in irritation.

'I've already told you, lad,' Matthias said loudly, his impatience not going unnoticed by either Brogar or Sholto. 'I've plans for it. Men to Oban, men to Corran, men to everywhere in between. Isn't the closing of the mines enough for you? It was you who promised that blasted man but me who'll have to damn well deliver!'

Matthias was not a man given to swearing or losing his temper and he was immediately aggrieved he'd committed both vices now, and in front of strangers, not to mention the colour that had suffused Jed's face at Matthias impugning Wengler.

'I'm sorry,' Matthias said. 'It's nothing. A local matter.'

'It's not nothing!' Jed shouted, standing up suddenly, his chair screeching out across the floor. 'Archie Louden's missing, maybe murdered by pirates or smugglers! And Gustav Wengler…'

Matthias grimaced. He didn't want to hear Gustav Wengler's name ever again. He'd stolen something from Matthias, he'd stolen Jed, and the bitterness in his heart because of it overtook him as it had done the night before.

'I said we'll find him, boy, and so we will.' Matthias thumped his fist on the table, such a knife edge to his voice that Jed stayed rock still.

Brogar and Sholto exchanged glances. The mention of pirates and smugglers piqued their interest no end, as had the evident undercurrent of unease separating their hosts on either side of the table. Jed stood for a moment more as they watched in anticipation, the colour high in his cheeks, Matthias's use of the word boy having chilled him to the quick. He sat down. He'd no idea of the ramifications engendered by the apparent switch of his allegiance from Matthias to Wengler; all he understood was that something had changed between him and Matthias since they'd returned from the island and he didn't like it, not one bit.

'That man over on the island,' Matthias continued, speaking to his guests, trying to keep his voice even, 'is mad as a cage of march hares.' He shot a quick glance at Jed, daring him to speak, to go against him. Jed held his tongue. 'Unfortunately he has us in his grip, being the owner of the mines. We are entirely at his mercy. And when I say mad, I don't mean mad in the conventional sense, more that he lives in a world of his own making. The simple fact of his assistant not returning as expected has had the effect of throwing yet more hares into the mix when there's hardly room for the ones already there.'

Sholto lifted his eyebrows. This colourful metaphor threw him slightly, but he got the drift. He cast a look at Brogar, saw his hard, square face in profile as Brogar gazed intently at Matthias, the slight narrowing of Brogar's eyes as he assessed the situation, perhaps recalling – as Sholto was – the ripped down flag, the burned-out bothy. Maybe it was entirely irrelevant. Maybe it was a commonplace occurrence for both to have been accidentally destroyed, but given the smell of burning that had been so pungent, so obviously recent, he thought it surely worth a mention. He waited a second or two in case Brogar should weigh in but he did not, so Sholto cleared his throat.

'I'm not sure,' he began, 'if this is in any way pertinent…'

CHAPTER 9

BURNED DOWN BOTHIES, RIPPED DOWN FLAGS

They arrived at Ardslignish in a clatter of hooves, horses soon hitched to the trees by the track, the men going down the rest of the way on foot to the burned-out circle where the bothy of straw bales and peat divots had once stood. Matthias was twenty odd yards distant when he caught the smell of smouldering strong in the air. He didn't really think it would be anything, for although it didn't happen often, it did happen – folk came, lit a fire, forgetting they were surrounded by everything fire loves, went to sleep without tending to it, left a candle burning, got distracted, got drunk. It was rare for anyone to be seriously hurt, the compacted straw of the walls not easily catching to an inferno, at least not without help. But then again, he thought, why hadn't he heard about this particular bothy catching alight? Surely any traveller would have said something of it and folk around here weren't usually tight-lipped about an event so exciting.

Unless it was smugglers, he thought. Matthias abhorred them and what they did, hated the stranglehold they had on the peninsula, the ease with which they carried on trading despite the regular incursions of excise men coming in from Fort William, tracking the whole of Ardnamurchan up and down – and its surrounding seas – like their own personal hunting ground. They didn't often get help from the locals and Lord knew Matthias couldn't blame them for that. Poverty made collusion easy, made folk turn a blind eye, thankful for the small gifts found upon doorsteps the following morning – a keg of fine French wine or brandy, a stash of tobacco, a crate of fruit whose name was unknown but made fine pickles and jams. What any of this might have to do with the disappearance of Archie Louden wasn't obvious at all. Yet Matthias was cautious, had everyone hang back while he went down alone to the burned-out bothy, or thought he had, because suddenly beside him was the bulk of Brogar Finn who wasn't a man to take orders from anyone, as Matthias would soon find out.

'There's a track going through the grass here,' Brogar said. 'Seems to be heading off to that ditch…' and away Brogar went on its trail before Matthias could stop him. He turned his attention instead to the flag pole at the water's edge and saw straightaway that Sholto had been right to believe it had been deliberately interfered with. The ropes were lowered to bring down the flag but no flag to be seen, only a few shreds of cloth and a sharp nick in the rope suggesting that someone had put a knife to it and ripped the flag away, and no one would do that unless there was no need nor want of being fetched from this tiny piece of land jutting out into the sea like a beak from a bird. *So, smugglers after all,* Matthias concluded.

'You might want to come take a look at this,' shouted Brogar Finn. Matthias did, and what he saw made him bowk and vomit, and up came all the stew and skillet scones eaten earlier, for down there in the ditch lay a man who looked to have been rolled in wet coal dust, so charred was he, and the smell was of rancid fat, burned cloth and skin. Brogar turned the body over and Matthias was broken from his body all over again, for the half of the face that had been in the icy water was obscenely intact compared to rest of him, and Matthias knew him straightaway. It was Archie Louden, and his stomach clenched and down went Matthias on hands and knees, retching like a cat with a fur ball in its thorat until all he was spewing was a deep yellow bile flecked with strings of red blood torn from the lining of his throat.

The others came down from the track at a signal from Brogar, Matthias having had to sit, too appalled to do anything but hang his head between his knees until he felt the blood begin to pump again around his body, Brogar taking charge, keeping everyone from away, except Sholto.

'So what do you think?' he asked, as Sholto knelt to take his look. A few months previously Sholto had been a bookworm in a basement office, one of those faceless, nameless researchers he'd mentioned earlier to Matthias and Jed. But since his first assignment in the field, with Brogar in Kildonan, he'd seen a few dead bodies up close, far closer than in the anatomy lectures he'd frequented back in Trondheim, and looking on the pitiable sight of Archie Louden Sholto felt no revulsion, only a need to find out who had been capable of putting him through such a horribly protracted death.

'At a guess,' Sholto said, moving his long fingers gently about the man's head, probing his skull through what little hair was left, 'I'd say he was hit on the head at least twice. There's an obvious fracture here at the back and his lower jaw is loose, several teeth missing, suggesting another attack from the front. Poor man,' Sholto added, looking back along the trail in the grass leading from the burned-out bothy to this ditch, noting the slight scorch marks left along its length, the blackening of the grass to either side, the remnants of ash and cinder that must have fallen from the burning man desperately crawling towards the water of the dyke that proved, in the end, not to be his salvation but his dying ground.

'So,' Brogar said, 'knocked out and left for dead, bothy set alight, but he comes round and tries to get to the ditch to put himself out.'

As matter-of-fact as always, a trait Sholto had found, on first meeting Brogar, a little disturbing, until he realised this was the way Brogar kept himself sane given all he'd seen during his long years working for the Company, all the dead men he'd encountered through all manner of accident and bad circumstance: men pulled limb from limb by a pack of wolves or who'd had their stomachs ripped out by bears looking for an easy winter meal, bodies lying side by side with the de-gutted dogs who had been their life companions and protectors out on tundra and taiga, or the rags of other men who'd disappeared through sudden cracks in the ice, surfacing only when a frozen lake had finally thawed, bobbing to the surface like corks, fingers, feet and face nibbled away by the char who survived in the dark, sluggish stream of water existing far below the ice.

'I think I've found something!' shouted Hugh who, with Gilligan, Brogar had ordered to rake around in the ashes of the bothy and its environs. 'There's an iron spike here for tethering horses,' he yelled, 'and hoof marks too. One set coming in and then away again, and looking lighter going than when they came. And there's something else...'

Hugh went down on one knee and studied the hoof marks. He wasn't the brightest lad on God's earth but he knew about horses and could see that one of the marks of one of the hooves was more sharply defined than the rest.

'It's had a new shoe,' he declared, 'and a bad nail, and not long since. I can see the mark of the dropped nail in one of the sets.'

'Good lad,' said Jed, who'd gone first to Matthias to check it really was Archie Louden in the ditch, which Matthias could not deny. Jed had kept glancing over to where Brogar and Sholto were studying the body but dared not approach. He'd not known Archie Louden at all but he certainly didn't want to see him now, not given what Matthias had managed to mumble out about what he looked like. Jed had been standing dithering at the flagpole ever since, more worried by how Wengler was going to react when they told him the news than anything else. Jed knew about the smugglers – you couldn't stay anywhere in Ardnamuchan for more than a few days without hearing some tale or other about them, but he'd never heard of anything like this. Even if Archie had stumbled on some secret handover or tryst he couldn't understand why they hadn't just incapacitated him before disappearing into the backwaters from whence they'd come. By all accounts they'd done the same before, and surely this level of violence could only serve to bring more attention to their activities, catching the interest of the excise men who would come crawling over the peninsula and out into the waters surrounding it, making it a far less safe place for the smugglers to carry on their usual business than before.

'Something here too!' came Gilligan's shrill cry from the dead circle of the bothy. 'Some kind of bag, and stuff in it!'

Not much stuff as it turned out, to Gilligan's great disappointment. He handed it over to Matthias, who was somewhat revived now he'd sluiced his face with seawater from the loch, so cold it left his fingers numb. The water in the dyke might have been marginally warmer but Matthias wasn't going anywhere near it, not with Archie having been in it. He shuddered to see the dark roll of his body lying a little way up, Brogar and Sholto having lifted him from the water, placing him face upwards on the grass. The black smudges were still evident on their clothes and hands from this moving, despite both having rubbed the latter in the wet grass to try to clean them.

'There's some normal traveller's supplies here,' Matthias said, once he'd cleared his throat, gained back a shred of voice. 'A rudimentary medical kit, a pick for hooves, a salve for girth-rub, another for blisters...'

He handled each piece of equipment with distaste. All were covered with a sticky tar-like substance that must have exuded from the leather of the bag under the heat of the fire, and he loathed the feeling of it on his skin, longed to drop the bag and run back to the sea to wash his hands again. He fought for control, passing each object he retrieved to Jed, who was standing by his side, Matthias finding his close presence a comfort, the younger man ramrod straight, carrying enough backbone for the two of them.

'And there's something else...' Matthias put his fingers into the deepest recess of what he assumed must be Archie's bag. The tarry substance had stuck the two sides of it together but, by pushing the leather apart, he had a corner of what lay at the bottom and then had it out.

'A book, I think,' he croaked, swallowing back the bile, extracting the sorry mess of what had once been a tidy package double wrapped in waxed linen, scraps of which still adhered to its surface.

'Right up your street, Sholto,' said Brogar, the two of them just then approaching. Sholto smiled involuntarily, but it was to Jed that Matthias handed the small oblong of char and tar, as he'd handed everything else, Jed reacting as he always did when given a set of unknowns, ordering all the objects on the ground in a tidy order, but he treated this latest find with more reverence. Back at Matthias's house Brogar had suspected that this Jed was almost as bookish as Sholto, and this suspicion was now confirmed, Jed handling the wrapped book with the greatest of care, pulling out a handkerchief from his pocket the second Matthias hinted what it might be, taking it within his kerchief and using the loose edges to rub gently at the linen wrappings and bindings that had stretched and curled with the heat.

'A journal, maybe?' Sholto asked, moving up beside Jed. 'It wouldn't be unusual for someone to keep one of his travels.'

'Maybe,' Jed agreed, looking up quickly as Brogar produced a vicious looking knife from the sheath at his belt.

'Can't we just hack into it and see or, even better, leave it until later?' Brogar asked, the only one of them who seemed to have noticed it had started snowing and that a vicious wind was starting in at them from the west. He wanted to get moving, to make sure they'd recovered all they could, get the body of the dead man properly seen to, check out those hoof marks, get everyone on the move before the snow covered everything up. Sholto shot Brogar a look and although Brogar rolled his eyes he handed the knife over to Sholto and took a pace back.

'I'll go take a look at those hoof marks,' Brogar said, 'but you'll need to look lively, Sholto; snow's coming down now, and only one way that will go.'

Away he went, Gilligan skipping at his side, a boy who never knew his father and in consequence was always eager for the attention of men he deemed worthy to take his absentee place.

'We'll need to go at it gently,' Sholto was saying, looking up briefly into the sky that had of a sudden closed in on them, aware now of the brief guffets of snow that were starting to fall, several flakes landing on his hand as he spoke. 'We'll look at it properly back at Matthias's but we can maybe take a brief glimpse at the title page, see what we've actually got.'

Jed nodded, holding the book still as Sholto worked the point of Brogar's large knife - more used to butchering frozen dogs and horses for food than slipping between burned coverings of linen - but Sholto was deft, soon had them away so he could make out some kind of impress on the book's cover, though could make nothing of it, blackened as it was with the residue of the fire. Working quicker now, as the snow began to fall with more intent, he sliced the top board from the spine and lifted it away to reveal the frontispiece, tainted on all four sides by scorch and burn, the printed words and illustrations hard to make out clearly, a dark shadow having fallen over them where the tannin and dye had leached from the leather cover into the pages from the heat. He was about to suggest they wrap the lot up and take a proper look at it later when Jed spoke.

'It looks like a copy of Chaucer's Astrolabe,' he said, sounding puzzled. 'But Wengler already has a copy… I saw it in his study.'

And then his mouth dropped open slightly as he thought about it.

'Unless,' he said. 'Unless… but surely it can't be…'

'Can't be what?' Sholto asked, as Jed began to shake his head.

'Chaucer's Riddle…' Jed's voice was quiet and thin, Sholto looking at him quizzically, having no idea what Jed was talking about. And then Brogar bore down on the two of them, clicking his tongue with impatience.

'We've to get going,' Brogar announced. 'This snow is going to cover everything. We need to get all we've found tidied up and ready to go. We need to get a few sketches of these hoof marks and mark their direction, for there'll be nothing left of them but mud if we have a fall and then a sudden thaw. And we've a body to arrange the transport of. You two need to look sharp. You can chatter on about books and riddles as much as you want later on, but for now there's things needing doing. Time to be moving. Hugh, with me.'

Hugh trotted up obediently, Brogar telling him to go and gather as many birch and alder branches as he could. 'Long as you can get them, and if they'll bend and not break, so much the better. Sholto, give the lad my knife. Good, there you go.'

Hugh's wide face cracked open in a wondrous smile as he took the huge knife, putting his thumb to its blade and immediately withdrawing it, sticking it happily into his mouth to suck away the blood before scampering off to the scrub to do as he was told.

'Gilligan will need to get the ferryman. Matthias!' Brogar was shouting now, although he was not aware of it. 'Get yourself here.'

Matthias was not far away. He'd sat down again, couldn't shake the sickness he was feeling right down in his throat, through his stomach, into his legs. He levered himself to standing, face white and gaunt as the falling snow.

'Point your fastest horse out to Gilligan,' Brogar commanded, 'then get yourself back to the bothy and fetch up what's left of that ripped out flag lying over there, and get the rope from the pole, as much of it as you can. Jed, you've an eye, so make sketches of all those hoof prints Hugh was talking about and you, Sholto, gather up the bag and everything that was in it, including that blasted book.'

Everyone, bar Sholto, was startled at Brogar's peremptory orders but none disobeyed and off they went to perform their duties.

'Is he always like this?' Jed asked Sholto quietly, as he took out notebook and pencil.

'Always,' Sholto replied with a conspiratorial grin. 'But don't let it put you off. Brogar might growl like a bear, but he's the growling bear you want by your side in adversity and you, my friend, are in adversity right now.'

CHAPTER 10

WICKER COFFINS, FLOATING CHAPELS

The snow continued falling, but gently. Every now and then, over the next few minutes, one of them would stop and stand, let the cold flakes fall upon their upturned faces, but not for long. Hugh returned from the scrub-line with an armful of branches at the same moment Brogar and Sholto arrived by the loch-side with Archie's body, Matthias already there with the remainders of rope and flag; and from these unpromising materials Brogar soon had a flexible mat made into which he and Sholto shifted the body of Archie Louden, ready for transportation. Brogar had already stripped Archie's body of every scrap of material that remained on him, a task everyone else was immensely thankful he carried out without need of their help. He handed the burned and stinking scraps to Sholto, who went through each piece with care. He didn't find much: a pair of spectacles in a hard-shelled, shark-skin-covered case, a few metal buttons and a belt buckle, several coins secreted in his trouser pockets carrying the unmistakeable impress of a Danish mint: yet more proof, if any were needed, that this was Archie Louden, and no other.

By the time all this was done, Hesketh Wood and his ferry could be seen scrawling up the loch, sticking to the landward edge where trees and scrub sheltered him somewhat from snow and wind, Gilligan having ridden his horse like the devil, leaving it lame for a few days afterwards – not that anyone minded, given the circumstances. Hesketh had hardly brought his ferry in before Sholto and Brogar were lifting the roll of birch, flag and rope, lowering it into the boat's belly, Hesketh quickly lifting out a couple of seat planks to make way. His face was solemn and grey. He'd been forewarned by an excited Gilligan, who'd accompanied him back, of what to expect, and although he'd transported corpses before he'd never had to carry one that was murdered and burned and his cheeks blanched as the men lay the wickered bundle down, clearing his throat again and again, not having bargained on the smell, nor the strange black sap that began to drip from between the roped-up birch twigs in which the body had been bound. He surely wasn't going to touch it but it looked sticky, like the pitch he used to caulk his boat, and he grimaced as he imagined a boat caulked with nothing but such a substance: literally a corpse boat, the stuff of many recurring nightmares during the following weeks. It made his trip back to Strontian acutely uncomfortable, bearable only because of the near constant chirruping kept up by Gilligan, sent with him on the return journey to keep the body from rolling around too much on their way back. Hesketh couldn't have expressed how glad he was of this extra company. He'd never liked carrying corpses at the best of times, but he was cheered by the boy who was seemingly made up entirely of curiosity, giving forth a constant barrage of chatter that kept Hesketh's mind occupied. The snow was being driven almost horizontal by the wind, not that Gilligan noticed, energised as he was by the whole adventure, which in turn kept Hesketh pulling at his oars all the way back down the loch to Strontian. And all those questions the boy asked, and the things he said, stayed in Hesketh's head for a long while, ticking over and over into his night-time hours as he formulated the answers he'd not been able to provide at the time.

Have you ever seen a dead body before? Gotta tell you I've seen a few. We had a pretty big time of it back in Kildonan that was fair gruesome. So what was your worst? I think mine was the poisoning – that was awful! And you must have seen plenty drowned men, what with you living here and being by the sea and all. Ooh, but wait! What's that over there? What kind of fish was it that just jumped? I bet that it thought the snow falling was insects. D'you think that's possible? And was that really true what Hugh told me, that you make your cattle swim over to the islands? How do you get them to do that? Back home we couldn't hardly get our kine over a river, let alone a stretch of water like this. So they can really swim? Who'd have thought it! And how d'you manage this boat anyway when the tide goes against you? And what if you lost an oar? And what if you lost two oars? How far down would we float before we grounded?

Questions and more questions, but they kept Hesketh's mind off his stinking cargo as he forged on down the coast, kept him dipping his oars in and out of the water, concentrating on the steady rhythm that formed the normal pattern of his days; made him wonder on things he wouldn't have thought on before, like maybe that's all life was: just one long string of questions until you got to the end of it, and no guarantee even then of anyone giving you any answers; and what this particular death really meant, the why and the how of it. Hesketh had met Archie many times, ferrying him back and forth from Havengore once a month at minimum. He remembered how Archie would fling himself into the water by Havengore to drag in Hesketh's boat so Hesketh wouldn't have to get himself wet, leave as dry as he came. He'd always appreciated that small consideration, and Archie always tipped him well despite him knowing Hesketh got a stipend through Wengler's lawyers for his services. And he always had a ready smile, did Archie, entertaining Hesketh with tales of the places he'd been, places Hesketh would never go. Hesketh's heart almost broke to think of Archie lying here in his boat, wrapped in that hard blanket of twigs and rope, leaking his dark pitch into the boards below. He was never so glad to see the minister's black form, shifting between white slats of snow, as he was on that late December afternoon. He liked Oswald Harlow, for the man was nothing if not kind, and kindness, Hesketh thought, was what Archie needed now.

Oswald Harlow himself was freezing, as glad to see Hesketh as Hesketh was to see him. The snow was of the kind you could brush off your clothes without it making a mark but the wind was driving it straight up his sleeves, down the gap between cassock and neck, and he was shivering badly, left ankle throbbing where he'd tripped over one of the snow-covered tram lines laid into the pier to take the raw lead ore to the barges and on to the workings at Bonawe. He looked out towards the Floating Chapel, the iron boat towed up from the Clyde when the local landowner, James Riddell, refused permission to have the tumbled-down church at Strontian rebuilt, not when it would be Free Presbyterian. There'd been a huge storm a few years back that drove the Floating Chapel right between two rocks just below Riddell's house, Riddell taking this as a sign from God and relenting, allowing a new church to be built at Acharacle and the chapel at Ockle to be reinstated. But the folk of Strontian liked their Floating Chapel, as did Oswald, and so it remained, and was the place the corpse would need to stay until it could be laid into the ground.

He hoped this new body wasn't like the one the lad Harald had found on the other side of the point at Ockle, a man without a name or family to claim him. It reminded Oswald that he must go visit Simmy, who'd not been at service on Advent Sunday, of all days. Most likely the dreadful man Simmy had the misfortune to have as a father had stopped her coming, was maybe sick again, though plainly hadn't died, more was the pity. Oswald winced, hating to wish a man dead, but Fraser McRailty was just plain wicked, especially to his daughter, working her like a mule and never showing her a lick of appreciation or affection, not that Oswald had ever seen; and by Christ, the fight he'd had to get him to release Simmy to school just once or twice a week, and she so bright; and then he'd stopped her schooling completely, probably fearing a daughter who could read and write when he could barely spell his own name. Either way, he decided, if Simmy didn't turn up to service next Sunday he'd go pay a visit, check she was all right and hadn't been beaten to a pulp, for it wouldn't have been the first time if she had.

And then the boat was in, and no time to think on Simmy for the moment, Hesketh standing up and throwing him a rope Oswald barely had the feeling in his cold hands to grasp. Luckily, the young lad who'd earlier delivered Hesketh's message about a dead body coming leapt into the water as if it was not so cold it had already begun to freeze at its edges, and was up the icy shingle in a trice and onto the pier next to him, taking the rope from his hands, pulling the boat in.

$$\Theta$$

Brogar was studying the rather bad map Matthias had laid out on the table before them, aware for the first time of exactly where they were on Scotland's west coast, the peninsula of Ardnamurchan sticking out like a bad foot, almost nudging the large Island of Mull that lay to its immediate south. Seeing it all just so, Brogar understood why the boat crew had deposited him and Sholto where they had, at Ardslignish, and why Archie Louden might have been at the same place, for Ardslignish was the obvious jumping-off point for both Strontian and Havengore, if you were going by boat. Sholto made the same observation.

'So I think we can assume Archie came by water up from Oban,' Sholto said, moving his long fingers over the map. 'The land journey from there to here is convoluted, and his letter indicated the opposite.'

'That was Archie,' Matthias smiled at the thought. 'Always wanting back on the island was his way. Always taking a boat if he could, which is so much quicker. He'd stop with me only when he got here too dark for Hesketh to take him across.'

'So,' Brogar said, 'it shouldn't be hard to find out where he got his horse, and if we can find out where, then we can find out when.'

'That would have been Kilchoan,' Matthias supplied. 'There's a man there breeds horses; workers, small and sturdy, but certainly strong enough to carry a man down to Ardslignish.'

'And what about farriers?' Brogar asked. 'Does he do his own?'

Matthias was struck by his own lack of logic, for Hugh had been certain the animal at the bothy had been newly shod.

'No,' he said, tapping his lips with his fingers, 'but there's a travelling farrier comes through these parts a few times a year, servicing the most outlying farms that can't easily get down to Strontian. And if there really was a loose nail, well, that doesn't surprise me. He's cheap and not the best, but that would please old Skinner up at Kilchoan, where I suspect Archie must have been.'

Matthias glanced at the window, the outside so dark he might have been inside a molehill. It didn't seem possible so much had happened in one day, nor that Archie was really dead. He had a sudden thought of Oswald Harlow out on the Floating Chapel with Archie's body, all alone, nothing to keep him company in his vigil but a couple of glasses of bad Communion wine.

'Jed,' he said. 'Would you gather up some vittals from the kitchen, take them out to the Reverend? I'm sure he'd be glad of them. I only wish we could get him something hot.'

'Well that's easy done,' put in Brogar Finn, the scar moving unnervingly on his cheek as he exhibited what Matthias correctly interpreted as a smile. 'Trick I learned out on the steppes. Cursed cold it can be at night for men watching their livestock, so the women put one vessel inside a larger one, stuff the gap between with moss or straw or felt. Mud'll do at a pinch. Stopper the lot up, wrap it in a sack, it'll stay piping hot for an hour, maybe two, if you're lucky.'

Matthias could have laughed, it was so simple a solution. He wondered why no one had ever patented it and made a fortune. Jed was more practical.

'I can do that,' he said and was immediately on his feet, Gilligan and Hugh up behind him, eager for anything new, and a visit to a chapel floating in the middle of a sea loch was something they didn't want to miss.

'Right then,' Jed said, leading his aides away, soon banging around the kitchen area and out to the barn, gathering what they needed, Gilligan fetching straw, Hugh happily gouging up some mud from outside the door with a spoon, Jed fetching an empty milk churn, and a few minutes later they were gone.

Sholto took the opportunity to take out Archie's meagre possessions and laid them out on the table.

'So, do you know anything of what this Archie was doing on his trip?' he asked Matthias, who shook his head.

'I don't,' he said. 'I've no idea what they worked on out there. Archie spoke about it sometimes, but only in the vaguest terms.

Jed might know more. He and Wengler struck up a kind of rapport, at least as much rapport as Wengler is able to do with anyone.'

There was a note of bitterness to Matthias's voice he couldn't disguise and he saw the two Company men raise their eyebrows, but did not at that moment care. All he felt was that everything was slipping from his grasp and he hated it; hated that Archie had died and nothing he could have done to have prevented it; hated too that Jed was gone from him, that he'd been stupid enough to look on Jed as some kind of protégé he could mould in his own image like some sort of ersatz son.

'Jed said something earlier about Chaucer's Riddle,' Sholto was saying, looking directly at Matthias. 'Does that mean anything to you?'

'Nothing,' Matthias said shortly, rubbing his temples with his fingers. A short silence then, before Sholto came at him again.

'And what do you know about the monuments on the island?'

Matthias raised his head, stopped his rubbing.

'Why would you want to know?'

'Because your man Wengler named his island after another, also called Havengore, in the Sound of Denmark. And that original Havengore is where Tycho Brahe built his Uraniborg in the 1570s, which is effectively a massive observatory built out of stone.'

Sholto could have said much more about Tycho Brahe and Uraniborg, but Brogar interrupted with familiar impatience.

'As gratifying as all these intellectual ramblings are,' he said, the tone to his voice making it quite clear that he was anything but gratified, 'I think we're rather getting off point. Let's not forget that this Archie Louden is dead, presumably murdered, and that he was coming back from a research trip in Denmark. Shouldn't we therefore have found on him something more than a couple of buttons and a few coins? Shouldn't we be asking what happened to whatever it was he brought back with him? And shouldn't we be asking the only other man alive who presumably knows what he was sent for?'

Matthias switched his gaze to Brogar and shook his head. Whatever big fish he'd imagined himself in whatever pond he thought he'd been swimming in all his life, had just been taken over, and rightly so.

'Wengler,' Matthias said quietly. 'I didn't even think to ask him. Why didn't I even think to ask?'

He got no answer, only the soft hand of Sholto patting his shoulder in a gesture of solidarity Matthias wasn't sure he could bear.

'Too late to go and interview the man now,' Brogar was saying, with a heartiness that had Matthias grinding his teeth, not out of malice but despair. He felt the presumption of his own intellect sliding away from him, for everything these Company men had done, asked and stated since they'd landed, was everything Matthias should have done, asked and stated himself. But instead Matthias McQuat had been found wanting, and not only did he know it but he knew that Jed must know it too, and that he found hard to forgive.

'Tomorrow morning,' was all he could say. 'We'll go over in the morning.'

And weak as it was, that was all he had.

Chapter 11

Consecrated Boards
on Unconsecrated Waters

Jed and his merry band of Gilligan and Hugh set forth towards the Floating Chapel, complete with one sack of bread and cheese and another bearing hot stew begged from a neighbour in its insulated churn. Their way through the snow-laden streets was not dark, for by now everyone in Strontian had heard the news, and every window was lit with vigil candles as people sat by their fires and mulled over the bad news that Archie Louden had died, and not well. He was wasn't exactly one of their own, but had been around and about the place for almost a decade and that made it their business, no matter he'd spent most of his time over on that island with the man they all knew was more than just a little out to lunch. Folk flitted from door to door as Jed and company moved through the silent streets, all eager to pass on the bad tidings or gossip a little more about it, everyone agreeing that it must be something to do with the smugglers who blighted their shores and what, in consequence, that would mean for the rest of them, which was the incoming of the excise men once they heard about it, and them stirring everything up, checking on taxes and illicit drink, and they none of them wanted that.

'So it's a church that's on the water?' Hugh was asking, as they left the main street and walked down the pier to the first of the boardwalks that had been anchored to its end, their boots squeaking in the snow, the same snow falling on them, though softer now, the wind having apparently retired for the night now the sun was well and truly down.

'That it is,' Jed replied, not that he'd ever visited it before. He'd seen it right enough and asked about it not long after he'd arrived, everyone telling him the story of the laird who refused the Presbyterians even an inch of space on his land and how the congregation had come up with an alternative that was so ingenious in its way that even said laird had been impressed, if not in a particularly godly way.

'There's planked rafts leading out to it,' Jed explained, 'that are put out whenever there's a service, assuming the tide allows it; otherwise you can only get to it by Hesketh's ferry, but only if you're willing to climb up the rope ladders on the outside.'

Gilligan nodded, knowing this already from Hesketh.

'So yon minister's out there on his own with the body?' Hugh asked, shivering slightly, remembering the corpses laid out in Solveig's barn and how she'd stayed with them the night through and alone, and how he'd thought at the time he should have given her company but hadn't dared. The dead might be dead, was his philosophy, but there was something undoubtedly spooky about spending time with them. Not that he could put his finger on exactly why that was, only that he felt it viscerally, a fear ingrained in him like a tattoo he couldn't shift. That fear wasn't being helped right now by the way Jed's lantern threw up strange shadows as they started across the narrow pontoons leading towards the dark bulk of the Floating Chapel moored out in the Sound, and took his first wobbling steps on the wooden slats, holding out his hands to the rope rails.

'Are you sure it's safe?' he asked, almost whispered, feeling pitiful because he couldn't go at it with the same gusto Gilligan was doing, already two yards in, his gait and feet making the walkways move even more than Hugh had anticipated.

'It's fine,' Jed said, offering reassurance, moving easily past him. 'Think on it as walking over…'

But Jed stopped speaking as he drew level with Gilligan because the walkway they were on suddenly parted company from the one behind and the one in front, the mooring ropes slackening, gaps appearing over fast running water, maybe only a couple of feet but enough to force a jump rather than a straightforward stride. Jed didn't hesitate, and his lamp dipped alarmingly as he landed on the opposite side, Gilligan alighting a second behind him, leaving Hugh alone on the landward side. The longer he hesitated, the larger the gap was becoming and it took Gilligan jumping back and giving his friend a shove before Hugh got up the nerve to take his leap of faith.

'All fine,' Jed said breezily, hastily grabbing and tightening the ropes as the three were reunited, unaware that Hugh's heart was beating so wildly he could feel it in his throat. 'Just means tide's turning,' he went on. 'We'll need to be quick if we want to get back again.'

And quick they were, leaping their way onto the last pontoon and scrambling up the rope ladder to board the Floating Chapel, barely having time to deliver their goods to a startled Oswald Harlow before retreating again, jumping the black depths of the Sound and back to land.

Θ

Sholto was in the barn, the finds from the bothy bag laid out on the couple of bails of straw serving him and Brogar as a table. Not that Brogar was with him. He was still in with Matthias, mapping down to the last inch the ways Archie Louden might have taken to get to the point on Ardslignish, so that on the morrow they could spend their time in the most efficacious way to track his progress, find out who he'd met, if anyone, and who else was around at the same time. Sholto hoped Brogar's presence would shake Matthias from the torpor he'd thrown himself into. After Jed and the boys had left he'd shut himself down temporarily, answering questions only in monosyllables. Grief, Sholto knew from experience, took people different ways, and this particular way was apparently Matthias's, inconvenient as it was, but if anyone could snap him out of it, that person was Brogar Finn. He wasn't glad of it, but was glad of the leeway it provided him to do what he did best, which was to analyse the evidence given him, seeking out the messages they might have hidden within their bounds. He focussed first on the practical travelling objects Archie had with him, wanting to get them out of the way before moving on to the more obvious goal which was undoubtedly the book that had so surprised Jed. He picked up the hoof pincers, brushing away the dried mud with his fingers. Some of it was still caked in its teeth, and stuck within these remnants was a single thorn, hard, sharp and unbroken, probably from a sloe.

Easy done, he thought, knowing how tough those blackthorn spikes could be, how shrikes often used them to store the carcasses of the smaller birds they'd caught, using them like larders. And this single thorn explained why Archie Louden might have been stopped in his tracks.

He hires a horse at Kilchoan, Sholto reasoned. *He rides it hard because he's keen to get back home. Probably late afternoon, wants to get there before the sun goes down. Horse steps on the thorn and because it's been badly shod the thorn stabs its way between shoe and foot, slows them both down. Too late now to get to Strontian, so straight for the nearest bothy to while out the night.*

So far, so obvious, but Sholto wasn't done. This was only Sholto's second outing into the field, and he hadn't Brogar's broad experience, but he'd read and studied a thousand reports from the Company's agents who, like Brogar, travelled so far and wide it was almost unimaginable. He had diligently sifted through all those diverse reports and notes, absorbing the experiences of unknown people and their unknown lives, understanding that - no matter how differently they appeared - underneath they all presented the same basic patterns of behaviour, and Archie would be no different.

Sholto picked up the several Danish coins he'd recovered from Archie's pockets. On one was imprinted with its denomination – *2 rigsdaler* – and on its other side a portrait of Christianus IX, dated 1868. So not much doubt Archie really had just arrived back from Denmark given that it was now December 1869, and little more doubt that what he'd been sent to fetch was important, at least to Gustav Wengler. What that might be, Sholto had no idea. Such property could have been intellectual, though Matthias had said already Wengler was in regular correspondence with other astronomers and mathematicians, so most likely it was a physical object or objects he'd sent Archie to collect.

So, he thought, *where would I carry something I'd gone to such great lengths to fetch for my employer?*

His immediate thought was a saddlebag, and it occurred to him only now that such an obvious accoutrement had not been found with Archie's body, only the satchel he presumably carried about his neck. He knew from Brogar that men who travelled often, often travelled light. *Take nothing with you that you don't need,* Brogar had told him back in Kildonan, astonished, and a little contemptuous if truth be told, that Sholto had gone to the bother of shipping over with him a hoard of books sitting unopened and unread in their sea chest, awaiting his instructions. It was no use Sholto explaining to Brogar that without his books he felt naked and vulnerable. Now Sholto had actually travelled he understood Brogar's veiled ridicule because he felt it too. Of all the things you want to travel with, a load of books is probably the last. What you needed was something small and light. One satchel in which to carry everyday essentials, and one other – a saddlebag maybe, if you know you'll be travelling with horses – in which to carry everything else.

Bring your wits, pack your necessities, but ditch the rest, was what Sholto had learned the hard way. And undoubtedly Archie had learned the same, and if he stuck to Brogar's principles he would have kept whatever was of most importance as close to his person as he possibly could. And the only things he'd had on his actual person were his spectacles and, in his satchel, that book that had so perturbed Jed. And so the most important thing had to be the book, disregarding anything else taken from him by his attackers, and so it was to that object Sholto now turned his attention.

CHAPTER 12

INSIDE THE SNAIL

Simmy made up her mind. The ring had to go to the minister. She'd missed Advent Sunday Mass and with it the blessing of the body Harald had found, before Reverend Harlow took it down to Strontian in case anyone there recognised anything of the scraps, and the most recognisable of those scraps had to be the ring. And she'd other things to worry about, like that Harald had been acting really, really strange, keeping his distance so she'd barely clapped eyes on him these past few days, and then there was that fearful bruise on his jaw.

'Got a kick from a horse,' Harald said when she asked, though that hardly seemed likely, as Harald was as good with horses as he was bad with people. 'It's going to get better, Simmy,' he'd added, 'if only you can wait a while.'

It was late now, all strength sapped from the sun, weak as it was. She'd done all her tasks excepting the worst, which was to see to her father. Not that she was feared of him, for he'd no more strength in him now than the limpid sun as it dropped below the horizon. He'd got a lot worse since Sunday, maybe because the temperature had dropped and the frost had begun to nip at the fields and his arthritic joints. His knees and elbows were swollen to the size of cooking apples and he'd been lying in his bed moaning and groaning, able to crawl no further abroad than the piss-pot Simmy had put in the corner of his room so he didn't have to go to the outside dunny – the pit in the back of the yard she and Harald used. It meant that every evening before she got the tea she had to go into his room to collect the piss-pot, empty it onto the midden before giving it a rinse and a bit of lime slake before returning it to its place. The stench was always vile, the pot swirling with dark yellow urine, the sediment from his faeces settled into a brown sludge at its base. She didn't want to look, but she'd been told she needed to check for signs of blood and even though she put her hand over her mouth, her fingers pinching her nose shut, the stench churned her stomach like it was trying to flip itself inside out. Which was why it was the last task she performed before she made the tea, because if she did it afterwards then all that tea, food and all, would have come straight back up again, and that was a waste in anyone's mind.

They'd no doctor here in Ockle, nor anywhere else on the peninsula, but Mr McQuat down at the mines arranged for one of the monks to come over the water every couple of months, wandering about the scattered homesteads and villages, checking on who was ailing and if he could do anything to help. The last time Brother Athanasius came to see Simmy's father he'd sat her down, told her things were bad and needed keeping an eye on, and looking for blood in his stools was one of the tasks he'd asked her to do. And so Simmy did it, not for love of her father – for him she did no love at all – but because she respected Brother Athanasius and Reverend Harlow, who always accompanied him on such visits. The Brother had left her a small book about diseases on that last visit on the advice of Reverend Harlow, pointing out the pages she might find most useful.

'Your father is very ill,' Athanasius had said, 'and is unlikely to get better. But if we can track his symptoms we might be able to make his end a little easier when it comes, and it will come, Simmy, before too long.'

Brother Athanasius had not been surprised Simmy was dry-eyed at this prognostication. He knew from Oswald that Old Man McRailty, if he could be called old at the age of forty six, was not a man anyone wanted living longer than he should.

'He mightn't have been good to you or your brother,' Athanasius went on, 'but he is your father, and without him neither you nor Harald would be walking this earth, so it behoves you to take care of him in his final days.'

It behoves me, Simmy had thought, finding the words strange, a commandment to perform a duty she'd never stinted at and had been obeying her whole life. She thought of those words again now as she went back towards the small house in which her father was encased, trapped like a snail within its shell, no way back out into the light. She felt the familiar stirrings of relief that he might soon die, and guilt to want it so. Fraser McRailty used to fill this house corner to corner, room to room, from cellar to ceiling, stamping his big boots all about it, his loud voice reaching the parts his boots could not, she and Harald trying to make themselves small and impenetrable as woodlice, rolling themselves up just to keep out of his way. But in the last few months all that had changed, their father confined and bounded by the illness that was eating him alive, making the entire house seem a smaller place. And it was pity instead of the usual anger that overtook Simmy today, maybe because she'd been thinking on the bones in the crypt, lonely and unknown; or maybe because she'd taken a decision about the little ring and to whom it rightfully belonged. She went inside, from light to shadow, and stood for a moment hoping Harald would be home; but there was no sign of him. She was alone.

CHAPTER 13

STRANGERS AND SUNDIALS

Brogar was having a difficult time with Matthias McQuat. His first meeting with the man had given Brogar the impression he was capable and intelligent and just as well, seeing as he was in charge of the mines he and Sholto had been sent to investigate. His persona as intelligent and capable persisted after they'd discovered the body of his friend, but the moment Archie was despatched to the Floating Chapel and later Jed and the boys, Matthias had apparently splintered into pieces, which Brogar found infuriating. He'd come across the likes of Matthias before, men good at their jobs, strong and commanding, who nevertheless couldn't think themselves into a straight line when something vaguely emotional came along, choosing to sit and brood instead of facing facts. And that was something Brogar could not abide.

'Maps,' he barked. 'Do you have any of the area?'

Matthias responded sluggishly, but eventually rustled an old Roy map out of his desk; a military map commissioned after the Jacobite rebellions more than a hundred years before. It wasn't especially detailed, but it was enough.

'Show me,' Brogar commanded. 'Tell me the way Archie Louden would have gone.'

Matthias sighed, but did as asked, moving a finger over the map from Oban up to the point, and from there to Ardslignish. Brogar was frustrated and was about to go around the table and physically shake some sense out of Matthias when he was interrupted by a timid knocking on the door.

'Expecting anyone?' Brogar asked.

'Maybe some Strontian folk, wanting to know what's happening,' Matthias said, shrugging his shoulders, visibly trying to haul himself back into the world, be the man he'd always been, the one to whom everyone came for answers. Such a small noise, that knocking at his door, and yet enough to blow some life back into him, and Brogar saw it.

'Who is it?' Matthias asked, as the knocking came again, louder this time, as if all the strange happenings of the day had rolled themselves into one and come banging at his door. When there was no answer Matthias stood up, went to the door and pulled it open to reveal the pale outline of a face he did not recognise, the rest of the man hidden by the night.

'Matthias McQuat's house,' Matthias said. 'Who are you and what's your business here?'

The apparition let out a long breath that was visible in the cold air as he put out a hand to the jamb.

'My name is Kurti Griffen,' said the stranger. 'I was looking for Gustav Wengler, and was directed here.'

Matthias blinked, but the shock of this announcement acted as the kick up his backside Brogar had a few moments back been about to administer himself.

'In,' was all Matthias said, stepping back, waving his arm, and in the man came. 'Can I get you some food? Something to drink?'

Matthias asked, the old Highland customs taking priority before all else.

'Thank you,' Kurti Griffen said. 'That would be most kind.'

Matthias noted straight off his English was fluent but accented just as the older Gustav Wengler's had been.

'You've come from Denmark,' Matthias stated, to general surprise.

'Why, yes,' Griffen replied, as Matthias hung the kettle, sticking the last of his bread onto a toasting fork.

'You ever hear of a man named Archie Louden?' Brogar butted in, Griffen's dark eyes skewing towards him.

'I am aware of that name,' he replied slowly.

'In what manner, exactly?' Brogar demanded.

Griffen cleared his throat, weighing what to say next, no point starting off on the wrong foot.

'He visited the Round Tower in Copenhagen two weeks ago, and came to my notice when he asked about a… certain artefact.'

This Round Tower being what?' Brogar went on, the answer coming not from Griffen but Sholto, who chose that moment to re-enter Matthias's house and caught the last of the conversation.

'The first stage of the Trinitatis complex begun by Christina IV for academic excellence…' Sholto began, until he saw the look on Brogar's face when he amended his information. 'Basically, a huge Observatory stuffed with one of the world's largest and oldest collections of astronomical instruments.'

He could have said more, like how beautiful the building was, how it has no stairs but instead a cobbled and ramped walkway taking seven and half rotations to go all the two hundred and nine metres to the roof top observatory – a feature unique in European architecture - but he, with the others cocked his head as he heard a chattering as of goldfinch on the wing, and out of the dark space of the door Sholto had neglected to close came Jed, Gilligan and Hugh, all red-faced with the rush of their return and the exhilaration of one of their number nearly having drowned, Hugh's clothes wet and dripping from where he'd failed to clear the leap from the second pontoon back to the first on their return journey.

'What've we missed?' Jed asked, going straight to one of Matthias's cupboards and pulling out a corked bottle of wine and a cup into which he poured a liberal dose, along with a slosh of tepid water from the kettle, handing it immediately to Hugh.

'Almost lost this young man,' he said in explanation, 'only just had time to chuck in a rope and pull him out.'

Gilligan shoved Hugh towards the fire, whose warmth soon made his clothes give out enough steam to fog the windows.

'Screaming like a girl, you were,' Gilligan added, rubbing his friend's back and shoulders to allay the shivering.

'Not half!' Jed added.

'Y...y...you'd've screamed too,' Hugh countered through chattering teeth, 'if you'd b...b...been in the drink. That w...w... water was b...b...lack as b...b...Brora coal and f...f...fierce cold. Th...th...thought I were a goner,' he added quietly.

Matthias shivered too because Hugh wasn't wrong. If Jed hadn't been so quick and if Hugh had got more than a few yards from the pontoon then there really would have been another body to be seen to.

'So what's the what?' Gilligan interrupted, 'and who the curse is this?'

'This, Gilligan,' Brogar said, 'is Kurti Griffen, newly arrived from Denmark,' he laid a slight emphasis on the last word, catching everyone's attention. Griffen politely removed his hat, the hair beneath being the exact same orange gold as crack willow stems in winter.

'Denmark?' Jed repeated thoughtfully, abandoning the kettle he'd been about to fill.

'Denmark,' Brogar went on. 'And Mr Griffen here was about to tell us everything he knows of Archie Louden, and why he has come to our doors.'

Griffen was not intimidated by Brogar's frankly menacing attitude, and instead found himself a little amused. He took his time, looking around carefully at the assembled company before he chose to speak.

'Well?' Brogar prompted, not regarding patience as a virtue.

'Well,' Griffen began, flexing his strong fingers as he removed his gloves. 'Before I answer that, I have a few questions of my own. Like who you all are and which of you is Mr Wengler.'

'Well said, sir!' Brogar laughed shortly, enjoying the fact that this newcomer was not intimidated but was holding his own. 'You've the right of it there. Matthias, will you do the honours?'

Matthias nodded and obliged.

'I am Matthias McQuat,' he began, 'manager of the Galena Ore Works on this peninsula. And these other gentlemen are Sholto McKay and Brogar Finn, both from the Pan-European Mining Company of Lundt and McCleery's…'

'Ah,' Griffen said, leaning forward, looking interested, 'now them I've heard of. You have an office in Copenhagen, I think.'

'That we do,' Brogar replied, raising an eyebrow, but Matthias was already continuing his task.

'And to your left is Jed Thornbrough, my temporary and very able assistant from London,' he said, smiling briefly at the lad, the fire back in his belly, thinking that Wengler could go hang, that he wasn't going to give Jed up without a fight. 'And over by the fire are Gilligan and Hugh who came with Misters Finn and McKay.'

'And you,' Brogar put in, 'who exactly are you, Mr Kurti Griffen?'

Griffen moved his head and gazed directly at Brogar. He'd had dealings with Lundt and McCleery men before, knew how tough and resourceful their field workers were required to be, had the feeling that this one was tougher and more resourceful than most. He tipped his head to one side.

'No one has told me yet of Gustav Wengler,' he stated, 'and I do not have to justify myself to anyone but him, but,' he added, raising a hand to forestall objection, 'presumably from what you've said you all know his associate Archie Louden, so my turn to ask a question. Why the interest in what he was doing in Denmark?'

'Because he's dead,' Matthias said flatly, rubbing his temples with his fingers. 'We found his body this afternoon.'

Kurti Griffen's expression did not change, but he turned his attention to Matthias in apparent surprise.

'And what does Gustav Wengler have to say of this?' he asked, a question which caught them all off guard.

'He doesn't know,' Matthias said after a small hesitation. 'We've to tell him in the morning, and it won't go well.'

'And why is that?' Griffen asked mildly. 'Do we consider his reaction might shift the wheel?'

Only Sholto understood the old Danish proverb and undertook the answer.

'That might be an understatement,' he said. 'Mr Wengler is... a tad eccentric, and very reliant on his helpmeet. The fact of his non-return has already upset him considerably, and the news that he will never return might be enough to shove the wagon right off the cliff, to further your metaphor.'

Sholto looked at Griffen and Griffen, rather unnervingly, looked right back.

'So before we go any further,' Sholto took a breath and went on, 'we need to know what Archie was doing in Denmark and how it is that you've so coincidentally turned up on his tail.'

Kurti Griffen did not miss the note of suspicion and possible accusation in Sholto's remark. He'd gained his position as Investigator for the Round Tower by being attentive and astute. This new information of Archie's death of necessity changed his role here. Time to give a little information in order to gain more back, decide where he should go from there. He nodded, kneading his cheeks with thumb and forefinger.

'All right,' he said, 'then let me tell you this. Thirteen years ago the man in charge of the Round Tower got the place into financial difficulties and only got out of them by selling off parts of the collection he had no right to sell. My role, for the past few years, since the new director came on board, has been to track them down and return them to the Round Tower where they belong. The piece I am particularly interested in at the moment is a sundial, sold to one Gustav Wengler twelve years ago, transported over to Scotland in April the following year, although the exact date and route by which it left and arrived are still unknown.'

A short silence then, as everyone tried to put together how this related to what had happened in the here and now of Ardnamurchan Peninsula. Brogar was first to get a glimmering.

'So Archie went to the Round Tower asking about this same sundial, and you questioned him about it.'

'I did,' Griffen replied. 'He told me that yes, he knew of the purchase but as far as he and his employer were concerned, it never arrived.'

'And despite his asking, despite the fact he plainly didn't know where your sundial was, you didn't believe him,' Jed stated.

'Men lie,' Griffen said simply. 'And considering the purchases I discovered Mr Louden made when in Copenhagen I have good reason to believe that either he or his employer were doing just that.'

A fox amongst the fold could not have caused more consternation. Jed jumped up from his seat, Matthias up behind him because a thought had just occurred that might turn this whole situation on its head.

'Sit,' he commanded Jed, a hand on his shoulder pushing him down. Jed obeyed, though his body was quivering beneath Matthias's fingers.

'You're wrong,' Jed said quietly, staring daggers at Kurti Griffen. 'Gustav Wengler would never lie. He's not made like that. Ascertaining facts is what he's all about and untruth has no part in it.'

Matthias kept his hand on Jed's shoulder as he recalled his wanderings over Wengler's island and that flat empty circle in the middle of it, thinking too on the unknown sack of bones Oswald Harlow had buried that morning in the old churchyard at Strontian, no one coming forward to claim them, after no one had at Ockle before, and Oswald telling him the few words he'd said: *Come from nowhere and nothing, and into the ground you go, my friend, unknown but not unremarked, and never forgotten.*

'Archie didn't lie,' Matthias said slowly, 'and neither more did Wengler. I don't think your sundial, Griffen, ever reached its destination, but I think I might know where it is.'

CHAPTER 14

BEING STRONG, BEING WEAK

Simmy had had it with Harald avoiding her. Where he was sleeping she'd no idea, certainly not at home and most probably with Aileen and her family. But their da was dying, Simmy was sure of it. He'd creaked like a squeaky door every time he pulled air into his lungs and what came out afterwards sounded like an old sponge being squeezed of its last drops. And there was blood in his stools, she'd seen it the past two mornings – thin trails of it floating in the sunk-below detritus and the dark yellow piss. If he died, everything would change. They could only keep the croft if Harald signed for it – sons having the right, but not daughters – and only if they could pay off their da's debts up front and make a clean slate of it. And Lord knew if that was possible. Simmy was unprepared. She should've figured all this out months ago, forced Harald to go see the Factor – the laird's general manager – and get things worked out. But that hadn't happened, and there was only one person she could think of to turn to for help. And so here Simmy was, standing on the threshold of Aileen's home, kicking her boots on the step to loosen the hard mud that had collected in their cracks, wondering whether or not to chap at the door. And then the door opened, Aileen standing there, apparently having heard Simmy without the knocks Simmy had yet to perform. She must have been patting butter, judging by the equipment laid out on the big wooden table beyond, and Aileen's eyes were as unnerving as ever, no sign of her parents anywhere.

'Folks away?' Simmy asked.

'Come in, Simmy,' Aileen replied, in that weird way she had of knowing who was there, even though she couldn't see them. 'And yes, folks away. Over at Fort William. Be there a couple of weeks, Advent Retreat and all that. Come on in. We've time for a blether.'

Simmy was embarrassed. She didn't dislike Aileen as such, but regarded her as an enemy as far as Harald was concerned and was uncertain where to cast her gaze, unable to look into those unseeing eyes, focussing instead on the rest of Aileen's face: the crooked tooth on the upper left side of her mouth, the little dimple in her chin, the fact that one ear was higher than the other, the slight curl of her hair as she brushed it from her forehead. Simmy wondered what it would be like to live all her life in darkness, how Aileen managed on her own without mother or father to look after her. And yet Aileen moved around her dark kitchen as if she could see every nook and cranny, pulling out a stool for Simmy, asking her to sit, fetching a cup of some elderflower cordial, the soft bubbles bursting as she poured it sounding loud in Simmy's ears.

'So what's on your mind, Simmy?' Aileen asked, smiling gently, 'for you've surely not made your way over here to ask the time of day.'

Simmy squirmed. Aileen's astuteness was uncanny.

'It's me da,' Simmy admitted. 'He's worse'n what he was just a few days since, and I think that... well, I think this might be it.'

'Oh Simmy,' Aileen said, her hand stretching out across the table and taking Simmy's free hand in her own, Simmy shivering at the swift and certain way Aileen moved towards it, like a dog scenting a bone beneath the earth.

'I'm so sorry,' she said, squeezing Simmy's hand, and it was all Simmy could do not to snatch it away because sympathy was the last thing she wanted. She shook her head, though Aileen couldn't see her, and spoke louder and with more boldness than she meant.

'It's not that. Nothing to be sorry about far as he's concerned. Soonest gone is soonest mended is what I say.'

'You don't mean that,' Aileen replied softly, letting go of Simmy's hand, Simmy forced to look at Aileen's face again as she went on. 'He's your da, no matter he's not been an awful good one.'

Simmy snorted. She couldn't help herself, for a worse da than Fraser McRailty didn't come along every day, but thinking on him Simmy found a choke coming to her throat and something that sounded horribly like a sob. She snatched up the cup of cordial and took a quick gulp to disguise her reaction, which only made it worse, and now there were tears coming from her eyes unbidden as the realisation that her da was really dying hit her like a sack of bricks. He'd not always been bad, hadn't Fraser McRailty, and there were parts of her that remembered him from long, long ago when he'd been a kinder man, one who taught her how to calm the chooks and take their eggs without getting her fingers pecked to shreds, who had shown both her and Harald how to fish right and proper, how to trap rabbits and birds, how to gut and cook their catches over a peat fire, how to clean the shit from a pregnant sheep's arse so the lambs wouldn't be infected when they fell.

Simmy took out a handkerchief and blew her nose.

'And what does Harald have to say about it?' Aileen asked, once Simmy had done the business.

'But that's just it,' Simmy snuffled, her voice high and tight. 'I don't know where he is. I've hardly seen him this whole week, and

BURNING SECRETS

I need him, Aileen, I really need him to be here.'

And then she spilled out all her worries about the croft, about the debts she knew her da had, how they would pay for the funeral, how unless Harald went to the Factor they would be destitute, with nowhere to go. And she told Aileen about the ring, about how she'd been about to give it up to the minister but now thought it might to hang onto it, deceitful as it was.

'Harald found it with the Ockle Bones,' Simmy confessed. 'He wanted to give it up to the minister for your birth date, for Saint Lucy's intercession, and then I was going to give it the minister anywise, 'case it turned out important, but we'll maybe need it…'

Aileen did exactly the opposite of what Simmy had expected and smiled, and Simmy saw in that smile what Harald had always done, and how kind Aileen was, and how forgiving.

'My darling Simmy,' Aileen said quietly, 'you've no need to worry on my account. I like my life just the way it is. I'm grateful for it, and manage very well. I've no need of saints to broker bargains on my behalf. My parents do that well enough. They're over now at the monks' retreat paying out good money I've told them countless times not to waste on prayers and masses that will do no good at all. What I'm more worried about right now is why your brother isn't with you, for I've not seen him either. He's not been here for days, and indeed I'd been thinking to come over to find you, it's so unusual. But I've never wanted to intrude, you and Harald being so close, and me the cuckoo in the nest, so to speak.'

Simmy looked into Aileen's face and no longer saw the dead eyes, saw only the tears brimming at their edges and understood why Harald had been so taken with the girl Aileen had been and the woman she had become, precisely because she didn't see what was on the outside – quite literally – and make judgements because of it. Here instead was a woman who marked her days by sound and silence and the subtleties of how the world moved about her, the intricacies of being and living in ways others overlooked, feeling for the currents that moved the water and not just what was on the surface for all to see. And it struck Simmy too that there must be something deep inside Harald that she, his own sister, had overlooked, because he'd always been able to understand this woman completely. Aileen might be as blind as a frog buried beneath the mud of a winter pool but she was all the better for it, and Simmy felt a rush of warmth towards Aileen as she finally grasped it.

'So what shall we do about Harald?' Simmy asked, hope creeping in like a cat before a stove.

'It's a problem,' Aileen said, 'no doubting it. But he'll have his reasons, and we've no cause at the moment to think they're bad. Trust is always hard, but I think we can spare him some, don't you?'

Simmy thought about that. Trusting Harald, she realised, was rather a novel concept. It wasn't that he was a hothead – far from it – more that making unilateral decisions had never come naturally to him. Big or small, he usually ran everything past Simmy before he took action, whether it was to take the animals to new pasture, change their feeding regime, plant one crop rather than another in a different rotation. Everything delivered to Simmy for approval. And now the one time he'd made some decision on his own she'd immediately assumed the worst. She was shamed by Aileen's words. Harald was her big brother and deserved Simmy's trust, at least until he proved otherwise.

'And the ring?' Simmy asked. 'What should I do about that?'

'I suggest,' Aileen said, smiling her wonderful smile, 'that you hang onto it, darling. For who knows how things will go. We'll call it salvage, and that's enough for the moment.'

Aileen moved with ease about the table and sat down on the stool beside Simmy and put her arm about Simmy's shoulders, hugging her to her breast.

'And I don't want you to worry, not about anything,' Aileen added as Simmy leaned in towards her. 'Whatever happens – if your da dies or if he doesn't, if Harald comes back or no, I can promise you this, Simmy: wherever I am there will be a place for you. So never fear, darling, never fear for anything, for you will always have a home with me.'

Simmy closed her eyes and folded herself into the warm curl of Aileen's body, forgetting to be strong, glad that for a few minutes at least she could let go the reins.

CHAPTER 15

EVERYONE GOING WHICHWAYS

There were a few things needed organising the following morning. Someone had to tell Wengler about Archie and this duty, Matthias knew, was up to him. He would take Jed with him because Jed was the only person he knew who might be able to cope with a Wengler falling apart at the seams.

Someone too needed over to Ockle to see if their sundial was the same one Griffen was seeking; Sholto was the one to go, taking Griffen with him, partly to keep an eye on the man but also because Matthias was certain he was holding something back, and it seemed to him that Sholto and Griffen were of an ilk and if anyone could winkle out such secrets, Sholto was the one to do it.

There was also the need to get to Kilchoan, ascertain whether or not Archie had really been there and, if he had, what kind of horse he'd hired to take him down to the bothy. If they could trace the horse they'd be halfway to finding who had taken it from Archie, presumably by force. Hugh, recovered from his ducking, was the obvious choice here, apparently knowing more about horses than anyone else, and Gilligan was not to be parted from his friend.

Last was the task of tracking down the other objects – aside from the book – Archie was presumed to have been carrying with him, purchased in Copenhagen on Wengler's say-so, at least according to Griffen. These comprised a Moon Dial and a Sun Brooch, so Griffen informed them, though exactly what these were Griffen either didn't know or didn't choose to divulge, only that their purchase was a strong intimation to him and his superiors at the Round Tower that Archie knew of the existence of the sundial.

These were hazy waters, Matthias understood, and precisely for this reason he decided the person best suited to the task of their pursuit was Brogar Finn, for even in the short time Matthias had known him he understood that Brogar had an intimate understanding of the underworkings of society, even if he was not a part of them, and was not a man anyone would wilfully choose to enter into conflict with. And so it was Brogar that Matthias sent back down the peninsula to Corran in the hope that whoever stole the brooches from Archie had tried to sell them locally, or at least made their existence known as being up for sale. The population was sparse along those desolate tracks that led to Corran – and from there over the ferry and on to Fort William – but Matthias had not lived here all his life without knowing several of the family names linked to the smugglers – and who better to approach with stolen goods? – and one of these was directly on the route, as he told Brogar.

He also checked in at the mines to make sure everyone was doing as they should and to his great relief found that his overseers had risen to the challenge, organised their day just as he would have done himself. He thanked them, then headed towards Hesketh's ferry, which took him to the Floating Chapel to ask how Oswald's vigil had gone, and some other questions besides.

'It went hard,' Oswald said, without preamble, when Hesketh had pulled his boat alongside the chapel and Matthias had scrambled up the ropes. 'But thank you for sending over those lads with their gifts. It was extremely heartening to get some hot food inside my skin.'

'I'm glad it was so,' Matthias said, 'but tell me something, Oswald. Those bones, the ones you just buried, how long do you think they were in the water?'

Oswald Harlow was perturbed. He'd been a minister for many years and had buried all sorts, young and old, in all sorts of states, and had a fair notion of how bodies decayed over time.

'Water's not so precise as soil, Matthias,' he said. 'But my best guess is they were there for quite a few years.'

'More than ten, maybe?' Matthias persisted.

'Quite possibly, quite possibly,' Oswald answered, looking closely at Matthias, noticing how tired the man looked, how pale, how dark were the circles beneath his eyes and the stubble about his chin, and Matthias a man so particular about being clean shaven.

'Are you telling me you know who he is?' Oswald asked, a slight rush of blood suffusing his cheeks. 'Because if you do, Matthias, there might be family…'

Matthias interrupted, shaking his head.

'An idea only,' he said. 'And one that needs some investigation yet. But tell me, what do you know of the sundial up at Ockle? How long it's been there, for instance.'

Oswald was mystified, and very curious. He'd been in this parish for just over a decade, and as far as he knew the sundial in the graveyard at Ockle had always been there, at least as long as he'd been minister, and so he said.

'But why are you asking?' Oswald didn't want to let it go. 'And what's it got to do with those bones?'

Matthias shook his head again as he moved back to the edge of the Floating Chapel.

'I've no answers yet,' Matthias said as he lowered himself down over the side. 'But come over to my house this evening, for by then we may have at least a part of them.'

The Reverend Oswald Harlow leant out over the rope rails of his Floating Chapel, raising a hand as Hesketh Wood pulled at his oars, wondering what on God's good earth was going on.

Θ

Gilligan and Hugh were enjoying themselves immensely. When they'd elected to leave Kildonan with Brogar and Sholto they knew they were being given the possibility to escape from a lacklustre existence tending cattle and sheep for the rest of their days. Previously, they'd dreamed of going off to the gold fields of the Suisgill and Kildonan, striking it rich, but that was all gone now, the Gold Rush well and truly over. They neither of them had extant family back home and were all the family either had needed for the past several years, and now here they were being sent out on detectival activities and they were tripping over each other with anticipation. There hadn't been enough horses in Strontian to supply everyone with their own and so the two of them had been downgraded – having the least far to go – allocated a couple of pit mules whose usual duties were hauling carts of rough ore down to the shoreline, ready to be loaded onto barges that would sail them down the coast to Bonawe. The comparative lightness of the load of these two young boys made the mules a little skittish and they kept snatching at the winter-wilted grass growing alongside the track, at least until Hugh broke off some hazel switches and showed Gilligan how to use them in conjunction with the basic rope bridles they were equipped with to keep them focussed and on the path.

'So what do you really think happened to that man in the bothy?' Gilligan was asking as they wound through the woods cladding that part of peninsula, broken only by several sandy braes tipping down towards the shores of the loch.

'Think he got robbed and left for dead,' Hugh said, matter-of-factly, Gilligan nodding sagely.

'Kinda got that bit already,' he said. 'What I was meaning was the way and the why of it. You saw them strange buildings over on that island same as I did. What if that weird hermit who lives there is some kind of maniac who comes out at night and goes around murdering people?' Gilligan shivered pleasurably, sure he was onto something. 'What if he's gone mad, what with being all on his own and the like? What if he's done it once and got a taste for it?'

Hugh looked over at Gilligan and smiled indulgently. Of the two, Gilligan had always been the one with the better imagination. Back at Kildonan, when they were sequestered for the night in their stables, it was always Gilligan who told the stories and Hugh who listened. There were plenty of wild folk tales told back in the day and Gilligan had the ability and disposition to snatch the sum of them and redistribute them as he saw fit. During the day it was a different story, for then it was Hugh who was in charge, the one who could see straightaway if a dam was in trouble, if a milker wasn't milking right, if a sheep was missing, if a horse needed to be re-shod or a dose of some medication or other. He'd felt real important the afternoon before when he'd told the others about the hoof prints, and more important still when he'd been taken seriously by no less than Brogar Finn, a man who'd been to Siberia and a load of other places Hugh couldn't remember the names of and no idea at all of where they were, but saw in Brogar the kind of man he would choose to be, if he ever got the chance.

'Not likely,' Hugh said, concerning Gilligan's rampant imaginings about the mad man on the island. 'But think on this: they was all talking about smugglers before, remember, at the house? Real life smugglers. Gotta be pirates too. Gangs of 'em roaming the waters just about here. Nothing like that over our way.'

Gilligan began jumping up and down on the blanket that served for his saddle, getting so excited he almost slipped right off and had to do a few gymnastic manoeuvres to keep himself upright.

'Pirates!' he exclaimed, once he'd steadied himself. 'Now that's got to be some sort of exciting life, don't you think? Maybe we could join 'em, take ourselves out over the seas. Think on what we'd see then, Hugh!'

Hugh was more sanguine.

'Not if they goes about murdering folk, we won't,' he said, having a sudden thought back to the Floating Chapel the night before, and Archie Louden's body wrapped in his wickerwork and how desolate he had looked, the dead man's face poking out the top where the minister had pulled away the wooden shroud to make his blessings. And Jesus, that had been bad to look at, half of it crisped up like a salmon fillet left on a fire overnight and only the minister's single candle for a light, flickering and jumping in the shadows.

'Not pirates, then,' Gilligan said, a little disappointed.

'Nor smugglers neither,' said Hugh, not disappointed at all.

'Straight and narrow for us both, then,' Gilligan added, wrinkling his nose at the stricture until Hugh added his rider.

'Straight,' Hugh said, 'but I don't think it's ever going to be narrow, Gilligan, not now.' Thoughts already blooming in his mind of following Brogar Finn to the ends of the earth. 'You mind that tale about Black Colin?' he asked, Gilligan smiling broadly. It came from one of the books Solveig McCleery had lent them; Black Colin who'd fought in the Crusades leaving his lady behind him on the islet of Loch Awe, coming back seven years later, making his return known by leaving his half of the ring he'd split with her on her door step.

''Course I do,' Gilligan replied happily. 'But why are you thinking on that just now?'

'Only that he set off not knowing what he was going to find,' Hugh said, 'nor if he was ever coming back. But he found plenty and lived to tell the tale, and so shall we.'

Brogar, the unknowing focus of Hugh's rather inchoate devotion, was by now quite a few miles down the track from Strontian village. Matthias had given him the name of one of the smuggler families and detailed instructions of where their homestead was and he was upon it now. He drew his horse to a stop as he contemplated the small black house teetering on a rocky bluff above him. Terrible place for a farmer's home to be, but a great place for a smuggler's house, the folks inside well able to spy out the land all around them and, more particularly, who might be turning off the main thoroughfare towards the house up above, approachable only by a muddy track that dwindled into a snake thrashing its way through the heather. Plenty of time on that approach for anyone in the house above to vacate or hide whatever they did not want seen. Brogar had no fixed plan on how he was going to handle this, but Matthias had been right about Brogar understanding much of the criminal world and his encounters with the marginalised. Most of these, Brogar knew, did not take such a path lightly, and only when they'd no other direction to go. Life could chuck up enormous odds in those badlands and he had much admiration for the men and women who survived them, however they could. He was the first to admit he'd been one of them on occasion, for you couldn't go to the places the Company sent him and get by without double dealings of one sort or another. Not that the Company acknowledged it. They wanted results, and weren't fussy how its agents came up with them. Sholto didn't understand this yet, too new to the game, but Brogar had been playing it far longer. He'd much to thank the Company for but knew first hand he'd sometimes acted in ways not entirely palatable, crossed the rubicon into a darker, shadier side of life than any of the board members would admit existed. He knew too about death and dying, and that the death of Archie Louden had been cruel, even sadistic. No one hit another man over the head and set him burning if he didn't want him absolutely annihilated, and it took a special class of man to do that, one who was usually accompanied by others unable to do the same – weak links, those others, waiting to be broken, waiting for Brogar to snap them to get at the truth. And Brogar cared about the truth. He knew he was not a particularly likeable or approachable man, not like Sholto was, but had enough self-awareness to turn this to his advantage, and both were problem solvers. They might go at it from different ends but both would go and go until they met in the middle and had it puzzled out. His dim-wittedness over at Kildonan had almost got Sholto killed, a debacle that made him re-evaluate some of his previous and most spectacularly foolhardy actions which had led to several earlier assistants not being so lucky. So, no better man than Brogar to tackle smugglers and understand why they did what they did, which boiled down to the same basic premise: I want what I want, and I don't care how I get it. Within Brogar's admittedly flexible notions of justice, poverty and the need to survive was one thing, greed quite another, and one he would not brook.

He took his horse up the small path towards the house on the rock at a gentle pace. Using his spyglass he'd already noted there were at least two people up there: women, one older, one younger, tying a few sacks over a stack of newly cut peat. He didn't want to spook them so called out warning of his approach.

'Hello there!' he shouted as he neared the house, the two women suddenly looking up from the task that had so consumed them they'd been oblivious to his coming. The younger woman turned towards him, the older one scuttling back into the house, Brogar recognising the thump of a piece of wood slotting into place to keep the door shut.

'Can I help you?' asked the younger woman, now stranded outside, her face blank, marred only by black smudges from the peat she'd been working with. She was not alarmed, realising straight off that the stranger couldn't be an excise man, not travelling on his own, and there was no one else down below or along the several hundred yards of track that were in clear view. It was undoubtedly unusual for her to get callers, but not completely unheard of. Tinkers came by from time to time, offering to sharpen knives or mend shoes or sell their pots and pans or any one of a hundred other goods and services. Brogar brought his horse to a halt a few yards from her, but did not dismount. He'd not seen anyone else in the vicinity but that didn't mean there wasn't another person – besides the old woman – in the house. He scanned its outlines, the hill that rounded up behind it, but could see nothing of a threat.

'Good day to you,' Brogar said amiably. 'I'm looking for a little information.'

The woman blinked but did not reply, merely held a hand to her forehead to cut out the sun and study this newcomer the better.

Definitely no excise man, soldier or tinker, she could see it from his clothes; but he was a hard-looking man, and she'd seen his kind before and was not about to welcome him into her home.

'I doubt you've heard it yet,' Brogar went on, 'but a man was murdered yesterday afternoon, down the peninsula at Ard...' he stopped momentarily, having forgotten the complicated tongue-ties presented by the names of Ardslignish and Ardnamurchan. 'Anyway, at one of the ferry posts beyond Strontian.'

The woman blanched perceptibly, and Brogar drove his point home. 'He was called Archie Louden, worked for Gustav Wengler. I gather he's been here a long time and folk down on the peninsula are rattled.'

The woman took a step back and glanced towards her house. Brogar moved his horse a pace closer and lowered his voice.

'I'm one of several men looking for who did it,' he said quietly, as the woman dragged her eyes back to his. 'And we'll not stop, I'll not stop, until I know what happened to him.'

The woman paled further, obviously frightened, but moved herself so that she was positioned squarely between Brogar and her front door.

'Don't come any closer,' she whispered. 'Ma will have a musket trained on you right this minute.'

Brogar raised his eyebrows but did not shift his ground an inch, nor did he shift his gaze from the woman. He'd already taken in all he needed, made note of the distance he was from the house, the height of the two tiny windows that were set into its walls. It would take a good shot to even get close to him. The horse might present a larger target but he rather doubted the musket's existence, at least not one an old woman could fire with any accuracy. That required strong and nimble fingers, and the old woman must have been in her sixties or even seventies, judging from the way her back was bent.

'It's not you I'm after,' Brogar said, keeping his head down so no one could read his lips from any eyeglass that might be trained on him from the heather. 'Just the person responsible for setting fire to a man for no other purpose than robbing him of a few trinkets. Brooches. Two of them. Have you heard who might be putting them on the market?'

The woman before him moved her hand from brow to throat, glancing swiftly at the house.

'Brooches?' she echoed, twitching slightly.

'Don't look back again,' Brogar told her. 'Just keep your eye line on me. We're talking about two brooches, and I'm certain you don't believe a man should be murdered for so little, or be the one standing between such a murderer and the noose.'

He'd hit home. He could see it in the woman's eyes, in her collapsing demeanour. She was desperate to speak, her throat pulsing as she fought to get out words, and then he heard the shifting of a wooden shutter as it was pushed wide open. He raised his face to find the older woman squared within its frame, an ancient musket levelled on its ledge, its sights pointed right at his head. The old woman spoke and although Brogar didn't understand the words he recognised them as Gaelic, uttered loud and fierce, the younger woman replying, holding up her hand, pointing first at Brogar and then down the empty road towards Strontian. Another exchange followed, and Brogar's horse chose that moment to stamp its foot, move itself a few steps to the left, impatient at being held motionless for so long. The older woman raised her weapon, swivelling her gun towards the newly presented target.

'Stop!' shouted the younger woman, striding swiftly into the path between the old woman and Brogar. 'It's no use, Ma,' she went on. 'He's gone too far this time, and I'll not be a part of it. A couple of brooches! Why would anyone kill a man for that?'

A shot rang out, going wide, going right up into the sky, but Brogar's horse was startled and would have run if the younger woman hadn't quickly grabbed at its slack reins and caught it still.

'Get off,' she whispered urgently. 'Get away right now, soon as I let go. She's off her head, man, and anyways it's Dunstan you want. My husband's brother. I'll not say he did it, but he was round here last night asking me to hawk them brooches for him down in Fort William.'

The old woman cursed out of the window as she struggled to reload and the younger woman let Brogar's horse go and started back towards the house, keeping her body within the line of fire.

'Enough, Breda,' she cried out. 'Would you see us all hang for the sake of your worthless son? It's one thing when he brings in brandy and tobacco, it's something else when he starts killing people. And Archie Louden? He's practically one of our own.'

Another shot rang out and a pluffet of dust rose up just to the right of the woman's foot, making her retreat in Brogar's direction, lifting her face briefly so that he plainly saw the tears spilling from her eyes, wetting her cheeks. She took strength from the fact that Brogar had not budged, and turned back in defiance.

'He was one of our own, Ma,' she called out, and maybe the old woman heard her or maybe not, either way she disappeared from the window, withdrawing the musket, slamming the shutter behind her, leaving her daughter-in-law standing in the heather. Time for Brogar to get the hell out of there before someone got killed, but he was not without a few grains of compassion and understood the family dynamic in this tiny cottage in the middle of nowhere had just been struck right down the middle and split in two.

'Will you be all right?' he asked.

'She's angry,' the woman managed to say. 'But she's knows I'm right. Dunstan's ay been the bad one in the barrel, no matter how many times my Malcolm tried to set him right. But Dunstan'll be long gone. He's not a man easy to find; doesn't live here or anywhere I knows of…'

The front door of the cottage was suddenly flung open and there was Breda, Dunstan's mother, brandishing the reloaded musket.

'Get yourself gone!' she shouted. 'Or so help me, the wind will be whistling through the hole I'm about to blow through your head!'

'I'm stopping with Matthias McQuat of the Galena Ore Mines,' Brogar whispered urgently to the younger woman. 'Get yourself down there if you need help.'

She looked up and smiled a skewed smile, wrapping her arms about her skinny body.

'Thank you,' she said, 'but I've my own bed to lie in. But speak to young Harald McRailty over in Ockle. Poor boy's thick in with Dunstan. Has a beast for a father and chose a worse one to take his place.'

The musket blasted again and this time Brogar turned his horse smartly and raced it back down the slope, a sharp smell of burning in his nostrils where the line of shot had burned through his hair. Not so bad an aim then, this old woman Breda, but no whistling – at least not yet – through Brogar's head.

Θ

'So it's definitely the same one?' Sholto was asking Kurti Griffen, having arrived at Ockle and made their way up to the church, tethering their horses, wandering through the graveyard until they found the great shining face of the sundial at its farthest boundary, propped on several fallen stones and a wall that backed into a copse of ancient holm oaks, a huge profusion of denuded stalks of honeysuckle and bindweed keeping the wall up. Around the sundial itself the stalks had been hacked away, probably back in summer, leaving only the runners behind. The sundial was completely at odds with the paucity of its surroundings and yet obviously had been there for many years, verdigris covering much of its surface, hiding its many markings.

'I'm astonished,' Griffen exclaimed, 'but I really think it might be.'

He took out his notebook and studied a diagram he had there, comparing like to like, the copy of his illustrations to the reality lying in this churchyard in this most obscure part of a country he'd little idea existed until Archie Louden came into his purview. How the sundial had got here to Ockle and not to Gustav Wengler, its purported buyer, was a mystery, but after a few minutes scraping away at the sundial's face he was in little doubt. The Round Tower sundial was one of a kind, and Griffen ran his fingers with reverence over the engravings on its face. Of all the artefacts he had returned to their proper home this was the real prize, and he was already figuring out in his head what he would need to do to get it repatriated. Sholto was equally fascinated, for he could see at a glance it was no ordinary object. Even in its dilapidated state it was obvious how intricate were its markings, containing far more information than was usual. Many churches had sundials in their grounds or built into their walls, but never before had he come across anything as elaborate as this. There were lines of writing around its rim and a further tightly packed spiral of words leading to its centre, and in unusual languages, not the normal Latin or Greek that were so common. He would have a taken a closer look there and then had not both Brogar and Matthias cautioned him to keep alert around this

Kurti Griffen – about whom they knew nothing apart from the information he had voluntarily given, none of which they could verify. Sholto scanned his surroundings and caught sight of a young girl hovering at the edge of his eye line. He straightened up, pretending a yawn he had no need of, Griffen wholly engaged with the sundial and completely unaware of Sholto or what he was doing.

'Just going to stretch my legs before the journey back,' Sholto said, moving his way down the path towards the girl. She'd knelt down, unconvincingly tending to some anonymous grave. Sholto held up a hand in greeting as he approached her and the girl took it in good stead and stood up, though made no move towards him.

'Excuse me,' Sholto said, as he neared her. 'My name is Sholto McKay, and I wonder if I might ask you a couple of questions?'

Simmy looked at the man who was standing maybe ten yards away from her. She'd never seen him before, a skinny man, with dark hair through which ran a streak of white though he seemed too young for it, and a face that looked, she thought, rather kind. She was wary though, as was everyone in these parts, for strangers of any stripe usually meant smugglers or the excise men come to catch them, not that this man looked like either. Simmy's heart was beating fast but she stood her ground, glancing briefly at the poor scrap of her mother's grave – if indeed it was hers, for this part of the graveyard was for paupers, buried with only a piece of wood to mark them, most of which had long since crumbled and rotted completely away. She'd been on her way to the sundial herself after leaving Aileen's, in the vague hope Harald might be there.

'Why are you looking at our sundial?' Simmy asked, and Sholto's hand faltered a little as he lowered it, unnerved that the girl had clocked their intention so completely.

'Well, it's very unusual,' he said, 'and of a certain interest to my friend over there. More importantly, we think it might be linked to a death that happened near here.'

It was a bit of a leap, but Sholto wanted to catch the girl's attention before she thought better of the situation and ran away, and apparently achieved it. She stiffened but did not run. He'd no way of knowing that Simmy wasn't thinking of Archie Louden at all but on Harald's bag of bones, thinking that someone had learned about the burial down in Strontian and finally come forward with an identity, and therefore with possible questions about the whereabouts of the ring. She would give it up if she had to, and would not directly lie about it, but surely it would be easy enough for people to believe it had long ago been swept away into the water, never to be seen again. It might make selling it more difficult, but now she had Aileen on side it didn't seem quite so impossible.

'So what's your questions?' Simmy asked, putting her head to one side, studying Sholto, who was smiling at her directness.

'Well now,' he said. 'Let's start with something obvious. Do you know where the sundial came from, or how long it's been here?'

'Sort of to the first,' the girl replied elliptically, 'and I can find out the second. But why do you want to know?'

Sholto raised his eyebrows. He'd been expecting a vaguer answer of the type that said it had been here forever, and he looked at the girl more closely, saw an intelligence in those dark brown eyes that seemed as out of place in this little neck of Ardnamurchan as the sundial did. He was about to fumble in his pockets for a coin or two in an attempt to elicit more specifics when the girl turned on her heel and began to walk away.

'Come on then,' she said, a hint of impatience to her voice when Sholto didn't immediately follow. He glanced back at Griffen, still bent over the sundial, rubbing at it with a handkerchief, entirely engrossed.

'Meet you back at the horses,' he called out, to which Griffen replied with an uninterested wave of his arm, Sholto following on behind Simmy as she made her quick way through the untidy lines of graves.

CHAPTER 16

BROKEN EGGS, BROKEN MEN

Matthias was dreading the meeting with Gustav Wengler and absolutely didn't want to get stranded on the island with him, not again.

'Can you stay nearby, Hesketh?' he asked, once they'd drawn up on the little shingle beach of Havengore. Hesketh looked back over to the shore on the other side of the loch. It wasn't far. He could easily row back and out again, but he knew the news Matthias was coming to impart and thought the better of it.

'Could stop here, throw a line in,' he offered.

Matthias was mighty relieved and it showed on his face.

'Thank you,' he said. 'I don't anticipate we'll be all that long, but it depends rather…'

He trailed off, Hesketh finishing his sentence for him.

'On whether the horn daft man goes completely off his nail?'

'Quite,' Matthias said and smiled, interrupted by the horn daft man himself appearing over the knoll, having been eyes out for them coming and getting to the pier before they did themselves. Matthias nodded once at Hesketh and stepped from the boat, Jed jumping out behind him.

'You've news,' Wengler stated, the skin of his face looking even tauter and thinner than it had the last time, his eyes bright and feverish, making Matthias wonder whether Wengler had slept at all these past two nights, let alone had anything to eat.

'We've news,' Matthias said, without inflection. 'But let's get on back to the house,' he added, 'before we say any more.'

Jed moved up next to Gustav Wengler and took his arm, turning him gently on the track, Wengler looking absurdly grateful to have this one small decision taken from his hands.

'Happy fishing,' Matthias said, looking back at Hesketh, Hesketh nodding, pulling in his oars, tucking them tidily against the sides of his boat. But in truth he knew he'd do no fishing, not after seeing Gustav Wengler there on the shore of his little island, knowing how the news of Archie's death might shatter his fragile world into little pieces, like a bird's egg stamped underfoot. Most folk had family of some kind or another to fall back on, someone to comfort and cosset them in similar situations, even neighbours at a pinch. Wengler had none of this. No family. No neighbours. He was entirely alone, no matter it had been of his own making, and Hesketh regretted his earlier remarks about horn daft men, for who wasn't a little mad when it came down to it? Wengler was minutes away from having his world flipped sideways, and Hesketh wouldn't wish that on anyone.

Θ

Gilligan and Hugh arrived at Kilchoan without incident. It was an easy ride, straight up the track to the point with no possibility of going in the wrong direction, the only turn-offs being the main one to Ockle and several pitted paths leading to the few low-slung cottages to right or left of the track or down to the ferry points. The man who owned the croft at Kilchoan spotted them coming and was there to greet them at the gate of his paddock, nuzzled around by twenty or so black-felted ponies that had Gilligan giggling at their miniature size.

'But they're tiny!' he exclaimed, as Padraig Skinner opened the gate for them and brought them in.

'Small, lads, just as you are,' Skinner flashed back, 'but them horses are a damn sight stronger'n you'll ever be, and two of 'em'll pull a pleuch through bad ground more'n four of you could. But come on in. What can I do you for?'

Hugh took the lead, asking if by chance he'd hired out a horse to a man named Archie Louden not long since and if so when, and what horse it was, and when he was expecting it back. Padraig Skinner rubbed the stubble on his chin.

'Funny you should ask,' he said, 'only I's been wondering on that me seln. Knows Archie I do, and he's not one that's late, not normal. Was thinking on sending one o'me boys into the village next coupla days, see what was what.'

'So you hired him a horse?' Hugh dug the thread out of the talking. 'Had it been newly shod, on one hoof anywise? Maybe back right?'

Padraig Skinner gave the boy an appraising glance.

'Aye,' he said slowly. 'That it had. Had a few needed doing and tinker came in a few weeks back. Had him do what was needed before he was off again.'

'And what day was it, when you sent it out with Archie? And what kind of horse was it? Not one of these, surely…' Hugh taking in at a glance these were workers, not designed to carry anyone on their backs. Padraig Skinner didn't answer straightaway, wary now, rubbed his chin again before replying.

'Well now,' he said. 'I knows what I knows, but not rightly sure why I should tell you anything of anyone else's business.'

''Cepting 'e's dead,' Gilligan put in, having left off petting the small Highland horses he was rather taken with. Padraig sucked in his cheeks and blew them out again. This was news to him. He didn't like losing horses at the best of times, and couldn't figure out why the piebald he'd hired to Archie should've kicked the bucket on so short a ride.

'Hope he's not sent you looking for some kind o'compensation,' Skinner said after a few moments, ''cos he picked that one out himself, right enough, an' I tellt him then it weren't the best of 'em, but he wanted it fast and I'd not much else.'

Hugh looked puzzled, before clocking the mistake. 'No, no,' he said. 'The horse is fine, far as we know. It's Mr Louden who's dead, and that's why we're here. His horse wasn't with him, so we figured find the horse and maybe find the man who killed him.'

'Archie Louden's dead?' Padraig Skinner was incredulous.

'Dead as dead can be,' Gilligan said, unhappy memories resurfacing of Archie's face white one side, burned black the other.

'Dead as dead can be,' Padraig Skinner repeated thoughtfully. 'Then best come in lads. Maybe there's summat I can tell yous that might be of help.'

Θ

Matthias, Jed and Wengler were back in Wengler's usual room, everything the same except for the blackboards that, to Jed's dismay, had all been wiped clean; blank and empty as Wengler's face.

'So he's dead.' Gustav Wengler spoke the words, but it was anyone's guess whether he'd actually taken them in. He was sat

BURNING SECRETS

on his seat in the middle of the room, no finger-tapping going on now, no movement to him at all except for his lips mouthing those three simple words over and again, once out loud, the rest silently.

'He's in the Floating Chapel,' Matthias said quietly. 'And there's the funeral to organise. Did he have family, do you know?'

No reaction from Wengler.

'Would you like me to take charge of the arrangements?' Matthias offered, feeling uncomfortably large and out of place.

Still nothing from Wengler, who sat on his seat as if it was the lynch pin of his world. Matthias wasn't sure what he'd expected from Wengler, had been prepared for tantrums or some spectacular outburst of some kind, but not this silence, this untethering. He'd known it would be up to him to bury Archie, just as he'd buried Wengler's father. He couldn't help being irritated by this lack of response, no asking for details, as if the only thing of consequence in Wengler's world was Wengler himself, sitting on his stool in the middle of his perfectly ordered room, in the middle of his perfectly ordered house, in the middle of his perfectly ordered island. Except that it wasn't perfectly ordered anymore, not with Archie gone. Matthias moved over to one of the windows in Wengler's self-immuring tower, exchanging a glance with Jed as he did so, Jed taking the hint, kneeling down in front of Wengler's stool.

'Mr Wengler,' Jed said, soothing and calm, 'there are some questions we need to ask you. We need to know why you sent Archie over to Denmark and what it was he was bringing back for you; if we know the particulars then it's possible that what is lost might yet be recovered, and by recovering it we can maybe find out who killed Archie.'

No immediate answer from Wengler, though his lips stopped moving and Jed held his breath in anticipation. Matthias was trying to keep still, not break the moment, but looking out of the window he realised something he'd not done before, namely that Ardslignish was in direct line of sight. He turned back from the window and spoke very quietly.

'Did you see a fire, Mr Wengler? Burning out there in the night? The same night you expected Archie back, or maybe the night before? Did you see anything? Anything at all?'

Wengler unexpectedly lifted his head, looked towards Matthias and the bright light of the window behind him.

'Ardslignish,' he said, and began to rock back and forth very slowly.

'I think you saw it, Mr Wengler,' Matthias persisted. 'I think you were waiting for Archie, looking out for him out of this window, looking over towards the ferry points up and down in case he was there raising the flag. So did you see a fire at Ardslignish?'

Wengler stopped rocking, stood up, looking directly out of the window at Matthias's back.

'I saw it,' he said slowly, and now he was finally moving he had more to say. 'I put it in my log. I saw it first at thirty minutes past four on Thursday afternoon. I looked again exactly an hour later and it was still burning. I looked again an hour after that and it was smouldering only. I was looking out for him because I knew he'd be here before his letter said. He always is, tries to surprise me. But I don't like surprises, so I looked out for him...'

So, Jed had been right. Archie – the perfect assistant – built time-lags into his letters so he would always be on time, Wengler realising the ruse so the time-lags were never time-lags at all.

'He should have been back,' Wengler's words came slow and then slower, like a pendulum decreasing its momentum, 'but he wasn't... and he wasn't... because... because...'

His mind was jumping gaps, making deductions, and he suddenly marched to the window, shoving Matthias roughly out of his way, staring out of the glass intently.

'I saw someone there,' he said, a catch in his throat. 'He was coming out of the fire. He was moving across the grass… I made a note of it,' he whispered, 'in my log.'

Matthias felt a surge of acid from stomach to throat, put a hand over his mouth to stop it going any further. Wengler had seen it all; Wengler had been standing here at this window watching a man stagger out of a burning bothy and done nothing more than make a note of it in his wretched log. Granted, he may not have realised what he was seeing, for it would have been dark and indistinct. And no way to get word to the mainland, but why in Heaven's name hadn't he raised the alarm the following morning so someone could go and investigate? But of course Wengler hadn't. He had the emotional depth of a water vole. Everything seen and experienced having to be filtered through the mesh of mathematics that made up his mind. Witnessing without understanding, not on any conscious level, maybe knowing it and not knowing it at the same time, an explanation for why he'd been so anxious about Archie's non-return, his tenacious belief that something was really wrong without being able to voice exactly why that was. Matthias looked anew at Gustav Wengler, who was gripping hard at the ledge of the window; left it to Jed to voice the awful truth.

'You saw him die,' Jed said, hollow and chilled. Gustav Wengler, with all his mastery of complex mathematics, seemingly unable to add two and two together when it was right in front of his eyes. Wengler turned away from the window and fixed his gaze on the last blackboard in the line, the one that had held a few squiggles of Archie's handwriting until that morning when he'd wiped all his boards clean, when he'd wiped away the last trace of Archie.

'I saw him die,' Wengler repeated Jed's words mechanically, a full three seconds passing before he folded up his body and collapsed onto the hard floor, his head cracking as it hit, Jed running over and crouching quickly down beside him, taking him by the shoulders, trying to haul him up.

'Come on, Mr Wengler, let's get you to your bed,' he said, but Wengler would not be moved, curling his body up into itself like a ball of silver elvers caught in a net. Matthias's throat constricted with compassion, Wengler obviously not the emotionless automaton Matthias had taken him to be and so he moved too and bent over the fallen man and between them they managed to lift him and shift him to Archie's bed, covering him with blankets, Jed sitting by him while Matthias went downstairs and raked the cupboards for anything he could find, which wasn't much.

'We can't just leave him,' Jed was saying, once they'd forced some of the wine they'd left the night before down Wengler's throat and Wengler had closed his eyes, dropping immediately into nightmare judging by the constant twitching of his limbs, the flickering of his eyelids. Probably looking out of that window again, at the wobbling, burning torch that had been Archie Louden. Matthias was loathe to stay any longer on the island than was necessary, but Jed wouldn't give up on his broken hero, paining Matthias with his pleas.

'We can't just leave him,' Jed kept saying. 'Christ knows what he'll do when he wakes up again.'

'Probably go straight back to his books,' Matthias snapped back before he could stop himself, Jed looking up at him with such hurt and accusation in his small face that Matthias could have bitten out his tongue.

'I'm sorry,' Matthias apologised, for there was no doubting Wengler was suffering some deep emotion, maybe for the first time in his life.

'Stay here,' Matthias said, as if Jed would have done otherwise. 'Let me go speak to Hesketh, see what can be arranged.'

And off he went, an empty vessel who had to grip at the rails of the spiral staircase to stop himself from falling, Jed such a bright spark when he'd tumbled into Strontian, illuminating Matthias's life, revealing the dark shadows that lay in every corner, forcing Matthias towards the realisation that he wasn't so unlike Gustav Wengler: that he too kept other folk at a distance, kept himself apart on account of his background and position, considering a family life unviable, at odds with his work and studies.

I mayn't have bought an island, Matthias thought, as he walked down the short track to the pier of Havengore, *but I've made one of myself, God help me.*

Θ

'I did a project on it,' Simmy was telling Sholto, 'for Reverend Harlow, and he's always kept my work in the chapel because he knows I can't keep it at home. He's got them all in the cupboard in the back room where he stores his vestments and books and stuff.'

Sholto followed the girl inside the chapel, a plain square space barely twenty yards in length, nothing more than a lectern raised on a rough dais and several rows of uncomfortable looking pews; a place less likely to have a large ornate sundial in its grounds would be hard to find.

'Here we are,' said the girl, leading him into a tiny anteroom, going straight to a cupboard, taking from it a bundle of folders she laid down on the table that took up most of the room along with some rather miniscule chairs that must serve for Sunday school, or at least for people much smaller than himself.

'So your name is Simmy?' Sholto guessed, reading from the neat and careful lettering on the front of the folders Simmy was now sorting through, laying each one out side by side as if keen to impress Sholto with her magnum opus.

'That's me,' the girl said brightly. 'And you said you were a McKay, though not one from around here, I don't think.'

'Sholto,' Sholto said. 'You can call me Sholto. And no, I'm not from around here. My family were from the east coast a long while ago, but we were lucky enough to be moved to Scandinavia during the clearances.'

'Ah,' said Simmy, studying Sholto with interest. 'I know about them, and Reverend Harlow told me too that lots of people shifted the other way – from Scandinavia to Scotland – hundreds of years ago, so maybe we're related after all.'

The idea seemed to please her, for she smiled so disingenuously that Sholto found himself smiling back. He liked the girl, and he liked her self-assurance, her interest in what was going on around her, evident from the titles written in the same painstaking script upon the front of each of the folders on the table: *A Description of the Trees that are found in and about Ockle; Some of the Birds I've Seen; Different Ways of Fishing for Different Kinds of Fish; A History of the Peninsula of Ardnamuchan, as told to me by the Reverend Oswald Harlow and his books.*

'You like your learning, then?' Sholto asked as he moved about the table, studying her folders one by one.

'I do,' Simmy said brightly. 'I'd do it all day long if I could, but, well…'

Her voice tailed off, the smile slipping from her face, but she picked up one of the folders and handed it to Sholto with the same air of formality she might have given to a board of examiners.

'Here's the one you'll want to see,' she said, and Sholto took it with the same formality with which it had been given.

'*The Ockle Sundial,*' he read out loud its declamatory title, '*and how it came to be in our chapel's graveyard.* That's a good way to start,' he said, and was rewarded by another smile, though the girl began to fidget and plainly wanted the folder back so she could explain it. Sholto obliged. He sat down on one of the tiny seats, his spine jarring as he went down further than he'd been expecting before hitting base, Simmy placing her work before him, opening it to the first page.

'Let me show you,' Simmy said, enthusiastically. 'I wrote this years ago and I always meant to go back and get it redone, because it was my brother Harald who was so much to do with it, and when he and Aileen get married, well, I thought that if I could do it a bit more and with some better illustrations it would make a good gift for them.'

'Has to be better than another toasting fork they'll not know what to do with,' Sholto remarked, but the girl didn't seem to notice, having already begun turning the pages for him.

'Look see, here's a picture I made of the broomway. I doubt you'll know what that is…'

Sholto didn't, but happily he had Simmy to explain.

'All the coast around this way is full of sandbanks and most of them you only see when the tide is really low. Some are really dangerous, so when at neap tide years back when I was, I don't know, but quite young, and we saw the edge of a barge a few hundred yards out, well we had to go back to the oldsters, the ones that knows which bits of the sands will sink and which won't, and they marked it for the rest of us by the switches of broom they'd pulled from the banks.' Simmy flipped a page. 'That's a drawing I did of my ma's da, best as I can remember him anyway. He was one of the ones could always make out the broomway, not that he was there when they found the old barge, but they called on my brother Harald to go out with them and help them in with it, because that was where they found it...'

Questions quivered on Sholto's lips but he didn't want to stop the girl mid-flow and let her go on, so evidently proud was she of her project and having someone to show it to.

'The sundial, I mean. Not that anyone knew it straight off. Everyone thought it was going to be smugglers' stuff, barrels of drink or some tobackee, 'cos them smugglers are always hanging around here. Anyway, just below the water line they saw summat glinting, and fine glinting, and knew it was big and they'd need the biggest men to bring it in, and my brother Harald was big even back then...'

The girl stopped for a breath and Sholto managed to get a line in.

'And when was this?'

'Dunno exactly,' Simmy said. 'Maybe when I was six or seven? Year before Reverend Harlow came anyway, that much I'm sure. Anyway, like I said, it was a huge day when they brought the sundial in, Harald dragging it like an ox back over the broomway, and they couldn't have done it without him.'

She turned the next page to reveal the drawing she'd made of her brother hauling in his great catch, a broad-faced boy with huge shoulders, ropes strung around his body, heaving the sundial from the sand-silted barge, and unmistakeably the same sundial that was out there in the graveyard for Simmy had added a further drawing – and a remarkably accurate one – of the sundial once in situ.

'It's such a marvellous thing,' Simmy said, pointing to her drawing. 'Lots of words on it I don't understand. Lots of different languages too, though I don't know the names of them, but there's Latin in there, and some French I think.'

Sholto nodded his head, for this indeed was so, but inevitably his questions started spilling out.

'So why hide such a marvellous thing at the back of the graveyard? And what happened to the barge's crew? Didn't anyone wonder who it belonged to?'

'The old minister was going to do it,' Simmy answered quickly. 'He was going to go over to the monks at Fort William to ask on it, said we were to park it in back beneath the walls and cover it over to keep it safe.'

'And?' Sholto prompted, when Simmy did not continue the tale.

'And nothing,' she shrugged. 'The old minister never got to Fort William. Got some kind of sick hernia on his way there, and that was that. Never even made it to the monks, I don't think. And so the sundial's been here ever since.'

CHAPTER 17

TAPPING A WAY BACK TO LIFE

The solution to Matthias's problem of who should stay with Wengler came from an unexpected source. He left Jed temporarily with the prostrated Gustav and went down to the jetty to ask Hesketh to bring over a couple of womenfolk from the village to see to Wengler's needs, now that Archie was irrevocably gone.

'Ach, but he'll no be liking that at all, Mr Matthias,' was Hesketh's firm response to this request.

'I know that,' Matthias replied, 'but what else can we do? He doesn't function well with people he doesn't know but I certainly can't stay, and the only other option is Jed, and I have need of him over the water.'

Hesketh nodded, understanding the problem better than Matthias gave him credit for, thinking of little else than the oddity that was Gustav Wengler since Matthias had left him, and on how Hesketh himself had felt fifteen odd years back when his wife had died, how intrusive he'd found the folk coming in left-wise and sideways with their sympathy, and how much more Wengler would hate it.

'Better he's with folk he knows,' Hesketh said.

'But he has none,' Matthias said.

'Ken that,' Hesketh answered shortly, 'but he knows me, and I knows him. Been doing his errands for nigh on twenty year and I mayn't be a pal, for Lord knows he's none of them, but times like this you don't always want a pal, you just needs someone's been through it all before.'

$$\ominus$$

Jed wasn't happy with this arrangement, but was easily over-ruled once the plain truth was pointed out to him that Hesketh was better known to Wengler than Jed was himself. Hesketh took Matthias and Jed back to the mainland before returning, tying up his boat, going up the track to Wengler's fortress and opening the kitchen door. He was nervous but not intimidated, in fact felt strangely as if he might be about to do the best thing he'd done for a while. He went up the spiral staircase and located Gustav Wengler, still trussed up in his blankets, a cup of cold tea and a partly filled wine bottle by his side. Hesketh took one look and retreated, going into Wengler's study and returning with the stool from the centre of the room, placing it next to Wengler's bed, sitting by him the rest of the day through and the night that followed. Occasionally Wengler cried out and Hesketh jumped into action, stroking his hand over Wengler's forehead, easing him back into untidy sleep. Once, during the night, Gustav Wengler woke up, recognising first his stool and then the man sitting upon it, though could not conjure up his name.

'Who are you?' Wengler asked, voice coarse with catarrh and anxiety.

'Just a man's already been through what you're going through,' Hesketh said mildly, and Wengler was satisfied with that. He sighed, turned himself over and went back to sleep. Hesketh must have nodded off himself because suddenly he was jerked awake by something hitting the window, his heart fluttering at the sound.

Just a bird, he reasoned, but was spooked – too late in the year for the pufflings who routinely crashed into anything on the first dark night of their flying, recalling his grandmother's stories of the ghosts of the dead visiting on All Hallows Eve, although that night was also long past.

Only a bird, he thought again as he stood and went to the window, looking out over the dark island into the dark night. No lights anywhere but the one by Wengler's bedside, only the snow falling lightly, covering everything, suffusing the world with a gleaming that made it seem a better place than it was. He moved softly from the bed chamber into Wengler's study, going directly to the east-facing window, unlatching it and bending his body out as far as he could safely go, delighting at the soft touch of the snowflakes falling sporadically from above. He saw Wengler's monuments – what they called over the water the White Cathedral – and by God how white they were now, and how monumental, and how utterly alien. He was so captivated by their strangeness that he didn't hear Wengler coming in behind him, padding softly over the boards in his socks, bringing with him the stool Hesketh had earlier removed, Wengler replacing it exactly on the spot Hesketh had taken it from. Hesketh turned at the soft scrape of wood on wood and the slight clinking of the lamp Gustav placed on the floor as he sat himself down, eyes open to the darkness as if he could clearly see all his shelves of books and his blackboards and everything that was about him.

'You think it's beautiful,' Wengler stated, as Hesketh drew himself back in and fixed the latch.

'I do,' Hesketh said.

'More beautiful than the wife you were telling me about?' Wengler asked, which caught Hesketh off guard because he'd supposed Wengler asleep when he'd started talking quietly about his Elissa, expressing the grief he'd never before articulated, finding that he could say anything into the night in this strange place on this strange island with this strange man, saying the words he'd never spoken aloud, not to anyone. Hesketh swallowed but did not speak.

'There's no comparison,' Wengler went on. 'Wives are just people and people die, but those monuments out there have a life apart, a higher purpose. By the time these ones crumble and fall they will have been built again somewhere else in the world with the same comparative dimensions. It's been like this for hundreds of years, because collectively they form a key for opening up the universe, and all we builders seek is the lock into which that key will fit.'

Hesketh had nothing to say. He was experiencing something he had no words for. He knew his own life was never going to amount to much, would come and go like the proverbial light of a candle – here one minute, gone the next – that everything he'd ever been would be forgotten the moment he ceased to take his last breath – no children to regret his passing, no one to pay for a stone with his name and dates scratched upon it. He stood by the window watching the snow, looking at the monuments outside that looked even more like a White Cathedral than ever, before switching his gaze back to Gustav Wengler who was sitting on his stool like some kind of gnome, hunch-backed, open-eyed, staring into the darkness as if Hesketh's nana's ghosts had risen up out of the ground and were looking right back at him. It took Hesketh a few minutes to catch his breath, bring himself back to the normal.

'So where is the lock?' Hesketh asked, his voice sounding eerie and strained in this dark night of the soul, Wengler's outline wavering slightly as the breeze coming from the window swayed the light of the lamp. Wengler didn't move, kept staring at the empty boards, seeing the words again in his head, everything figured out from that slim volume he'd had for years on his shelf but never read, not until Archie asked about it, curious about the unusual gold lettering on its spine: Ձոռուռ'ս Հաննիկ. What a morning that had been! Such excitement as so much was explained that had previously been hidden, that empty circle once more given meaning and purpose; the reason Wengler sent Archie to Denmark, hot on the trail.

'It's out there in the darkness,' he said, in his oddly unintonated voice, Hesketh looking out again as if it might be there, hovering in space. The clouds from whence the snow had fallen were being gathered by the up-there wind, revealing a sky so black and filled with stars Hesketh's heart quickened in his chest. So many nights he'd seen those stars, but never such a multitude as now.

'So how will you find it?' Hesketh asked, his voice quiet, reverential, imbued with the feeling that if only he knew where to look and what he was looking for then he would go and fetch it himself. He'd never been a religious man, but there was a numinosity to this night that bordered on the mystical. Wengler began to tap his fingers on the base of his chair: a rhythmic sound, the taps coming in groups that were sometimes longer, sometimes shorter, as if his fingers were following some music only he could hear.

'Do you know where to look?' Hesketh asked.

'Not yet,' Wengler replied slowly. 'But I know it's near, and I'll not let it slip from my fingers, not again.'

Tap, tap, tap, came Gustav Wengler's fingers, and beat, beat, beat went Hesketh's heart. Verse and refrain, but all one song.

CHAPTER 18

THE LION FLEXES ITS CLAWS

It was well past three thirty in the afternoon and almost dark when Gilligan and Hugh arrived back at Matthias's house just as Brogar was hitching up his horse, combing it down, giving it some hay, duties the boys happily took over. Sholto and Griffen arrived a half hour later, their own horses hungry and thirsty, thrusting long necks into the trough at the end of Matthias's yard. Once the horses were tended and returned to their respective owners scattered about the village, everyone gathered in Matthias's house and began tucking into the hearty barley broth Matthias's housekeeper hooked above the fire before leaving them to it. Gilligan and Hugh formed a bannock-making machine, one mixing flour and milk together, another slipping them onto the skillet and from there to the hungry men at the table. There was much to say but five hours in the saddle makes hollow stomachs and the way was to eat first, talk later. They were mopping up the last dregs of broth with the last crumbs of bannock when Oswald Harlow arrived, bearing a couple of bottles of tonic wine brewed from blackberries and birch-sap.

'Welcome, Oswald,' Matthias said, Oswald squashing himself in at the table, looking at all the strange faces seated about him.

Matthias made introductions, followed immediately by Sholto asking if Oswald knew a girl named Simmy from Ockle.

'That I do,' Oswald said, puzzled by what was going on and what any of these unknown people had been doing over at Ockle, of all places.

'She seems a remarkable girl,' Sholto commented, Oswald nodding his head in agreement.

'Indeed she is, but…'

Matthias held up his hands.

'Excuse me, Oswald, for interrupting, but we'll get to all the details in a moment. Let me first explain a few things to you and then, if everyone's in agreement, we'll go round the table, see what everyone has learned.'

It was an admirable strategy if only they'd stuck to it, but Gilligan was too quick, jumping up and starting to speak before anyone else had the chance.

'We found a lot out at Kilchoan,' he said, eager as a bee on a hot summer's eve. 'The man there definitely hired a horse to Archie Louden and Hugh was right about the shoe, for it was not long mended.'

'Last couple of weeks,' Hugh put in.

'Right,' Gilligan chirruped on. 'So Archie got there, landed off a boat from Oban and super eager to get over to the island, and the man… I've forgotten his name…'

'Padraig Skinner,' Hugh put in.

'Right, Padraig Skinner. He's got lots of little black working horses. Ponies really, but he calls them horses. Anyway, none of them would do…'

'He wanted a fast one, picked a piebald mare,' Hugh interjected, 'the only piebald Mr Skinner had. Said he'd get the animal back in a couple of days by the usual means…'

'The usual means?' Sholto interrupted.

'Archie would come to me and we'd send a lad back with it to Skinner's in the morning,' Matthias put in. 'And if he'd gone over from Ardslignish he'd have got Hesketh out first thing to arrange the same.'

'And it's branded,' Hugh chirruped. 'A cross on the back right rump.'

'Aha!' Brogar said. 'Branded is excellent news. Even if they try to disguise it.'

'Probably just add another brand over it,' Hugh suggested, Brogar nodding.

'I think you're right. So we're looking for a piebald mare with a new branding mark over an old one and with a bad shoe at the back, going on the market two, three days back. Where would anyone go with that, Matthias?'

'Not far, given the state of its shoe,' Matthias said. 'Can't think whoever pinched it would want to draw attention by getting it re-shod. Best guess is down towards Corran where someone could get it over the water to another ostler's. Did you see anything like it, Brogar, on your travels down there?'

'I didn't,' Brogar replied, 'but I did find a possible name for our thief, if not our murderer.'

This was big news indeed, and everyone leaned forward.

'There's a woman in that house you pointed me to, Matthias, the one way up back in the heather, built on a ridge.'

'Malcolm Pirie's,' Matthias affirmed.

'That's it,' Brogar said. 'His wife said that Malcolm's brother Dunstan tried to palm a couple of brooches off on them a few nights back.'

Oswald Harlow let out a sigh.

'Dunstan Pirie,' he said and looked over at Matthias, who nodded in confirmation.

'Long been known to be in with the bad sort,' Matthias explained. 'Every time the excise men come, they come looking for him, but he doesn't seem to live anywhere in particular, at least not for long, so they've never caught him.'

'That's precisely what she said,' Brogar added. 'But I don't think her husband is involved, not directly, she made that quite clear. The mother, on the other hand, she was pretty near blowing my head off with some musket she must have had since the dawn of time.'

He didn't draw attention to the burn line through his hair, but everyone noticed it anyway.

'That'd be Breda Pirie,' Oswald put in. 'Not the most trusting of women, and she's had that damn musket out at me before now.'

He smiled briefly, but not when Brogar had said what he said next.

'Best line of enquiry is a lad named Harald McRailty who lives over at that place you went today, Sholto. Ockle, was it?'

Both Sholto and Oswald Harlow started at the name.

'Oh my Lord,' Oswald was the first to speak. 'Oh please no, not Harald.'

'Simmy's brother,' Sholto said quietly.

'You mentioned her earlier,' Matthias stated.

'I did,' Sholto agreed. 'I met her today when Griffen and I were there looking for the sundial. She was very helpful, showed me some project she'd done for you, Oswald, when the villagers first found the sundial.'

'You never told me about that,' Griffen accused Sholto, turning a hard stare upon him, Sholto looking right back.

'I didn't,' Sholto said calmly, 'because it struck me then, as it strikes me now, that there's far more going on here than we've been led to believe. And the one part of it that makes very little sense is you, Griffen, turning up right when you did.'

All eyes turned to Kurti Griffen then, who stiffened under their collective gaze.

'I told you why I came,' he said, after a few moments.

'That you did,' Sholto went on, 'but I don't think you've been honest with us. That Simmy child had drawings in her little project of the sundial and I can tell all of you right now that it's no ordinary thing.'

'So what is it?' Brogar asked, looking directly at Kurti Griffen. 'You've a choice,' he added, with a bluntness even the dullest of people could not ignore, and Griffen was no dullard. 'Either tell us right now,' Brogar continued, 'or we'll chuck you out into the snow and let you do your own investigating from here on in, though I can guarantee you'll not get further than you can crawl.'

'Now wait just a minute,' Matthias tried to intervene, but one look from stone-cold Brogar was enough to shush him.

'You've thirty seconds,' Brogar said to Griffen, 'and if I had my choice you'd not get even that.'

'All right!' Griffen said after a breath's interval. 'All right. You've made your point. And yes, the sundial is something special. Not that we knew it immediately, but when we saw where it had been headed – namely to your Gustav Wengler – it aroused a certain amount of interest.'

'You think it's to do with Chaucer's Riddle,' Jed said slowly, the first words he'd spoken since he and Matthias had left the island, angry that he'd not been allowed to stay with Gustav Wengler, then remorseful to think he'd had the arrogance to presume he should be the one to stay, and then desperately sad to know that Wengler had, with all probability, witnessed the death of the one man in the world he'd trusted, and sadder still to think it might be enough to tip him over the edge of the madness he was plainly teetering on the brink of, and what would happen to that great intellect if he did.

'What's Chaucer's Riddle?' Gilligan asked, breaking into Jed's thoughts like a hammer thrown through a pane of glass.

'It's nothing but a mathematical conundrum, rumours of corrections to Titius's flawed Law of Numerical Relationships written in the margins of Chaucer's Astrolabe,' Griffen replied, as if he was reading off a crib sheet, which indeed he almost was, following the line his superiors had told him to take.

'But it's not!' Jed shouted, suddenly come to life. 'It isn't that at all, and you know it! And I think Wengler's working on it, so it can't be nothing. Titius's name was definitely on the boards that first morning we went to the island. I didn't think about it then...'

Jed looked at Matthias with such pleading, such asking, that Matthias couldn't bring himself to remind Jed that the last time they'd seen those boards they were wiped as clean as a stone on the shore of the Sunart after the tide has come and gone.

'There *were* writings there...' Matthias said, noncommittally, 'but I confess they meant nothing to me.'

'Aren't we rather getting away from the point here?' Brogar said. 'Top of our list should be who murdered a man, not some maths puzzle or the provenance of a sundial.'

Sholto shook his head.

'I'm not sure they're so unconnected,' he said. 'The fact is, I think the one predicates the other. One of Joseph Lundt's gathered proverbs goes like this: *aithnicheaar an leomhan air scrib de iongann,*' he pronounced the Gaelic words clearly and with care, 'the lion is known by the scratch of his claw.'

How any old Gael would have known about lions, let alone their claws, was anybody's business but Brogar knew when Sholto was onto something, however obscurely he chose to make it known.

'And?' he prompted.

'And I think it's significant that the one book we found with Archie's body was a copy of Chaucer's Astrolabe,' Sholto replied, 'presumably acquired in Copenhagen, probably just before he went to the Round Tower on Wengler's behalf to ask what had become of the sundial he purchased twelve years ago but never received. And that,' Sholto said, tapping his fingers on the table, 'is when Griffen became involved and came scurrying over here to find out exactly the same thing.'

CHAPTER 19

AND NOW THE RIDDLE

Everyone had questions, mostly about the sundial connection: why Wengler had never enquired about its non-appearance before, why he'd chosen to do so now, and how it had ended up grounded on a sandbank outside of Ockle. Sholto stemmed the flow and insisted all these questions wait for the moment.

'First,' he said, 'we need to establish what we know and what we don't. And what we know is this: Wengler is an astronomer and mathematician, and a good one by all accounts.'

'Not just good,' Kurti Griffen added. 'He's one of the best in Europe, when he chooses to contribute.'

Jed nodded emphatically, about to chip in until Sholto stopped him.

'Quite,' Sholto agreed. 'Let's take that as read. And let's make a leap of faith and assume the sundial was intended to take centre stage in that complex of monuments over on his island, judging from what Matthias said earlier.'

'Well, I'm not sure about that,' Matthias said nervously. 'I'm no astronomer.'

'No,' Sholto said. 'Neither am I. But Wengler's White Cathedral, as I believe it's widely known…' Matthias nodded. 'Very well, the White Cathedral. Well, I've seen depictions of monuments very like them, most notably Tycho Brahe's on another Havengore over in Denmark, and I know they were built to emulate the ones erected by Jai Singh in the 1720s, which in turn were built to emulate those designed by Ulugh Beg at Samarkand many years before that, and due to their great size can take measurements down to the millimetre, tell time to the second.'

Brogar was impressed but not as surprised as the rest of them by this demonstration of knowledge far beyond their usual ken. Griffen narrowed his eyes in suspicion. It was one thing for Sholto to have kept his silence about a schoolgirl's essay, it was quite another to have knowledge of a topic so obscure, a possible leaning towards the provenance of the sundial he'd only recently learned himself. He needed time to rethink, re-plan; he needed to find out how much these people knew and, more importantly, how much Gustav Wengler knew. It beggared belief that anyone in this backwater had stumbled over the truth of Chaucer's Riddle, though the appearance of Archie Louden had certainly raised suspicions Wengler might be on the trail. How, they'd didn't know. Presumably from another source, given that it had only just surfaced in the Round Tower papers, and everyone sworn to secrecy, at least until they got the sundial back.

'So what else do you know about it, Sholto?' he asked, keeping his voice casual. 'About the sundial?'

Sholto didn't turn his head towards Griffen, spoke instead to the wider group.

'I don't. Not about its specific design or usage, but presumably Wengler saw it as part of a larger complex of instruments. My guess is they collectively provide an extremely accurate look at the stars, but I don't know much more than that.'

He hesitated, for he'd seen the sundial and it looked like something more to him, its own conundrum, nothing so hum drum as a mere cog in a wheel. Griffen saw the hesitation and gripped his glass in anticipation, but Sholto didn't go on. Plainly the man was vastly more well-read than Griffen had previously given him credit for and knew he was going to have to tread far more carefully from here on in.

'The real question remains,' Sholto went on, oblivious to Griffen's scrutiny, 'is why Wengler's interest in the sundial has suddenly revived, why he sent Archie to Denmark to ask about it and also came back with that particular copy of that particular book. Twelve years ago he was apparently unconcerned by the non-appearance of the sundial, or possibly had no means of following it up.'

'It was around the time his last assistant left,' Matthias said, for the same idea had already occurred to him.

'And before Archie joined him,' Sholto continued for him. 'So why now? And why the book and the brooches come to that? And why did Archie's queries about the sundial suddenly jolt the Round Tower in the form of Kurti Griffen here, who immediately sets forth on the trail of both it and Archie.'

Sholto leaned back in his chair, looking around at his audience, gratified to see every face fixed on his as if he were the elder of some tribe telling them their history about a glowing fire. The silence was absolute, the night outside dark and complete, the snow falling softly once again against the windows, gathering at their edges, and it occurred to him just how perfect the world could be, and how grateful he was to be out in it, experiencing it for himself.

'And did our Kurti Griffen here,' Brogar suddenly put in, 'find Archie Louden before we did?'

Griffen's eyes widened as the implication dawned on him.

'If you're suggesting I murdered him, you could not be more wrong.' Griffen's voice scratched through the silence, his left eye spasming in a rhythmic tic he was unable to stop.

'Maybe not, Mr Griffen,' Brogar sounded amiable but his face told another tale. Griffen shifted in his seat. 'But you've been keeping secrets,' Brogar went on, 'and we don't like that. And now is your opportunity to redeem yourself.'

'Why not tell us about the brooches?' Sholto put in quietly, the two Company men performing a double act of such menace that everyone about the table felt a shiver go up and down their spines.

'They're nothing,' Griffen said shortly, glad they seemed to be as far away from the truth as they could be. 'A distraction. A couple of pretty gewgaws. Gold-set pieces of smoky quartz you use like miniature telescopes to study the sun and the moon. Nothing more, and nothing to do with the Round Tower, and certainly not the sundial.'

'Nothing,' Matthias interjected quietly, 'except they were most probably the reason Archie was murdered. Exactly the kind of things a man like Dunstan Pirie would think worth stealing.'

'But they've no special value,' Griffen argued. 'Like I said, they're toys. Faceted to magnify the craters of the moon, look at an eclipse without blinding your eyes.'

'And yet you told us quite specifically that when you learned of Archie's purchases you doubted his word about the sundial,' Sholto said, 'so why is that?'

Griffen hesitated, annoyed to be caught in a lie, wondering how to go on. He chose to persist in the line given him by his superiors, for a little longer at least.

'An old wives' tale,' he said. 'One that says the three things go together: brooches, sundial and ring.'

'What ring?' Matthias asked, Brogar interrupting.

'What the hell does any of that mean, Griffen?' Brogar put in. 'Did the brooches come from the Round Tower or not?'

'Absolutely not,' said Griffen in return. 'We've examples there, of course, but not the ones your Archie Louden purchased. The fact is I've no idea where they came from.'

'So you've lied again,' Sholto stated. 'You know perfectly well they are nothing to do with the sundial, so it must have been the book that piqued your interest.' Griffen eased his head upon his neck, realising his mistake. 'So how is Chaucer's Astrolabe connected to the sundial?'

Griffen moved in his chair, cleared his throat, annoyed that Sholto had made the connection so quickly.

'Let me be frank,' he said. 'Yes, Mr Louden came to ask about the sundial, and when I interrog... when I asked him,' he amended quickly, 'what else he'd been doing in Copenhagen, who he was working for, he did happen to mention the book, yes. But I don't see why...'

'Because that's when you knew,' Jed cut Griffen off, a growl in his throat that sent an undercurrent of unrest about the room. 'You knew!'

Jed stood up, banging his fists upon the table with such anger that everyone drew back with perturbation. Everyone except Kurti Griffen.

'I didn't know!' Griffen said loudly. 'We didn't know anything for sure. We only suspected.'

Hoping the lie would hold.

'Suspected what?' Matthias asked, completely baffled, as were the rest.

'That Wengler might be about to solve Chaucer's Riddle!'

Sholto stood up, holding out a hand towards Jed who was having none of it and pushed him angrily away.

'He knew!' Jed repeated. 'And maybe he did kill Archie! Just because he said he didn't doesn't make it so!'

Jed lunged across the room and grabbed Griffen by the shoulders, pulling him backwards so both Griffen and his chair tumbled to the floor, Brogar and Matthias immediately on their feet, Brogar there first, prising Jed free without difficulty, leaving Kurti Griffen to right himself, rub the back of his head where it had hit the floor.

'My God, Jed,' Matthias said, reaching his young protégé, taking hold of him, dragging him away from Brogar. 'What's got into you?'

'But he knows,' Jed repeated, though the fight was gone from him, allowing himself to be pulled across the floor and onto the seat next to Matthias, who put an arm about the young man's shoulders, keeping him close.

'So what is it he knows?' Brogar demanded. 'You really need to tell us.'

Jed took a few deep breaths as Griffen regained his seat, the tic in his eye the only clue to his agitation.

'No harm done,' Griffen said, 'but I can see why there might have been a misapprehension.'

'Then for Christ's sake get on and spell it out for the rest of us,' Brogar went on. 'Because I for one have had enough and I'd be quite happy to strangle the relevant information out of the two of you if you don't do it on your own.'

Brogar looked daggers alternately at both Jed and Griffen, neither in any doubt he meant what he said. The wind outside rose as if in agreement, lifting a couple of roof slats and slapping them down again.

Kurti Griffen blinked, and then spoke.

'You're right about the brooches,' he said quietly. 'They have nothing to do with the sundial, mere sideshows to the main event.'

'The main event being what?' Sholto put in, Griffen hesitating only a moment, sticking to the truth as far as he could, but no need for any extras.

'Mr Louden telling us the sundial never reached Gustav Wengler. It got everyone riled, at least everyone in the know, because we thought we knew where it was. And when I questioned Mr Louden I found out about the Astrolabe and what the two had in common, namely Gustav Wengler and Chaucer's Riddle.'

Oswald Harlow hadn't said a word all this while. It seemed to him he'd been shoved onto the stage of one of those puppet theatres the travelling men sometimes brought around the villages, unable to see the strings attached to the marionettes or who or what was directing them. The earlier mention of Simmy and Harald had distracted him but the discussion of the sundial had him focussed, had him making some deductions of his own, specifically of when and how the sundial had arrived in Ockle and the bones Harald found, the bones he'd only just buried. More information was what was needed, and so he asked for it.

'This Chaucer's Riddle,' he said. 'Am I alone in not understanding what it is?'

He was not, and Gilligan shivered in anticipation, the very words sounding odd and intriguing, as they were to Oswald himself.

'It's this,' Jed said quietly, casting a murderous look at Griffen before taking the floor. 'Johannes Titius thought he could predict the appearance of new planets with his Law of Numerical Relationships. No one took him seriously, except Johannes Bode who took it on himself to publicise Titius's work. It was clear to everyone that the Numerical Law didn't work. Even Titius admitted it, but he kept on going at it, trying out new formulae, jotting down all his corrections in the margins of his copy of Chaucer's Astrolabe.'

'Chaucer's Astrolabe being, specifically?' Brogar asked.

Jed shrugged. 'It's nothing. A handbook the English poet Chaucer wrote for his son about the workings of the solar system.'

'Hardly nothing,' Griffen put in. 'Chaucer died in 1400 and his Astrolabe has been used as a primer ever since, and in lots of different languages.'

'So far so good,' Brogar said. 'But none of this explains a damn about why the blasted scribbles your Titius wrote in his book near had Jed ripping Griffen out of his skin.'

Jed blushed.

'Because the Astrolabe and sundial belong with Wengler,' he said with passion, 'and Griffen's here to take them away.'

'And what would Wengler do with them?' Brogar was becoming impatient.

'Solve Chaucer's Riddle!' Jed spoke up immediately, Griffen smiling half a smile, letting Jed do the work for him, keeping the tale of Titius's ridiculous law alive, and all to the good as far as he and the Round Tower were concerned.

'I don't quite see where the sundial fits in,' Oswald said quietly, Griffen clicking his fingernails, eager to get in the lie.

'Nothing that matters anymore,' he said loudly. 'Not if you've got the Astrolabe.' Sholto looked at Griffen with interest. He had a strong feeling that whatever Griffen said next would be a fabrication, but maybe a fabrication giving a clue to the truth, like badger scat points to the direction of the sett. 'Because,' Griffen pushed on regardless, 'there've long been rumours circulating the Round Tower that Titius, working with a pupil, designed the sundial to incorporate the main body of his Laws of Numerical Relationships.'

'Like a back-up plan!' Jed jumped in, Griffen nodding, rubbing his beard with his fingers.

'If you want to put it like that, then yes. That's the essence of Chaucer's Riddle: Astrolabe and sundial, two ways of working out the corrections to Titius's Laws.'

'And if they are correct then they'll lead to the discovery of new planets!' Jed went on with enthusiasm, 'and that would really be something!'

'Something worth killing for, perhaps,' Brogar stated flatly, looking at Griffen before breezily going on, 'although I rather doubt it. And if Archie was killed for that book by some rogue mathematician why didn't he take it with him? No. What were stolen were brooches and a horse, and we've got to start at the beginning if we're ever going to reach the end. And we've a dead body, people, a man who didn't die easy, and it would serve you all well to remember that.'

CHAPTER 20

THE MISDEEDS OF THE DYING

Simmy's father was dead. She was later to his room than was usual owing to her visit to the graveyard and her strange encounter with Sholto McKay, so proud that someone apart from Oswald Harlow was taking her projects seriously, meaning she'd stayed away from home far longer than she'd meant. Once back, she saw to the animals as usual, got the dinner ready – some spuds and kale and a scrawny chicken she'd wrung the neck of, it being obvious it had no more eggs left to lay. She'd been thinking on her da the whole afternoon, ever since she'd spoken to Aileen, bringing back a load of memories she'd all but forgotten from when she and Harald were younger and their da had been a da to speak of; how he'd not always been the way he was later when he'd beaten them both black and blue about something and nothing. Early doors, he'd been a good man who'd taken them fishing and taught them all sorts, and she was trying to get it all right in her head, and also where the hell Harald was and what he'd done that he thought he had to keep away from her and even from Aileen. And then, just as she'd been making up her da's dinner tray, she'd heard an ungodly noise coming from his room and went running to find her da lying on wringing wet sheets where he'd sweated himself dry as well as peed himself. His face was different, all soft of a sudden, almost welcoming, and she went to help him, about to roll him onto his side so she could wash him clean, pull away the soiled sheets. And that was when he'd placed a weak hand on her arm.

'Stop, Simmy,' he said, the first time he'd used her name for years. Not *my useless slattern of a daughter*, or *my shitty little bookworm*, or the more usual *whore, come here*, which was his favourite command. Nothing but her proper name, putting his skinny hand on her arm and beginning to cry. Her da, Old Man McRailty, who'd used his fists like pistons before he got ill and eyes so hard they could almost hammer nails into wood, Old Man McRailty was crying. Simmy subsided, sat down on the bed beside him, never mind the piss and stink.

'Never wanted,' he croaked, voice dull like he was speaking from underwater, 'never wanted,' he repeated, 'to do you wrong.'

Bad breath, bad enough to make Simmy blench, but his fingers not as strong as they'd used to be as they closed about her wrist. She could've broken free at any moment but that softness in his face said maybe he knew it was all over, that he too was maybe remembering better times when things had been good between them; and so Simmy leaned in, waiting for the final words, waiting for reconciliation. Her da tightened his grip about her wrist as she leant in, whispering in her ear with his last few breaths.

'Girls ain't meant to be too clever, always known it, always will.'

Simmy recoiled, tried to pull her arm away but Old Man McRailty was back, strong as ever.

'Good girls,' he croaked, 'know how to cry. But you've never cried, have you Simmy? Never about me, anywise. And you've never been a good girl.'

He wheezed a sad simulation of laughter as Simmy wrenched herself away, his hard yellow nails scratching through her skin, heart beating hard in her chest.

'Good girls,' her da repeated as Simmy took a step backwards, holding her bleeding hand to her mouth in shock and dismay, 'never been one, never will, never…'

Whatever barbs he'd been holding onto for this last moment got stuck in his throat as a spasm ran violently through him, the only thing on his blue lips being bloodied spit. Once, twice more, went those bad breaths through him and then he was still. No more words. No more nothing.

'Harald!' Simmy yelled, running helter skelter from the room.

'Harald!' she yelled again, so loud her voice broke and she coughed with the effort of getting his name out.

'Harald…' she tried again, little more than a whisper now as she heaved open the kitchen door and went out into a world now desolate and dark, lightened only by the snow that was falling, Simmy glad for its coolness on her burning cheeks. But Harald was nowhere to be seen and Simmy starting running from the house, running from her da, from his cruelty, from the last words he'd delivered to the one person who'd cared for him in his last months, his last hours, his *whore come here* beginning a desperate run into the night, no idea where she was going, knowing only that she could not go back.

CHAPTER 21

LIKE FLEAS ON A DOG

Oswald Harlow was standing at the shore end of the pontoons drawn in for the while, nothing to do but stand and stare, tide too high to put out the walkway, Hesketh Wood apparently still with Wengler on his island so not able to take him over, Archie's body only twenty yards distant but nothing Oswald could do to get to him. Despite the morning being cold as an icebox he felt a keen urge to get across, make sure Archie was not alone, minister as he was able before the burial that would soon take place. He knew this anxiety would seem absurd to other people, but given what he'd heard last night about Chaucer's Riddle, about the possibility of new planets, Oswald was having doubts about his God, about how He could be so interested in this one small world amongst the many. It would explain a lot, especially about the nature of evil, a problem he'd often struggled with. He felt a sudden tug at his elbow from some child he recognised, but couldn't put a name to.

'You're needed over at Ockle,' the child said breathlessly, the boy's name suddenly popping into Oswald's head because of the way he spoke his words: the son of Anna, the woman who cleaned the chapel at Ockle once or twice a week.

'It's Hector, isn't it?' Oswald asked.

'Right enough,' Hector said. 'And you're needed over soonest. Old Man McRailty's popped it. Mam found Simmy in the chapel this morning, almost froze she were, all curled up in a corner crying her eyes out.'

'And where's Simmy now?' Oswald asked, far more perturbed about Simmy than her father, whose demise – God help him – he didn't regret at all.

'Mam took her home to warm her up,' Hector supplied, 'and Simmy says she'll not budge till you gets there.'

Θ

Brogar and the others had their breakfast and were working out a plan for the day. They still needed to track down the brooches, the horse, and Dunstan Pirie, and it was imperative someone went over to the island to speak to Wengler, get his side of the story about what Archie's trip to Denmark was really all about. They'd come to the general assumption that Griffen hadn't murdered anybody. He even had an alibi of sorts, namely that he'd been travelling all that while and if they dug hard enough someone would remember him. If Griffen himself was in the clear that didn't mean some other stranger from Griffen's homeland hadn't come racing on ahead of him, eager to claim the glory of the sundial and Chaucer's Riddle for himself, but it seemed far more likely Archie had simply been robbed, bumped into some clutch of smugglers, and that was the line they were choosing to pursue.

Brogar, by common, if tacit, consent, took charge. He never pushed himself forward, never had the need to; it was simply that he had a personality like a roaring waterfall that swept everyone else out of the way, and them glad of it. Griffen might have spoken up against him the night before, but not once it was plain Brogar was better at making plans than anyone else.

'Jed and Griffen,' Brogar started barking out his orders. 'Get yourselves over to the island. See if you can get any sense out of Wengler. Take a look over those monuments first, never mind what he says, and see what you can make of them, especially that empty circle Matthias saw.'

'They should take Archie's copy of Chaucer's Astrolabe with them,' Sholto put in. 'There might be some dispute about the ownership of the sundial but that book is Wengler's rightful property. But first I suggest you both take a damned good look at it. Once Wengler's got a hold of it, it's unlikely we'll any of us see it again.'

Sholto had his doubts about the links between Astrolabe and sundial. Something wasn't right. The idea of using the sundial as a back-up for the notes in the Astrolabe struck him as faintly ludicrous. He needed a library but didn't have one to hand, and anyway, it could wait. There were more practical matters to be dealt with first.

Griffen and Jed nevertheless got up at his suggestion, Jed rushing to get his pencils, notebook and magnifying glass.

'Quite right, Sholto,' Brogar agreed. 'I don't care why everyone is so enamoured of a blasted book, but Archie would certainly have taken a damn good look through it himself. Plenty of time on his sea voyage over from Denmark.'

And it will keep Griffen and Jed out of our hair, he added silently in his head, his mouth breaking open in a smile that had Griffen wincing, not that Brogar noticed.

'Sholto has already organised with the minister to go back to Ockle,' he went on. 'If we're to find this Harald then we might need to do it through the sister, and Oswald and Sholto will be the only ones of us she'll likely trust.'

'What about us?' Gilligan asked, a bit jittery in the confines of his chair. If there was any action going he wanted in, and by him he meant Hugh too.

'I think, lads,' Brogar said, 'you'll be coming with me.'

A quick clap from Gilligan who got to his feet.

'Shall I get the horses ready?'

'Do that,' Brogar agreed, 'but Hugh, you stay here with me for a moment.'

Gilligan was off, Hugh staying solemn in his chair as if glued to it, his awe of Brogar Finn complete.

'You're the horse expert amongst us,' Brogar said, 'and we really need to find that piebald, and I think I know who might be able tell us where to look.'

He was thinking of Malcolm Pirie's wife in that little cottage laid up in the heather, though they'd need to be circumspect about it if they didn't want to get shot to pieces by the woman's blasted mother-in-law; a couple of small boys in the advance party might just do the trick, especially Hugh, who had a way with people.

'Whatever you say,' Hugh said, and meant every word.

'What about me?' Matthias asked. He would be glad to have time to go to the mines and make sure everything was in order but he was aggrieved that he seemed, at this point, to be the spare wheel.

'Ah,' Brogar said, exchanging a furtive glance with Sholto. They'd spoken about this the night before out in the barn, agreeing that although unpleasant there was yet another task that really needed doing. Matthias caught the look, an uncomfortable clamminess leaking into his armpits as he did so.

'What?' he said. 'Just tell me. Anything I can do.'

He sounded more confident than he felt, especially when Brogar told him the task they had in mind.

'We need you to dig up that body Oswald Harlow just buried in the graveyard. The one they found at Ockle.'

Matthias's blood drained into his boots.

'Dig up a body? I can't dig up a body...'

'It was long dead before it got there,' said Brogar calmly. 'About as long dead, in fact, as that sundial has been up at Ockle and you, Matthias, so Jed told me, are a very learned man, taught by monks no less. And if I know monks, which I do, then I'm guessing they taught you the rudiments of anatomy and medicine, so who else better to take a proper look?'

Anyone but me, Matthias was thinking. *Anyone but me.*

Θ

When the Reverend Harlow came along the road from Strontian he was surprised to be met by Matthias and Sholto, apparently already on their way to seeing him.

'Ah, Reverend,' Sholto said, ill at ease on his horse but nevertheless quite jovial given the circumstances, Oswald suddenly aware – as he'd not been before – that although neither this Sholto nor his companion Brogar had actually known Archie Louden they were far more intent on working out why and how he'd died than anyone here would ever have been, if left to their own devices. Archie's body would have been found eventually by somebody, Wengler would have been informed, Archie would have been buried, and that would've been that. A tragic end to a life that should have been longer but no delving into the details. All that had been turned on its head by these two men who between them figured out in the space of twenty four hours what no one else in Strontian would have even thought to look for. It felt to Oswald, as to Matthias before him, as if he'd been judged – and found also wanting.

He'd volunteered to come to this out-of-the-way parish in the guise of a crusader, arriving with the Floating Chapel. It had been the merest chance he'd heard of Ardnamurchan's troubles at all, having caught a tiny article in the diocesan magazine he only ever read sparingly, seeing in it a way out of the inner-Glasgow parish he'd been consigned to, hating every minute of it. Not the people. Not the people at all, but he was an east coast lad at heart and, quite simply, he missed the sea, grabbing this chance to get back to it.

When he heard what Sholto wanted him and Matthias to do he was horrified and perplexed.

'You want to dig up those old bones?' Oswald asked. 'But why?'

'I'm sorry, Reverend, but it has to be done,' Sholto replied, pulling at his horse as if he didn't know what way to properly keep it still, which he didn't, so that Matthias had to put out his hand and catch the reins to keep the animal from turning itself around and going home.

'But why?' Oswald repeated, his voice plaintive, aware he was now juggling not two dead bodies but three, but also that the living came before the dead, and Simmy before any of them. 'I'll not be able to help you,' he said, shaking his head. 'I've a body to see to up at Ockle. Simmy's father, it's Simmy's father, and I'll not abandon the girl, not after what that… man put her through all these years.'

Sholto looked at Matthias and then at Oswald. He'd no idea what Oswald meant by that enigmatic statement but he understood Oswald's deep concern for the girl. He'd only met Simmy briefly but she was not someone you forgot in a hurry. She appeared to be a girl in charge, a girl who had much to give and yet also – now that he thought about it – there was perhaps too much order and acuity to her projects, too much concentration on tiny details, and he was not blind to the implication, which was that maybe those projects were a way of controlling the one part of her life she felt safe with, and that one part of her life lay squarely with Oswald. So if her father had just died Sholto was not going to be the one to deny young Simmy anything she needed.

'All right,' Sholto said, 'me and Matthias will manage. You go see to Simmy and I'll catch you up in a short while. But Oswald,' Sholto added, 'you know we need to speak to Simmy's brother and if the father's dead then no doubt he'll be there, and the last thing we want is for him to bolt before I've a chance to talk to him.'

Oswald nodded. He led Sholto and Matthias to the graveyard hidden away behind the main habitations of Strontian.

'As it happens,' he said, 'they're not far down. We've not much room, so those Ockle bones are buried on top of another unknown and he's only two foot under. You'll find spades in the little hut over there and the ground will be easy enough to dig, having only just been filled.'

And so it was. Matthias and Sholto had the bones up within a half hour, laid out as Sholto directed on the shroud they'd been wrapped in, Sholto poking through them with a stick, much to Matthias's distaste.

'Matthias,' Sholto said. 'I know you don't want to do this, but I need you to look.'

Matthias had already almost boked up his breakfast, but he took a step forward and did as Sholto asked.

'We need to get them in some kind of order,' Sholto said, picking up one bone and then another. They were old and brittle, the colour of smoked fish, and all in a muddle, pelvis huddling next to bits of feet, leg bones leaning on arm bones, ribcage open and scattered, small lengths of vertebrae lying like they'd been thrown for a game of dice, and a skull that was filled at eye sockets and mouth as if the man had been buried alive. Sholto prised each bone away from the next, noting particularly the ribs and several vertebrae.

'I'm no specialist,' Sholto said, rather belying his own actions, 'but what do you make of this?'

He prodded several neck bones with his stick and then again at a couple of the ribs that hadn't altogether broken away from the sternum. Matthias put his hand over his mouth and looked as directed. Brogar had been right about the monks teaching him anatomy. He'd been curious about it back then, the way a man was put together beneath his skin, the cast of the bones, muscles and sinews at their hidden work.

'In order to heal,' the monks had explained, 'you need to know what you are healing; think of the body as a township, the veins running through it like streets, the stomach the market place where fuel and food are bartered for, heart and liver the seats of government, the brain the vessel of communal identity – the church, if you will. A broken-down hovel in the lowliest part of town can catch fire and cause a blaze – a fever, we would call it – that can set fire to the next hovel and the next house, running through the streets in a moment, uncaring whether the inhabitants are rich or poor. Each part has its right place and disruption to the one can cause disruption to the many.'

To illustrate their point, and to further their medicinal researches, they had permission from the Provost in Fort William to dissect the bodies of any prisoners who died whilst in custody, or the few who were executed for their crimes. It was rare for either option to occur, happening only once in the whole time Matthias had been at the monastery, but he'd been obliged to attend that one dissection and it was the vilest thing he'd ever participated in, the dead man split open from groin to neck, from one side of his chest to the other, a horrid reflection of the cross of Christ hung above their heads. And there was no ordered township within as he'd been led to believe, only an indistinct shamble of guts and rancid looking fat, his adolescent curiosity wandering to the man's puckered, shrunken genitals, appalled by their nakedness that reminded him of new born birds, the same blue goose-bumped veininess to their skin, revolted by the thick crimp and curl of the dark hair that nestled them. The man had been taken apart before his eyes, intestines and organs removed and examined before being placed in bowls on a bench where the students could sketch and poke them, cut them open to see what lay inside; every last square inch of skin flayed, followed by an excision of the muscles; sinews and tendons pulled away to display their elasticity before being snipped off at either end. All that was left in the end were the bones, clad in the merest shreds of flesh. And the head, kept for last, face still intact with moustache and beard, skin sagging from mouth and cheeks, hair thick and dark, eyes rolled back in their sockets. Matthias hadn't stayed to see the taking apart of this final prize. He'd had enough.

It had been a ghastly but oddly exhilarating experience for the younger Matthias, and although he never wanted to see or smell such a thing again the lesson was proving its worth to him now, because he could see an anomaly.

'It looks like the smaller neck bones have been crushed,' he said, mouth dry, words coming out a little short and cracked.

'Aha!' said Sholto, apparently delighted, his stick now poking irreverently at the bones in question, seeing Matthias was right. Matthias spat out the bile that had accumulated in his throat.

'So, strangled you think?' Sholto commented. 'And aren't the ribs cracked too, like he'd been hugged by a bear? Or wait a minute – a knife wound perhaps?'

The images Sholto's words were conjuring up were grotesque.

Matthias faltered but forced himself to look where Sholto's stick was now pointing.

'Restrained by the neck, possibly,' he said quietly, 'and yes, maybe a couple of knife strikes on that rib and the one above it. But I can't think, Sholto… I just can't think…'

'You don't need to,' Sholto replied, looking up at Matthias with sudden compassion, causing Matthias to blink furiously to keep back his tears. Sholto understood and removed his gaze back to the bones. 'So don't think about it, Matthias,' he said. 'You've done what we've asked you to. No need to do more. Take yourself away. I'll stay, take a few sketches and tidy everything up. Why don't you go home?'

For a few moments Matthias couldn't get out any words. He stood up, watching Sholto's deft movements as he separated the damaged bones from the rest, suddenly aware that by standing he was casting Sholto into shadow, the sun having come out briefly from the snow-laden clouds that cloaked the most part of the sky.

'We'll figure this out,' Sholto said, smiling up towards Matthias as Matthias took a step to the side, and there was such gentleness and reassurance in that smile of Sholto's that Matthias found himself nodding, before turning and walking away, troubled by why Sholto and Brogar had directed to have these old bones dug up at all, that maybe they'd come to the same conclusion he had. And a name and face was surfacing: that of Neal Gillespie, a fresh faced lad from Edinburgh, the assistant who had come and gone, everyone – Matthias included – assuming that two years of Gustav Wengler was enough for anyone, that he'd taken advantage of heading out on one of Wengler's errands to instead take himself home to Edinburgh. But what if he hadn't gone home? What if he'd been here all along up at Ockle? Strangled and stabbed, tied up in a sack and dumped in the water. They'd never heard a word from his family and the folk of Strontian hadn't given it another thought. Matthias was thinking only now that of course they'd not heard from the family, because any concerns would have been sent to his employer, Gustav Wengler, and Wengler would have ignored them. Neal had neither the intellect nor the aptitude to work well with a man like Wengler. His initial awe quickly palled into boredom and irritation and within a few months he was found frequently over in Strontian, bitterly complaining about his lot. The miracle was not that he'd disappeared, but that he'd stayed so long.

Matthias swiped a hand across his brow. He left the graveyard but did not go home, nor did he go to the mines. Instead he went down to the pier and looked out over the Sunart to Havengore, seeing Hesketh sitting idly on the small knoll above the tiny beach, having landed Jed and Griffen there a short while before. Matthias raised a hand in greeting but Hesketh did not see. Something had shifted during the previous night's snow and quiet speaking; a feeling of propriety and a duty of care towards Wengler, annoyance that other people were now descending on Havengore like fleas upon an ailing dog.

CHAPTER 22

THE BLIND AND THE NOT-SO-DUMB

Oswald Harlow couldn't get to Ockle fast enough. Once arrived he wasted no time, going straight to Hector's mother's house where – just as Hector had said – he found Simmy huddled in a corner of Anna's kitchen, a badly crocheted blanket around her shoulders, eyes and nose red with weeping now stopped up.

'Oh my dear Simmy,' Oswald said, as soon as Anna brought him in.

'Reverend!' Simmy said on seeing him. 'You came!'

Her face lit up with a smile and she jumped up immediately, the blanket falling to the floor as she ran the few short steps towards him, flinging her skinny arms about his waist.

'But of course I came,' Oswald said, his voice a little hoarse. 'But why didn't you let me know earlier that your father was taken so badly?'

'I didn't know,' the girl wailed, the tears starting up again. 'I just came in last night and there he was and oh, you should have heard the things he said!'

Oswald hugged the girl to him and then prised himself free, sat himself down on one of the rickety kitchen chairs and bade

Simmy do the same, which she did, her fingers twiddling with her apron that was spotted with little flecks of blood. Anna bustled away in the background, filling a kettle, preparing tea, unwilling to leave this small drama playing out in her own kitchen. Hector was nowhere to be seen. He'd done his bit, accompanying the Reverend back the way, and wanted no more to do with it, unlike his mother, who was always one for blethering, and this would keep her going for weeks.

'And where is Harald in all this?' Oswald asked, not thinking at all about Sholto's insistence that he needed to be talked to, only that the lad had not been here when his sister needed him most. Simmy was shaking her head.

'I don't know, Reverend,' she said. 'I haven't seen hide nor hair of him for the past few days, and neither more has Aileen. But I think he's in trouble...'

She let the words hang. She didn't mention the fearful bruise on Harald's jaw the last time she'd seen him, nor the promise he'd made that things were going to get better for them both, if only she could wait.

'And has anyone been back to your house, to your father?' Oswald asked.

Simmy shook her head again.

'No,' she said. 'I went straight to the chapel. I just couldn't bear being there alone with him. Not after those awful things he said just before, well, just before...'

Oswald put his hand out and took Simmy's in his own.

'Death is never easy,' he said. 'When people are balanced on its dark horizon they say things, Simmy, things they don't really mean.'

This wasn't strictly true. He didn't doubt for a second that anything Fraser McRailty had said with his dying breaths had been meant to wound, as they obviously had. His face and voice were calm, but down below he was cantered to the bristles: angry at Fraser McRailty for being a bastard to the last, angry at Harald for being who knew where doing God knew what, angry mostly at himself for not having been here when Simmy had been so feared she'd fled her homestead for the chapel and stayed there freezing and crying alone, the whole night through.

Θ

Sholto finished his examination and sketching of the Ockle Man's bones, wrapped them back up in their shroud, reburied them beneath the earth, wondering briefly about the two unknown, unnamed men, one on top the other. He supposed it wasn't that odd, this peninsula's waters patrolled by men who valued commodities over life. He truly hoped Simmy's brother wasn't as neck deep in such activities as Brogar's source suggested for, if true, it hardly bore thinking on what would happen to Simmy now her father was dead. He brushed his hands with snow to rid them of the last of the corpse dirt, got onto his horse with as much grace as he could muster, thanking God no one was looking to see him take several inexpert turns and twitches of rein and rod to get the blasted animal going in the right direction. Next stop Ockle, unless the blasted animal chose to throw him at some indeterminate point on the way, and break his neck.

Θ

Brogar was at the bottom of the lane leading up to the house in the heather. He'd sent Gilligan and Hugh on before him, confident the old biddy Breda wouldn't let loose her shotgun at a couple of lads on foot. It was nigh on twenty minutes later when Gilligan came running partway back down to signal Brogar up. He reached the house, dismounted, was brought this time straightaway over the threshold to find the younger woman he'd spoken with before sitting by her fire, Hugh standing companionably by her side, no sign of the older woman anywhere.

'You're all right,' said the woman, whose name she now gave as Orla, 'ma-in-law's away for the day, and I don't know one end of a shotgun from the other.'

Orla looked weary, as if she'd not slept well for days, which she hadn't, her skin pale apart from the places where the smoke from the fire had darkened the fine lines in her forehead and the sides of her eyes. She waved a hand to Brogar.

'Sit down, please,' she said, pushing a cup of something vaguely resembling coffee towards him. 'Your lads have already told me what's been going on and I can tell you this. Yes, Dunstan was here, like I said before, banging on about them brooches. Had the bloody cheek to… well, I've already said.'

'And she knows about the horse too,' Hugh put in, his small face tight and earnest as he placed a hand upon Orla's shoulder as if he'd known her all his days, Orla smiling at the lad's touch but keeping her head down, not looking directly at Brogar Finn, whose face reminded her disagreeably, if unreasonably, of Dunstan's own, both hard and dark, scarred and closed.

'Couldn't say it before,' she said, 'but this's all gone on long enough, with a man dead an' all. My Malcolm's aye been a good man, but his brother's always been wily and takes advantage, being the older of the two. And he's a bully. Has beaten down on me more than once when Malcolm's not been here, and he's often not. And he's done more besides… well, you can guess. I'll not spell it out while Hugh is with us.'

Hugh's forehead creased in concern. He'd liked this woman immediately he'd met her and didn't like to think of anyone doing her harm. Thankfully he didn't fully comprehend the implications of her last words as Brogar did, Brogar having known men like Dunstan Pirie before and what they liked to do to women when their husbands were away. It was all about power and intimidation and he despised it, and began to look at Orla in a different light: a woman so familiar with violence it had almost beaten her into the ground and yet here she was, standing up against it, no matter the cost.

'Anything you can tell us will go no further,' Brogar said. 'We'll not say it came from you.'

Orla looked up at Brogar then, seeing beyond the superficial similarities to her brother-in-law, the blazing in his eyes that told her here was a protector not an abuser, no matter how powerful he was. She held his gaze for a moment and knew he understood, and her face reddened.

'Anywise, on the horse problem,' Orla went on, shifting her gaze from the dark eyes of Brogar Finn. 'Yes. Dunstan spoke of that too, with his mother, mind, not with me. But this is a small house and I hear things. Mind I spoke of Harald McRailty?'

'I do,' Brogar said. 'And you should maybe know that he's the brother of a girl called Simmy over at Ockle, and that their father died last night.'

Orla closed her eyes briefly. She didn't know Simmy directly, but everyone knew of everyone else on this peninsula one way or another. News could be slow or fast but there were only so many families in so isolated a place, and all were related, branch or root, all tied into one another's lives.

'That's not good,' she said. 'I've only met Harald a couple of times but both times he was with Dunstan, and both times he was about as underneath that man's thumb as it is possible to be, no matter him saying he wanted out.'

'Tell Mr Brogar about the piebald,' Hugh said, his voice soft, almost cajoling. Orla sighed.

'He's always on the up, is Dunstan. Said he'd money coming in and that Harald was to bring it. Said they'd found a runaway and that Harald had found a buyer over Corran way.'

'But Padraig Skinner branded all his horses,' Gilligan chipped in. 'We saw it when we were up there, so how come no one knew where it had come from?'

'How does anyone know anything?' Orla murmured, suddenly putting her hands to her face and closing herself off, brought back only by Hugh, who knelt down before her and patted her arm.

'Please tell us,' he said, such gentleness in his voice that she did so, wiping a hand against her eyes before she went on.

'I'm sorry,' she said. 'But I've just about had it with the lot of them, what with Dunstan and his mother and his dirty...'

She stopped short, feeling Hugh tensing before her like a man getting ready to do battle, that one last word giving away far more than she'd intended, certainly to this young boy. She shifted her gaze to Brogar and looked him bang in the eye.

'I'm done with the lot of them,' she said again, 'and your Harald has too. He was here last night, wanted me to tell Dunstan he'd sold the piebald as asked but that was it. He wasn't going to do it anymore.'

Orla looked at the floor and shook her head, before turning back to Brogar.

'Well, that fired the mother off, even while she was pocketing the money, and I can tell you they're alike, her and Dunstan, like as two as bees in a hive, and Dunstan's not the man to take no from anyone. All he ever hears is his own voice or his mother's, which are one and the same. And if that lad's father's died, well…'

'You're thinking Dunstan will step up whether Harald wants it or no,' Brogar finished for her, Orla letting out a breath.

'Mebbe. He's aye for the in,' she said, 'and Harald's just a boy looking for someone to lead him on, and I'm worrying for him now even more because Dunstan's a mean man and not one to be crossed and not one to leave tracks behind him when he goes. The Piries,' she added, 'at least Dunstan and his mother's part of them, always clear away their mess.'

Brogar nodded his understanding. Dunstan had cleared away Archie Louden and obviously wasn't above clearing away Harald too, or Orla come to that, if he took the notion.

'You should come to the village,' he stated. 'Come stay with Matthias or Oswald Harlow. Get yourself away, onto a better track of life…'

Orla smiled, but there was no warmth to it and no life either.

'I can't have my husband and boys coming back from the fishing to find me gone.'

'Come with us,' Brogar tried again. 'We'll get word to your family, keep you safe until they get back.'

Orla shook her head.

'This is my home,' she said, 'my family's home. I can't just leave. Where would you have us go?'

Brogar had no answer, not for the long term. He thanked her, told her the offer still stood if she chose to take it up, motioned Gilligan and Hugh to follow him; and out they went and down the track and back onto their horses, all three of them worrying about Orla with every step away from her that they took.

⊖

Sholto got to Ockle chapel where he'd arranged to meet Oswald after Oswald's duties to Simmy and her father had been done. While waiting, he went into the little schoolroom and found Simmy's projects laid out just as he had left them. He sat down on the same miniscule chair he'd sat on before and picked up Simmy's project on the sundial. Now she wasn't hovering at his shoulder, flipping the pages for him, telling him the story, he was able to go through it at leisure. He began at the beginning, reading about how the barge had first been sighted: a piece of wood sticking out of the sand one neap tide when the sea had retreated to its farthest point; the villagers of Ockle quickly mustered, hoping it was the visible edge of a few crates of smugglers' cargo somehow lost overboard or maybe deliberately jettisoned if excise men had been spotted. The old folk had marked out the broomway and off across the sands had gone several men to investigate. Simmy had added an evocative drawing at this point that she'd skipped over before. Her hand was good, and she'd added details of the shovels and ropes the men were carrying, a couple of oystercatchers nibbling at the shore's edge, the group of onlookers waiting eagerly for news. Next came the description of the discovery that the wood was in fact the prow of a small sailing boat or barge.

No mast, Simmy had written, *but places for oars clearly seen on the one side of the boat that was left.*

Another drawing then, a close-up that was so realistic Sholto wondered if she hadn't scampered up beside the men and taken a look for herself. She said she'd been young at the time, but yes, he thought, a girl like Simmy might well have done exactly that. This picture showed what they found once they started digging around – some frayed edges of sacking and the round edge of an object stuck beneath the visible edge of the boat, sunk right down in the sand.

A cry went up, she wrote dramatically. '*We've found something, and it's big!*'

Another picture, this time of a large-shouldered lad harnessed to the rope looped about the wood to pull it clear, other men digging at the sand with their shovels.

And then it rose from the sand like the sun: a huge round disc that was so grand we all on the shore let up a whoop as Harald started to drag it out, because he was the strongest of the lot.

Sholto smiled at the unveiled pride she had in her brother; he turned the page, and there was the sundial lying on the shoreline. She'd shown him this before, but not the next page: the sundial again, an almost perfect circle, probably made by Simmy running a pencil around a saucer that only just fitted between the margins. He let out a breath, for it was far more detailed than the previous sketch, and beneath she'd arranged five long columns of the words inscribed on the sundial's face, all grouped by what she must have judged to be their commonalities; and the more Sholto looked, the more he realised what a remarkable and intuitive job she had done. He bent his head closer to read the words she had painstakingly copied out, despite not understanding their meanings or even the language nor, in the case of the last column, even the letters of those languages that were so unlike a Roman script. Still, she'd grouped them almost as Sholto would have done: twelve different languages in Simmy's five columns; Italian, French and Spanish in one; German, Dutch, Danish and Swedish in another; English had a column to itself and was the shortest of them all; the next comprised Latin and Romanian, the last with Greek and Armenian in their alien scripts. Surprising to Sholto, a linguist by trade, was that none of the individual words made much sense when related to the one before or the one after. There seemed no logic to their construction and yet he was certain there was a pattern, given form by the way Simmy had written them down. He studied Simmy's depiction of the sundial but, as detailed as it was, it was impossible to tell from it which words came from where, only that growing in from the outer edge of the sundial to its centre was a concentrated spiral of small and fine inscriptions, first in one language and then another, apparently at random. He sat back as far as his tiny seat would allow. The column of English words seemed out of place on a sundial: mass, velocity, infinity, large, small, speed… and Simmy's dissection of the words on the sundial pointed out to Sholto what had not been in evidence before, namely that a great many were the written words or symbols for numbers and their mathematical equators: multiply, divide, plus and to the power of. Beyond that, he wasn't sure where to go or how to proceed, except that all roads seemed to lead to Wengler and his island, and to the Round Tower and possibly back to Titius and his supposed Riddle, although Sholto was still harbouring his doubts about that.

Θ

Aileen was effusive when Oswald Harlow brought Simmy to her door, and more so when he explained why she was here, namely that Simmy's father was finally dead.

'Oh my dear,' Aileen said, once apprised of the facts. 'Come in, child, come in by the fire and get yourself warm.'

Simmy obliged, Oswald hovering by the door. He'd always been impressed by Aileen, never more so than now as she drew Simmy into her care, knowing he'd brought the girl to the right place. The house was dark as a rabbit hole, the shutters having been drawn closed against wind and snow, the day already losing light despite it being only just past noon: yellow-grey clouds heaping up in the sky, blocking out the sun, a distinctive scent in the air that meant more snow before the day was done.

'I need to go on to Simmy's home,' Oswald said, declining Aileen's offer of food and drink.

'Oh, but of course, Reverend. You've no need to worry about Simmy. I'll be glad to keep her here with me and if you need any help with the laying out, well, you've only to ask.'

Oswald Harlow didn't reply, but Aileen detected his hesitation.

'I know what you're thinking, Reverend,' she said, 'but as long as someone can get me there and provide me with the necessaries then I'll have no problem washing him down and getting him ready.'

They were both cut short by a stifled sob from Simmy.

'I just want to know where Harald is,' she whispered. 'Oh, tell me you'll look for him, Reverend. Please tell me that.'

Oswald spread his hand over his chin, rubbing his nose for a moment with forefinger and thumb, taking a deep breath, unwilling to lie but neither willing to tell her Harald had to be found one way or another, and not just because of their father. He found himself fixing his eyes on Aileen's unseeing face, and it was she who gave a reply in his stead.

'But of course he will,' she said. 'And Harald'll hear the news soon enough and come running, because you've always been his girl, Simmy, and no matter what happens, you always will.'

CHAPTER 23

GOD FORGETS HIS DUTIES,
BUT OSWALD DOES NOT

Jed didn't bother knocking on Wengler's outer door, assuring Griffen it would be in vain. Instead, he led Griffen straight in and through the kitchen and up the spiral staircase to the upper rooms. He was unsurprised to find Gustav Wengler on his stool in the middle of his study just as Hesketh had left him. What did surprise Jed were the several piles of books and papers on the table that hadn't been there before, obviously riffled through and not quite in their customary order – unlike Wengler, who sat stock still, staring at his blackboards, though there was not a jot of chalk on any of them.

'It's just me, Mr Wengler,' Jed said, 'Jed Thornbrough. We spoke before?'

Gustav Wengler let out a breath but didn't speak, just carried on staring at the blackboards on which were nothing but the wipes of a cloth forming a series of dusty arcs across their empty surfaces.

'I've brought someone with me,' Jed tried again. 'He met with Archie when Archie was in Copenhagen.'

Wengler twitched.

'Do you see those arcs?' he said, nodding towards the

blackboards. 'It strikes me how like they are to the corona seen during a partial solar eclipse.'

Jed frowned, unsure how to reply.

'We've brought the book Archie bought in Denmark,' he added. 'We think it might be Titius's actual copy of Chaucer's Astrolabe.'

That caught Wengler's attention. He turned his head towards Jed as Jed brought the burned-edged book from his jerkin and placed it in Wengler's outstretched hand, Kurti Griffen choosing that moment to speak.

'I need to ask you about the sundial you purchased from the Round Tower,' he began, but was cut off sharply by Wengler.

'Not now. Ask me later.'

He swivelled himself on his stool, leaving them staring mutely at his back.

Jed sighed.

'We might as well leave him be for half an hour,' he said, motioning Griffen to the door, Griffen shuffling his feet, unwilling to go. 'Just give him a while,' Jed said as they closed the door behind them. 'Let's take a look at the monuments instead.'

'I thought he'd be more interested in the sundial,' Griffen said as they went down the spiral staircase.

'It's not that exactly,' Jed explained, 'more that he can only focus on one thing at a time.'

'You seem to know an awful lot about him,' said Griffen at his back, seeing Jed shrugging his shoulders.

'I've been following his work, spoken to a few people who regularly correspond with him from London,' Jed reached the floor and started off across the kitchen, turning back to speak again to Griffen.

'They all say how extraordinary he is, how completely he can concentrate. It's like he lives entirely in the present, absolutely occupied with whatever he's working on, unable to let his mind move on to something else until the task in hand is done. They envy him, living here on this island with no family, no menial tasks, nothing to distract him.'

'I'm assuming he sleeps, changes his clothes and goes to the bathroom every now and then,' Kurti Griffen commented, 'so he can't be so completely focussed on mathematics all of the time.'

Jed let out a breath, annoyed.

'Well of course,' he replied, 'but he'll be doing them by rote, not actually thinking about them. He knows they have to be done and so he does them. Simple as that.'

'You make him sound like a piece of clockwork,' Griffen said.

'Only if a piece of clockwork can come up with a workable demonstration of Goldbach's Conjecture up to $n=311$ and describe different levels of infinity in terms of their relative countability... Oh, I don't know why I'm bothering.'

Griffen raised his eyebrows, not having the faintest idea what Jed was talking about. He was well aware of Wengler's reputation, having asked about him before he came on this trip; he'd also been one of the few schooled in the recently uncovered provenance of the sundial, and how imperative it was they got it back before Wengler could get his hands on it. Despite his jibes, he'd met men like Wengler before – you could hardly turn a corner in the Round Tower without tripping over one or other of them – and so he held up his hands in submission, bowing his head.

'I apologise,' he said. 'You're the one who should be talking to him, not me. Go back up, see what you can get out of him. The monuments are more my area of expertise anyway, so I'll go take a look. But,' he added as he gained the door, 'make sure you ask him about the sundial and make sure to tell him that legally it is still the property of the Round Tower. As is the ring.'

'Fine, thank you.' Jed was relieved. 'But what ring? You mentioned one before when you were talking about the brooches, but if they were nothing, what makes a ring any different?'

'Never tell anyone everything at once,' was all Kurti Griffen said, smiling as he pushed open the kitchen door, going out to view Wengler's snow-white monuments in a snow-white world, thinking how wonderful it was to be alive.

⊖

Harald was scared. More scared than he'd ever been in his life. He'd been hiding out the last couple of days, hadn't even been to the croft, unable to face any more questions from Simmy, and certainly not any from Aileen. He'd surfaced only once, to give Dunstan the money from the piebald, immensely relieved Dunstan himself wasn't there so he didn't have to tell him face to face that Harald was now out. He'd gotten in way over his head with Dunstan. Christ! A man had been killed, and he'd been a part of it. A simple robbery was what Dunstan had told him, take advantage while you can, and Harald had been happy enough to go along with that. Pinch a horse, a few valuables from folk who could afford to lose them, that's what he'd gone in for and nothing more. And them brooches had been fine looking things, far more than they'd expected, and them only at the bothy because the smuggling boats were due – fine French brandy was what they'd been waiting for, ten barrels of the stuff, their part to offload it, shove it in the bothy overnight before another boat took it on a few days later to Port Glasgow, where the real money was to be made. Then, only minutes after they'd got the flag down, they'd heard a horse coming along the track which was a miracle, given that hardly anyone used Ardslignish these days, now that the Skinners had shifted to Kilchoan. And that was when Dunstan made the quick plan to knock the traveller out, rob him of whatever he had, tie him up, leave him sitting somewhere off in the bushes while the real business of the evening went down. But that wasn't how it'd gone at all, and maybe Dunstan had never intended it to. And now Harald was a murderer – if only by proxy – his whole life hanging in the balance. All he'd wanted was a bit of money so's he and Aileen could get a good start. They'd been planning on getting wed for years, but neither had the means to leave their families behind and start over. And right when he'd thought it was never going to happen that man had cosied up with him in the Corran tavern, going on about all those years back when Harald had dragged the sundial along the broomway.

A lad with your strength, the man had said, *is always going to have uses. Us could put you onto better things than shoving sheep around a fold, if you're minded.*

And Harald had been minded. That had been a year back, and at the time he could hardly believe his luck. Just a few jobs here and there had been his thinking, a bit of lugging, a bit of carrying, amass a bit of money – and so he had – and then he'd wanted out. But Dunstan Pirie had other ideas, kept him in, kept saying *Look on me as your da. I'll never let you down, not like the one you've already got.* And Jesus it had swayed him, that wanting, that needing a strong man to tell him what to do, where to go, how to act. A bit of rebellion against his own da that had seemed like a lark at the time. But not after the bothy, when everything had gone so wrong. He was convinced he was going to hang for it and was terrified at what would happen to Simmy when he did. Sad truth was that when he'd finally got up the courage to stand against his da, the old man just switched all his attentions onto Simmy. No matter how many times Harald beat the sweat out of him because of it, he just didn't seem able to help himself. Soon as Harald's back was turned, he was as mean with Simmy as a stoat is to a rabbit, like he had a river of rage running through his veins that had to find a way out, and that way out was Simmy.

Harald bit his lip. He was stopping up at his mate Tom's cabin in the hills, listening to the drip, drip, dripping of the illicit whisky still in the shed, wondering what the hell he was going to do and how Simmy was faring back at home. Their da might be bedridden, weak as a reed before the wind, but he still had a voice and Harald knew how well he used it, how it had been used to break their mother just as well as his fists. Harald wanted back, wanted to be the boulder standing fast between Simmy and their father, but Harald didn't want to hang. His head reasoned that no one could connect either him or Dunstan to the affair, but he knew how folk tattled and that they'd be talking of nothing else. Sooner or later someone would find out about Harald selling the piebald to that farmer out at Corran, and then the new owner would blurt out Harald's name, and all would be lost.

Θ

Oswald left Aileen's house but didn't go directly to Simmy's. The dead could wait, for a short while at least. He was due to meet Sholto at the Ockle chapel and wanted to know what he and Matthias had discovered from their disinterment of the Ockle Man's bones. He got there just in time, Sholto on his way out the door to go look at Ockle's mysterious sundial.

'Ah!' Sholto said, delighted at the fortuitousness of their meeting. 'Just the man I wanted to see.'

'How so?' Oswald asked, not so delighted, his mind on dead bodies, finding this bonhomie out of place.

'How much do you know about your girl Simmy?' Sholto asked.

'Hardly my girl,' Oswald replied shortly, 'but I have ascertained that Harald is nowhere to be seen.'

'Quite. But the sundial,' Sholto went on unperturbed, 'Simmy's project on the sundial. How much study did you ever give it?'

Oswald was irritated, not seeing the relevance.

'She wrote it years back,' he answered. 'The last one she did before her father curtailed her schooling so much she…'

'You really should have looked at it more closely,' Sholto interrupted merrily, 'and I really need to take a proper look at the sundial itself.'

He began to move past Oswald but Oswald stopped him, grabbing Sholto hard by the arm, all that anger coming out in one devastating diatribe that stopped Sholto in his tracks.

'And you, sir,' Oswald said, face hard and set, 'don't know the first thing about Simmy or what her father's dying means for her, but let me tell you this. Whatever you think your calling is here, mine takes precedence. When we find Harald, if we find him, it's Simmy first, you after. And if you want to go off dallying to look at your precious sundial then so be it, but I, sir, will be no part. I've others to think on. I've Archie Louden for one, berthed all alone on the Floating Chapel with no family to perform vigil or mourn him and only us to do him right, and now I also have Simmy, her father dead, her brother missing. And she's not just the author of a project you find interesting but a young girl who has been abandoned. Abandoned! Do you understand the word? I hope you do, sir, because as of last night she is all alone in the world unless and until we can find her brother. So blast your sundial! Blast your sundial into hell! My duty is to Simmy, whose life is about to be swerved right off track unless Harald is found, and swiftly.'

Sholto moved back a step, shocked by Oswald's outburst, but he saw the right in it. He'd been so caught up in the mystery of the moment he'd forgotten there were real people with real lives involved. He'd not known Archie Louden at all but Simmy was a different matter, someone he'd met and liked.

'I apologise,' Sholto said, 'and am truly sorry for Simmy's loss and for my putting you in such a predicament. And of course, the very first thing we must do is locate her brother, and not for our own ends. But where are we to look?'

Oswald's blood pressure returned to normal, as did his manner. He released his grip on Sholto, ashamed of his verbal and physical assault, rubbed his nose again, would have been a hopeless hand at poker. He shook his head.

'I don't know,' he replied. 'And I'm sorry for my shouting, but there are so many questions and I don't know how to find the answers.'

Sholto understood. God could be a hard partner, asking much, giving little in return. Not a bargain he'd ever undertaken himself but he was sympathetic, and suddenly saw the way.

'Maybe all we can do is wait,' he said, 'but in a place such as this it's my experience news travels fast and wide. Perhaps if we announce Simmy's father's funeral as taking place tomorrow?'

'But of course!' Oswald's face lit up, could have kicked himself for not thinking of it himself. Announce the burial and Harald would be here in an instant, wherever he was hiding out, even if that was miles away, for he'd break every bone in his body to get back to the funeral on time. 'There's one thing I have to do first, though.'

'Anything,' Sholto said, sundial forgotten.

'Simmy's house, I need to go to Simmy's house, see what's what.'

'Only lead the way,' Sholto said, and Oswald did.

Harald wanted the last few days to undo themselves, dissolve the knot and tangle his life had become because of them. He was no great thinker, but even Harald knew that God Himself, even if He wanted to, could not turn back time. The selling of the piebald was going to do for him; even if he gave up Dunstan's name Dunstan would conjure up alibis from his friends in the smuggling game to put him far away from Ardslignish when the bothy man had been killed. He heard a soft footstep outside and immediately ducked out the back door of the stilling shed, pulling at the rope that lifted a square of overgrown heather hiding a tiny underground chamber beneath, into which he threw himself. There was barely enough space to contain him, and once the lid was down again it was dark as blood pudding inside, smelling strongly of mud and his own bad sweat. He tried not to breathe too loudly, to stop himself moving, couldn't help but think how like a coffin this hidey hole was, how much it was like being buried alive. He waited one minute, two, and then the trapdoor was suddenly tugged open and Harald braced himself, his heart beating too hard within his chest.

''S'only me,' said Tom, Harald glimpsing the outside world beyond the dark form of his friend: the cloud-heavy sky, the ends of Tom's hair wisping in the breeze coming in from the west.

'Thank God,' Harald whispered, heart subsiding back to normal rhythm as he gripped at the hole's edges and pulled himself back out into the world.

''S'all right,' Tom said, in his habitually understated way, Tom spending most of his life out here in the hills with no one but his dogs for company and, in consequence, saying nothing that didn't need saying, preferring the sounds of the wind and the burn from which he drew the water for his still to other people's voices, his own included.

'Just got news,' Tom said, as Harald brushed the dry earth and twigs from jacket and trousers. 'Could be good, could be bad, 'pending on how you looks at it. But it's your da, Harald. Thrown his last punch, mate, finally gone to that great paddock in the sky.'

CHAPTER 24

THE BRIARS THAT BIND

Sholto and Oswald arrived at Simmy's house to find her father in his bed, his room stinking of urine and rancid faeces, and no doubt at all the man was dead: skin turned a waxy yellow, beginning to sag away from his bones, lips drawn back from several stumps of rotting teeth in an unpleasant snarl. One hand lay upturned on the coverlet, clawed and rigid with rigor, eyes open, opaque, their pallid blue filmed over as scum does a pond.

'Definitely dead then,' Sholto said, not moving from the open door, a hand across his mouth as a choke of vomit rose in his throat, before subsiding.

'Quite so,' Oswald sighed. 'It makes you wonder what Lazarus must have been like after three days lying in the grave.'

'At least there's no flies,' Sholto said. 'This place is like an ice house.'

'I don't think closing doors was high on Simmy's list of priorities,' Oswald commented. 'Poor girl. I can't…'

'Sshh,' Sholto hissed urgently. 'I think I hear someone out in the yard. Quick, get behind the door.'

Oswald did as bid, the two of them standing shoulder to shoulder, backs against the wall, no time to push the door to as they heard footsteps entering the house and some indistinct clinking as someone brushed against the table and set the crockery on it juddering as cup hit plate and plate hit cutlery. A few moments later the bedroom door was pushed right back into their faces and a young man took a couple of hesitant paces inside the room. Sholto put the flat of his hands against the wood and shoved it hard, slamming the door closed behind the newcomer, who reacted by spinning around, fists at the ready, alarm in every limb and feature, eyes darting back and forth from the two men to the suddenly closed door.

'It's all right, Harald,' Oswald said, holding up his hands in appeasement. 'It's only me, come to see to your father.'

Harald did not shift his posture but his fighting muscles relaxed a little, a slight slump to his shoulders as he switched his gaze from Oswald Harlow to his dead father in the bed.

'So it's true then,' Harald said. 'He's finally gone.' And looking at that sad carcass crumpled beneath his sheets Harald found it hard to believe it was the same man who'd once been knotted with muscles from neck to foot, hard and strong as a clout of blackthorn, as slack now as they had once been tight and taut, like mooring ropes left too long in the water, getting skinnier and more frayed with every passing tide.

'And Simmy. Where's Simmy?' Harald asked anxiously, before fixing his eyes on Sholto. 'And who's this with you, Reverend? What's his turn here?'

Before either Sholto or Oswald had a chance to reply Harald suddenly paled and collapsed to his knees, retching so hard he might have been trying to sick up a month of suppers. Oswald moved quickly, hooked his hand beneath the lad's elbow.

'It's the smell, Harald. It's no good, and no good for you to see your father like this. Come on back to the kitchen and let's all sit down and discuss what needs to be done.'

Harald could only nod. He hadn't expected any emotion at all on seeing the old man dead but for the moment it hit him hard, his world collapsing like someone folding up a telescope.

'Simmy, where's Simmy?' was all he could say, allowing himself to be taken back into the kitchen and forcibly sat down, Oswald speaking soft as he could, going against his own earlier words and bringing in the bigger picture.

'I know it's a bad time to talk about this, Harald, but there are things needing sorted. And yes, Simmy is one of them. She's fine. With Aileen. And I know we need to speak about your father's funeral but there's also your dealings with Dunstan Pirie that have to be made clear.'

Harald lifted his head wearily as if he'd been walking non-stop for a week.

'Dunstan? What of him?' Harald's voice was dull and unconvincing, his worst nightmares coming to life.

'Please don't make things more difficult than they already are,' Oswald said as he stood across the table from Harald. He'd not meant to intimidate but that was the effect, Harald looking up at the Reverend's sparse, black-clothed body, the knife-edge of his companion; the fight going right out of him, if it had ever really been there at all.

'If I tell you everything will you promise to look after Simmy, and make sure my father is buried right?'

Oswald and Sholto exchanged glances. Neither had expected this quick collapse into collaboration, but were glad of it.

'Tell us about Archie Louden,' Sholto said, 'and we'll see what we can do.'

Harald furrowed his brows, not looking at Sholto, directing his confusion instead towards Oswald Harlow.

'I don't know who that is,' Harald said, shaking his head slowly from side to side.

'He's the man,' Oswald explained, 'who was burned alive in the bothy at Ardslignish a few days ago, and whose unpleasant remains are even now on the Floating Chapel at Strontian.'

His purpose with these blunt words had been to shock and they hit their mark. It didn't seem possible that Harald McRailty's face could have gone any paler, but paler it went.

'Burned... alive?' he repeated slowly.

'Alive,' Sholto reiterated. 'His name was Archie Louden,' he went on without remorse, 'worked for Gustav Wengler over on the island of Havengore in the Sunart Sound. Just got back from a trip to Denmark for his master when he was set upon, robbed, beaten up in the bothy and then set alight. But not yet dead, Harald. Alive enough to get himself out. Twenty yards he dragged himself, towards the dyke. That's twenty yards of burning, Harald, twenty yards of thinking he might make it, twenty long yards of crawling through the grass with his clothes and hair on fire and no one to help him. And he made it to the dyke, God help him, but he got to the water too late. And Lord knows, no one should go like that, so if you know anything, Harald, then please, please tell us.'

The geese that had been circling somewhere above the cottage took a collective decision at that moment to land, and the whiffling of their wings as they did so and the contented grackling once they'd got their feet on the ground filled the air. It was all so everyday that Harald was having difficulty comprehending the seriousness of the situation he was in. His mind was trying to think but kept latching onto the ordinary, normal everyday things about him, like the grain of the wood on the table, and the fact that the fire had gone out in its grate, and the chickens were making that noise they always did when they wanted feeding. And that his father was lying dead only a door away, and Simmy wasn't here to help him.

'Harald,' Oswald tried again, Harald making a noise like a dog that has just been beaten, a whimpering that admits defeat and desperately wants to please.

'I didn't know,' Harald whispered, but as soon as the words were out of him he knew he was lying, because in truth he'd known it all along. He'd known it when Dunstan told him to lead the piebald garron away, and he'd known it when he'd heard that strange whooshing noise and looked back to see the light going up into the evening sky. He could tell himself anything he wanted but he'd known it, in his boots and his bones, that Dunstan would not leave a man behind who'd seen their faces, heard their voices. And he'd done nothing to stop it. He'd remained the coward, unable to stand up against the likes of Dunstan Pirie even if he had eventually stood up against his father. He might have dragged a sundial practically singlehanded from the sand and back along the broomway but when it came down to tacks and nails he was still the same cowering, snivelling lad he'd been for the first fifteen years of his life. Harald took a deep breath, laid his hands down upon the table, looking fixedly at them.

'He told me to take the horse away, and so I did,' Harald said quietly. 'But I should have stayed, I should have stayed...'

Harald's *mea culpa* was interrupted by the clopping of a donkey cart coming into the cobbled yard, by people decanting themselves and heading for the door, and Harald was already on his feet because he knew those noises and those voices and into the kitchen came the two people in the world he most wanted to see and yet simultaneously the two people he was most feared of facing up to. And here they came, Simmy first, followed a few moments later by Aileen, swishing the stick Harald had so painstakingly picked, sanded and painted, fixing onto its end a metal ferrule, so Aileen would always find her way without obstacle. And now the greatest obstacle to her life was him.

'Harald!' Simmy shouted joyously the second she was through the door, running to him and flinging her arms about her brother's waist. 'And Aileen's here too,' she added unnecessarily, as Aileen tapped herself efficiently through the door, ignoring all offers of help from Oswald, who tried to lead her on. She smiled once in Harald's direction, but didn't intrude her own intense gladness to find him safe and well on the reunion of brother and sister, instead going straight to the nook and feeling around for the kettle, filling it from the jug that stood to one side, getting it on its hook, holding her hand over the embers and finding them wanting.

'If someone could get the fire alive again,' she said, 'that would be a real help. We're going to need something hot for ourselves, and a lot of warm water for washing down with. Simmy's going to pick out some clothes, and...' Aileen stopped speaking suddenly and moved her head, rested her cane against the table, listening to what no one else could hear, the tense way the other two men in the room were holding themselves, the quick breathing of Harald as he stroked Simmy's hair, the tightness to his movements, the feeling of his eyes fixed on Aileen as she moved.

'But something's wrong,' she said. 'Something's terribly wrong. Harald? No use hiding behind your sister. You have to tell me what's wrong.'

Θ

Jed watched Griffen walk out the door, relieved he was gone. He waited twenty minutes before going back up to Gustav Wengler and was astonished to see Wengler scribbling away on the blackboards with his chalk: *Titius/Bedrossian*, he read at the top, *Chaucer's Astrolabe* underneath, though scored out again, Archie's name below in slightly wobblier letters, a tightly wound spiral, a single perfect circle, a tall skinny rectangle, some odd lettering he'd never seen before. Jed took a breath and held it, unwilling to break Wengler's concentration, but Wengler had already heard him enter.

'What?' he said shortly.

'It's me again, Jed Thornbrough.'

'And why are you here?'

Jed swallowed. The last thing he wanted was to interrupt Wengler's train of thought but far better it was him asking the questions needed asking than Kurti Griffen, ready to gut Gustav Wengler like a fish.

'Um, there's a few things we need to ask you,' Jed said, shifting nervously from foot to foot.

'Ask then,' Wengler said. 'But make it quick.'

'Chaucer's Astrolabe, the copy you sent Archie to Denmark to fetch?'

'What about it?' Wengler said. 'I've been looking for it for years and now I have it, thanks to Archie.'

'Do you know if anyone else knew?' Jed asked, taking an emboldened step into the room. 'About Archie's errand, I mean?'

Wengler shook his head, obviously frustrated.

'No one.'

'And does anyone else know about the significance of the book? About Chaucer's Riddle, I mean?' Jed swallowed nervously, wondering if he'd overplayed his hand.

Wengler stopped writing, remained completely still.

'As far as I'm aware, I'm the only person working on the problem.'

'But you know we've found the sundial,' Jed said, and took back one of his steps as Wengler wheeled round and actually stared directly into his face.

'You've found my sundial,' he repeated. 'Where have you found my sundial?'

Jed swallowed again, feeling like a moth pinned to a collector's table.

'We think it's at Ockle, sir, in the graveyard there. And the man who was with me earlier? Kurti Griffen? Well, he's come here to find it too, says he knows you bought it in good faith but that it's going to have to go back to the Round Tower. I'm sure you'll be able to study it first…'

'The sundial belongs here,' Wengler stated. 'It's the last piece of the puzzle.'

Jed's blood was beating in his throat. He looked again at the blackboards but could make nothing of it.

'Griffen asked me to ask you about the ring, sir,' Jed said, suddenly remembering Griffen's entreaty. Wengler tilted his head, looking unnervingly like a pike baring its teeth in the belly of some dark pool.

'And what does he know of the ring?'

Jed blanched. He'd no idea.

'I don't know, Mr Wengler. It would be best to talk to him about it yourself. He'll be here momentarily.'

Wengler looked at Jed for a few more heart-searing moments and then turned back to his boards.

'Very well then,' was all he said, Jed removing himself, knowing he'd been dismissed, practically bowing himself out. He was halfway down the spiral staircase when Griffen came blowing in through the door.

'Cold as a bitch out there,' Griffen said, rubbing his hands together. 'So you've spoken to him then?'

Jed nodded noncommittally.

'And?' Griffen pursued. 'What did he say?'

'Not much,' Jed said, truth on his side. 'But enough.' A small lie, but he was eager to scribble down all he'd seen on the blackboards before he completely forgot it. 'I'd like to get back over to the mainland, talk a few things through with Matthias.'

'Then on you go,' Griffen said. 'Don't mind me. I'm going to get a cup of tea on, warm myself up.'

'Was there much in the monuments?' Jed asked politely, keen to get away, and get Griffen away too if he could. He didn't like the man, and he didn't trust him, this person from Denmark who'd turned up from nowhere and spoke better English than he did himself.

'Some,' Griffen nodded. 'I've no doubt he meant the sundial to rest here and nowhere else.'

He didn't know this at all, but it suited him to plant the seed.

'So you'll let him keep it?' Jed was almost jumping. Maybe he'd misjudged Griffen... but that hope was immediately quashed.

'I can't do that. I'm here to bring it home. I can see the extraordinary extents to which Wengler has gone to give it a place, make it a part of something; but we have the same facilities in Denmark and if there's discoveries to be made on the back of it, then that's where they should be made.'

'But you don't have the Astrolabe,' Jed countered, 'and you don't have Gustav Wengler. Can't you give him leave to finish what he's working on?'

He could have bitten out his tongue, but too late now.

'So it really is the right copy, then?' Griffen just had to say it and Jed quailed.

'I didn't say that,' Jed said, miserable now, feeling helpless, outgunned, needing backup, needing Matthias or maybe even that Sholto McKay, to fight his corner. 'But maybe it's not the right sundial,' he tried, desperate now. 'We should speak to that girl Simmy. The one over in Ockle Sholto was talking about? She seems to know a lot about it.'

'Go back to the mainland,' Kurti Griffen said, not unkindly. 'I can ask my own questions.'

'Go soft on him,' was all Jed could muster before he left Wengler to Griffen's mercy, walking from the kitchen and the house and going down the track, luck being on his side on that point at least, for there was Hesketh Wood on the other side of the loch, oars at the ready, as if waiting for an excuse to come over, which indeed he was.

Θ

'So where's Dunstan Pirie now?' Sholto was asking. Aileen had made a huge pot of tea and was now sitting by Harald's side, her thin fingers entwined with his far larger ones, as if neither ever wanted to let go.

'I don't know,' Harald said. 'He told me to get gone and not to look for him. That we weren't to meet up for a while. Maybe over to Fort William,' he added, with a note of desperation. 'He had them brooches. Maybe went to flog 'em there. There's a man there sometimes buys stuff…'

He trailed off as Aileen clicked her tongue and closed her eyes for a moment, swapping one darkness for another.

'Why did you do it, Harald?' she asked softly. 'Never mind the brooches, but you mind well enough what folk around here think of thieving horses.'

Sholto, unlike Simmy, had no difficulty looking at Aileen, eyes included. On the contrary, he found her fascinating. The way she'd moved about the room was extraordinary, as was her deftness, the surety of her fingers going at their tasks, touching, always touching, flittering about like butterflies on flowers, and if you discounted her eyes she was really rather beautiful. No wonder a lad like Harald had latched onto her. She was as certain of herself and her place in her surroundings as he seemed jittery and uncomfortable, even here in his own home, as if he didn't quite fit and couldn't wait to get out. Quite what she saw in him was more difficult. From what Sholto had seen of Harald so far he didn't have many engaging qualities. Certainly he was physically impressive, with shoulders even broader than Brogar's, but his manner suited one much younger than his apparent age, and there was a molten, aimless energy in him that he didn't appear in control of, as if he was a thundering stream that needed to be guided and led. But maybe, Sholto thought, it was precisely this need Aileen found attractive.

'I jis wanted us to get a good start,' Harald whispered. 'Thought if I went in with the smugglers for a year or so we could get up and out.'

'It wasn't the way, Harald,' Aileen said gently, and Harald looked as if he might cry. Sholto was shuffling this latest information in his head.

'So that's why you were at Ardslignish,' he said, finally enlightened. It had struck him previously how odd it was that Archie was attacked in so isolated a place, presuming no one could have known he was there – unless they'd followed him for the specific purpose of robbing him, which then turned on the fact they knew what he had with him and saw a profit in taking it; yet if that was the case, why not pinch the book too? Apparently by far the most valuable item he'd been carrying, at least to the right person.

'We was supposed to have been offloading a load of barrels,' Harald said. 'Hiding them in the bothy till they could be fetched. No one uses Ardslignish anymore, everyone knows that. It was all supposed to have been so easy… and then, well, then it all went wrong.'

Simmy had been quiet all this while. There was so much to deal with about her father dying, about what he'd said before he'd finally croaked, about Harald being involved in the smuggling – which explained an awful lot, now that she came to think of it – about what might happen to Harald when people found out, because Aileen was right. Smuggling was one thing, thieving horses another. Horses were livelihoods, and people had been hung for less. Her whole life was teetering on the brink, as was Harald's.

'But we don't need to tell anyone,' Simmy said quietly. 'About any of it. It was Dunstan murdered that man and made Harald do what he did. And with our da dead we could persuade the Factor to move the lease to Harald and Aileen and Harald could get married and we'd all go on as we did before.'

Everyone looked at Simmy, at her small head bowed over the table, not daring to look anyone in the eye, at her hands knotted together on the table that were reddened and calloused from years of mixing chicken feed and milking goats, querning corn, slopping out her father's stools, planting and pulling tatties and turnips when the weather was at its worst.

'We don't have to tell anyone,' she said again, and Oswald felt a great lump in his throat as he looked at her, at this young girl who had so much promise and so bright a mind, sprung up like the brightest yellow aconite from the hardest of soils, and yet was going to be ground right back into it if things went as he feared they must go.

'We can't just ignore what has happened,' it was Aileen who spoke for the rest, saying what none of the others could bring themselves to. 'A man has died, Simmy, and that cannot be allowed to pass unnoticed. And whether we like it or no, Harald is in the thick of it.'

Oswald cleared his throat and lifted up a hand. He couldn't bear seeing Simmy so broken, so utterly without hope as she was now.

'Maybe there's a way between these two paths,' he said, 'a way to work this to our advantage. Dunstan and Harald were supposed to offload the barrels that night into the bothy but after Archie's unexpected appearance and what happened next, well, there was no bothy left and Harald and Dunstan were long gone. So where did the smugglers go? What did they do? Presumably their parent ship would have already sailed on, not wanting to raise suspicion, leaving the locals to hide the booty until it could be taken on. Did they have other people they could contact at such short notice? Surely they couldn't risk being found with contraband on board when dawn came, so isn't it more likely they waited elsewhere for Dunstan to contact them?'

Sholto nodded with approval. 'Lines of communication,' he said. 'Not easy to re-establish once broken by chance. So how did you communicate, Harald?'

Harald shook his head. 'I didn't. All that was Dunstan and his crow of a mother. She was the one did all the directing when it came to the likes of that.'

Sholto and Oswald looked at each other, and then back across the table at the broken almost-family sitting on the other side. That Harald was a bit of a blockhead was not in doubt; a shambling, misguided blockhead maybe, but one who was the lynch pin of both Aileen and Simmy's lives and it was their lives Sholto and Oswald were thinking on now.

'I think Oswald was suggesting we catch the smugglers in the act,' Sholto proffered, Oswald nodding his assent.

'And make it so that Harald leads us to them,' he added. 'Think Harald. Where else would they go? They can't stay out at sea forever.'

Harald looked perplexed, and they all listened to the crackling of the peat on the fire and the grackling of the geese out in the field as his mind moved maddeningly slowly towards a possible solution.

'They used to use the back of Eilean Glas years back,' he finally said, 'after the Skinners shifted to Kilchoan when Ma Blaizie died. Bad blood there for some reason, Skinners shifting, and the island off bounds for grazing.'

Sholto knew all about family feuds, how they grew and rooted, tangling themselves together like bramble briars, keeping them locked in and everyone else outside.

'So where and what is Eilean Glas?' he asked.

'The Grey Isle,' Oswald interpreted. 'But you'll know it better as Havengore.'

CHAPTER 25

TALKING, AND TOWERS THAT
MIGHT NOT BE SO IMPREGNABLE

It didn't take long for Brogar, Gilligan and Hugh to get to Corran from the home Orla Pirie didn't want to leave, nor to the farmer who'd bought Padraig Skinner's piebald from Harald, following her directions. He was a stoop-shouldered, squinty-eyed man, suspicious immediately on their arrival, but it took Gilligan and Hugh only a few moments to pull the one nag from the paltry crowd of working animals, and only a second more to point out the new branding placed upon the old. Brogar saw no reason to castigate the man. The fact that he'd parted with good money and was about to lose a valuable animal was going to be punishment enough, but he saw the opportunity to gain more information and wasn't about to let that slip.

'We'll be taking the horse back with us to Kilchoan,' Brogar told the farmer. 'But whether or not we inform the authorities is up to you.'

'Oh God! Don't do that!' the farmer grovelled, plainly horrified. 'We're hardly scraping by as it is, and I handed over every last coin I had for it. I'd no idea the horse was nicked,' he added unconvincingly, 'and you have to understand we lost our best 'un a couple o' months back, and us not knowing what we was going to do without her.'

'You'll need to be making other plans,' Brogar replied sternly, though he was not without pity. He knew how hard a crofter's life could be, and all about the Destitution Roads that awaited them if they failed. His own family had been lucky by comparison, and they'd had a hard lot.

'So tell me everything about the man who sold you the piebald,' he said, 'and maybe we can open negotiations with Padraig Skinner, let him give one of your own mares a shot at his stallion, get you a new foal in the spring.'

'He didn't tell me his name,' the man said, pathetically grateful for this chance. 'Or no, that's not true. He told me his name, but it was a bad one. I knew it and he knew it, because it was that Harald McRailty from Ockle. Ayebody knows him hereabouts, the one as has fallen in with Dunstan Pirie this last while. And I can tell you he weren't too happy doing what he was doing. Jumpy as a hen on an ant hill he was.'

Brogar pulled at his reins, making his horse step back a pace or two, a tactic he knew was intimidating. He already knew about Harald and wanted more.

'Tell me about Dunstan,' he said, 'what he's like, where he might be.'

The squinty-eyed man pulled at his sparse beard, wondering what to say, weighing up the odds. But the offer of a foal from Kilchoan was well placed and he didn't think long.

'Aye, well then,' said the farmer, rubbing his hand beneath his nose to remove the excess drips. 'Had a few dealings with Dunstan before,' he said vaguely. 'Not that we ever knew he was on the fiddle, mind, only that he'd been worried when the excise men began combing through his croft a while back, needed to offload a couple of nags for the time, so he told us.'

'And?' Brogar prompted as the man began to shuffle his feet, plainly uncomfortable.

'Can definitely tell you this,' he finally decided to say, 'and that word hereabouts is that Dunstan Pirie's gone to ground on Eilean Beag Gras. He might be a big man so far as his own boots is concerned but he was all for running after Harald flogging me that pony excepting for old Ma Pirie, who telt him to stay put, and so he's done.'

'Eilean Beag Gras?' Brogar asked.

'We call it the Wee Grey Isle,' said the farmer. 'That lump of stone out in the Sunart as is covered over in cormorant shite, right next to the big one – the one with the White Cathedral on it. Gotta feel a little sorry for Dunstan,' the squinty-eyed farmer added, though neither Brogar, Gilligan nor Hugh shared the sentiment. 'Sounds like maybe he should have run when he'd the chance. But old Ma Pirie's the hardest kind of woman you'll ever meet, and she'd lock down her own son if it meant she could get her own way.'

'Did he ever mention anything to you about brooches?' Brogar asked. The man shook his head.

'Ain't clapped eyes on Dunstan since that last time with the excise men,' he replied, wiping his nose again, this time on his sleeve. 'Twas his sister-in-law came to fetch back the nags a couple weeks afterwards. But I seen old Ma Pirie last night. She was in the wee tavern at Corran ferry telling anyone who was anyone to keep their mouths shut about Dunstan if anybody asked.'

Old Ma Pirie, Brogar thought, not the rattled old biddie he'd taken her to be the day before, not at all, and possibly more dangerous than Dunstan. The bigger question being, to Brogar's mind, where the hell she was now.

Θ

After Jed had gone over to the mainland, Griffen thought at first it was a mistake – Wengler simply refused to answer any of the questions Griffen fired at him, just carried on staring resolutely at his blackboards as if they held the key to the universe. Most galling for Griffen was that they actually might, seeing what was there. What puzzled him most was Wengler's complete disinterest in the sundial, given its importance. He'd expected the man to come back with questions of his own, argue his corner, his ownership. At first he couldn't understand how the sundial had been in Ockle all those years and yet Wenger had never heard of it, for plainly he hadn't or he'd have brought it to the island quick as he could sneeze. On the other hand, the lack of gossip filtering through to a hermit like Wengler was not so incredible. It struck him that this godforsaken peninsula was not so dissimilar to the place he'd been born, equally closed and insular. He'd had to fight tooth and nail to get out and over to Copenhagen, another two decades before he finally made it to the Round Tower, another eight before he reached the position of prestige he now so immensely enjoyed. He was boiling with frustration, but recognised the need to come at the situation from another angle, get his objectives clear, make a new plan of attack, especially now it was obvious Wengler knew the truth, or at least a part of it. That single name on his boards was sign enough.

'I know you think I'm intruding,' he said to Wengler's back, 'and I know you don't want to hear what I've said about the sundial going back to the Round Tower, but maybe we can compromise. We both know Chaucer's Riddle is so much more than Titius's discredited Numerical Law, that Titius and Bedrossian figured out something far more important. So how about I offer you some information of my own? How about I mention a girl named Simmy and her brother over in Ockle who found your sundial, and later a bag of old bones that were probably those of your previous assistant?'

Wengler stiffened and slowly turned around.

'And how about,' Griffen went on, now he'd snagged Wengler, ready to reel him in. 'How about I tell you I think it highly likely they also found the ring, not that they've told anyone about it. But you and I know the ring would never have gone far from the sundial. It left the Round Tower on a chain about Gillespie's neck – that much is in our notes of your initial purchase. So how about I fetch the ring, take it with the sundial back to Copenhagen, give you first crack at both?'

Wengler stared just over the top of Griffen's head, obviously thinking hard, weighing things up, working things out. Griffen in turn looked at Wengler and had a new idea. If he could manage to inveigle sundial, ring and Wengler all to the Round Tower, all at the same time, that would really impress the Big Men at the top. He swallowed with anticipation, already envisaging his promotion. He cleared his throat.

'How about I go for a short walk and let you have a think about it?' he offered.

Wengler spoke for the first time since Griffen had entered the room.

'That sounds fair, Mr Griffen,' Wengler said slowly. 'Go take your walk. Let me think about it, as suggested. But don't expect miracles, not from me.'

Griffen lifted his head and said a silent hallelujah to whatever gods were up above.

'Very well then,' he said, suppressing a smile of triumph, having to physically restrain himself from breaking into a skip and a jump as he left the room.

Θ

'This whole situation is becoming very complicated,' Oswald was saying, as he accompanied Sholto back from Ockle.

'I don't see how,' Sholto replied, in jocular mood. He'd had a bit of time to take a look at the sundial – and a good idea of how it got there and when – and had witnessed the small and satisfying family reunion of Simmy, Harald and Aileen, and the possibility of a way out for them all; the murder of Archie Louden was solved, so all in all, Sholto reflected, the day could not have gone better.

He felt light and merry, taking pleasure in everything he passed. There was enough snow lying from the night before to make the entire landscape look new and fresh, but not so much as to impede their travelling. A few twitchy-tailed wrens took low flits across their path from time to time, and they disturbed a flock of snow bunting who'd been foutering about in a patch of crowberry, rising up in a pretty hue and cry as they passed. And when they were just in sight of the Sunart, Sholto could hear the faint lulling calls of eider duck as they tipped off one by one from their sea-borne rafts, dipping into the waves with the same synchrony as the crowds of turnstones wheeling through the evening sky. He was even enjoying being on horseback – a recent skill acquired over in Sutherland – and Sholto was more at peace with the world than he had been for a long time, and rather resented Oswald's doom laden presence beside him.

Θ

It was with huge relief that Kurti Griffen stepped back out into the crisp Scottish air, certain he now had the upper hand with Wengler. He began to thread his way again through Wengler's monuments, which really were remarkable and, as Sholto had said, were the spit of some of Tycho Brahe's Uraniborg, his Castle of the Heavens on Hven – the proper name of Havengore – at least from the drawings of them he'd seen. He knew a fair bit amount about Brahe and Hven, as every Danish child did, not least the fact that Brahe's nose had been sliced off in a duel when he was nineteen and that he'd worn a silver replacement strapped about his head for the remainder of his life. Nothing astronomical about that of course, although he also knew that Brahe had catalogued the positions of seven hundred and seventy seven stars from the massive turrets of his observatories with such accuracy that his work had never yet been superseded, even to this day. Uraniborg was now in ruins, but not Wengler's monuments, and so he stopped once more at the empty circle hammered into the bedrock with such efficiency that the thrift and rockrose inside it had not managed to encroach more than a few inches over its line, wondering if perhaps the sundial really should take its place here, at least for a short while. It was too cold to stay in one place too long and so he left the monuments, judging he'd maybe wait ten more minutes before going back inside, strike a formal bargain with Wengler: agree to the sundial staying here for a single month as long as Wengler then agreed to return to the Round Tower with him and complete Griffen's coup.

He made his way towards the shore – intending to splash a little of its water on his face to liven himself up, get his thought processes sharpened – when he became aware of a small aberrant movement down in a tiny bay that lay between two rocky promontories. A boat, he realised, pulled as far up the short spat of shingle as it could go, only the tip of its prow visible, swaying back and forth at the water's edge. He was intrigued, certain he'd been told previously that the only landing space on this island was on the other side. He clambered down the small incline to the miniscule bay and, as his feet hit the shore, saw a flattened area of marram grass to one side of the boat marred by drag-lines that disappeared round the end of the rocky outcrop, appearing again on the other side. He scrambled onto the rocks and bent down, saw there was a cave-like hollow further up, cupped and sculpted by the sea, hidden to view unless you were standing right where he was now, and furthermore he was sure he could see a line of barrels stashed right at the back. It was inaccessible at the moment, the narrow channel between him and the cave steadily filling with water. He retreated back up the cliff and scrambled down the other side of the channel and was starting back down again when a shadow fell over him. He turned his head up towards it, saw something swinging down fast down from above, enough time to register it was coming, not enough time to get out of its way. The sack-wrapped rock caught him full on his right temple, knocking him from his clinch against the rocks so he fell back onto the promontory, precariously propped up by his sagging knees. It was so fast and unexpected an attack that Griffen couldn't figure out what was happening. He was confused and dizzy, a curl of bitter vomit coming up his throat from his stomach. He tried to turn, drag himself back up the cliff but could find no purchase, his movements only making it easier for the sack-wielder to strike at him again, this time coming down with full force on the top of his head, splintering his skull into five pieces, popping out an eye, forcing shards of bone deep into his brain, blood blooming like bog water into a footstep once that foot has passed. He curled himself instinctively into the crevice between the boulders of the promontory but it didn't stop the next blow, nor the last, but by then Kurti Griffen was as dead as the seven hundred and seventy seven stars Tycho Brahe had catalogued so assiduously several hundred years before. His murderer squatted briefly to make sure the deed was satisfactorily done before dropping the sack onto Griffen's head, straightening quickly and striding with urgent purpose towards Gustav Wengler's house.

CHAPTER 26

PERFECT DAYS, NOT-SO-PERFECT PROBLEMS

'So, complicated how, Oswald?' Sholto finally asked, more out of duty than care, when Oswald remained silent after his first announcement, Sholto a little put out that he couldn't go on enjoying his almost perfect day. Oswald did not reply immediately, as they were by then ducking through some trees that were scattering snow upon their backs, but once out the other side he pulled his horse abreast of Sholto's and began to speak.

'We're going to need far more than Harald's word that Dunstan Pirie killed Archie Louden,' was his opener, 'and as for what you told me about the Ockle Man... well... if he was murdered,' he went on, Sholto listening closely, if a little irritably, 'then I have a conundrum, because I know what was found with those bones, but the sanctity of the confessional means I cannot talk about it, even if I think it might be of some significance.'

'So what was it?' Sholto asked, Oswald the one to be irritated now.

'I've just said I can't tell you. But it's all the most holy mess I've ever been involved with.'

Sholto said nothing, his ebullience swiftly fleeing. If there was a connection between the sundial and the bones – as both he and

Matthias suspected – then he was mighty curious about what had been found with them. He glanced at Oswald, who was hanging his head, taking none of the joy in the late afternoon Sholto was, and understood his dilemma. Being a clergyman was not a job he envied, and being one in a place like this must surely require a man to be as tight lipped as a limpet sucked against a rock: betray one secret and everyone would know about it soon enough, and then you'd be a clergyman without a congregation, and next without a parish. But Sholto could see an easier way to get the information he needed. It didn't take a genius to figure out that it must have been Harald who found whatever Oswald felt unable to disclose, and Harald might be strong in body but he'd already proved himself weak in mind; throw Brogar into the mix, was Sholto's reasoning, and Harald would open up like a dandelion in the sun and let fly his secrets to the wind.

⊖

Brogar was feeling quite as cheery as Sholto, for his day too had panned out well, gleaning more information than he'd any right to expect. On the way back from Corran to Strontian they made only one stop, at Hugh's behest, and so once again Brogar was left waiting at the bottom of the small heathery track that led up to the Pirie house, though this time he had Gilligan for company. They'd both dismounted to let their loose-reined horses forage for whatever they could find amongst the snow-shivered heather, Gilligan a little embarrassed at Hugh's impassioned plea to pass on what they'd learned to Orla Pirie; not that Brogar had rebuked Hugh, had just raised an eyebrow and agreed to the stop, as long as it was brief.

'He's jis like that, is Hugh,' Gilligan said after a while of kicking the snow about with the tip of his boot.

'Just like what?' Brogar asked after a moment. He'd sat himself down on a boulder and hadn't moved since, nor made any enquiry of Gilligan as to his friend's movements.

'Like he can't help but take care of folk,' Gilligan said, not meeting Brogar's eye but going on nonetheless. 'Alwus has done, ever since his folks died. Tried it first with his sister but then she was gone too, and after that it was the horses – and he's always been good with them. And me. He's alwus taken care on me. We kind of grew up together and it was alwus just normal kind of caring but since, well, since all that stuff over the way with Mrs McCleery, it's like he feels things a bit deeper...'

Gilligan stopped, screwing up his eyes. He would never have said that he loved Hugh but knew they were closer together than most families, and more so since what had gone on in Sutherland and then leaving there to come here. He felt a desperate need to defend his friend in case Brogar should be thinking badly of him, because Brogar was their hero, and he couldn't bear for Brogar to think Hugh was acting soft and out of turn. Brogar listened quietly, pinching his nose with forefinger and thumb before laying both hands out on his knees.

'He's a good lad,' Brogar said. 'I know it as well as you do, and he's a good heart, and nothing wrong with that. Only problem with having a heart as wide as the sky is that sometimes, and usually when you least expect it, the sky doesn't want to have anything to do with you.'

Gilligan nodded as if he understood, which he sort of did. Solveig McCleery had been like that, and look what had happened to her. All of a sudden he wanted to launch himself up the path towards the Pirie house and express his brotherly solidarity, but he didn't have to, for here came Hugh himself, running down through the heather as if he had a snake on his tail. He couldn't get his breath at first, stood panting beside them with hands on knees before turning towards them, his eyes shining a little too brightly.

Brogar was already on his feet, reining in his horse, getting up on its back with a single agile movement.

'Tell us, lad,' he said once up, and Hugh did.

Θ

Jed was fretful. He'd got to Matthias's to find the place deserted, apart from a leg of mutton carefully coffined in pastry and laid on the table by their housekeeper. He busied himself with burying it in the ashes of the fire, covering it over with the flat stones piled by the side of the grate for the purpose before stacking on more peat and getting it lit, so the meat could properly cook through. He filled the large kettle with water and hung it above the flames; he pounded a load of barely flour with water and butter and left it standing so it could be later boiled quickly into dumplings or griddled into bannocks. After that, he began fidgeting, kept going outside to look at the Sunart, studying the tide like the enemy it was, seeing the water rising and lifting the kelp from the rocks on both sides. Once the water had set the Floating Chapel bobbing on its anchors and the had sun dropped below the horizon, he knew it was too late. Griffen would not be back tonight and was probably bullying Wengler even now. He glanced over to the island, Wengler's tower dark as a tomb, picturing Wengler sitting in the blackness of his room, staring into space, pushing his obsessive mind around the obstacles Archie's death had placed in its way. He couldn't see any lights and figured Griffen was down below in the kitchen, hidden from his view, helping himself to the paltry supplies Hesketh Wood had brought over when he'd come to fetch Jed, Jed cursing himself black and blue he'd not thought to do the same. He'd been thinking to offer himself as Wengler's new assistant but already he'd fallen at the first hurdle on a mere matter of practicalities. He'd seen for himself how bare Wengler's cupboards were and had done nothing about it, Jed being such an idiot it had never crossed his mind. He'd wanted over to Havengore to face Kurti Griffen down, demand the sundial be moved from Ockle to the island, that Wengler be allowed time and space to do what he did best and figure it all out, whatever all that was. Wengler would work it out and then he, Jed Thornbrough, would be the one to guide Gustav Wengler through the maze of the scientific community, be his buffer and spokesperson when they finally announced they'd the means to discover new planets. He was not put off by the obvious caveats: that Wengler might not want him, that Jed was still bound by his present contract of employment, that the sundial and Astrolabe might yet prove to be without worth, just like Titius's first Law of Numerical Relationships, no guarantee that Chaucer's Riddle would actually do what it had been so long rumoured to do. But hubris was not a concept easily grasped by the young, and Jed was no exception.

$$\Theta$$

'So when did Orla say old Ma Pirie came back to the house?' Brogar asked, Hugh being as filled with news when he'd bounded down the track as a sea squirt is full of water.

''Bout the time we was down at the farmer's, asking about the stolen horse,' he said excitedly. 'Orla was doing the chores, said we'd been gone maybe an hour when old Ma came bundling through the door demanding this and that, got Orla to pack up a bunch of supplies in a sack and then she was off again. And Orla saw the gun was gone with her, and a load of ammunition too.

What are we to do, Mr Finn? We can't leave her there alone. What if the old woman comes back?'

Brogar calmed the lad as best he could.

'She's taken supplies,' he said, 'and she's taken a weapon. She's not coming back, Hugh, at least not for a while.'

'They'll be over together on that wee grey island,' Gilligan put in. 'Dunstan and his mother, so wheesht your panic, man. Your lady friend is safe.'

Hugh's face blushed red as a cowberry and Brogar intervened.

'Gilligan's right, Hugh. The old woman's gone. She's a son to protect and she'll not be back until she's done doing it. Seen bears doing exactly the same. They'll risk their lives ten times over making sure their cubs are safe, and that's what old Ma Pirie is doing now. Orla's in no danger.'

Hugh was assuaged, but he looked back many times towards the house in the heather as they made their way on to Strontian, because – just as Gilligan had said to Brogar – that was just what Hugh was like. Some people have a nature they can't escape from, no matter how hard they try.

$$\Theta$$

Jed didn't even realise he'd fallen asleep. He'd rested his head on his folded arms on the table for a couple of minutes and the next thing he knew in came Matthias, who'd been at the mines, and then Sholto – Oswald having gone on to his manse – followed not long afterwards by Brogar, Gilligan and Hugh. It was well after five o'clock, completely dark outside by the time they'd all gathered about the table. Enough time for the mutton to have cooked and Jed pulled it from the fire, laid it on a huge platter, broke open the pastry crust to release the aroma of mustard and dried wild garlic, got the griddle scones on and off the skillet quick as they were needed, which was when the information started flying.

'So Dunstan Pirie definitely murdered Archie Louden?' Brogar was asking.

'Harald's not got the wit to lie, at least not well,' Sholto said. 'Simmy and Aileen would have seen through any subterfuge in a moment.'

'And it would explain why Dunstan's gone to ground,' Hugh chipped in, 'and why his mother is so intent on protecting him.'

'Right again,' agreed Sholto. 'And now we know where they're hiding out, it's time we made a proper plan.'

'Action at last,' Brogar said, a broad smile creasing his scar in a way that had Matthias's teeth itching even as he agreed to the statement.

'You're right,' Matthias said. 'No time to wait for the excise men. It would take a day, maybe two, to get a message to the garrison at Fort William, and another before they arrived. And that's assuming the snow isn't far worse over the water, which it usually is. I never thought I'd be glad to see the excise, but I truly wish they were here now.'

'Up to us, then,' Brogar said amiably, Gilligan and Hugh exchanging glances, eager for more adventures yet to come. 'I'll need to take a proper look at the lie of the land,' Brogar went on, 'but from what I remember seeing of the Wee Grey Isle, as you call it, it's not very big, which is to our advantage, but not easily boarded without being seen, which is not. Our best shot is going to depend on distraction and deception, have an obvious approach from one side while we launch a sneaky attack from the other.'

'What are we going to do about boats?' Sholto asked, forestalled by Matthias who began speaking almost before Sholto finished his question.

'Not a problem,' he said. 'There's many folk have at the fishing hereabouts and although a lot of them take out and away for several weeks at a time, dropping their loads off at Kinlochbervie or Oban before they come home, there's usually a few at rest and I can commandeer them. Only problem is that I'll have to give an explanation of why we want them.'

'The more the merrier,' Brogar commented. 'Can't have too many bodies at a task like this.'

'That's not my main concern,' Matthias replied. 'What I'm worried about is that someone might take umbrage at what we're doing and tip the Piries off.'

Brogar creased his brows. This was a complication he should have foreseen, smuggling a way of life to the poorest who had no other source of income, especially when you factored in kinship.

'That's a problem,' he said. 'But not one that's insurmountable. What we need is a ruse.'

'And we have one!' Jed chipped in brightly. 'We've got the sundial! It's going to need bringing over from Ockle, so why don't we hire a couple of boats under that pretext? Tell folk we need to go out first to Havengore to check the best way to get it in, take a couple of practice runs up and down the Sunart so's we know the handling of the craft we'll be using.'

Brogar clapped one large hand down on Jed's skinny frame, setting him rocking in his chair but leaving Jed with a grin on his face the size of the plate he'd not long cleared of food.

'That, my lad,' Brogar said, 'is a very sound idea. But it's going to be up to you, Matthias, to convince these people to give up their boats without insisting on piloting them themselves.'

'Hesketh would surely help there,' Hugh offered. 'If anyone knows how to pilot a boat it's him, and folk'll trust him like they mightn't trust us. And he already knows a fair bit about what's going on.'

'You're a born strategist, Hugh,' Brogar flashed the lad a smile that had Hugh glowing like he'd been set on fire inside his skin. 'Must be all those stories you've been reading.'

'Thanks to Solveig,' Gilligan said.

'Indeed,' Brogar commented, thinking on that woman, who had been one of the strongest and strangest women he'd ever come across, and one who had a mind that could sort this whole situation in a flash.

'The plan,' he said, 'needs a bit of burnishing, so this is what we'll do…'

CHAPTER 27

LOYALTY, AND LIVING UP TO IT

The following day they all rose early, Jed being up a good half hour before the rest, getting breakfast ready so they wouldn't be slowed up. No more snow had fallen, for which all were grateful, and soon as they were washed and fed Jed and Matthias set out into the village to hustle up the boats they would need and get Hesketh Wood on side. What no one had figured into their plans was Oswald Harlow turning up at the door just as Jed and Matthias were about to leave.

He was clean and tidy, in full clerical regalia, but his face was sallow and drawn. He'd been turning over and over in his mind what he'd spoken about with Sholto the day before and the problem of who the Ockle Man might be and what had been told him in the confessional, and coming up with a plan of his own.

'I need to speak to Sholto McKay,' he said, on meeting Jed and Matthias as they were hurrying out of Matthias's yard.

'We've a fair bit on today, Reverend,' Matthias said, a little breathlessly. 'Is it not something that can wait?'

Oswald shook his head repeatedly before replying.

'No,' he said. 'I really don't think it can. I need to speak to Sholto now, before I head back over to Ockle to bury Simmy and Harald's father. And I've still a dead man decomposing on the Floating Chapel whom I hope no one has forgotten about completely.'

Matthias was embarrassed because yes, he had entirely forgotten, despite all the chatter about Dunstan Pirie the night before, and hated to think what state his body was in now, mortified he'd not spared Archie – a man he'd known and liked and spent many an hour and a drink with – a single thought over the past day and night.

'Oswald,' he said. 'I'm so sorry. I've been negligent. There's such a lot going on that we're both so unused to, and I'm entirely to blame for my non-thinking. But…' he stopped a moment, an idea popping into his head, 'if you can get Archie's body ready for burial before you go out to Ockle, then so much the better. I'm calling in some favours. I need to garner a few boats and, whilst I'm at it, I'm going to garner one for you. If Sholto agrees, why don't you and he take Archie's body back out to Ockle with you? It's a beautiful spot, that graveyard, and one I'm sure Archie would be happy in. The Mine will pay for any expenses, and if the lawyers refuse when they hear about it later then I will pay the money myself. But Oswald,' Matthias stood stock still, one hand across his chest, 'Archie was a friend, and I know you don't think I've done right by him but please, please, a good burial in a good place, and I will be in your debt.'

Oswald nodded. He'd no idea what was happening in this backwater of a parish he'd been assigned to, but since he'd been here he'd loved it like he was born to it, caring deeply for the people within its bailiwick. He also had a high regard for Matthias and could plainly see how distressed he was and agreed.

'So to Ockle,' Oswald said. 'I surely don't think Archie would be displeased with that.'

Matthias nodded his thanks.

'I would come with you if I could,' he said, 'but there are other urgent matters needing attendance, most notably the apprehension of Archie's murderer which we hope to resolve this very day. Please forgive me, Reverend,' he said formally, 'and if you return now to the Floating Chapel I will have Sholto with you as soon as he is able.'

And so it was arranged, Sholto agreeing to Matthias's swift change of plans, being in no great hurry to engage with an unstable, armed harridan and her murderous son on a piece of rock in the middle of a sea loch, and more than happy to accompany Oswald back to Ockle. In fact it couldn't have worked out better, for it would give him the opportunity to question Harald again, try to get out of him what Oswald could not divulge, assuming it was Harald who had divulged it. He was no Brogar Finn when it came to interrogation but he'd learned a thing or two since being in his company, and this was the day Harald was burying his father, so if ever there was a time he'd be vulnerable, this was it. He was glad too that he would be there when Archie Louden was finally laid to rest. He'd not known him, but finding a man's corpse leads inevitably to certain bonds of duty. He certainly wasn't looking forward to sharing a boat with Archie's remains, but it would give Matthias another reason for commandeering boats and also give him time to air out his theory with Oswald as to the identity of the Ockle Man.

Just another day of death and dying, Sholto thought, uncomfortably exhilarated. It was less than a quarter year since being released from his airless, windowless office in Trondheim, but already going back there was an impossibility he could not, would not, contemplate. He'd found his way at last. He'd found Brogar Finn, and he'd found Scotland, the place his parents had come from. It had taken a long time but he felt a strong echo of family in this land across the sea where he'd been born and partially raised, whether he remembered it well or no, realising with an odd kind of pride that he finally understood the Gaelic word his mother had used to explain the hankering for her homeland that had never left her, no matter how bleak that homeland had been: cianalas. He felt it bleeding into his bones, taking its rightful place in mind and body, drawing him into the fold of the diaspora in a way it hadn't done before.

Θ

While Matthias went about commandeering the boats they needed, all the rest – barring Sholto and Oswald – piled into Hesketh Wood's ferry and went over to Havengore. No sooner had they landed than Jed was scampering up the track like a hound after a fox, intent on seeing Wengler and finding out what wrongs Kurti Griffen might or might not have done him. Gilligan and Hugh were given free rein to do whatever they liked. Last time they were here they'd been told they couldn't go anywhere but the landing beach, but no one gave a damn now about what Wengler would have to say about their roaming, there being far more important matters at hand. So off they went, scampering like rabbits over the stones, eager to explore the island and its strange buildings, the like of which they'd never before encountered. Brogar had other things to do, mostly speaking with Hesketh Wood, explaining what they were about and how they needed his help to do it.

'So, they're over on the Wee Grey,' Hesketh said thoughtfully. 'That's not going to be easy. Ain't no bays nor beaches on which to pull up. Best you've got is a few anchor points drilled into the rock on north and south ends of the island. Folk used to graze the odd sheep there, though mostly swam them over at low tide. To get a boat in you need a man already on the island so's you can throw the rope over and get it tied and pulled in to the rocks. If old Ma Pirie went out there then I'm guessing she'd use the north side, 'cos that's what she used to do as a bairn, for her family – along with the Skinners – had the grazing rights. If Dunstan's already out there then he must have swum himself over like the sheep, probably from here, from Havengore. But he's aye strong enough, if he went on the turn, when tide's pulling in towards it.'

'So what's the best way to land someone, or several people, so they can't be seen?' Brogar asked.

Hesketh thought for a moment, stroking his bristly chin. He was aware of the stakes and no lover of the Piries or the smugglers they dealt with and wanted to help Brogar best he could, so took his time.

'They mightn't worry about a direct approach from me,' he said. 'They knows me, might assume I'm bringing news or more supplies from friends back on shore. Mind, I'd have to be alone. Even if we had a man lying prone in the boat they'd be sure to see him. They've height on their side. That place is just rocks on rocks, and the only shelter they'll have is the shepherd's bothy tucked down to the east on the low side, out of the wind. But if I can bring them both around and away from it, and if you're quick and quiet, send one man into the water to climb up and bring you in, then you might be able to get a boat in and reach the bothy or some other shelter before they realise something's amiss.'

'Well then,' Brogar said. 'That will have to do. But sketch it out for me precisely.'

He drew his foot through the sand to create a circle.

'If this is the Wee Grey Isle, show me exactly where the bothy is and the anchor points in relation to the sides you and we'll be coming in at.'

BURNING SECRETS

Hesketh hunkered down, taking up a small handful of pebbles, placing them as accurately as he could, erasing one part of Brogar's circle and replacing it with a more accurate rendition of the island's shape.

'There's something else you should know,' Brogar said, once Hesketh finished explaining what was what and the approximate distances between one part of the island and the other. Hesketh stood up, tipping his head towards Brogar, shielding his eyes from the sun that was lying in the sky above Brogar's shoulder.

'Tell on,' Hesketh said. 'I'll not baulk, sir. Them smugglers've cut the legs out from under me as far as my business is concerned, and Dunstan's a man I grew up with and never liked since we was knee high.'

'She's a shotgun,' Brogar said baldly, 'and I doubt she'll fear to use it. She knows Dunstan's neck is halfway in the noose and I suspect she's a woman who'd stick her own head in it rather than see him swing.'

Hesketh kept his hand to his brow, studying Brogar Finn, the hardness to his face, the scar that ran down one side like a broken arrow. On other men it might have been taken as the token of a violent nature, but not on Brogar. On him it meant honesty, or not honesty exactly. Loyalty, that was it. That's what Brogar's scar said to Hesketh: loyalty taken beyond the point of reasonable expectation, an impression given more gravitas by the intensity of Brogar's gaze, the way he held himself, the way he could be so still while he was waiting for an answer to a question, as he was now. Someone, Hesketh concluded, who would be unswerved by even the most extreme of circumstances; someone, Hesketh thought, that anyone in a fight needed by their side, no matter the outcome. And he, for one, was willing to take that chance.

Θ

Archie Louden's body was far more unpleasant than Sholto had expected, Oswald right to be concerned about its non-interment. They'd been so keen to go after the facts of his death that they'd all, Sholto included, forgotten about the physical remains of the man their investigations had left behind. The moment Sholto was halfway across the pontoons that led out to the Floating Chapel the wind changed direction, and the smell was appalling. No other word for it. Sholto baulked, retching over the ropes of the gangway into the water, could not go on until he'd tied his scarf around his face. How Oswald had stuck it out as long as he had was nothing short of heroic.

'I've wrapped him in several sheets already,' Oswald said, 'but as you can tell, I don't think it's done much good.'

'Must have been the fire,' Sholto managed to say. 'Heated his core temperature, accelerated decomposition inside…'

'Like a cockle on the fire,' Oswald said dourly. 'But eventually even a bad one splits open, and I'm afraid that's what's happened here.'

Sholto coughed at the analogy and the truth of it.

'Have we anything else we can put him in?'

'I took the precaution of bringing a couple of waxed tarpaulins I begged from the mine workings,' Oswald said in reply, 'they're already on board.'

Sholto nodded shortly, trying to prepare himself for what he was going to have to see and do once he stepped on board the Floating Chapel. The journey over to Ockle was going to be as foul as it was necessary, but Sholto blessed Oswald's foresight and, once they'd landed, he did his utmost to help, and eventually they had Archie rolled from off his bier and onto the tarpaulins, the two of them working quickly to roll him up and tie him fast. Sholto couldn't help but think of the mutton they'd had the night before, encased in its pastry coffin, left to smoulder and cook in the ashes of the fire. Life could be cruel, as could death, as Sholto well knew, but Archie Louden's passing from the one to the other seemed the cruellest of all.

Θ

Over on Havengore, Gilligan and Hugh had run their riot. The White Cathedral was both as fascinating and mystifying as they'd expected, but they weren't astronomers and so, once they'd run their eyes over the huge monuments and their feet up and down the steps and across the thin corridors of stone that Matthias and Griffen had so admired, they moved on towards the shore, hoping for rockpools, caves and other places to explore. They discovered a spill of rocks leading down to a small shingled beach no wider than the width of a boat, with a creek to one side and another tumble of rocks on the other. They were about to clamber down, for they could see a small hollow to the left that wasn't exactly a cave but was the closest they'd ever come to one, when Hugh held out his arm, keeping Gilligan from going any farther.

'Wait,' he said. 'Look at that.'

He pointed down the short cliff to a spray of some substance, dark and thick, splattered across the rocks below.

'What is it?' Gilligan asked, craning his neck down as he pushed against his friend's skinny arm to see the better.

'I think it might be blood,' Hugh whispered, and the two lads looked at each other for a moment before turning as one and racing back across the island straight towards the little pier, where they found Brogar and Hesketh apparently drawing figments in the sand.

Θ

Secrecy was not a commodity much in use in Strontian, and the moment Matthias started asking for the use of boats to take the body of Archie Louden over to Ockle for burial, and bringing the sundial back, folk started passing on the news, with the result that by the time Oswald and Sholto had staggered down the pontoon with their burden they had as many boats as either of them could have wished. Most were filled to the gunnels with men, women and children, all eager for a day out: funerals, like secrets, being open affairs hereabouts. Most of the village had come into contact with Archie in one way or another and all wanted to pay their respects, even if his funeral was to be in Ockle, maybe even the better for it, for it gave them the excuse to abandon quotidian affairs and pack themselves up for an excursion. While Matthias made himself scarce with the two boats needed for Brogar's planned assault on the Wee Grey Isle, Oswald Harlow's heart was full at the sight of everyone gathering around the shore.

'You don't need to tell me your plans,' he said to Sholto, 'but if there's anything I can do to help...'

Sholto had the same slight burn in his throat as Oswald did on witnessing the solidarity of this small community wanting to send someone off right, even if he was not entirely of their own.

'I can't tell you everything,' Sholto said, 'but the boats Matthias has taken? Well, we've a fair idea where Archie's murderer is hiding out and we mean to find him while everyone else is away.'

Oswald looked at Sholto. 'Can you not tell me where? Or how you're intending to apprehend him?'

'I cannot,' Sholto said. 'One word comes out about it and all could be lost. But this gathering, this wanting to mourn, we can put it to our advantage if you heed me.'

Sholto was thinking fast, finding angles. This mass turn out of Strontian folk was making him form another quick plan in his head and he needed to get it carried through, and quick.

'So be it,' Oswald said. 'Whatever you need me to do or say, it will be done.'

Θ

The small flotilla of boats set out from the Floating Chapel a quarter hour later. As soon as Archie Louden's body, tied up from foot to scalp in his tarpaulin to keep him in, had been loaded onto his allotted boat, Oswald stepped back onto the wavering pontoons and addressed the crowd.

'We are all here today,' he began, 'because one of our number has passed over into a better life, and I can't thank you all enough for coming out to witness his burial. His name, as I'm sure you all know, was Archie Louden, and he has been for many years in our midst. What you may or may not know is that the manner of his passing was as brutal an act as I have ever seen. We all know about the smuggling that goes on in these parts and, God forgive me, I have sometimes partaken of the benefits they have afforded us when times have been hard and luxuries scarce. But I'm certain I'm not alone in regretting deeply that it was as a direct result of those activities that Archie Louden died a death so horrible we would none of us wish it on our worst enemies. But what is done is done. Archie is dead, and the awful truth is that it might have been you or me, yours and mine, in Archie's place, dying as he did. Brothers and sisters, mothers and fathers,' Oswald was right in the flow and meant every single word, 'let us not have to do this again. Let us not put up with what is corrupting our small community. Let us bring up our children to know what is right and what is wrong, and murder is always wrong, no matter the circumstances. And Archie Louden was murdered, and did not deserve what happened to him. If we any of us learn anything by it then let it be this: ill-doing begets ill-doing. Archie was in the wrong place at the wrong time, but it might have been any one of us lying here in this boat, waiting to be buried far from his home.'

There were murmurings then upon boat and shore but Oswald was not quite done.

'We'll be leaving in just a moment but, before we go, I need to thank you for relinquishing several of your boats for our purpose. Matthias McQuat has already taken two over to Havengore to offer transport to the funeral to Gustav Wengler and our visitors.'

There was a definite charge in the crowd as folk looked over towards Havengore, wondering if this could truly be the case, if the man who lived there – who none of them had clapped eyes on for almost two decades – was really about to come out of hiding. Oswald noted the collective direction of their gaze and tried to draw them back.

'I also need to thank,' he said loudly, 'the visitors we have in our midst,' he nodded briefly at Sholto who took a small bow, 'who took upon themselves the responsibility of investigating the circumstances of Archie's death when we were found wanting. Archie's murderer is as yet unknown,' he hoped the Almighty would overlook the lie, 'but we are getting there, so if anyone knows anything, anything at all, then please, please, come to me. Whatever you tell me will be treated with the utmost confidence. Your name will not be spoken of nor mentioned to anyone else, and your testimony will not be called upon in a court of law, that

BURNING SECRETS

much I will personally guarantee. And I will say only one thing more, from the Good Book, from Exodus 10:17. *Now therefore forgive me my sin, and take this death from me.* And so let us do just that together, and take this death from our midst. Let's be done with it! Let's be over to Ockle!'

Immediately everyone bustled and scrambled, stirred by their minister's words, swiftly rearranging themselves to best advantage in their boats, one coming alongside and hitching Archie's boat to their own, for which small mercy Sholto sighed his relief. He'd been standing at Oswald's side during his address, scanning the crowds for anyone perhaps not taking what Oswald had said about not knowing the identity of the murder at face value, sneaking off to get a warning to the Piries. He saw nothing suspicious, nothing but a kinship of eager faces ready for the off.

CHAPTER 28

BAD DISCOVERIES, BETTER PLANS

Jed tore back down the track from Wengler's house, running into Brogar, Hesketh and the boys as they were halfway up it.

'He's not here!' he shouted, soon as he saw them. 'Gustav Wengler! He's not anywhere in the house, and all his papers have been moved about in his study like someone's been there and looked through them!'

Brogar moved an arm, catching Jed before his momentum barrelled him past the little group who were moving purposefully up the track, about to veer away to the right towards the small bay Gilligan and Hugh had just come from.

'Hang fast, Jed,' he said, propelling Jed towards the path the rest of them were taking. Jed was out of breath and, like Gilligan and Hugh, had to run to keep up with the great strides Brogar was taking.

'But he's not there,' Jed persisted, hanging at Brogar's elbow. 'He's always there. He never leaves. Why isn't he there?'

'And you've checked everywhere?' Brogar asked. 'The entire island?'

'Well, no,' Jed answered.

'Isn't it possible,' Brogar posited, 'that Wengler occasionally wanders about to take the air, check on his great monuments?'

He wasn't going to say what he was actually thinking, that he could envision a few scenarios in which both Griffen and Wengler might have posed a threat to both smugglers and Piries alike, at least if Havengore really had been used to stash the smugglers' goods after Ardslignish became untenable, and if Dunstan and his mother were holed up on the Wee Grey Isle. Who knew what either Wengler or Griffen might have seen and what might have happened if they'd intervened?

They arrived at the small bay.

'I think it's blood,' Hugh said, Brogar immediately going down on all fours to check.

'Right enough,' Brogar said, rubbing forefinger against thumb, ascertaining the facts before straightening up in one lithe movement. 'And there's a lot more of it down there. See that sack that's been tucked into the rocks?'

He nodded at Gilligan and Hugh who took their cue and, nimble-limbed, were down the short cliff in a moment and over to the rocks and lifting up the sack. The two of them did a swift kick-back upon their heels as they did so, neither expecting to find Kurti Griffen, his orange-gold hair shockingly drenched in blood, his head and face a messy pulp, one eye popped out of its socket and burst in a gelatinous mass partway down his cheek, his jaw broken open to display several splintered teeth.

'Oh God,' Jed whispered, immediately turning to one side and boking into the heather.

'Quite,' Brogar commented, as Hugh and Gilligan began to skitter their feet back upon the rocks in their shock. 'Take care, boys. No falling, and don't disturb anything at all.'

He was too late in his warning, Gilligan already losing his balance and landing with a thump onto the sand below the rocks.

'All right?' Brogar asked, as Gilligan pushed himself up on his elbows seeing more clearly as he did so the small cave that lay underneath the sea-carved rock.

'Aye,' he tried to shout, the word coming out in a frightened squall. 'I'm fine, but there's more down here. Barrels I think. Looks like you can get to them when the tide's right out, but not now, not unless you're a midget more'n me.'

Θ

'I need to ask you something,' Sholto said to Oswald, 'just between me and you and, like you said yourself, this will go no further.'

The flotilla had got speedily, if erratically, underway, their two allotted oar-pullers concentrating on getting into their rhythm, not listening to what was going on in the stern.

'Does it have to do with Harald?' Oswald asked.

'It does,' Sholto said. 'Or more specifically with what he found. I suspect the Ockle Man might have been Archie Louden's predecessor, accompanying the sundial back from Denmark to Havengore, when something went very badly wrong.'

Oswald Harlow nodded, but did not look surprised.

'Yes,' he said. 'I wondered about that myself. If so, he was called Neal Gillespie, an Edinburgh man, I believe. It was not long before I first arrived here so I didn't know him, but I heard he'd gone off on some trip for Wengler and never come back.'

'Did no one ever think to ask what had happened to him?' Sholto asked.

Oswald shrugged. 'Everyone knew Gustav Wengler was not the easiest man to work with. I gather it was assumed Neal had gone off on that last trip and chosen not to come back. There was never any inquiry from his family, so I was told.'

'Assuming he had one,' Sholto commented.

'Well yes,' Oswald said. 'Assuming that.'

'But didn't anyone query his disappearance when the sundial was discovered?' Sholto persisted.

Oswald sighed.

'Why would they? Why would anyone? No one knew why Wengler had sent him off, or to where. And from what I've gathered since, and from what I knew of Archie Louden, Wengler's assistants' usual purchases were books, caches of journals, the odd small artefact here and there. And the sundial wasn't discovered until a while after Neal Gillespie failed to return to Havengore.'

'But now you're rethinking that version of events,' Sholto said, 'as am I.'

'Pounds to pennies it was those blasted smugglers,' Oswald said quietly. 'I thought it not long after Harald came to me. I've looked at that sundial time and time again and wondered how such a wondrous object came to be lodged in such an isolated backwater as Ockle. I was brand new here, and at the time Ockle wasn't part of my ministry. But I heard about it, how everyone was hailing it as a miracle, a blessing given to Ockle like other places have visions of the Virgin Mary. But the truth is that after a couple of years everyone forgot about it, myself included.'

Oswald stared intently at the oars of the men who were plying them over to Ockle, at their going in and out of the water, the bright flash as the sun caught the water before the oars descended back into darkness. Just like the Ockle Man, he thought: first in the light as a living man and then into dark waters as a dead one, then dragged out and buried again, hopefully for the last time.

'So you really think the Ockle Man – or Neal Gillespie, if it is he,' Oswald asked, 'was murdered?'

'I do,' Sholto said. 'I think he brought the sundial over from Denmark and called on the wrong men to transport it on its last leg, from Oban maybe, to here. I think whoever was carrying it realised the sundial was a big prize, worth a lot of money, even if just for scrap. Maybe killed Neal for the chance at it, shoved him in a sack and sent him into the water before being shipwrecked themselves.'

He might have said more, but just then they rounded the point and were soon in, the flotilla of boats crowding into the small bay at Ockle, disgorging like ants onto the sand.

'So what do we do now?' Oswald asked.

'We do exactly as planned,' Sholto said. 'But I need to get Harald on his own, soon as you get the service over with.'

Θ

'So if that's Kurti Griffen, where's Wengler?' Jed was asking, absolutely distraught, unable to think straight, not focussing on Griffen at all, only on Wengler.

'There's marks in the sand here,' Hesketh called up from the small bay. 'Looks like a small craft has been moored and pushed out again cupla times, last time not long since. Drag marks still dry.'

'They've taken him,' Jed said miserably. 'I'm sure of it. They've taken him.'

Brogar was worried, for Jed could well be right. He didn't know what had happened here, but could make several guesses: Griffen interrupts the smugglers offloading or attempting to retrieve their wares, or maybe sees one or both of the Piries hop-skipping their way over to the Wee Grey Isle next door and comes to investigate; Piries kill him, so why stop there? Wengler's also a liability, might see something from his tower, and he's wealthy: owns the mines, owns the island, in possession of more than the collective citizens of the entire peninsula put together, the Piries included; Dunstan and old Ma already desperate. No hard task then to take Wengler with them as a bargainer, and how easy thereafter to make him sign any number of promissory notes once away from his home, as eager to get back as they are to get away, cash-in-hand; only concern then being to make sure Gustav Wengler is not found – alive or dead – until that can happen. Hence no dead Wengler lying next to dead Griffen. And that was only one possibility.

'Right,' Brogar said decisively, gathering everyone up. 'Back to the pier. Matthias should be there by now so we'll go ahead as planned. We'll need to go slow and careful, keep ourselves hidden as much as we can. If we've not already been seen then it must stay that way. Jed, I want you in one boat with Gilligan and Matthias, and I'll take Hugh with me. You already know what I've discussed with Hesketh Wood. He'll be our diversion. We'll both need to row off in the opposite direction, circle right around Havengore and go into the Wee Grey Isle to get landed without being seen. And listen up, all of you, and listen well. I want no heroics. Those Piries are dangerous and desperate, and if Wengler is with them, if we've got any chance at all of getting him back alive, then you must do exactly as I say.'

Brogar's army was small and unarmed, shocked and frightened, but all were ready for action and ran like a scourge back across the island, the great white monuments towering above them, hiding their shadows in the late morning sun.

CHAPTER 29

RESPECT AND RETRIBUTION

The men and women of Strontian filed their way up the small streets of Ockle towards the chapel. All the way up the Sunart and around the point they'd been laughing and treating this excursion like a huge family day out, but the moment the funeral boat came in they became sombre, taking Archie's body upon their shoulders, carrying him through the small hamlet with all the solemnity required. Oswald led the way, and even before they'd got halfway from bay to chapel they were greeted by a knot of Ockle men buzzing with the new arrivals, unable to figure out why Strontian folk were here, and with another body. But all were related, boot and buckle, and soon all was clear and the two villages melded into one, rather glad to have a worthy body to bury and not just one as disliked as Fraser McRailty.

Sholto kept to the back as the crowd jostled and pushed its way up the village street, catching sight of Harald, Simmy and Aileen, all dressed in their best, as everyone poured into the small chapel, pushing into the sparse pews, everyone shuffling and coughing and trying to make enough room for everyone else to get in. Sholto did not attempt to gain ingress, content to hang at the back, one of the twenty or so folk who couldn't find a seat. He'd never enjoyed funerals, excepting that one over in Sutherland that had been an unexpectedly joyous occasion, despite the circumstances. There was none of that here, which smacked more of sightseeing than anything else. He was surprised, therefore, when he felt a small pressure at his elbow and turned to see Simmy in a pretty, if faded, floral dress at his side.

'What are all these people doing here?' she asked, smiling wanly up at him. 'Surely not to see my da off?'

It struck him how out of place she seemed, how out of step with the rest as if she'd been plucked up from where she was meant to be and dropped down into the wrong place entirely.

'A man was murdered on the other side of the peninsula,' he explained. 'Oswald thought it best to bury him here today, alongside your father.'

Simmy dropped her gaze, studying her boots, the same boots she always wore despite having on her Sunday best.

'Didn't suppose they'd've come here for the old man,' she said. 'But he wasn't always like he was,' she went on. 'He was mean at the end, and for years and years before that, but he wasn't always like it. Used to take us fishing, me and Harald, and for picnics, like we were real people, proper children. It was only after me mam died that it went really wrong, like the world went black on him, and he wasn't never the same again.'

Sholto nodded. Such a strange child, this Simmy. From what Oswald had told him of her father, about how miserable he'd made her life, he couldn't fathom how she could conjure up forgiveness for him, and yet plainly that was so. He wanted to say something profound and comforting, but no words came, and so instead took Simmy's hand in his own.

'It's going to be a hard road from here on in, Simmy,' he said, thinking about Harald, how he might yet hang for his part in the death of Archie, if Brogar's scheme didn't go to plan. 'But I want you to know that Oswald Harlow will always help you, as will Matthias McQuat over at Strontian, and you can always call on me,' he offered, somewhat rashly, 'and I will come running from the ends of the earth if you have need.'

He was rewarded by Simmy giving his hand a light squeeze before releasing him.

'No need to worry about me, Mr Sholto,' Simmy said. 'I've Aileen now, and Harald, and once we put my da in the ground we'll all be free to set up home and be a proper family, like we was before.'

And then she was gone, back into the chapel, leaving Sholto truly wishing that it could be so, hoping he wasn't going to be the one to rip Simmy's new family apart at the seams.

Θ

Hesketh Wood took his way slow as he was able from Havengore towards the Wee Grey Isle, dallying a short while in the midst of it to throw out a few pre-baited hand-lines to draw the Piries' attention, assuming they were really there and watching. He even snagged a few mackerel which surprised and delighted him, their iridescent blues and greens flashing as he pulled them in. It was old Ma Pirie spotted Hesketh first, catching the bright flash of light and colour out in the Sunart when Hesketh's mackerel leapt and shone as he whipped them up and into the boat. She was simmering like a kettle on the go, angry at her son for getting them into this situation in the first place but protective enough to go to any lengths to see him right.

'What's he doing?' she asked of Dunstan, as Dunstan brought his eyeglass up.

'Nothing, Ma. Him is jis fishing. Ye ken what Hesketh's like.'

'I ken and I ken,' she retorted, 'and that man's no fisherman as I ever knew. So what's he doing here?'

Dunstan handed the glass over to Breda and she looked a while and, as she did so, she saw Hesketh raise a hand, and nothing to do with fishing.

'He's a-signalling us,' she said. 'Think your brother's Orla suddenly found herself a new friend?'

Dunstan grimaced. He'd no love whatsoever for his brother Malcolm but he liked Orla right enough, harboured fantasies about him and Orla getting it together, preferably with some enthusiasm on her part. Not that she'd done so before, being good and gooder right down her boots, which only made her all the more desirable.

'Bring him in,' Dunstan said, and although his mother looked at him badly he insisted. 'Might have news. I've men out there listening and looking, so bring him in.'

Old Ma Pirie acquiesced. They'd both seen the boats heading out from Strontian to who knew where and for what purpose, and so if ever there was a chance for a message getting to them, this was going to be as good as it got. She threw Hesketh a gesture that meant he should go about to the bluff and bring himself in close enough to speak.

'He must have summat for us,' Dunstan said for reassurance. 'Ye ken how hard up the man is. Must surely be carrying a message in from one of me friends.'

Ma Pirie was more suspicious than her son. She'd known smugglers all her life, had been running them for almost as long as she could remember, Dunstan brought up in her wake, so for once she took his word for it, but not before she'd checked her musket and made sure it was loaded, ready to fire.

'Over to the west side then,' she hissed, and Dunstan complied, both too canny to stand up and welcome Hesketh in with open arms, whatever news he might be bringing. Hesketh understood, had been expecting it, took his time putting his oars back onto their rollocks, thanking God they'd taken the bait and were moving to the opposite side of the island from where Brogar and the others were hopefully already coming in.

They were. As he shouted a loud *Halloo* to the Piries, Gilligan and Hugh were already leaping into the freezing water and clambering up the seaweed-covered rocks, looping the boat-ropes through the anchor rings hammered deep into the rock, Brogar, Matthias and Jed soon brought in and jumping onto land, able to hear the gist of the shouted conversation going on, on the other side of the island.

'News?' Dunstan said loudly, voice cracked and deepened by years of rough tobacco and being on the salt water in gale and strife.

'Some,' Hesketh said, a slight splashing as he manoeuvred his boat close as he could to shore.

'Well spit it out man,' Breda Pirie shouted. 'Time's a-wasting. And what you're doing here anyways is what's riddling me.'

A short pause then, during which time Brogar motioned to Jed and a dripping Gilligan to head along to the left towards the bothy while he, Matthias and Hugh took off stealthily onto the main bluff of the island.

'Got word from one of your workmates,' Hesketh was saying, keeping his voice light, sticking to the lines Brogar had primed him with. 'Excise men is heading this way, up from the Fort. Don't know why in particular, only that they'll be here next day or two. Thought you might want to know.'

'Shit,' Dunstan cursed. 'What do you think, Ma?'

'Think it's time we were shifting,' said old Ma Pirie, her eyes scanning the Sunart and Hesketh Wood and then the island of Havengore behind him, when she caught a quick movement of something right out of place. 'And think there's a rat out there on that boat, and where there's one rat another's sure to follow.'

She pivoted swiftly on her heel and lifted her gun, sure now she'd seen one of those rats, in the form of Jed Thornbrough, moving quickly over the other side of the island.

'Attack!' she skirled into the wind and got herself and Dunstan down prone into the heather, would have let fly a couple of shots at the traitor Hesketh Wood if she thought she'd had the time.

'Anyone comes near us and I'll blast 'em!' Ma Pirie shouted for everyone to hear, and despite everything Brogar had said earlier Jed was blazing with such indignation and fury that he stood up.

'We've come for Gustav Wengler!' he yelled. Ma Pirie pulled the trigger, the shot ricocheting wildly from the rock only a couple of inches from where Jed was standing, Brogar dragging him swiftly out of sight.

'Gotta figure you've come in over the north side,' Ma Pirie was screeching, 'So get you all over to the bothy and stay there till we're in your boats and away or I'll put holes in every last damn man jack of you!'

Dunstan, like Jed, was wanting to up and fight but his mother had a grip on his sleeve like a vice.

'Wheesht your while, child,' she spat in his ear. 'We'll not go down like this. We've a gun and they've not, so we've to shift our way over towards th'other side. Only place for them to have got on here like the vermin they are.'

Dunstan did as he was told, the two of them stomaching it over the heathery tussocks, Breda keeping her gun up all the while and at the ready, him keeping his head down, feeling sick, skin pale and sweaty, so fearful his teeth were chattering like the flag fixings at Ardslignish had done in the wind before he'd ripped them down.

Jed blessed old Ma's direction to go for the bothy, he and Gilligan streaking across the spiky, orange-wintered grass as they ran for it, the only place on this godforsaken half acre of earth where they could be holding Gustav Wengler. They rammed through the small opening in the wall where the door should have been, Gilligan's heart hammering like a blacksmith at an anvil, eyes wide and panicked, wishing he knew how far around the island the others had got, finding out soon enough when another blast of Ma Pirie's gun came hollering towards them out of the day. He'd been limpet-stuck to Jed throughout their short run, but now they were in the bothy itself they both saw it was empty, except of ancient sheep droppings, and then Jed was bolting past him, running out the doorway, already shouting.

'But he's not here! He's not here! Oh please God he's not dead! I'm going to kill that old bitch of a woman if...'

Cut short by another almighty round of shots as Brogar, Hugh and Matthias ran from one bluff of rocks to another, having seen Ma Pirie and her son squiggling their prone circuit through the heather. The sounds jumped and echoed, Brogar signalling his two companions to get down and stay down before nimbly crouching and leaping his way over to the cover of the next boulder behind which the Piries had just moved and, swift and flexible as a stoat, whipping his body round to the other side, grabbing Old Ma by the ankle and giving her such a yank the gun went flying from her grasp. Dunstan was less than the length of a pinafore string behind his mother, the gun landing right front of him. He picked it up, put his non-too-steady hands about its barrel and an even shakier finger upon its trigger.

'Let me ma go,' he shouted at Brogar, voice high and tight with panic, 'or I'll have you!'

Hugh took his moment and upped from behind his rock, Dunstan catching the movement, finger pressing in reflex upon the trigger, the shotgun's recoil pushing him backwards, ears deaf with the sound; Brogar leapt to his feet, picked up the gun and pushed its stock hard into Dunstan's neck.

'Got you,' Brogar said, even as he was shaking off Ma Pirie as she rolled herself over to clutch at Brogar's leg, giving her a quick kick that sent her reeling into a few moments of unconsciousness, enough time for Matthias to arrive on the scene and fling himself upon her, get her immobilised.

'All done, Piries,' Brogar said, breathing hard, shaking off the loop of rope he'd carried with him about neck and shoulder.

'Hugh,' he ordered. 'Get them tied. Hugh!' he repeated, but there was no response, no answer, because that last wild shot of Dunstan's had caught Hugh square in the face and Hugh was lying dying in the heather looking up at a patch of blue sky and the cloud of red coming in from the west that was so bright, so fast, so vivid, he knew it was the last thing he was ever going to see.

CHAPTER 30

FROM THE ENDS OF THE EARTH

Holding two funerals at the same time in the same chapel was always going to be hard, but Oswald had meant what he'd said about bringing death out of life and bringing everything to a close. He'd been a minister for over thirty years and had the capacity, therefore, to tie both funerals neatly the one into the other, Ockle with Strontian: two places, two burials, and in so short a space of time. He spun a masterpiece of a sermon and kept everyone enraptured by the poignancy of the moment. Except Sholto, who made no effort to crowd in with the rest and instead sat outside, thinking things over, wondering when and how it would be best to go at Harald once his father was safely within the ground. He could see the grave from here, a neat heap of black dirt beside stark white snow and could also see two gravediggers working frantically to get another prepared for the unexpected arrival of Archie Louden's body. About halfway through the sermon, as far as Sholto could guess, he was surprised by Simmy suddenly appearing by his side.

"Spose you're wondering what I'm doing here, with it not being over yet," she said.

'I'm guessing you're not one for sermons,' Sholto replied, wondering how she'd extricated herself without knocking up some disturbance inside.

'I nipped out through the sacristy,' Simmy said, as if reading his mind. 'But Harald and Aileen's all right with it, Mr Sholto. They knew I mightn't be able to stick it. I just want a little time to myself, especially now all these Strontian folk are involved. A little space to breathe, take a walk without everyone else. Can you understand that?'

Sholto could.

'It's been a bad time for you,' he said. 'And everyone handles it differently. Do you want me to come with you?'

Simmy smiled, but shook her head.

'No thanks,' she said. 'But I do want to see the sundial one last time, before you take it away with you.'

Sholto was surprised.

'What makes you think we're taking away the sundial?' he asked.

'No other reason you'd all be here,' Simmy said simply. ''S'all right though,' Simmy added, making Sholto feel worse than he already did. 'We always knew it never belonged here, but we was glad of the loan of it while we had it.'

$$\Theta$$

The shock of finding Hugh with his face a blood-born mess was tremendous, most notably for Gilligan, who fainted on the spot, Matthias almost as bad, legs giving way, crumpling him to his knees. Brogar yelled for Jed to run back to the bothy, find any receptacle he could and fill it with sea water, Jed back a few minutes later, trickling the water over Hugh's face as Brogar swabbed gently at the wounds with a ripped off portion of his shirt. Hugh was breathing, lips moving but no sound coming out. Brogar ordered Matthias to his feet, told him to go signal Hesketh Wood in, which didn't take long, Hesketh having heard all the shots and already around the island, pulling in and about to launch himself into the water to come and give them aid.

'Stand by!' Matthias shouted. 'We've one wounded; got to get him back over to the mainland. It looks bad,' he added, Hesketh wasting no time, chucking his rope over to Matthias.

'How bad, and who?' Hesketh asked as Matthias hauled him in.

'One of Brogar's boys,' Matthias said, shaking his head in distress. 'Need to get him over, and soonest. Get him to my place, get him seen to. I know most of Strontian's over to Ockle but Elspeth won't have gone.'

'Like as not,' Hesketh agreed, the two of them knowing that Elspeth McGrury, Matthias's housekeeper, had refused to step foot in a boat since her husband and sons were lost at sea and not a splinter of them or their boat ever seen again.

They carried Hugh gently but quickly into Hesketh's boat, Gilligan going with him, holding his friend's hand, crying all the while and yet talking too, because Hugh had once or twice flicked open his one moving eye and indicated he was conscious, if only barely. All the way back to Strontian Gilligan kept up a garbled retelling of some of the stories from Solveig's books, trying to keep Hugh focussed, trying to keep him awake, fearing that if he went to sleep he might never wake up. And Gilligan couldn't cope with that. Matthias, sat opposite him, could see it too, a gut-wrenching guilt chilling him from the inside out that he'd involved all these extraneous people in what had been his problem, and his alone. If only he'd dealt with Archie's death as efficiently as Brogar and Sholto had done then none of this would have happened. But instead Kurti Griffen was dead, Hugh dying and Gustav Wengler probably floating face down in the Sound. And gone with Wengler would go the mines, and that would be the end of everything. Only the smuggling left, and that meant disaster.

No way out, he was thinking, *no way out for any of us,* shaking his head, trying to stop the tears and the awful despair that was creeping its way into him like water drawn inside a drowning man.

Θ

Simmy left Sholto and wound her way through the cemetery, glancing briefly at the gravediggers going hard at their work to dig a second grave, Simmy shuddering at the thought that she would one day end up in a hole just like that, hopefully not next to her da. She went quickly on, soon wending her way through the oak copse towards the sundial, surprised to see someone there already: a stoop-shouldered skinny man she'd never seen before, presumably one of the folk over from Strontian who hadn't managed to squash himself into the chapel.

'Hello,' she said. 'That's our sundial. Quite something, isn't it?'

The man didn't reply. He was resting both hands on the edges of the sundial's surface that he'd brushed free of snow, obviously contemplating what he'd revealed thereby with much thought.

'It was my brother Harald as dragged it from the sand,' Simmy went on, eager to talk about it, eager to talk about anything that distracted her from the empty graves and the bodies in the church. 'I made a big project on it a few years back, copied down all the writing and everything. Not that I could make much sense of it.'

She was rewarded by the stranger nodding his head in apparent comprehension.

'It's a non-sequential group of words in twelve languages,' he said, though did not look up.

'Like a puzzle!' Simmy was delighted at the prospect, coming up beside the man in her curiosity. If the sundial was going to leave Ockle she would dearly like to understand all the strange squiggles on it before it left.

'I always thought that,' she went on, staring down at the sundial's face in imitation of her companion. 'I mean not what you said exactly, only that when I was copying it I sort of split it up, like you do with algebra. And even the words I understood were strange. I mean, what's a time interval when it's at home? And I didn't even know what velocity meant, or infinity. Had to ask the Reverend.'

'Algebra,' the man repeated slowly, the word starting a cascade in his head, flashes coming in as he strung Simmy's words together: velocity, infinity, time interval...

'I learned that with Oswald Harlow,' Simmy added proudly. 'Said I was real good at it, that I had a knack. Guess it was all that counting out of cups of corn for the chickens and figuring out where they were laying their eggs.'

The man continued staring at the sundial, unmoved by her attempt at humour. *Sholto would have smiled at that*, she thought, and cast a glance back towards the chapel, not that she could see him, even if he was still there. The trees might be denuded of leaves but their trunks were gnarled and stunted, all pushed in one direction by the wind, weaved up together like someone had deliberately laid a tangled hedge.

'Algebra, velocity, infinity...' the man said again, which Simmy found a little vexing.

'But if it's a puzzle,' she said, after a couple of moments, wanting to please, not knowing how to do it, 'then it's like we're missing the piece that tells us where one part starts and the other ends.'

The man did not reply, nor did he look at Simmy, but reached out a hand and traced a finger from beginning to end of the long tight spiral of words that covered the majority of the sundial's face, stopping momentarily on some of the English ones, and more in Latin and Greek.

'If it's a puzzle,' he repeated Simmy's words slowly, his finger reaching the sundial's centre, where the sail-shaped gnomon stood proud, a small uneven rim of snow gathered on its edge like the crenellations of a tiny castle wall.

'If it's a puzzle,' he said again, slower still, 'then there's a key, and the key to this sundial is its ring.'

He turned suddenly, removing his hands from the sundial.

'Griffen said your brother found it,' he stated with such certainty that Simmy was momentarily confused, blurting out her answer without thinking about it.

'Well yes, with the Ockle Man's bones. But how did…'

She stopped suddenly, took a step back.

'Well,' she said. 'It's been nice meeting you, but I've really got to get going. It's me da's funeral back there, after all.'

'Wait,' said the man, putting out a hand, gripping hard at Simmy's arm. 'You have to tell me about the ring.'

Simmy was frightened. He was grabbing her tight and it hurt and she really, really hated that he was talking to her and yet wasn't exactly looking at her, not like a normal person at all.

'Let me go!' she shouted, trying to pull away, but he wouldn't let her go. She would have pulled out the ring in a second and given it to him if she could, but she'd come dressed in her Sunday best for her da's funeral and the ring was sewn up inside that special pocket she'd made for it in her normal daily smock while she thought on what to do with it.

'I've not it with me,' Simmy said, wriggling, squeezing out the words between clenched teeth. 'It's at home, sewn into my smock.'

The smock patently wasn't on her now, but this man was, suddenly and scarily right up in front of her, twisting her around and pushing her back against the sundial, and she could see there were dark stains on his sleeves and had slaughtered enough chickens to know that it was blood. And then she really struggled but couldn't get free and all she could think to do was to let out an ear-piercing shriek into the mid-morning air and hope that someone – Sholto, if he was still waiting for her outside the chapel – would hear her and come running.

From the ends of the world, he'd said, and Christ, Simmy hoped that was true.

⊖

'You've bloody nothing against my boy,' Old Ma was croaking. Brogar would have found it mildly amusing that she was referring to her son as a boy – for Dunstan was at least in his mid-forties – if the situation hadn't been so urgent. She and Dunstan were trussed up with rope so they could hardly move, dragged back to the bothy. She cocked her head towards Brogar like a bird puzzling out a worm.

'It's that lad Harald's word against his own, and I can rustle up ten men as'll say Dunstan was drinking himself silly down at Corran when it came to pass.'

'I don't doubt it,' Brogar said, 'but who's to give either of you an alibi for Kurti Griffen and Gustav Wengler? There's folk knew you were out here and when you came, and no one else has a mote of motive to bring harm on either one of them, excepting you.'

Ma Pirie narrowed her eyes.

'I dinna ken either of them names,' she said, 'an' no more does Dunstan.'

Brogar feigned surprise.

'You've never heard of Gustav Wengler? The famous hermit who's been living on that island over the way with his eyes on you the whole time you've been here?'

Ma Pirie shook her head. She had an almighty ache in it from Brogar's boot and a bruise coming up on her right temple because of it, but she still had her wits about her.

'Well aye, I ken of him living there. So does anybody, but anybody knows too he lives inside his walls same as a crab stays inside its shell.'

Brogar sighed.

'You might as well just spill it out,' he said. 'There's a heap of Dunstan's wet clothes just outside these walls and I've no doubt we'll find blood on them and, when we do, that'll be that.'

Ma Pirie let out a short laugh.

'Them isn't wet with anything but water from his jumping off and pulling me in last night. And if there's a scrap of blood on'm then I can tell you right now it didn't come from whatever you said his name was, the one before the mad bloke. And who is he anyway, this dead person you don't seem to be able to walk a mile without tripping over?'

Brogar rubbed his chin, beginning to have doubts about the extent of what the Piries had done. Not about Archie Louden, about that he was certain. Dunstan had done him in, sure as day follows night. But Griffen's death was different. It was no bungled robbery gone wrong but carried out in a manner that suggested planning. Certainly the Piries were capable of it, but it didn't feel right. Ma Pirie wasn't worried a tad by any blood that might be on Dunstan's discarded clothing, but then again she could have drubbed them against the rocks to remove any trace. She was a canny woman and he wouldn't have put much past her, but Brogar was no lumber head when it came to perspicacity and he could have sworn he'd seen a flicker of surprise in her eyes at the mention of another dead man, namely Kurti Griffen. More worryingly, there was no sign of Gustav Wengler anywhere. Jed and Matthias between them had scoured Havengore and the Wee Grey Isle top to bottom and found not a scrap of him, alive or dead. Certainly the sea loch was large and it was tidal, and it would be an easy thing to chuck a body in and for no one to find it, at least not for a while. But if they'd done that to Wengler, why hadn't they done the same to Kurti Griffen? Yet more troubling was that he'd personally searched the bothy, Ma Pirie and her son and all the meagre belongings they'd brought with them, and found nothing even vaguely incriminating. If they'd forced Wengler into writing and signing promissory notes for monies due then there was not a sign of it, not a hint, no evidence of a piece of paper, pen or ink, nor even any reason to suppose either of them could read or write. And that was when Brogar began to formulate another idea entirely of what might have happened to Gustav Wengler.

'Ever felt like doing something good with your life?' Brogar asked Dunstan Pirie.

'Not until now,' Dunstan said, chaffing against his bonds, eager for the out, any out at all.

'I'm going to put you in a boat and make you row, you and me, double oars, and if we get to Ockle soonest,' Brogar said, 'then I'll be at your trial swearing you're just a poor boy gone wrong.'

Dunstan needed no more push than that, held up his wrists so Brogar could untie the ropes.

'You try anything,' Brogar warned, as he began to unpick the knots, 'Jed still has your mother's gun, and he'll use it.'

Jed nodded emphatically, but Dunstan was past any form of rebellion, despite his mam sending him daggers.

'Sorry, Ma,' he said, as Brogar freed him, 'but life is life, and by Christ I mean to live it.'

'You're not a Pirie anymore if you do this!' Old Ma shouted after them. 'An' I'll see you swing, boy, if you leave me here!'

But by then Dunstan and Brogar were already jumping into the boat and pulling up the spare oars from its base, fitting them into the second pair of rollocks, Jed unwinding the rope that was keeping them tethered to the Wee Grey Isle, tying it in knots about Dunstan's ankles before pushing them off. Only Jed and Ma Pirie left behind and both of them carrying a grudge, the one against the other, but only Jed with the gun.

CHAPTER 31

DEAD MEN ALIVE, AND LIVE MEN ROWING

My God, that scream. It came out of nowhere, out of a solemn, silent day. Sholto looked up the path, saw the two gravediggers stopping their shovelling, cocking their ears.

'It's Simmy!' Sholto shouted as he passed them on the run. 'It must be Simmy!'

And off he went towards the trees that were bent over like old men with rheumatics, no way through them, only around, the gravediggers looking after Sholto, not sure what to do. They'd no idea who he was but knew Simmy right enough, took a quick glance at the new grave, wondering if it would do. It certainly wasn't as deep as it should be, but by common and tacit consent they nodded at each other, threw down their shovels and followed on in Sholto's wake.

Θ

'We need to go faster,' Brogar kept telling Dunstan. 'And try to keep your oars in step with mine.'

'No offence, man,' Dunstan grumbled, 'but I'm the one should take the lead as I ken where we're going.'

Brogar knew it was so, and there followed a few awkward moments as they shuffled places, Dunstan taking first point, Brogar moving behind so he could keep to the rhythm of Dunstan's rowing and, once the order was established, Dunstan rowed like he'd never rowed before, like he was back at the gala days he'd competed in when he was a younger man, folk rowing right across the Sunart from one peninsula to the other, the highlight of a young man's year and a competition Dunstan had won several times over and was still immensely proud of it. He was stronger now than he'd ever been back then and was a driven man, not wanting his neck in a noose if he could help it. He had a wild thought about kicking himself free of the ropes and jumping into the water, making a dash for it; but where would he go? Not far, was what. Cards marked well and true. The plan on the Wee Grey Isle was to join the smugglers coming back for their booty, head to Glasgow, disappear. But that option was long gone. He grimaced, swung the boat so close about the point that Brogar winced, couldn't believe they wouldn't be wrecked on the rocks or grounded on the sandbanks, but Dunstan knew this coast better than just about anyone and took them in, reaching Ockle in record time, had anybody been there to make note of it.

Θ

Stars above Simmy, scattered and distant, like dewdrops on hidden leaves. A cold night, clouds, a moon ringed with ice, geese rankling in their lines, following hidden pathways, maybe tracing the curvature of the earth, maybe the line of lochs that swept down from the mountains through the rivers into the sea below the village. Simmy didn't know. All she knew was that there was grass somewhere below the metal on which she lay, grass that would keep on pushing upwards even if she never did. Soil below grass below Simmy, run through with worms, raddled with mole-holes and quick-pulsing shrews who would not, could not, stop, not even for an hour, or they would die for lack of food.

She was having trouble focussing, wondering if her eyes were even open, for surely it could not be night. Surely there should not be stars above her. Surely it was not that long since she'd left her father's funeral, come out for a breath of air, found Sholto, the open graves, that strange man at the sundial. That strange man at the sundial. She opened her eyes. There was the sky, but it was clouded and blue beyond. No stars. No moon, no geese, and no man either. Only Simmy, looking ever upward, unable to move, a terrible pain in her chest, her mind a mess of thoughts as she tried to figure out what had happened. The man at the sundial. She tried to remember him, but he was just a shadow who'd been holding onto her arm one minute and then pushing her back the next. He'd been asking about the ring, but she couldn't remember what that ring might be, couldn't remember anything at all, felt a single warm tear slipping from her eye and sliding down her cheek. It tickled, but there was nothing she could do about it, and the tickling of that tear was almost worse than the pain in her chest because she thought it might be the last warm thing she would ever feel. She tried to move again, tried to move anything, an arm, a hand, a fingertip, but nothing about her was working. She heard footsteps running, maybe towards her, maybe away, and must have closed her eyes because once again, because high above her was the moon and the night, and the sounds of geese whiffling down into a field, and she thought again of those cold dark graves. She couldn't remember who the graves were meant for, only that she didn't want to be put in one, not now, not ever, and so she made one last effort and flicked open her eyes. Blue sky above Simmy, and clouds, but then those blasted stars kept reappearing one by one as the night blurred in from either side and she knew she was going to die, that all she was ever going to see from here on in was darkness, just like Aileen; except that unlike Aileen she would be six foot under and no way of getting out, no way of getting home, no way of seeing Harald, not ever again.

Where are you, Harald, Simmy thought. *Why aren't you here to keep me safe?*

And then she saw him, saw Harald, like she'd just wished him into being, for there he was, standing right above her, his pale face drawn and oddly thin. She tried to speak his name, lift her hand towards him but hadn't the strength. Still, at least she'd seen him one last time.

Hang on Simmy, Harald was saying. She couldn't hear his words but she could read his lips, read his mind, like she'd always done. *Hang on Simmy. Don't let that bastard grind you down. I'll only be away a while and then we'll be together. Just you and me Simmy, always you and me.*

Θ

Sholto McKay was appalled to find Simmy struck through on the sundial, the tiny wedge of the gnomon's tip protruding from the middle of her chest.

'Hang on Simmy,' Sholto said, 'you hang on in there.'

But even as he spoke Simmy's eyes were flickering closed, Sholto standing above her, arms stretched out but with no aim. He didn't know whether to pull her up or leave her be, and below her, across the round face of the sundial, blood was spreading and pooling and he didn't know how much more could come out of her small body and her still be alive.

Θ

Dunstan and Brogar arrived at Ockle just as the funeral cortege was beginning to process from chapel to grave, Oswald at the lead, the two bodies held high on the shoulders of the men who had volunteered for the task. Oswald kept up his prayers as he led the way, keeping in step with the clanging of the chapel's bell, the men behind him steady at their duty, despite the stench coming from Archie's un-coffined corpse, Oswald hoping they could bear it the few short yards to Archie's grave. Not far to go, Oswald knew, but no sign of the gravediggers, just a couple of shovels lying on the ground as evidence of their recent work. It didn't stop Oswald. He went on intoning his prayers until the men had unburdened themselves of Archie Louden's corpse, dropping it straight into his grave with a horrible thump, Oswald noting it was not as deep as it should have been, but close to the tree line and maybe the men had hit roots or a layer of rock. He was about to signal the mourners to step back a little, towards the better prepared grave of Fraser McRailty, when one of the absentee gravediggers came running back along the path, pushing his way through the crowds.

'Oh Jesus, Jesus,' he cried, trying to get his breath. 'Oh but you're not going to believe it, and it's only just happened, but young Simmy McRailty's impaled upon the sundial and no one knows how to get her off without her dying!'

There were a couple of moments' stunned silence before a terrible roar broke from Harald's throat and he began pushing and shoving everyone out of his way, running for the trees and the path that led to the sundial.

'Everyone keep calm!' Oswald shouted before anyone else had the gumption to follow, his shout so loud he felt his throat protesting. He'd always been a measured man, had built his entire career on being just so, never sticking his neck out an inch more than was needed, not until he'd argued so fiercely for the Floating Chapel and ended up in Ardnamurchan, a calm and secure place he'd been happy in, until now, when it seemed that God Himself had decided otherwise. And so be it. Oswald raised his arms. Halted the few who were about to set off after Harald.

'Everyone,' he said loudly, 'remain where you are. A mob running loose is not what we need.'

And everybody halted, excepting Aileen, people moving away from her to give her free passage.

'Reverend,' she said, calm as ever, though her skin was white as a razor clam pulled fresh from its shell. 'Let's you and me go see what this is all about, and if everyone else could stay here, see to Mr McRailty's burial, that would be much appreciated.'

Astonishingly everyone did as she asked, Oswald hooking his arm about her own as they hurried forward towards the trees.

'You should have been a minister,' Oswald found himself saying.

'In another life,' Aileen shot back, 'when women are not viewed so much as chattels but as valuable human beings in their own right.'

Oswald could have said much at this point, about the better way women were treated in post-Old Testament times, about how them being amongst Jesus's most trusted companions – a sermon he'd been working on for many years but never had the courage to come right out and say. He kept quiet, merely led Aileen quick as he thought safe for her through the complicated humps and bumps of graves until they hit the path that led straight to the sundial, seeing what she could not and that Harald was already there, slumped on his knees, Sholto McKay dithering, the second gravedigger off to one side, his fingers pulling again and again at his long beard. And then Sholto moved to one side and Oswald saw Simmy and let out an involuntary gasp that had Aileen quickening her steps, and his with her own.

'Tell me,' she said, but Oswald couldn't find his voice.

'Tell me,' Aileen said again, and this time Oswald swallowed hard, managed to get out a few words.

'It's like the man said, Aileen. It's Simmy, and she's lying on her back on the sundial, and oh God, oh God...'

'Tell me exactly,' Aileen was remorseless, her world different from his own, seeing it from somewhere else entirely.

'She's on the sundial,' Oswald explained as he got Aileen within a yard or two. 'And so help me God, she's stuck on it, on the sail, and I think she's dying. I really think she might be dying.'

This was Harald's opinion too and he let out another roar that quickly tailed off into a whimper to hear his thoughts being voiced, a noise as recognisable to Aileen as the drawing in of the sea or the blowing of the wind.

'She's not dead yet, Harald,' Aileen's voice was soft but curt, like a mother, like a teacher, like someone you would never go up against. 'Simmy is strong, and Simmy would never leave us like this. I don't know who else is here, but can I ask of them this? How much blood is there?'

Sholto moved back to make way for Aileen. He was shocked, couldn't understand how this had happened, not to anyone, certainly not to Simmy, who seemed to have held the sun in every breath. But he had words, and spoke them.

'There's a lot,' he said. 'A pool spreading out a few inches to either side of her. And I don't know whether to move her or leave her be. She was trying to talk earlier...'

'No talking,' Aileen was decisive. 'That can come later. How far down is she on the dial?'

'Oh Jesus,' Harald wailed. 'I can't bear it! What if Simmy dies? Oh Aileen, what if Simmy dies?'

'Simmy,' Aileen stated, pulling her arm free from Oswald's, 'is not going to die. If the gnomon is gone through her chest then obviously it hasn't punctured her heart or she would be dead already. Possibly it has damaged a lung. Is her breathing ragged?'

Sholto leant down towards Simmy. Her lips were beginning to turn blue, but her breathing, shallow and thready as it was, seemed regular, and so he said.

'Very well,' Aileen said. 'When I give the word lift her, do it as gently as you can, but only up an inch or so, and get as much snow packed beneath her then as you can. It's going to hurt her, so do it quick. And pile more snow onto her body up above. The colder we can get her, the slower her blood's going to flow and the more chance she's going to have.'

Everyone set to scraping up snow and squeezing it tight into ice-balls, getting them lined up and ready to go when, at Aileen's command, Harald and Sholto took Simmy by either side, the gravedigger holding her head, and they eased her up an inch or two so Oswald could shove in as much ice as he could. They were aided by the natural arch of her back, and it didn't take Oswald more than a couple of minutes to complete his task, working first from one side and then the other. Once done, the others let go of Simmy, who sighed as her body rested back onto the ice, curving like a bridge, head and calves resting against the dial, the tip of the gnomon no longer visible, only a neat round circle of blood on her dress to indicate it was still in there somewhere. Then that was covered too, more snow piled directly onto her torso and lower body.

'All done,' Sholto said quietly, Aileen nodding.

'First part over,' she said. 'Next we're going to need needle and cord to sew her up when we finally lift her off.'

'How long should we wait?' Sholto asked anxiously, knowing there would be a very fine line between Simmy been cooled enough to slow the blood flow and being too cold to fight against it back into life.

'Not long,' Aileen said, 'but long enough to get the necessary equipment. I need someone to run swift as they can to my house and bring me my sewing box. It's a wicker basket kept in the cupboard two doors along to the right side of the stove, and whoever fetches it, make sure you bring a candle and flint with you. We're going to need to heat up the needle to let it slide easy through the skin, and we're going to need hot wax to cauterise the wounds once they've been sewn. And I need the strongest thread you can find. There's some in the basket on a spool wrapped round a tup's horn,' Aileen said. 'Fetch all this to me and we'll go from there.'

⊖

Fraser McRailty was not being buried with the reverence he might have expected. After Oswald and Aileen had left, his pall bearers ditched their burden with speed, dumping him without ceremony into his grave. The crowd was twitchy, not knowing what was going on up at the sundial, Strontian and Ockle folk mingling as kin came to kin, and what started as a murmur of puzzlement and shock soon rose into a cacophony of everyone demanding to know what exactly was what. Just as they were about to break away and go see for themselves they were interrupted by the sudden and extraordinary arrival of Brogar Finn and Dunstan Pirie, coming running up the lane that led to the churchyard to find the lot of them breaking away into knots as they discussed whether or not they should go on up through the trees, no matter what they'd been told. The newcomers were spotted a good minute before they arrived, Dunstan's running impeded by his hands being boumd with rope, huffing and puffing, and this latest development enough to keep them all rooted to the spot. At least until Brogar opened his mouth.

'I'm looking for Oswald Harlow,' he said loudly, 'and Sholto McKay. And what the hell is going on here?'

Brogar knew who was being buried here today but he'd noticed, as he'd run towards the milling crowd, that neither Oswald nor Sholto were anywhere to be seen. There were the two open graves into which the relevant bodies had apparently already been placed, but no sign of active service on the part of a minister, and none of the usual prayers and codswallop that always went with such interments. The appearance of Dunstan Pirie at his heels caused a quick and very disapproving stir amongst the crowd, but that was of no concern to Brogar. They could pick the man up and lynch him from the nearest branch if they so chose, but first he wanted answers.

'Oswald Harlow, Sholto McKay,' he repeated. 'Tell me where they are or by God, I'll horsewhip the first one of you that gets in my way.'

'At the sundial,' someone mumbled. 'Back of the cemetery.'

'Been a bit of an accident,' another added.

'Young Simmy,' put in a third, and would have said more but Brogar cut him short.

'Which way?' he demanded, the crowd giving him direction by involuntarily turning their faces and bodies towards the trees. Brogar was off like a hare, Dunstan hard on his heels, tugged on by the rope tethering him to Brogar, wondering what was going on, how he might put it to his advantage, certain only that he didn't want to be left behind with a crowd of uncertain temperament. Of his mother, out on the Wee Grey Isle, he spared not a thought, for weirdly his head was filled with Brogar's words: *want to do anything good with your life...* And maybe it was just the rush of having rowed so hard, or maybe because he'd finally gone against Old Ma Pirie, or maybe because he finally *had* done something good in that rowing; but whatever the reason, Dunstan had the odd delusion of being on the right side for the first time in his life.

CHAPTER 32

LIMBS FROM LIMBS, SKIN FROM BONE

The gravedigger with the beard volunteered to go back to Aileen's house, halfway down the path to the chapel when Brogar and Dunstan came racing past, out of breath when he got to the folk by the chapel where he passed the baton on.

'She's badly,' he puffed. 'But Aileen's an idea and we need someone quick as lightning to her house. Wickerwork basket, two doors to the right of the oven, and something to light a candle. Bring it all back and young Simmy might yet be saved.'

Within a half second of his pronouncement three young lads separated from the throng and went careering off to Aileen's home just down the way, shoving and pushing to get through the door and in. The first flung open a cupboard and found it empty, the second opened the right one and snatched up the basket. This happened to be Hector, son of the chapel cleaner, a boy in command of his troops.

'Get a light!' he shouted, and the third boy did just that, pulling out some dull red coals from the stove with his fingers and got them into an empty milk churn, the first boy grabbing a couple of candles from the niche by the front door.

'Back, quick as you like!' yelled Hector, the wicker basket tucked under his arm.

'Can't believe this happened to Simmy,' said the third boy, keeping up with Hector, blowing on the tips of his fingers that were already blistering from the coal as he swapped the milk churn from one hand to the other.

'Jis cos she was alwus better than you at school,' gasped the first boy.

'None o' that,' the lad replied. 'Even if she's aye been smart. But I'd not've let anyone push me down on that sundial, and that's what must have happened.'

'Right or wrong,' gasped Hector, 'we've her life in the balance, boys, so let's see it done.'

Θ

Gustav was trapped. The narrow focus of his mind would not let him swerve, kept him in its narrow tunnel, no light at either end, the only solution being to go on; not such a non-listener as everyone supposed, fitting everything together into a logical sequence of events starting from the day Archie found that book sleeping on Wengler's shelf. The fact that he'd arrived at the sundial just before Simmy – and it had to have been Simmy, for she'd said her brother's name was Harald – seemed nothing short of the harmonious universe falling into place, telling him he was on the right track and not to stop.

The only flaw to his logic was that the girl Simmy hadn't had the ring with her, but every equation has its workings out and she'd told him it was at her home, in her smock. He wasn't sure exactly what a smock looked like, or where was her home was, had pushed her away the moment she'd let out that shriek. He wasn't keen on noise of any kind, and certainly not of that ilk, and immediately moved away from it, intent on his new goal. He could hear a load of people down by the chapel and instinctively went in the opposite direction, climbing over the cemetery wall and going down a lane lined either side with naked, snow-bearing trees towards a cluster of low-lying cottages at its base. Everywhere seemed deserted, apart from one old woman sitting on a three-legged stool outside her home, clay pipe clutched between her gums as she gazed up the lane with lazy indifference.

'Simmy's house, if you please?' Gustav Wengler asked.

The old woman didn't shift her posture other than to suck down on the pipe a time or two. She showed no interest in Wengler or where he'd come from or what was going on at the chapel, but she jutted her chin towards a small wooden bridge that crossed one of the skinny arms of the sea loch as it tapered inland.

'The one as backs onto the corn field beyond,' she croaked, Wengler looking in the direction she had nodded, seeing only one small croft lying beyond the bridge, away from the rest of the village. He didn't thank her and she didn't appear to expect it, just kept on gazing up the path towards the chapel, her mind as empty as the painted lady shell hanging on a string about her neck, given to her thirty seven years before by a lad she'd been sworn to before he'd gone off to some war or other and not come back. She fingered that shell sometimes, wondering why she still wore it, the memory of that boy long since gone. Several minutes after Gustav Wengler disappeared down the road, she only vaguely remembered she'd seen him at all, and only because someone else arrived, who she mistook for him.

'I telt you already,' she said. 'It's the one yonder over the bridge.'

⊖

Brogar took one look at the girl splayed out on the sundial, at the snow and ice packed beneath and around her, and nodded at Sholto.

'Quick thinking by somebody,' he said.

'Not me,' Sholto said, shaking his head, ashamed such a course of action had never occurred to him. 'It was Aileen's idea.'

Brogar turned towards the woman. If Brogar was put off by her boiled-egg eyes he made no show of it, shifting his gaze instead to the large lad standing at her shoulder who had left off his noisy weeping at the sight of Dunstan, when his face paled and distorted with the shock.

'Well done then to Aileen,' Brogar said. 'I'm not sure anyone could have done better. I take it we're about to lift the girl off and sew her up?'

'That's the idea,' Aileen said, glad of this newcomer's steady calm, the note of authority in his voice, its lack of panic or squeamishness. A man, in short, who was more than capable of doing what she could not.

'But not by me,' she said. 'I can darn socks and broad-stitch patches, but perhaps you?'

Brogar bowed briefly, not that Aileen could see it, but she felt the short swish of air as he moved.

'It will be my pleasure,' Brogar answered, 'and here, I suspect, come the necessaries.'

As indeed they did, Hector and his friends skidding to a halt beside the small group. Aileen repeated her instructions about candles, needles and thread, and as soon as she spoke them they were done, the slender wicks being lit from the hot coals in the milk churn, a long, sharp needle passed through the flame, the tup's horn brought out, its thread rubbed with candle grease to keep it smooth. They were about to start proceedings when the gravedigger with the tugged beard reappeared, several Ockle folk coming on behind, no longer content to stay behind, not with Dunstan Pirie inexplicably thrown into the mix.

'Um,' said the gravedigger, pulling ever more fiercely at his beard. 'Don't know if this is worth the mention, but think it probably is. My mate just went down the hill to his nan's to get some, well, a little fortification shall we say…'

He glanced at Reverend Harlow, fearing disapproval, but Oswald was not standing on ceremony.

'Just say it, Jacob,' Oswald said.

'Well she's a brain holds nothing more than the last leaf that blew her by, can't mind much more'n what's just happened, but when he went in for some revivements, if we can call it that…'

'We can call it anything you want,' Oswald said a little sharply, 'just get on.'

'Well she doesn't mind at all who asked her,' Jacob obliged, 'but the second her grandson got there she chided him for having forgotten, which is a bit rich coming from her, anyway she said what she'd said before and that it was the house over the bridge.'

'The point being what?' Brogar asked.

'The point being,' Jacob answered slowly, 'that the house over the bridge is where Simmy lives.'

Harald had got it too and let out a roar, almost pushing Aileen over as he came past her, running down the path towards the chapel. She held out a hand into empty space and Brogar caught her, put her back on her feet.

'Want me to stop him?' he asked, Aileen nodding.

'Aye,' she said. 'If he thinks that's whoever did this to Simmy he'll not bother asking questions, he'll just tear the man limb from limb.'

'I'll go,' Dunstan said, surprising even himself by volunteering, flinching when Aileen swung her head towards him, staring at him with her two blind eyes.

'You'll do no such thing, Dunstan Pirie,' such ferocity in her voice she almost spat, her composure suddenly under threat. 'I don't know what you're doing here or why you're not swinging from the nearest gallows, but if you go anywhere near my Harald ever again I swear I'll plait that noose and put it around your neck myself.'

Brogar felt Aileen's arm trembling beneath his own and held out a hand, shoving it squarely at Dunstan's chest.

'I don't think we're looking to let you loose any time soon,' he said, nodding to a couple of strong looking men who came forward to make sure that didn't happen. 'We've Simmy here to worry about first and foremost. Sholto?'

'You want me to do the sewing up,' Sholto stated.

'I do,' Brogar said. 'I'll go after Harald, see if I can stop him before he rips the hide right off Gustav Wengler's bones.'

Sholto's mouth fell open in shock, and Oswald took a step forward.

'Gustav Wengler? What do you mean, Gustav Wengler?'

'I mean exactly that,' said Brogar. 'But no time to explain it now. Aileen and Sholto, do your best for the girl; Oswald, take charge of Dunstan, and Dunstan,' Brogar turned towards him and said something no one expected, least of all Dunstan himself. 'We all know what you did to Archie Louden, but there's no need for Harald to go down with you. And what you did today? That rowing over to Ockle? Well, maybe there's some forgiveness due you yet.'

And then Brogar was off. He didn't bother to pelt down the path after Harald, he merely turned away from the others, went behind the sundial, vaulted the high stone wall and disappeared into the scrub on the other side from where they could hear his fast and determined boot-steps scrunching on compacted snow and fallen leaves, going quicker still when he saw Harald running past the house at the bottom of the tree-lined lane, hoping he could get to Simmy's house before Harald got his very large and strong hands around Gustav Wengler's not so large, not so strong, neck.

Θ

'I don't understand,' Aileen spoke into the shocked silence, breaking the spell left by Brogar's sudden departure and announcement, the Ockle men immediately closing in around Dunstan and dragging him back towards the chapel, Hector and his two buddies departing too, scrambling over the wall, hot on Brogar's heels, eager to be in on the end of the most exciting day of their lives.

'I don't understand,' Aileen said again. 'What's going on? Where has everyone gone?'

Sholto moved up beside her. 'It's all right, Aileen, me and Oswald are still here.'

'An' me too,' added Jacob, the gravedigger, 'an' we're not going anywhere, miss, not until we've seen to young Simmy.'

And with that, Aileen had to be content. Brogar was right. Explanations could wait, all that was important now was Simmy. Her face recovered its usual colour, her voice its usual calm command.

'All right then,' she said. 'Sholto, Oswald, Jacob, let's get Simmy lifted. Do it quick and do it fast. Put her straight over on her front. It's the back wound that'll need cleaned and sewn first. Mr Sholto?'

Sholto nodded, then realised the futility. 'I'm here,' he said, 'and I've everything to hand.'

'Tear away the dress first,' Aileen advised, 'rub the wound clean with snow.'

'Of course,' Sholto said, moving past her to take up his position,

Aileen putting out a hand to catch at his arm.

'You know this mayn't work,' she said very quietly.

'I know,' Sholto murmured in return. 'But we have to try.'

CHAPTER 33

WELL, THAT'S ONE WAY TO LEARN

Harald could feel the world spinning beneath his boots. He wished it could turn the other way, go back upon itself so the last nine months had never happened, that he'd never met up with Dunstan Pirie, that he'd never found the body in the mud. He didn't have the sharpest mind in Ockle but he figured out a couple of things whilst he was running back towards his home as fast as heart and feet could carry him, mostly that Simmy was dying, and that Simmy was dying because of him. He couldn't join the dots of why it had happened but he knew it was all his fault. He'd been terribly unnerved to see Dunstan Pirie – of all people – arriving at the sundial, but knew in every stretching sinew, every juddering bone as he ran that he was at the centre of everything awful that was happening. One minute Simmy had been by him in the chapel, the next she'd excused herself and gone. He couldn't blame her for that. He'd no grief at all about his father's passing, not after the initial shock of seeing him dead. He'd only been held in place because of the other man they were burying, the one he and Dunstan had done to death. He'd felt sick, tasting again the burning from the bothy, remembering the look in Orla Pirie's eyes when he'd delivered the money from the horse as arranged, only understanding that look now, and that she knew.

And now his mess had entangled Simmy, like the root that grows the leaf that grows the poisonous stem that strangles the better fruit-giving plant growing beside it. Their da might have been an evil, bitter bastard but in the end it was Harald – Simmy's protector – who'd cut the wood for Simmy's coffin, hammering in the nails one by one with every misspent action and deed.

He was running across the bridge now and could see his house and that the door was open wide and all that anger, all that self-recrimination, burned in him like the brand he'd burned onto that horse, and spurred him on; over the rattling boards he went and along the lane by the paddock, flinging open the gate to the yard with such force one of the hinges fell off as it hit the fence. He tripped over a chicken desperately trying to get out of his way and stumbled, almost fell, but got his way up and ran the few yards to the door, his large bulk filling the jamb as he barged his way through, cutting off the light from the man who was sitting at the kitchen table, a large knife in his hand, a couple of Simmy's dresses laid out upon the wood in pieces.

'At last,' Gustav Wengler sighed, a note of relief to his tired voice. 'Someone who can tell me the difference between a petticoat and a smock.'

Harald saw the knife, saw the dresses, saw the man calmly sitting there and came to an abrupt stop. It took him a few moments to bring all the pieces together: man, knife, Simmy's clothes, and then his body reacted all on its own and he was leaping towards Gustav Wengler like a man possessed.

Θ

BURNING SECRETS

Brogar reached the village end of the bridge just as Harald was running off the other side and down the short lane. He saw Harald fling aside the gate to his yard, saw him trip and stumble. In the few seconds more it took Brogar to follow in his wake the chickens had clucked and chided, fluttered themselves out of his way, and Brogar got to the open door and moved himself in.

Θ

'Are we ready?' Aileen said.

'Ready,' said Sholto, and on his nod Jacob and Oswald lifted Simmy quickly up and away from the point of the sundial. There was a ghastly grating as the gnomon caught at her sternum, the edges of her ribs, and she groaned like trees blowing in high wind. But they'd been prepared for that and didn't stop, lifted her and rolled her, and there she was, back soaked with blood. Sholto used Aileen's sewing scissors to cut away Simmy's dress, exposing the straight-edged gash made by the gnomon's sail – six inches wide at the base before tapering to its tip. Oswald was at the ready with handfuls of snow to rub the wound clean, astonished to see that Aileen's earlier ministrations had worked, the wound clear of blood, purple-tinged at its edges, Simmy's skin white as the snow he was rubbing it with, but little bleeding, even after she'd been moved.

'Keep her still,' Aileen commanded, 'you have to keep her still.'

Sholto was quick and deft, brought out the needle, carefully ran it through the flame of the candle he'd set on the dial, began to pinch Simmy's flesh between his fingers and push the needle's point through, in and out, in and out, Simmy all the while letting out a heart rending moan like seals singing on the sand, which even on a good day sounds like they're all being murdered.

'It's good she's still conscious,' Aileen quavered, hating to hear those noises coming out of Simmy, hoping Sholto would be confident and not take too long about his task. He did not. Simmy's obvious distress did not distract him, only made him faster and surer, needle in, needle out, on with the wax to seal stitch and wound.

'Flip her,' he said, after several minutes, Oswald and Jacob jumping to. The wound on Simmy's chest was ragged from where she'd tried to move, but barely an inch long, and it took Sholto only a few practiced movements – scissors, snow, needles and wax – and then he was done.

Θ

Harald was on Gustav Wengler like a weasel on a vole, big hands wrenching away the knife from Wengler's fingers, bringing it up and holding it to Wengler's throat.

'You're not to touch anything of Simmy's!' Harald shouted. 'Else you want me to slit you ear to ear!'

Wengler looked utterly confused.

'You've not come to help me find the ring?' he croaked, Harald letting out a short bark, pushing the point of the knife through Wengler's skin, making him squeak; would have pushed it further, would have pushed it right through one side and out the other if Brogar hadn't at that moment strode through the open door.

'Enough, Harald,' Brogar said.

'It'll never be enough!' Harald yelled back. 'This bastard killed my sister and all he can bloody well talk about is petticoats and rings!'

Brogar held up his hands.

'She's not dead, Harald. And you need to listen to me, because if you kill him then your life is really over. You might as well slit your own throat too and have done with it.'

'Ha!' Harald shook his head vigorously, voice suddenly low and without edge. ''S'already over, int'it. Nothing to save me now, not now you've Dunstan to spill out his lies and put it all on me.'

Brogar took a step inside the room, Harald turning his head away so Brogar couldn't see the tears running down his cheeks from useless rage, sorrow and self-pity.

'Look at me, Harald,' Brogar said. 'Look at me,' he commanded. Harald sniffed, bent his head down to rub his face against his sleeve, but he did look, saw Brogar standing as a monolith framed by the door, the light behind him shining exactly like the picture of an angel he'd seen years back in Simmy's Sunday School book.

'Listen to me, Harald,' Brogar repeated, softer now, taking a small step forward. 'We already know it was Dunstan killed Archie Louden. He's said as much, and in front of good witnesses who'll not be ignored. And Simmy's alive, Harald. Aileen and Sholto are seeing to her right now. Don't go down this path. Don't kill this man. We've only got Dunstan because of you and I swear to God that's going to count in your favour.'

Harald wavered, thinking never his strong point and Brogar could see it. There was a sudden and unexpected disturbance at his back as Hector and his mates came tumbling through the door, a distraction Brogar took immediate advantage of, lunging forward, grabbing the knife from Harald's hand.

'Enough, Harald,' Brogar said.

And it was enough.

Harald was done.

He slumped onto a chair and began to weep, great heaving sobs coming from his large body that were so incongruous it was impossible not to feel his distress.

'All right, Harald,' Brogar said, placing a hand upon Harald's shoulder, nodding the boys in, not that they moved, far too shocked at the scene before them: at Gustav Wengler's throat trickling with blood despite the hand he'd put against it to stop its flow; at Harald – the strongest man they'd ever known – curled up over the table weeping like a baby; at the ripped up dresses for which there seemed no adequate explanation; but mostly at the daunting sight of Brogar Finn with his face scarred like a side of beef ready for the spit, huge knife in one hand, blood bright on its tip, his other hand on Harald's back.

'That's it, Harald,' Brogar was saying, one huge man patting another huge man on his shuddering shoulders. 'You've done well, and your sister will be proud.'

Jesus. Talk about life lessons. This one was going to last Hector and his friends their whole life through.

CHAPTER 34

BLACK SLUGS, WHITE CLOVER

It was a rare day in Ockle, starting with two empty graves, ending with a celebration the like of which they'd never seen, their mood of gaiety fuelled by news that Simmy was going strong; taken to Aileen's home, she'd been stripped and slipped into a clean white nightdress and into Aileen's bed. Several hours after her impromptu surgery she'd opened her eyes to find Harald, clumsy and tear stained, on a stool beside her, holding her small hand within his own.

Meanwhile the Ockle folk had taken possession of the chapel – the only communal space in the hamlet – drawing their Strontian neighbours in, filling the pews with food scraped out of cupboards and potato cellars, wishing they could have run to a roasted ox or two; but times were hard and the most they could manage were a few scrawny chickens and an elderly ewe who had run her course, ceremonially butchered and cooked in the open fire pit Oswald had been delighted to allow being dug just beyond the chapel's outer walls. The whole place was thronged with people mingling freely, the day warmer than anyone could have expected given the snow lying on the ground, the sky blue and clear, great phalanxes of geese and swans passing overhead but no clouds to speak of. They all, to a man, lifted their faces to the meagre sun, overjoyed to be alive and in such a place as this.

There was a lot they collectively had to talk about and make decisions over: what to do about Harald, Dunstan and Gustav Wengler being top of the list. The latter two were holed up in the sacristy, the outer door nailed shut to prevent escape, not that either seemed in a mind to attempt it, not with the scrum of folk on either side.

Before closing the inner door and leaving them to it, Oswald explained to a totally baffled Gustav Wengler what he was being accused of.

'You nearly killed Simmy McRailty,' he said, 'up at the sundial. Don't you remember?'

Gustav frowned but was saying nothing, had chosen instead to fixate upon Simmy's little project on the sundial that was lying open on the table, one hand spread over it as if to suck it all in, the other held against the tightly bandaged hole in his throat.

Dunstan Pirie appeared stoical at his incarceration: a minor miracle to everyone from Strontian who'd had dealings with him, every previous encounter characterised by belligerence, intolerance and the kind of simmering rage that had to have been years in the making. It was as if the tide of that anger had finally reached its upper limit and had nowhere to go but back down again, like an ebbing sea. Nor had Dunstan asked about his mother stranded out on the Wee Grey Isle, and no more concerned was anyone else. Let her sit there and suffer was the common opinion, and if she happened to die overnight then good riddance to bad rubbish.

Sholto was of a more humane and common sense disposition, especially considering Jed was there with her.

'We can't just leave her there,' he said to Oswald, once he had him cornered. Oswald was exuberant, never having seen his two flocks, his two parishes, come together like they were doing now and he was bright with the Light of God and expectation, filled with hope and human kindness.

'By all means,' he said happily, 'bring her in. But who's to go for her?'

Sholto could see the problem; no way any of these men and women were going to leave the day that had turned into the biggest party of their lives. He didn't push the matter, couldn't begrudge them that: old folk talking to old folk they'd not seen in a couple of decades, young folk pairing off and sidling away to one side or another, groups of children hop-skipping over graves, mouths greasy from the roasted meat of the mutton and chicken they'd not tasted in months; others sitting and leaning back, gossiping in their pews or around the fire pit, smoking pipes, sharing drink – which was surprisingly lavish given the general air of poverty, undoubtedly due to someone having raised Harald's friend Tom, returning with several kegs of Sholto knew not what, only that it was pale, a little cloudy and indubitably alcoholic.

Getting no quarter of help from Oswald, Sholto went in search of Brogar, mildly surprised he was not supping with the crowds, chatting and tattling; even more surprised when he began down the track to Aileen's house only to find Brogar coming up the path towards him, his face contorted by a frown.

'Simmy?' Sholto asked, aware that his breath had left him, that he was expecting the worst of news.

'She's doing fine,' Brogar said shortly as they fell into step together back towards the chapel. 'You did a good job. Sewed her up neat and tight and no sign of infection.'

'But?' Sholto said, for he knew the signs, and they all pointed to Brogar not being happy.

'But,' Brogar said, 'everyone seems to have forgotten she wasn't the only one to be injured in all this. There's Hugh to worry about too.'

Sholto blanched. This was the first he'd heard of it.

'What happened to Hugh?' he asked, his mouth going dry. He'd not known the lad over-long, but long enough to like him and admire his seriousness and the way he always did everything with a purpose.

'Dunstan shot him,' Brogar said with a bluntness that stopped Sholto in his tracks, made him put out a hand to grab at Brogar's elbow, but Brogar was already stepping out of Sholto's reach and on up the track.

'Why didn't you tell me before?' Sholto shouted hotly, catching Brogar up, looking over at his friend, at the scowl on his face, the slight tug of scar at the corners of eye and mouth as if there was a great battle going on just below Brogar's skin.

'Because I forgot, Sholto,' Brogar said, exhaling slowly. 'I forgot. There was so much going on here that I forgot. And never mind the Dunstan Piries and Gustav Wenglers of this world; the fact remains that I should have got back to Hugh hours ago. God knows how he's doing, but I mean to find out.'

Brogar brooked no shilly-shallying and once he'd made up his mind there were very few who would dare stand in his way. He'd thought first to get Harald's help but Harald was a wreck, glued to his seat beside Simmy's bed, not even Brogar able to shift him from her side. As he and Sholto approached the chapel it was obvious to both that all able bodied men, Oswald included, were either drunk or on their way to being drunk, and only one man up to the task of taking them safely back around the point.

'Are you sure?' Sholto asked, but Brogar obviously was for he went straight to the back door of the sacristy and began pulling at the wood with his bare hands.

'Dunstan Pirie,' Brogar said, the second he had it opened, Dunstan standing up as if a coiled spring had been released beneath his seat. 'I need you to row us back. Are you up for it?'

No explanation, no argument, no pleading, but Dunstan needed no more motivation. A possible means of escape if he could manage it, another point in his favour at his trial if he could not.

'I'm up for it,' he said quickly. 'But what about him?' pushing a thumb towards Gustav Wengler.

'Leave him be,' Brogar said. 'Where's he going to go?'

He had the right of it. Wengler had not reacted at all at the sudden entrance or departure, and the three of them were soon off, Dunstan's hands once more tied by a rope whose other end was secured about Brogar's waist, running down the lane towards Ockle harbour, chucking themselves into a boat. They were about to push off – Dunstan's feet tightly tied now, to leave his hands free - when to their annoyance they saw a figure racing down the track after them, waving his arms wildly about his head: Gustav Wengler. Not so inert as they'd thought, but no time to be wasted taking him back again. Brogar roughly grabbed the man and threw him in and they were off, Brogar and Dunstan strong at the oars, Sholto in the bow giving direction, Wengler at the opposite end, eyes closed, mind blind to everyone and everything around him, all those phrases from the sundial running through his head like sprinters eager to clear the final hurdle and get to the finishing line before it was too late.

☉

In Ockle, most folk were soon sleeping soundly after the exertions and excitements of the day. Night came early this time of the year and their bodies were attuned to it. The few lamps and candles that could be spared had been lit and long gone down and extinguished, and every home in Ockle opened to their Strontian neighbours, those who couldn't fit inside their walls given blankets and bedded down in the chapel.

Oswald Harlow was alone in noting the prisoners were gone but was not alarmed, as gone too were Sholto and Brogar, no doubt spiriting them away so they couldn't be summarily lynched in the morning when everyone might not be so forgiving as they'd been the night before; his surmise backed up by the fact that he could see from the little knoll on which the chapel stood that there was a gap in the crowd of boats huddled in Ockle's tiny harbour. He'd drunk more than he was used to and walked it off, wandering the hamlet of Ockle before returning to the chapel, astonished all over again by how quickly his two communities had melded into one: no arguments, no family feuds raising their fearsome heads after years of being apart – despite all the drink that had been flying – immensely proud of his dual congregations because of it and thinking just how lucky he was to have come to this peninsula.

He sat for a while by the dying embers of the fire pit, looking up at the stars, marvelling at the enormity of his God. The possibility that other planets, other worlds with other people existing on them out there no longer seemed threatening, but rather comforting in a manner he couldn't adequately articulate, only that the problem of evil no longer seemed so intractable as it had before, it seemingly suddenly obvious that if that was the case then it was the church's job – his own job – to stand guard against it in God's absence. He pulled the blanket about his shoulders and glowed in the moment, cocking his head when he saw a couple of lights bobbing towards the chapel and then beyond.

'It's just over here, I think,' Oswald recognised Harald's voice and was curious, put his head above the wall, saw Aileen holding a lamp to light Harald's way, her own steps going easy in the darkness: all the same to her whether it was night or day. Harald looked bulkier than usual and it took a few moments for Oswald to realise he was carrying Simmy cradled in his arms.

'It's really close,' Aileen said, stopping for a moment, moving the lamp from side to side. 'I can smell the damp earth. Do you see it?'

'I do,' Harald replied. 'Two yards off the path to your right, but take your steps careful, so's you don't trip on anything.'

Aileen did as directed, Harald coming on behind her, slipping Simmy down so she was sitting on the ground by Fraser McRailty's open grave.

Oswald's heart skipped a beat. This was far too personal a drama, one not meant for him and yet here he was, barely ten yards distant.

Harald was first to speak, his voice oddly formal and hoarse, like he'd spent a long time crying, which indeed he had.

'To my father, Fraser McRailty,' Harald said, 'I've brought the belt and baton you were so free with.'

There was a thud as Harald threw both onto Fraser McRailty's coffin, no one yet having filled it in, and Oswald curled up inside. He'd seen the bruises so often on both Harald – when he'd been younger – and latterly on Simmy, but a baton? He knew the one. It used to hang on the outside of the McRailty house, and not so much a baton as a lead-tipped cosh for stunning livestock before slaughter, or so he'd always supposed. That it had been used on someone as precious as Simmy hardly bore thinking about.

Aileen spoke next, as if she'd been reading Oswald's mind.

'He was a wicked man but, like all men, good or bad, he's come to his end. Simmy, do you want to say anything?'

There was an ache of a pause that dragged into the silent night before Simmy spoke.

'I think the best thing we can do is forgive him,' Simmy whispered. 'What's done is done, laid to rest like he is. And he wasn't always bad, Harald, you know that as well as I do.'

Harald didn't answer and Oswald, in his hidey-hole, had an upsurge of emotion at Simmy's words; as families went, the McRailtys had their share of crooked souls but Simmy was surely not one of them, straight as the gnomon on the sundial, and with those few words she single-handedly restored the slight wavering of his faith, giving him the understanding that any world that had people like Simmy in it could never be abandoned entirely by God, that good needed bad to give it meaning. He recalled how on his journey over to Ockle earlier that day he'd seen a fat black slug wrapped around the stem of a single white clover flower that had astonishingly grown far too late in the season and survived both frost and snow. He wished he'd taken the time to dismount and remove the slug, give the flower the chance to survive just one more day.

CHAPTER 35

SLEEPING VIALS AND VENOM

The sun sank itself out of the day's existence a scant half hour after three in the afternoon. For Sholto it was gone far too soon, one minute here, the next slipping away like a fish below the waves. He was immensely glad Brogar had taken Dunstan on for their crew, the man having an almost unnatural gift for navigating when all Sholto could see was darkness. There'd been one tiny glimpse of light as they turned from Ockle into the Sound, presumably coming from Kilchoan, and from that single light Dunstan had all the direction he needed, though he pushed them farther out away from the point in what seemed entirely the wrong direction.

'Couple of rocks beneath the surface,' he said by way of explanation. 'Have to go out before coming back in.'

Don't we all, thought Sholto, shivering in the darkness, bobbing on a boat in the middle of an ink black sea.

Θ

Hugh was conscious all the way back from the Wee Grey Isle, and Jesus, in such agony, as if his face was being ripped off layer by layer like someone peeling a rotten onion. He wanted to be a man about it but every movement made it worse, his only comfort being Gilligan clutching at his hand and talking all the while. He couldn't make out the words, but that didn't matter. Enough that Gilligan was there. He'd no concept of time or place, only the constant present of his pain that seemed to go on for ever. And then the strangest thing happened; he was convinced he could hear Orla Pirie's voice, feel her cool hand upon his brow, could smell something sweet, like honeysuckle opening on a warm summer's eve. The scent made him drowsy, made him realise he'd never been so bone weary in all his life, so when Orla told him to sleep he thought, *Why not?* He knew she could not possibly be there, that he was making her up in his head, but that was all right. Enough fighting for one day, time to let be what would be. He closed his eyes, loosened his grip, and let go.

Θ

'Almost there,' Dustan said as they passed by Ardslignish, its soft grey tongue of shingle laying out into the loch. He didn't look towards it other than to steer them by. Shame was not his way, no guilt weighing down his shoulders about how he'd lived his life. Let others scrimp and scratch like chickens at the earth to claw enough food into their mouths to keep them going another few joyless seasons, each one harder and thinner than the last. He'd thrown himself into the twilight world of smuggling without a second thought and by Christ, there'd been nights out here on the dark waters of the Sound when he'd felt life in every muscle and sinew; mates aplenty to play at dice or cards, booze flowing freely, no wife or bairns to drag him down. He'd enjoyed every minute of it, even when he'd been chased by the excise men, escaping by the merest lick of luck: such exhilaration in those extreme circumstances it made him want to throw back his head and laugh. And not many men could say that, certainly not hereabouts, though he guessed Brogar Finn – come from who knew where and for whatever reason – might be one of them. And even now, he regretted not a jot, found joy in his muscles working at the oars, at the night, at the shift of water beneath the boards of the boat. No chance of leaping overboard and swimming for it, not with the rope around his feet, and it still tied about Brogar's waist. He knew he would most likely hang but hell, he'd had a ball of it. And one last chance to enjoy the sea and the stars and being out here in the night.

Θ

It had been a hard crossing, bringing Hugh back over, with Hugh moaning and groaning all the while, making the rest of them sick with their inability to help, Matthias worrying all the while what they would do when they got back – Strontian being practically deserted. Elspeth would be there, of course, but Lord knew what she could do. Hugh had been blasted full in the face with maybe ten or eleven pebble-sized wounds resulting, one blowing the tip of his nose clean away and several others clustered dangerously close to his eyes, both of which were filmed over with dark blood leaking from their corners like mortuary tears. Matthias had seen plenty of deer shot through neck or haunch, but nothing, absolutely nothing like this.

No more had Hesketh, but he rowed steady and true and had them over the Sound quick as he could, him and Gilligan carrying Hugh gently to Matthias's house, Matthias running on ahead to prepare for Hugh's arrival, absolutely flabbergasted to find Orla Pirie sitting at his table, hunched in a shawl.

She stood up immediately, the shawl dropping to the floor to reveal her thin grey dress to all its disadvantage: the fraying cuffs and collar, the pinafore a mere scrap of white too often washed. On any other afternoon, at any other time, Matthias would have been struck by her desperation, but not today.

'Forgive me,' Orla began, 'but I was told…'

Matthias wasn't in any mood to listen and cut her off, pushing rudely by her as he struggled to get the kettle off the hook over the fire, his hand shaking visibly as he took up the jug by the sink, half of the water missing the kettle completely and dousing the fire instead – exactly what he did not need.

'Let me,' Orla said, taking the kettle from Matthias, getting it filled and back onto its hook, poking up the peats Matthias had just soaked, by which time Matthias had already rushed off again, this time to the small room that housed his bed, trying to smooth out the sheets and coverlet, pluff up the pillow. He didn't have an exact plan of action, but if Hugh was going to die then he'd damn well do it on a comfortable bed. And then in came Hesketh and Gilligan bearing Hugh, Matthias shouting them on, Orla at their heels, shocked by the sight of Hugh's bloody face as they took him through and placed him gently down.

'What's happened?' she asked, though she could see well enough, having treated many a gunshot in her time, what with the human detritus Dunstan occasionally brought back to the house after excise raids.

'Gilligan,' she took charge without thinking, 'stay by him, hold his hand, let him know you're there; Matthias, get back into the kitchen. Find me every herb under the sun you have in this house and any cleaning agent, even if it's only coal soap. And get a sheet cut up and in a bowl and pour on the water when it's boiled.'

'What's that?' Gilligan said shakily as Orla removed from the pocket of her apron a small vial.

'Something that'll help,' she said, thanking God she'd brought it with her, despite intending it for quite a different purpose. She poured a little of its contents into the half-filled glass of water on Matthias's nightstand and gently opened Hugh's mouth with her fingers, pinching shut his bloody nose, tipping the liquid down his throat so he had to swallow. The mixture of laudanum and poppy acted quickly anad should knock Hugh out for several hours – long enough for her to clean and treat his wounds. She placed a hand on Hugh's forehead and stroked his hair, whispering softly in his ear.

'You can go to sleep now, Hugh, and everything will be better in the morning.'

Θ

Out on the Wee Grey Isle, Jed was jittery, his fingers sweating about the musket he'd not the faintest idea how to work. He supposed it was as easy as pulling the trigger but wasn't sure the thing was loaded or how to go about checking. Old Ma Pirie had been venomous as a pit-adder the first half hour after the others had left with Hugh, cursing and griping; still cursing and griping when he shifted her inside the ancient bothy and got a fire going, and now he went back outside and ripped up several armfuls of heather from between the rocks, dumping them down beside her.

'It's getting dark,' he stated, 'and I'm needing away.'

'You're nothing but a bitch-born whelp,' old Ma Pirie spat, 'and if you let me die out here you'll be swinging on the gibbet next to Dunstan, and no more than either of you deserve.'

Jed gritted his teeth but didn't answer. He left her to it, going straight to the small cove where the second boat was moored. He pulled it in close as he could get it before chucking the musket as far out into the Sound as possible, and himself after it. The water was so cold it froze him into immobility and only once his arms began flailing of their own accord could he get his breath, enough to haul himself into the boat and get rowing, or rowing of sorts, never having done it before, going first one way and then another, oars splashing at the water ineffectually and out of tune, but eventually he had it and off he went, almost dark by now, taking his uneven way back across the water, seeming to get colder with every stroke.

CHAPTER 36

THE BUILDERS GO ON FOREVER

'How's he doing?' Brogar asked the moment he was across Matthias's threshold.

'He's sleeping,' Orla said. 'I've cleaned his wounds best as I'm able, and laid on compresses and bandaged him up.'

And so she had. The only visible part of Hugh's face was the lower third, from the stump of his nose – blown back to the cartilage but cleaned and liberally doused in witch hazel – down to his chin.

'So he'll be all right?' Brogar persisted.

Orla made a small movement of her shoulders but nodded.

'He'll live,' she answered quietly, back to her usual timid and shrinking self now her ministrations were for the moment at an end. 'But how strong his vision will be is another matter.'

Gilligan gasped and put a hand to his mouth.

'He'll never be blind, miss, will he?' he mumbled through his fingers. He shouldn't have been so shocked, not with the way Hugh looked when they brought him in, but it didn't bear thinking about that Hugh would never be able to read his stories again or see the sky or the hills and the sea.

'There's worse things, Gilligan,' Sholto said, laying a hand on the boy's shoulders. 'There's a woman over at Ockle, Aileen's her name, and she's never seen a damn thing in her life but she manages just fine.'

It was small compensation, Sholto knew. Certainly Aileen was blind as a boulder, but as far as she was concerned she was complete, having always been that way. Having sight and then losing it was beyond Sholto's comprehension. It seemed as impossible as taking a fish out of water and expecting it to start breathing air and walking on its fins.

'Let's not assume the worst before it happens,' Brogar said. 'I've been in plenty situations where it looks like there's no way out, but there always is. You just have to find it. And Hugh will find his way out too.'

Brogar's voice was so strong and optimistic that Gilligan allowed his worry to slide and he looked up and gave half a smile.

'You really think so?' he said.

'I do, Gilligan,' Brogar replied heartily, baring his teeth in what passed in Brogar for a smile. 'Don't count him out just yet. He's the best of care, and he's a fighter. And either way, he's you to count on, and myself and Sholto. And we'll none of us let him down.'

Sholto cleared his throat. 'We've other matters to discuss,' he said. 'Let's not forget we've Dunstan Pirie and Gustav Wengler locked out in the barn.'

There was a sudden stir at these words as Orla looked up sharply, feeling like she'd been punched in the gut, interrupted by the unexpected apparition of a dripping wet Jed stumbling through the door just catching the last of Sholto's words.

'Y…y…you've found Mr Wengler?' he said through chattering teeth as Matthias sprang up from his seat.

'Jed!' he cried. 'What on earth? Did you row over? And in the dark? And old Ma Pirie? What about her?'

Jed tried to grin but it was lost in a violent fit of shivering as Matthias brought him swiftly to a chair by the fire and shoved him down.

'S…s…she's fine. L…l…lit a fire. B…but d…d…did you say y… you'd f…f…found Mr W…Wengler?'

'He did, lad,' Matthias said quietly, 'and there's a lot we neither of us understand, but you need to get warm before we do anything else.'

He strode swiftly to his bedchamber and lifted the lid of the blanket box, casting a quick glance at Hugh – who seemed easy enough, thank God, breathing deep and even in his sleep – returning with a couple of rather ratty blankets, wrapping them about Jed's shoulders.

'The situation,' Sholto took up where he'd left off, 'is more complicated than we originally thought and yes, Jed, we found Gustav Wengler, but he wasn't kidnapped. He left under his own steam.'

'I don't understand,' Matthias supplied in place of the stuttering Jed, whose confusion – like his own – was as plain on his face as a swan swimming on black waters. 'How on earth could he have left the island? I mean, he never leaves…'

He left the sentence hanging and Sholto looked to Brogar for explication, for in truth he was a little hazy about how it had come about himself.

'He took a boat,' Brogar did not disappoint, 'but first things first. Some of you don't know what others do; for example that Kurti Griffen is dead.'

Matthias closed his eyes, dropped his head, Orla looking at him with concern. She wanted to be bustling, to be standing at the edge, marginalised as always, even in her own home, and was desperately uncomfortable having all these men about her, felt a scratching on her skin, a wanting to be gone.

'We found the drag marks of a boat by Griffen's body,' Brogar went on, 'and there's a load of barrels stashed in a small cave nearby.'

'So after the failed attempt to get in at Ardslignish,' Sholto added slowly, putting the pieces together, 'they went to Havengore, dumped their booty, probably left a small craft to aid later swift recovery...'

'And Dunstan Pirie knew it,' Brogar added. 'Every smuggler needs a back-up plan.'

'No. Wait a minute,' Sholto put in, holding up a hand. 'That can't be right.'

Brogar smiled broadly, stretching his head back upon his neck, waiting for Sholto to get there by himself. By God, but this felt good! He'd had plenty of assistants before but none like Sholto, the two of them fitting together as a double acorn in its double cup; his misgivings about coming to Scotland had been so wide of the mark he could have laughed. He was as eager to hear what Sholto would come up with as the rest were, could see them all juggling this new information, looking for the flaw Sholto had obviously already spotted: Orla Pirie, once again bowed and defeated; Gilligan, nervous and fidgety, worried about his friend; Matthias finding it hard to take any more threats to his village and his mines; Jed beginning to move his shoulders in his blankets, eager to be on, to get to the end of the story. Just like Brogar had been at his age.

'So,' Sholto began, looking over at Brogar who nodded encouragingly, eyes bright with expectation.

'Let's hear it, Sholto,' Brogar said, Sholto smiling briefly before going on.

'Let's just get all this straight,' Sholto said. 'Let's start at the beginning and move on from there.'

⊖

Dunstan and Wengler were bound hand and foot, a single lamp hanging from a hook in the beam hardly alleviating the gloom, and certainly not the irritation Dunstan had at Wengler repeating the same words over and over again.

'Why are they not taking me home? I need to get back to Havengore. I've work to do. Why are they not taking me home?'

After several iterations, punctuated by a breath or two, Dunstan had had enough.

'You ain't never going home, mate. We've killed people, you and me, and when you does summat like that it's a game changer. No going home ever again.'

No reaction from his companion prisoner, just like out at Ockle. It was going to be a long night.

'Best chance is transportation,' Dunstan went on, thinking on Brogar's promise to speak on his behalf. A slim chance, but no harm grasping at it. How the hell Gustav Wengler had ended up in the same situation as him was a mystery. Dunstan knew about the mad hermit – everybody did – but trying to kill a girl was a step too far, even for Dunstan. Men were fine – put yourself in that line of work and what do you expect? But shoving girls down on sundials? Even Dunstan had his limits. He eyed his fellow prisoner with distaste, remembering there was that other fellow, murdered on Havengore. Brogar had accused him of that killing too, and probably no way to prove otherwise. Hanging for his own crimes was one thing; hanging for someone else's was another; and it couldn't have been his smuggling buddies either, for they'd been long since gone and not yet due back. So no one left but Gustav Wengler to do that particular deed. Dunstan was weighing things up, taking Brogar's words on board, wondering if there might not be a better way to get things done.

Θ

'We know Dunstan killed Archie at Ardslignish,' Sholto was saying, teasing out the threads as he went, 'and burned down the bothy, so nowhere to hide the contraband. So instead they chose to land their goods at their old spot on Wengler's island, stuffing their casks into the little overhung cave we know is only accessible at low tide. They left a boat there, dragged up into the small bay to make the retrieval so much the quicker when the coast was clear.' Sholto coughed, cleared his throat. 'And that'll be why Dunstan and his mother went to ground on the smaller island next door, all part of the plan when things went wrong. And they wouldn't have risked having their own boat bobbing off the Wee Grey Isle for all the world to see. They'd have friends take them over. Right, Orla?'

Orla flinched, wrapping her hands in her pinafore, feeling the small vial there.

'Aye,' she whispered. 'Always good for back up plans are the Piries.'

Remembering her own back up plan to finish off Dunstan and old Ma for good, saved from joining the fold of Pirie murderers by Hugh needing her help more than she needed to bring it all to a stop, that little vial in her pocket put to better use. Immensely glad for it now, for it seemed it had come to a stop all by itself.

Sholto nodded.

'So, halfway there. But then we have the riddle of the sundial, bought by Gustav Wengler in good faith as part of his White

Cathedral – in essence a giant observatory – mislaid on its way to Havengore over ten years back. We know from Griffen that it left Denmark and we know it ended up in Ockle. We also know it was accompanied by Wengler's previous assistant…'

He stopped, struggling for the name which would not come.

'Neal Gillespie,' put in Matthias, remembering the gangling blond-haired lad so proud of his job, and then so dispirited.

'Neal Gillespie, that's right,' Sholto said. 'And if we assume the bag of bones found at Ockle was the body of Neal Gillespie then we can also safely assume all did not go well on that trip.'

'But those bones could have belonged to anyone,' Jed protested, coming back to the normal, warmed up, head getting back into gear.

'I don't think so,' Sholto said. 'They fit the timeframe, and they show clear evidence of having come to a violent end. The sundial was a very valuable piece, so it's no stretch to assume the men accompanying it decided to take it for themselves.'

'And then they foundered themselves,' Matthias sighed. 'The weather can be vicious here, come out of nowhere, nothing standing between us and the Atlantic, and 1857 was worse than most, especially back end of April. Isn't that when Griffen said the sundial left Denmark?'

He closed his eyes, remembering those storms well: the rain coming down like the second flood was upon them, the ground so wet it was hard to take a step without slipping, like the older Gustav Wengler had done – going headfirst down a shaft and breaking his neck.

'It is,' Sholto agreed, 'and I'd guess you never heard anything after that April from Neil Gillespie?'

'Nothing,' Matthias breathed, but did not open his eyes, Sholto nodding briefly before going on.

'Which brings me full circle to Kurti Griffen.'

He took a breath, and Jed shook his head, fearing what was coming next.

'There was a ring found with the Ockle Bones, and a very unusual one I would bet, given by Harald to Simmy for safekeeping. And there are only two people we know of who had any notion of its provenance, namely that it originated from the Round Tower, sent with Neal because it was an integral part of the sundial, or at least an integral part of how to interpret it.'

Jed was shaking his head.

'I don't see how that matters a whit,' he argued stubbornly. 'Sundial or no sundial, ring or no ring. You've still not proved to me anything bad about Gustav Wengler.'

'Because he knew about the ring, Jed,' Sholto said sadly. 'We found him in Simmy's house looking for it, and the only way to Ockle from Havengore was on that boat that disappeared from the cove. Think, Jed. What did Griffen say to Wengler when you two were over on the island?'

Jed swiped angrily at his eyes to staunch unwanted tears. He'd not been there when Griffen spoke to Wengler but certainly the ring had been mentioned, for he'd mentioned it himself.

'Griffen may have thought Wengler wasn't even listening,' Sholto tried again. 'You know better than anyone how he can cut himself off, doesn't like to talk, but also that he's a very clever man, one who can grind his attention down to a single point when he needs to.'

'And what is the bloody point?' Jed said, louder than he'd intended. 'What are you trying to say?'

He scrunched up his face, pummelling his forehead with his fingers, putting the pieces together, refusing to believe the implications.

'He's trying to tell you,' Brogar put in, 'that Wengler wanted the ring and sundial so badly that when he saw an opportunity to kill Griffen – the man who was threatening to take them away – he took it.'

Enough pussy-footing about. No chance of proving this statement unless Wengler confessed, and best chance of that being Jed coaxing it out of him, and no chance of that if they couldn't convince Jed that Gustav Wengler was in the worst kind of shite, and right up to his neck in it.

'But why?' Jed whispered miserably, tears falling in dribs and drabs down his young face.

'Because he's looking to unlock the universe,' came a quiet voice, Hesketh Wood unfolding himself from the shadows, previously so silent, so immobile, everyone had forgotten he was there. 'Wives are only people,' he quoted Wengler's words, 'that's what he told me. And people die, but the builders go on forever.'

CHAPTER 37

THE NOCTURNAL AND THE NIGHT

Hesketh's words, and his sudden reappearance, shocked everyone into silence, for a few moments at least.

Matthias was exhausted, eyes open again but seeing nothing but Old Man Wengler when they dragged him out of the flooded shaft, head lolling, neck broken clean at its base. A terrible day, one he'd hoped never to repeat, but here was another day just as terrible. He saw it all: Wengler looking out of the window for Archie coming home, Wengler witnessing him dying without knowing it; Wengler seeing the smugglers turning up on the other end of his island, their lights bobbing in the darkness of the night. He'd no interest in other people's lives unless they intruded on his own, as they were doing then, and come the morning he would have gone to investigate, found the boat they'd left behind. And if he'd taken the unprecedented decision to take himself over to Ockle and the sundial, only Griffen would have been standing in his way.

Matthias's shoulders sagged, finding it hard to understand a man so driven. Folk might protest that Wengler didn't know one end of a boat from the other but Matthias knew this wasn't so, that when he'd first shifted over to his island he'd gone out hour upon hour into the Sound making charts of all the tidal depths and currents, day and night. A matter of some concern to the older Wengler, fearing his son's naivety, that he'd hand all this information over to anyone who asked – namely to the likes of the Piries and their disreputable contacts.

He's a mind roams the universe like you or I would roam the hills; that's what the father had said of the son.

Matthias breathed deeply, looked out of the window into darkness, doubting Wengler would ever roam freely again. Reminding himself too that what was left of Kurti Griffen was still out there on the island, but nothing to be done about that, not tonight.

'I need to go speak to him,' Jed said, the first to break the silence after Hesketh Wood's dramatic and enigmatic pronouncement that jolted Jed's tears and self-recrimination right out of him. He just couldn't believe Wengler was capable of murder, no matter what Brogar and Sholto thought. The Piries must be responsible for Griffen's death, and what had happened to the girl Simmy just an accident.

'All right then,' Brogar was next to speak, unexpectedly agreeing. 'But go careful. Ask him if you can about Griffen and the girl.'

Jed didn't answer, merely shook off his blankets and headed to the door, soon out, shutting it behind him.

'He's in for a fall,' Sholto commented as he went, Brogar nodding, hoping it would be so, hoping Wengler would say the words Jed didn't want to hear.

'Best he gets it from the horse's mouth,' he commented. 'No real chance of getting him for Griffen if he doesn't.'

'He did have blood on his sleeves,' Sholto pointed out. 'We all saw it when we shut him up in the sacristy.'

'I know,' Brogar agreed. 'But no way to get him for murder on that. Simmy lost a lot of it, and Simmy's not dead.'

'Thank Christ for small mercies,' Sholto commented, and nobody could disagree.

Θ

Jed approached the barn with trepidation. The frost was hard down, his boots crunching on it as he went, trying to think what to say and how he was going to say it. He tapped politely but unnecessarily on the door of the shed before withdrawing the bolts and pushing it open to see Dunstan and Wengler both tied hand and foot, both leaning their backs uncomfortably against the opposite wall of the barn, the single lamp out of reach above their heads. It shocked him to see Wengler so ill-treated – head-bent, stoop-shouldered – convinced more than ever this was an injustice he needed to counter and fight.

'A bit of company at last,' Dunstan growled into the half-light as Jed made his way over to Gustav Wengler, sitting himself down on the floor a few yards apart.

'I've not come for you,' Jed snapped sharply. 'I've come to talk to Mr Wengler.'

'Good luck with that,' Dunstan commented. 'Stuck like a bad face in a storm, and been like it all the while.'

Jed ignored him.

'It's me, Mr Wengler. Jed Thornbrough. I came to see you this morning, over on your island?'

No reaction.

'He's no more wit than a fox without a snout,' Dunstan put in, Jed turning angrily towards him and putting a finger to his lips.

'Aye, right,' Dunstan grumbled, but he quieted and said nothing more, waiting to see what would happen next.

'You went to see the sundial,' Jed said, inching a little closer towards Wengler, whose head twitched at the word. 'But we've no need to talk about that now. What I'm really curious about is what happened to that man who came over with me: Kurti Griffen, the man from Denmark...'

Jed held his breath. He could see Wengler's face more clearly now, his eyes having adapted to the gloom, and saw that Wengler had moved, was listening to every word he said.

'So what really happened?' Jed tried again. 'I know you didn't kill him...'

Dunstan barked out a laugh into the darkness.

'Oh my Christ! But you're so wrong there!'

'Will you bloody well shut up for more than a minute!' Jed was angry, spat his words at Dunstan, and just at that moment Wengler chose to speak, Jed leaning in closer to catch his words.

'Have you ever seen a star clock?' he asked of no one in particular. 'The earliest ones are Egyptian, long sticks carved with inscriptions, calibrated by watching the horizon, noting the coincidence of bright stars rising or setting with the rising and setting of the sun.'

Jed frowned, but didn't stop Wengler, who carried on regardless.

'They recorded such transits against a water clock, created a time system. The *bay en imy wenut*, they called it, *the palm rib of the observer of the hours*. And that's what I do: observe the hours, observe the stars, observe the way time moves through the universe, picking at the problems it leaves behind. There's an instrument called the nocturnal, very simple, very elegant: a fixed midnight mark put against the date of the calendar on a stationary circle, a pointer on another rotating circle lined up with Polaris – or two or three bright stars, depending on your position on the earth's surface. And *res ipsa loquitur*. The facts speak for themselves. The time is discovered from where the pointer intersects the stationary hour disc.'

'Like a sundial without a sun,' Jed said slowly, Wengler nodding, apparently glad to be understood.

'A precursor, if you will. Seemingly simple, and yet quite complex. Consider the sundial: a circle, a gnomon and a shadow. And for all that someone has to work out the figures beforehand, take into account the polar axis, the plane of the equator, the plane formed by the horizon of local latitude, the way the sphere of the Earth inclines on its axis and revolves around the single star of the sun. Everything changing and yet staying the same, season following season, coming back upon itself. No doubt why many of the ancient Chinese sundials depict snakes eating their own tails.'

'And where does the Round Tower sundial fit in this?' Jed asked, wondering where this was going.

'I'm just saying that was how we started out,' Wengler said, 'measuring time with a stick. But what if the universe isn't standing still? What if it is moving, expanding? If that's the case, then one day we'll be able to look right back to the beginnings of the universe, and right on to its end. And the sundial is a step on the way, fitting into the puzzle like the ring fits into the sundial.'

An odd turn of phrase, Jed thought, about to ask when Dunstan got in first.

'Oh for Christ's sake,' he muttered, exhaling loudly. 'What the hell are you two bloody on about? Why the shite don't you get down to tacks and nails? Make him bloody well tell you he killed that man you were on about earlier!'

Dunstan blew out his breath and turned his head away. This wasn't how proper men talked or acted, not in the real world. And Dunstan had landed back into the real world with a God-

Almighty thump, anger back in him like a fire stoked up in the grate. All that bloody rowing, all that feeling like he was on the right side? What a shitting load of crap that had been, realisation hot in him that he was all lined up for swinging, and not only for the man in the bothy but for some other bloody murder he didn't even do.

'Just get him to spit it out, man,' Dunstan said, blinking into the gloom, a great lump rising in his throat to know he really was done for but was damned if he was going to die while the likes of this bloody madman went free. 'He did it, boy. You just need to make him say it.'

Dunstan closed his mouth. Last words he was going to say to either of these nut jobs, rage closing in on him like the fog that came off the Sound sometimes, creeping up from the water and up the heather braes, enclosing the house and sifting through the gaps and cracks inside so nothing could be seen, not even the hand in front of your face.

However Wengler felt about Dunstan's words – and it didn't seem likely he felt much – he responded, answering as if he'd been asked a noncommittal question about the weather, about what he'd just been reading, about what he might have had for supper.

'He tried to make a bargain,' Wengler said in his dreary monotone. 'Said I'd no right to sundial or ring, that I'd need to go to the Round Tower to study them. And that was unacceptable.'

Jed's insides contracted, wanting to shove the words right back down Wengler's throat, unwilling to be witness to them, to admit the admission. The lamp's light had weakened, not that Jed noticed, more aware of Dunstan's evident animosity and the bad smell of his sweat, despite the cold. He shifted himself back against the wall, now sitting side by side with Wengler.

'And so,' he said softly, 'when you saw Griffen down by the boat?'

'And so,' Wengler said, without hesitation, 'I had to get rid. I needed to see the sundial, get a look at the ring, if only once.'

'Did you know what you were going to do before you did it?' Jed asked quietly, everything for Jed hanging on Wengler's answer, which was the worst.

'It was an equation,' Wengler answered, 'just like everything else. And with that man against me, it was never going to work out right.'

'Told you so,' came Dunstan's hoarse voice, despite his earlier decision not to speak. His back was aching. He didn't want to be here, was only just twigging to the fact that the bolts on the door had been drawn from the outside and therefore that the door must still be open; equations, just like Wengler said - or betting the odds as Dunstan would have put it - spilling into his head. Escape would be hard, foot-tied as he was, but worth a shot; just one last mess to clear up before he made a break for it.

CHAPTER 38

SHEEP AND LAMBS

Hesketh and Brogar were weighing up their own odds, leaving Matthias not long after Jed went out to the barn, going to see the lay of the land, figure out if it was possible to get over to the Wee Grey Isle and bring old Ma Pirie in, even in the dark; Gilligan and Orla also deserted, retiring to sit by Hugh, taking with them a replenished bowl of hot water infused with herbs to change his compresses. Only people left then about the table were Sholto and Matthias, who sat for several minutes in silence until Sholto noticed a strange object on the shelf above the inglenook.

'What on earth is that?' he asked, intrigued, standing up and moving towards it, seeing a flat-bottomed figurine of a boat about eighteen inches long, carved out of wood with a dragon's head at one end, a tail at the other, piled with fifteen or so metal balls, the whole lot suspended above a pewter bowl. Matthias sighed before he could stop himself, looking up apologetically, only to be reminded once more of the terrible days he so feared.

'It was given me by Gustav's father,' he said quietly. 'An alarm of sorts. Chinese,' he sighed again, so weary he was finding it hard to get out any words at all.

'Fascinating!' Sholto said, undeterred. 'So how does it work? I'm guessing it's to do with the balls dropping into the bowl?'

Matthias rubbed the base of his neck with his fingers.

'Indeed,' he said. 'You place a stick of incense on the holder you'll find beneath the spheres and you drape the holder over with a series of cotton threads. As the incense stick burns down it goes through the threads at regular intervals, which in turn release the wired balls that drop and clatter into the bowl below.'

'Ingenious,' Sholto commented, eager to get it all set up and try it out, not that he had any sticks of incense about his person, and was about to ask Matthias whether the gift had come with supplies when he noticed several small clatters of his own.

'Did you hear that?' Sholto asked.

'I heard something,' Matthias replied absently. 'Night birds maybe, bumping the windows, or possibly bats.'

He was tired to the bone, staying awake only out of deference to his guests, would have lain himself out by the fire if he'd not been obliged to stay awake until either Sholto chose to retire for the night, or Brogar got back, with or without old Ma Pirie.

'There it is again,' Sholto said, cocking his head towards the small sound. 'Surely not a bat, at this time of year?'

'They come out all the time,' Matthias said with effort. 'They get disturbed or hungry. It's a myth that they hibernate the whole winter through.'

'Ever the scientist,' Sholto said, giving a small smile that went unacknowledged, seeing suddenly that Matthias was almost asleep where he sat. He made a move towards the coffee pot but, as he returned with it from the inglenook he stood quite still, listening intently.

'I can definitely hear something,' Sholto said. 'Some kind of scuffling...'

'I hear it,' Matthias answered, tipping back his chair, getting slowly to his feet, listening hard. 'It's coming from the shed!' Matthias shouted, coming alive, moving swiftly past Sholto, inadvertently knocking the coffee pot from Sholto's fingers so it fell to the flagstones, its metal clanking and plinking as the lid came loose, setting free the dark liquid to spread around Sholto's feet like a pool of rusty blood.

The two of them were across the yard in moments, Matthias getting to the barn first, shoving at the door with his hand, but it didn't budge.

'Out of my way,' Matthias shouted, pushing Sholto roughly to one side as he took a pace backwards and then reversed his trajectory, using his forward momentum to kick hard as he could at the door to get it open, mind racing, uppermost thoughts about Jed, for how on God's good earth had he let Jed go in there alone with those two men, those two murderers, and with only an unbolted door between them and escape? Matthias hadn't known he'd the strength within him but he kicked at that door as if it was separating a father from his only son.

'Jed!' Matthias shouted into utter dark and silence. 'Jed! Where are you? Are you all right?'

Θ

'Listen to me, Mr Wengler,' Jed had been saying, minutes previously, 'I'm going to tell no one what you've just said, and you've not to say it, not to anyone, not ever again.'

Jed stared hard at Gustav Wengler and Gustav Wengler looked right back.

'Now just a fecking minute,' Dunstan intervened. 'Does my word count for nothing?'

His mind was shifting, as was his body, slowly sliding his back up the wall. His feet were tied together, as were his hands, but the latter were tied at his stomach so he had some movement at least.

Jed didn't shift his gaze from his precious Wengler.

'It might come to that, but if it does then I'm going to say I did the murder myself. And either way, your word against mine.'

Ah Jesus, Dunstan thought, *why are the young so stupid?*

And up he went against the wall a little more, was almost up to standing, flexing his knees, checking all his muscles were working, looking over towards the door he knew must be unlocked.

'In fact that's what I'm going to do,' Jed went on feverishly. 'I'm going to tell everyone I killed Griffen, and no matter any evidence to the contrary I'll stick to my story. And the girl was an accident, wasn't she?'

Wengler nodded, Jed going on fast and bright, words out in a tumble, not thinking them through.

'And then you'll be free to study the sundial for as long as you want.'

Dunstan snorted, but Wengler apparently took the idea seriously and came to an opposite conclusion.

'You would be doing science a great service if you did. I think it might break the bounds, stretch the limits of physics and mathematics to places they've never been.'

And oh, so holy a voice, as if the man had been in church and Dunstan had never been one for preachers, and that did it for him. Doing science a great service? Letting someone take the rap for something they didn't do? Well bugger the lot of them, Dunstan wasn't going to stand for it. He was a bad man and he knew it, but Jesus Christ there were always lines drawn in the sand. He'd been his mother's lackey since early doors but she'd never given him a lick of appreciation; always Malcolm this, Malcolm that, the good boy who wasn't good at all. All these years he'd kept his tongue about it, kept Orla in the dark about Malcolm working one of the biggest smuggling circles the north of Scotland had ever seen. Diminished by it, made small by it, needing to keep his family close and under his thumb, needing to keep his enemies – his brother top of the list – far away as possible, keeping his brother's secret, bound by blood, bound by jealousy; Malcolm managing to do what Dunstan hadn't: getting out from under old Ma's thumb, going elsewhere, making a better living than Dunstan could ever aspire to; everything closing in on him, in this barn; everything coming to an end, one way or another.

The lamp sputtered and died, darkness on them in a blink, and in that moment Dunstan took his chance, moved swiftly along the wall, kicking out blindly at Jed, catching him square in the face, knocking his head down into the dirt. Dunstan stumbled but didn't stop, bent down and found Wengler's rope-tied feet and shuffle-hauled him into the empty centre of the room, looping his bound hands around Gustav Wengler's neck and pulling the rope tight, squeezing hard as he could.

Θ

Jed resurfaced, confused, feeling sick, head spinning, trying to croak for help but not getting far. Instead he put out a hand – no Wengler – and pitched himself forward, finding it hard to coordinate his limbs, crawling on hands and knees, couldn't see anything but a faint shiver of non-existent stars flickering into being one moment and then gone again. The stench of Dunstan's sweat, though, was acrid and strong and he headed towards it, couldn't understand that creaking noise, that dry kind of whining, but knew it meant something bad. He could faintly make out something darker than the dark, something more substantial, like a black stone in a black stream detectable only from the slight swish of water about its bulk. Dunstan, had to be Dunstan, trying to reach the open door; Jed crawled on, holding a hand out in front of him, catching at an upright leg and grabbing it hard, loud crash like a tree falling in a forest and then a rhythmic kind of thumping that must have been his heart, and then no – not his heart at all – but footsteps running across the yard, pushing at the door, a gust of fresh air blowing through Dunstan's sweat and then Jesus, such an awful pain in his side as the door was kicked open, Jed going with it, the wood catching him full on his hip as it swung, shoving him two foot across the floor. And then Matthias calling his name and nothing more to do but lie back and hope Dunstan hadn't got out, that he was somewhere in the darkness behind him.

⊖

Sholto had the presence of mind to leg it back to the house and snatch up a lamp, back in time to see Matthias heaving at the door, pushing away some obstruction on the other side, holding the lamp high as Matthias went in, first thing Matthias seeing being a prostrate Jed, aghast to realise he'd been the obstruction Matthias's boot had dooshed out of the way as he'd kicked in the door.

'Jed, lad,' he cried, sinking to his knees, lifting Jed's head from the floor, leaving Sholto to the rest, which was Dunstan, who was rolling from his front onto his back the other side of the open door, perspiration popping from his forehead like dew on Lady's Mantle. His entire body was shuddering as if he'd just performed some great feat of strength, presumably in a doomed attempt at escape. Sholto swung his lamp around to locate Wengler and there he was, lying prone a few yards down, right cheek to the earthen floor, head moving spasmodically, tongue horribly extended, bringing unwanted to Sholto's mind the image of a flaccid horse penis after a long piss. He'd no idea what had happened here but recognised a man in distress and hurriedly moved forward, setting down the lamp. Wengler's face was blotched and purple, lips blue and moving slowly, spasmodically, like a fish lipping at the water; whether he was getting any air in was moot, and Sholto put his fingers to Wengler's throat but could detect no pulse. His heart might still be beating inside his body but it wouldn't do so for long; if he was ever to be revived then something needed doing and needed doing now: Brogar's territory, but no Brogar here to help. He cupped his arms about Wengler's body and shifted him wholly onto his side, cricking up Wengler's knees to take the pressure off his diaphragm, figuring that if Wengler could still breathe this might be the position he could best do it in.

'Matthias!' Sholto shouted. 'Go get Orla!'

No response from Matthias until Sholto yelled again.

'Right now, Matthias! He's going to die if he's no help.'

'Go,' Jed croaked, not understanding what was going on, only that it could not be him Sholto was talking about so might be Wengler, and Matthias moved, springing to his feet, going for the door before changing his mind and coming back in, going right up to Dunstan Pirie.

'You did this,' he said, 'and so help me I'll make sure you never do it again.'

'You dinna ken…' Dunstan began, explanations stopped short by Matthias's fist swinging smack-hard into Dunstan's face, breaking his nose, blood beginning to pour, not that Matthias had a care for it, already turning away and racing for the door.

Θ

'So no hope of going over tonight?'

Brogar was sitting on the seat outside Hesketh's house.

'None,' Hesketh agreed. 'Tide's agin us and no moon to see us right.'

'So she's to stay there the night over,' Brogar commented, Hesketh replying with a nod but no words. They sat for a few minutes in companionable silence, enjoying the clean night air, the subtle scents of snow and the salt coming up from the loch. Unusually it was Hesketh, normally so tight-lipped, so used to keeping his opinions under wraps, who chose to speak first.

'So what do you make of this business with Mr Wengler?' he asked, looking up at the small bright patches of stars the shifting winds revealed occasionally as they shuffled the clouds way up in the atmosphere, clouds so high the water in them had turned to ice, lacing their edges with weird shimmers of green and blue that were entirely out of keeping with the everyday.

'I think,' Brogar said, weighing his words, taking his time, 'that he's probably the genius Jed believes him to be but, like the rest of us, he's flawed. I spend most of my time exploring instances of what turn out in the end to be the old flash in the pan. Not always, but often: people who believe they've a gold rush on their hands like, for instance, over at Kildonan. Maybe this is Wengler's flash in the pan, or maybe it's the real thing.'

'And if it is the real thing?' Hesketh asked. 'What then?'

Brogar looked up at the night sky, at the enormity of it. This wasn't his area of expertise, far happier grubbing deep and dirty in mineshafts where he could tell for certain what might or might not be found if they carried on digging. He shrugged.

'I really don't know,' he said. 'But he's people who have faith in him. That young Jed for one, and I don't think Sholto's far behind, and if Sholto's taking his theories seriously then there's got to be something in them. Maybe that island really is like Brahe's Hven, a place where great discoveries will be made.'

'Complete with one dead man too,' Hesketh replied, nodding over towards Havengore, Brogar suddenly remembering the mess of Kurti Griffen jammed between the rocks, shaking his head, wondering how he could possibly have forgotten.

Θ

Dunstan was shuddering against the wall of the shed, unable to rationalise what he'd done or why, so transfixed upon the act he barely registered the raw welts about his wrists where the ropes had burned into his skin as they'd done about Wengler's throat. The door opened again and in came Matthias, accompanied by Orla, face white and ghost-like, drab clothes dissolving into the darkness as if they belonged.

'Where is he?' she asked, her voice thin and reedy, Sholto lifting his lamp, exposing Gustav Wengler to her unprepared eyes.

'My God,' she said, hands going to her mouth, muffling her next words. 'But surely he's already dead?'

Sholto shook his head.

'I don't know,' he said. 'There wasn't much time, only a few minutes between when we heard the first noise and when we got here. Maybe there's something can be done to help him.'

To her great credit, Orla went down on her knees, placing her hand directly over Wengler's mouth and nose despite the ghastly extrusion of his tongue, which seemed to Sholto to have retracted, if only a little.

'There's still breath in him,' she said quietly, and quickly set to massaging Wengler's throat to free his airways, trying to persuade his tongue back inside his head where it belonged, and it went –

not wholly, but at least enough not to look so obscene as it had done, for which Sholto was profoundly grateful.

'I dinna ken if he'll last much longer,' Orla said, 'but mebbe if he's somewhere warmer, somewhere softer, he'll have a better chance.'

'Got to try, missus,' Jed whispered, getting up on wobbly legs, Matthias quick behind him, lending support.

'We can put him in with Hugh,' Matthias said, eyes wide and glittering, oddly exhilarated, despite feeling like he'd been put through a mangle and spat out the other side; but Jed was alive, the same lad he'd always been, never being still devoted to the blasted Wengler, no matter what the blasted Wengler had done.

'To the house then,' Sholto agreed, Matthias taking charge, lifting Wengler by the shoulders, Orla and Jed taking one leg each, Sholto lingering, looking over to Dunstan who was leaning against the barn side, broken-nosed, blood partway staunched by a scrap of sacking he'd found on the floor beside him, Sholto having a stab of concern for the man, going to replace the dead lamp on the hook above them with the live one in his hand.

'Dinna bother,' Dunstan said gruffly, spitting out a gobbet of black blood. 'Cannae get any darker for me than it already is.'

Sholto hesitated but didn't argue, went back to the door, about to pull it shut, draw the bolts, close Dunstan in, but turned one last time, unable to reconcile what Dunstan had done without the why of it.

'I don't understand – what you did to Wengler, I mean,' he said, 'because it must have been you.'

Dunstan turned his head, keeping to the shadows, sniffing back the blood, not sure how to explain it, even to himself.

'Might as well be hung for a sheep as a lamb,' he offered eventually, the idiom lost on Sholto, Dunstan sighing, closing his eyes, next words softened by the blood-soaked sacking draped over the lower half of his face.

'Take one and you might as well take the other,' he said. 'Whose gonna care?'

Sholto frowned, unsure what Dunstan was trying to say.

'But you might have got off with transportation for Archie and Hugh,' he countered. 'Brogar would have spoken for you, as would I. But now? Well…'

Dunstan took the sacking from his face and ground it angrily into the sandy floor beside him, nose throbbing badly, teeth clenched with the pain of it, suddenly grasping the root of his own actions and shouting it out.

''Cos that young pudding head of a boy you sent in here was gonna fess up to it! Take the rap for summat he never done! And that ain't fair and that ain't right. Me? 'S'different. I ken what I done and no regrets on it. Did what needed doing. But a madman piece of shite like your Wengler feller getting away with murder? Well that just ain't right, and no way I was gonna stand for it.'

And at last Sholto understood: sheep and lambs, and only one man to die for them both; Gustav had told the two of them he'd done for Kurti Griffen and Jed, the pudding head, had been willing to throw himself away to allow Wengler to go free. Proof nothing to do with it. Nor common sense. Confess to a killing like that and you'd hang, no matter what anyone said to the contrary – especially not on Dunstan's say-so – Jed not truly grasping the implications, convinced he had something special going with Wengler, believing he was intellectual family; and families were dark forests, as Sholto well knew. Dark and deep, tangled root and branch, traversed by hidden pathways others couldn't see.

The strangest thought of all was that Dunstan had put an end to it: Dunstan Pirie a hero. It beggared belief, but Sholto had nowhere else to go.

CHAPTER 39

HANDS THAT NEED TO BE WASHED

Two days later, Dunstan Pirie, hero or no, was sitting in the gaol at Fort William barracks. The garrison was occupied by only a handful of men, but more soon arrived from the Excise House in Oban to scour the land as they did periodically and no better time than now, with smugglers once again purported to be abroad. At Dunstan's initial hearing, a few weeks later, it was made plain to gallery and court that the Pirie family had long been implicated in the smuggling that had blighted these Highland waters for at least a hundred years. Much was made of the fact that old Ma Pirie was closely related to the Cummings family of Inverness who had been consistently mentioned in excise reports for many years for various offences, including the illegal introduction to the West Coast of tons of contraband tobacco, Italian walnuts, iron screws and nails, salt, numerous ankers of Dutch gin and hogsheads of wine from Burgundy and Portugal – ten barrels of the latter having being recovered from Havengore, along with the body of Kurti Griffen, the smugglers' sloop long gone, and not coming back once they'd heard news of murders and that the law would soon be crawling over Ardnamurchan and its surrounds like maggots on a carcass.

Dunstan made a full confession. Yes, he'd killed Archie Louden, who'd stumbled upon his illegal activities at Ardslignish, and yes, he'd inadvertently blasted Hugh in the face with his mother's shotgun, and yes, he'd launched a murderous attack on Gustav Wengler for reasons he would not divulge, unable to articulate the rage boiling in his blood to think that Wengler might go free and clear while he went under.

Ever done anything good with your life?

He couldn't fathom how Brogar's words had buried themselves so deep inside his head, seeds sprouting into unwanted weeds at every turn, but they were there all the same. He tried to add them up, but there wasn't much to add. He'd never told Orla othe truth about Malcolm for one, but that had been down to pride and spite, and nothing good in that; but he'd not dropped Harald McRailty in it like he could have done, and the young pudding head Jed had ceased to air his stupid confessions, so maybe that was good enough. Maybe someone somewhere, maybe that Sholto fellow, would remember him, and not all for the bad.

Θ

The trial lasted several days, what with shuffling the three accused, the various witnesses and their statements; the introduction of Hugh to the stand, and the full extent of his wounds so apparent, being the clincher. It took judge and jury less than an hour to deliberate their verdicts: Dunstan Pirie guilty of the murder of Archie Louden and the attempted murders of Hugh and Gustav Wengler: sentenced to death. Old Ma Breda Pirie – brought in from the Wee Grey Isle, sadly not frozen into submission but still screaming bloody oaths on all and everyone who had interfered with her life – convicted of running a smuggling ring for the past thirty nine years, harbouring a fugitive, firing her musket indiscriminately at the men who came to apprehend her: handed down ten years' hard labour for her crimes. She tried to put the blame entirely on Dunstan's shoulders for the smuggling but that had been a betrayal too far, Dunstan speaking up loudly against her and being believed, Orla backing him to the hilt. And ten years' hard labour would do a woman her age in, no one having sympathy, a cheer going up in the gallery as her sentence was passed, her shouting out a torrent of abuse at judge and jury not helping her cause.

Old Ma Pirie to the last.

Gustav Wengler was a different matter entirely, presented by his Edinburgh lawyer as a lunatic, and with ample evidence. Dunstan hadn't managed to kill him but had damaged his vocal cords beyond repair, Wengler able to speak only at so soft and low a register it was hard for the court to hear him, a problem made worse by Wengler's decision – possibly at his lawyer's instigation – to speak only in Latin, a fact that infuriated everyone. Sholto was brought in to interpret, at which point Wengler switched to ancient Greek – learned aged fifteen so he could read Euclid's Elements in its original language – when even Sholto gave up.

Then it was Matthias's turn to stand and talk on Wengler's behalf – though only under duress, and only because Jed and the lawyer forced his hand – giving a sworn statement listing Wengler's numerous contributions to the advancement of mathematics, physics and astronomy, ending by stating that – if the court would agree – he would personally guarantee that Wengler would remain under permanent house arrest on Havengore and make sure he never again crossed the water from his island for any other reason than that he'd died and needed burying. The court agreed, deeming Gustav Wengler an irredeemable madman despite Matthias's words, in fact precisely because of Matthias's words, which put Wengler's intellect so far beyond their own he patently inhabited a different universe and good luck to him, as long as he stayed as far away from them as possible. They did add a codicil to this arrangement of domestic house arrest, all of the opinion that should the Danish authorities choose their own path of prosecution for the death of Kurti Griffen, then no one would protest against it.

And thus they washed their hands.

CHAPTER 40

AND SO HE CRIES

Matthias was peerie-headed, all at odds, overwhelmed by Orla's skill and kindness in tending first Hugh and then Gustav Wengler – whether the latter deserved it or no. She and he had given their statements on day one of the trial, after which he'd been eager to get away, offering Orla to come back with him, she agreeing; a small time shared on the small cart as they travelled, speaking little, Orla shining with the chance of her new life now that Dunstan and old Ma were done for, talking about how Malcolm and the boys could come back home and they could all start again, despite her knowing it could never be so, Malcolm practically spelling it out for her years ago when he'd said he was taking all his fish in with the McGilligans at Wick. Still, she'd hung on so long to the illusion of husband and sons coming home it was hard to let go and kept popping from her lips at every turn.

Once back at Matthias's, Orla started preparing a celebratory meal for the others due back the following evening, sending Matthias running up and down the village to exchange the latest trial news for a bit of sage and parsley, some of the good pepper they'd only ever got from the smugglers, Orla bustling all the while around his kitchen, as if she belonged. And oh God, how he wished she did, loneliness crashing down on him like a collapsing wall. He spent the following day wandering aimlessly about the mines, afraid to be alone with her, all he could think about being what he didn't have, the inkling he'd already had with Jed's arrival becoming stronger now with every day. He wanted family, wanted to be a part of other people's lives and for theirs to be a part of his; certain he couldn't slip back into his old life, but no idea where to go from here.

Θ

Orla was standing by the sink, washing out a pan, when she saw Matthias return from his errands. He hesitated a moment before crossing the yard and coming in.

'Will you sit?' she asked. 'Take a cup of tea?'

'I cannot,' said Matthias, suddenly formal, taking off his cap, bringing a letter from his pocket and holding it up, chewing the inside of his lips. He'd done some digging since Orla had arrived and had the answers, but not ones Orla would want to hear. 'I've had it a couple of days,' he said. 'I know I shouldn't have kept it from you, but I did. It's about your husband. About Malcolm...'

'It tells you he's a bad sort,' Orla interrupted calmly, 'that he's working for the McGilligans who are notorious smugglers in the north, and you don't want to break the news to me.'

Matthias started with surprise and Orla moved across the room, taking Matthias by the arm, pulling him down so the two of them were sitting side by side at his table.

'I already know it,' she said quietly. 'I think I've known it a long time, deep inside, sitting there like a toad in the dark that won't come up until it's poked or until someone goes looking for it. And you went looking, didn't you?'

Matthias found it hard to speak, her nearness too much to bear, exacerbated by the possibility occasioned by what she'd said.

'I looked,' he managed: strangled words, tangled emotions, 'but only because I wanted to tell you good things, Orla. I couldn't bear that you were so unhappy. I simply couldn't bear it.'

He meant every word, and Orla put out her hand and took his in her own, as Matthias – the kindest man she'd ever met – closed his eyes and wept.

CHAPTER 41

TIGER TAIGA

'Strange days,' said Sholto on the night they got back from the trial, where both he and Brogar had been required to give statements along with the rest.

'Strange indeed,' Brogar replied, casually picking at his teeth with a sharpened stick. The mutton Orla had prepared had been exquisite, flavoured with a myriad of herbs she appeared to have conjured out of nowhere, and the butter-cooked potatoes were just as good, far better than anything they'd tasted since they'd been here.

'She's a resourceful woman, that Orla,' Sholto added, glancing at Brogar, 'don't you think?'

'I think the whole of Scotland's awash with them,' Brogar said. 'Can't seem to turn a corner without tripping over one or another.'

Sholto kept his silence a while, completely at home in this barn, Brogar by his side, nowhere else in the world he'd rather be, but something needed saying, questions that had grown in him the few months he'd been with Brogar but afraid until now to ask.

'Do you miss the company of women?' he said slowly, glad the lamp was turned away from him, his face in shadow.

Brogar let out a short laugh. 'Can't say I've noticed. Don't overestimate their powers of companionship, Sholto. I've known plenty, and there's plenty I can do without.'

Sholto blushed. He'd never talked so intimately with Brogar before, or with anyone come to that.

'I didn't mean like that,' he said. 'I meant more like… well, that's to say… I meant…'

Brogar flicked his toothpick aside with his thumbnail and looked over at Sholto. Despite the gloomy interior of the barn he could see Sholto's pale skin had become hot and uncomfortable and Brogar shook his head.

'In our line of work, friend, having relationships is not easy. Or rather,' Brogar corrected himself, 'there are plenty of outlets if you want to go looking for them, just none you might consider long term. So what's brought all this on? Are you reconsidering the job? Do you want home to Norway to find yourself a wife, a swarm of podgy children who can never get enough of you?'

Sholto's turn now to let out a snort of derisive laughter.

'Lord, no!' he said quickly. 'That's not what I want at all, far from it. It's just that seeing Matthias here and how he lives, and how he was with Orla tonight, well… it set me to thinking.'

Brogar nodded. He'd seen it too, the way Matthias could hardly look Orla in the eye, the way he softened at the edges whenever she was close to him, the slight shake to his hands as he took a bowl of food from her, nodding his thanks, unable to get out a single word.

'Their world is different from ours,' Brogar said. 'We're free to choose our own path, go where we want, do whatever we like. But women are not like us, at least not many. Sooner or later they're doomed to push out progeny, and that will do for them every time, for there's no going back once it's done. Orla's a prime example,'

Brogar went on, nodding towards the barn door and Matthias's house beyond. 'She's had a terrible time of it, living with old Ma Pirie and Dunstan,' Brogar said. 'We could have walked away, but she can't. She's family, Sholto, and she won't leave if there's a chance of them coming back.'

Sholto nodded. The heat in his face had subsided and, as embarrassed as he was to broach this area of human relationships, Brogar had given him the answers he required.

'So there's no in between,' Sholto said.

'Not with any ease,' Brogar replied. 'Twenty years I've been working for the Company and I've never regretted a second of it. But if you've doubts, Sholto, then now is the time to turn back.'

'I'll not go back,' Sholto said stoutly, *not while you're alive and kicking*, he thought, but did not say out loud.

'Thank God for that,' Brogar replied jovially. 'So maybe we can at last get down to some proper work, now we've successfully brought another murderer to book and solved the riddle of humankind.'

And that was all Sholto needed to hear. He'd never been much fussed with women, occasionally troubled by his lack of interest that had only increased since he'd come to work with Brogar when his life had suddenly been given a new dimension, one filled with colour and adventure and endless possibilities. He'd pondered previously what it all meant and how he would cope, how Brogar had coped all these years, and he'd wondered more so since he'd met Matthias and the monk-like way the man lived his life, Matthias doing as Sholto had done previously: filling every unoccupied second of his life with learning, books and business. But he'd not been slow to recognise Matthias's behaviour changing since Orla entered his life, no matter so peripherally, and that Matthias was teetering on the edge of an unnamed cliff, suddenly aware that his life was lacking, just as Sholto had the moment he'd been given the chance to leave his own little dungeon behind. Furthermore, it was clear to all that Matthias treated Jed more like a long lost son than a visiting scholar, and Sholto thought how much better, how much fuller, all their lives would be – Matthias's, Jed's and Orla's – if they teamed up into a single familial unit. It brought to mind Aileen, Simmy and Harald – another triad far stronger together than they were apart, seeming to need each other to make their individual lives complete.

But Sholto felt no urge to follow in their footsteps. He was with Brogar now, and knew he was on his right path after half a lifetime living half a life, as Matthias still was, and he was sad for the man. A brief taste of happiness was a wonderful thing, but not if it was snatched away with no hope of recovery when Jed and Orla left. Too sad for Sholto, and so he switched to an entirely different topic of conversation.

'Do you think there's any hope of Dunstan's sentence being commuted?' he asked. 'I know you brought up the possibility of transportation when you spoke to the court, but do you really think that might be an option?'

Brogar clicked his tongue. 'I doubt it,' he said, 'not after they heard the details of Archie's death and him trying to strangle Wengler, not to mention blasting Hugh in the face, even if it was an accident.'

A couple of tawny owls commenced a timely exchange of tu-whit tu-whooing somewhere close by and Brogar tipped his head towards the sound.

'Hear that?' he said.

'I do,' Sholto replied. 'But what of Dunstan? And Wengler, come to that, who's not only going to be set free but sent back to the only life he ever wanted.'

'We're not their judges, Sholto,' Brogar said. 'It's just like those owls. One man does one thing, another answers in kind. Out in Primorye, on the border between Russia and China, the insects are more vicious than the worst of the mosquitoes on the Norland lakes. The Chinese call the place *shuhai*, the forest sea, and anyone condemned of murder there is simply stripped naked and strapped to a tree. Two days later, he's dead. Sometimes there's nothing left of him at all, because a tiger has come out of the forest and eaten him head to toe.'

Sholto recoiled. 'But that's vile, Brogar. Killing someone is one thing, torturing him to death is quite another. It would make the one who did it as bad as the man who committed the crime in the first place.'

'How so?' Brogar answered easily. 'It's the law of survival, and survival – at least in a place like Primorye, where it's hot as a jungle in summer, and minus forty below in the winter – is all you've got to hang on to.'

'And there's tigers living there?' Sholto was incredulous.

'There are,' Brogar said, 'ones who can kill a man with a single swipe of their paw and leave nothing behind but a spot of blood, a few footprints, and the boots the man was standing in because for some reason they don't like eating boots; and usually the feet are still inside. Often the only thing left to bury.'

Sholto blinked. He'd seen a dog snuffling and digging its way down into a warren, coming back to the surface with a tiny rabbit quickly dispatched by crunching off its head and then proceeding to rip at the rest until there was hardly a scrap of fur left. The idea of a man being stalked and entirely consumed by a tiger was terrible, being disarticulated limb from limb, maybe still alive while some of it was going on…

Too much.

'So Dunstan deserves what he's got coming? Is that what you're saying?' Sholto said slowly. 'But what about Wengler? Where's the justice in all this? Where's the balance?'

Brogar didn't immediately reply. Everything he'd said to Sholto was true. He'd been there when it happened, spending a winter in Primorye a decade or so back. The inhabitants of the place had been sparse and few between, spending most of their time – depending on the time of year – fur-hunting, keeping bees and collecting pine-nuts until, on the twenty first of December, just before Christmas, a tiger attacked a hunter, Brogar turning up the following morning with the hunter's friends for a bit of a shindig to celebrate the season. As they approached the man's cabin they'd heard the roaring of that tiger somewhere not too far away in the unnavigable thicket of trees, his heart chilling at the sound, his blood becoming sluggish in his veins so he found it hard to move. The others stopped moving too, until that terrible sound stopped and not long afterwards they spotted the scrappy remains of Ilya Trush and his dogs: a few tatters of cloth and fur, a broken rifle, Ilya's sweaty feet inside his even sweatier boots, three yards apart, the left from the right. Men were always so convinced of their superiority, at least in towns where they were barricaded inside their walls; but out there, on the taiga, in the forest sea, men were just like any other animal: fair game to those larger, stealthier and more deadly than they were themselves, even with their guns.

'The strong will always take the weak,' Brogar said a minute later, when Sholto had almost forgotten what they'd been talking about. 'It's the law of the world,' he added, 'and so it's always been, and if there's one thing you need to remember if you work any longer for the Company and with me, Sholto, then remember that law, because sometimes that's all there is.'

CHAPTER 42

AND EVERYTHING CHANGES, ONCE AGAIN

In the couple of weeks gone since Dunstan's trial, Brogar had set to work with a dedication and stratagem Jed greatly admired. Previously, he'd gone at the same task with equal fervour, his plan being to map out the mines, making notes off all the different minerals the mining of the ore threw up, marking out squares of land with strings and pegs where such minerals had been found, checking on each of these every day, digging at them methodically with trowel and hammer, but coming up empty every time.

Not so Brogar, who asked Matthias where the original samples had been discovered, Matthias telling him what he'd said to Jed and that he simply didn't know, not for sure. Brogar had not been discouraged, but took quite a different approach to Jed's.

'You've done a thorough job,' Brogar said, as Jed pointed out his peg-and-string squares, 'but you have to remember that minerals don't just pop up out of the earth for no reason and finding one sample in one place doesn't mean it originated there. Think of the glaciers that once covered the whole of Scotland, scouring deep between and over the mountains, dragging rocks with them over tens, sometimes hundreds of miles. Minerals, like plants, grow where the underlying situation is just right for them to shift from one form into another. And Strontianite the mineral, Strontia the oxide or Strontium the element, will be no different. I've read the reports of the first two known findings, and they have certain markers in common…'

⊖

Sholto took no part in Brogar's looking. Geology was Brogar's field, Sholto's duty writing up whatever Brogar found and sending it back to the Company in a succinct and understandable manner, along with the statistical probability of whether or not his discoveries might merit further investigation. Which, in Company speak, meant: would it make them any money? Was it commercially viable as a product or mining enterprise and worth them expending any more time and effort to heave it out of the earth?

Sholto rubbed his hands together. It was cold, and he was still thinking hard about all that had happened, and more specifically about the diverse sentences meted out to Dunstan and Wengler and the implicit injustice of it, never mind tigers in the snow. He turned his head, looking out over the Sunart towards the startling monuments of Wengler's White Cathedral rising high above the grey granite of his island and, as he did so, he realised there was still one more mystery to be solved, and one more pot of justice to be poured out because of it, and that it was all to do with the ring Wengler had been so desperate to find and that everyone had entirely forgotten about since, himself included. There was a bit of digging to be done, not like Brogar's digging in the earth, but digging all the same, and Sholto rubbed his hands again, suddenly realising where and how he might find answers.

He needed to speak to Oswald, get off a couple of messages, get over to the island and back again. Jed was already on Havengore with Gilligan, getting the place aired and stocked, Wengler due for return as soon as an armed guard became available. He'd set off for the village when Matthias came running from the mines waving his arms.

'I've just come from a meeting with the lawyer!' Matthias shouted eagerly. 'It's a miracle! You've got to come back to the house!'

Matthias grabbed hard at Sholto's shoulder and tugged him forcibly in. 'I need a witness,' he gasped. 'In fact I need two, and soon as possible. The lawyer's on my heels. I'm afraid I left him standing, because as soon as he sits himself down at this table I need everything to be ready. And that includes you.'

Orla emerged from Hugh's room at the commotion.

'How's the lad doing, Orla?' Matthias asked, still a little out of breath.

'Well,' Orla said. 'I'm not sure the trip to Fort William did him any good, but he's not too badly for it.'

'Good, good,' Matthias said, motioning both Orla and Sholto to sit down at the table. 'I've such things to tell you I feel I'm about to burst! Can we get some drinks prepared? Perhaps something to eat?'

Orla stood up immediately and took charge of Matthias's small domestic domain.

'Now then,' Matthias said, wiping his brow, but hardly had he spoken than there was a knock on the door and he was up again.

'And here he is!' Matthias said warmly, ushering the newcomer deferentially in: cheeks pinched pink by the cold, moustaches wilted at the ends and beginning to freeze over.

'This is the lawyer from Edinburgh,' he said, unnecessarily, for they all remembered him from the trial though were a little surprised he was still hanging around a couple of weeks later. 'Tell them what you just told me,' Matthias went on, excitement evident in every limb. Andrew Fitzsimons, representative of MacWilliam, MacWilliam and Fitzsimons, acting lawyers for the Wengler family, coughed. He wasn't moved by Matthias's pleasure, had always been dry as a cinder and proud of it. He put his fingers to the ends of his moustaches to knock away the melting ice, twirl them back into some kind of order. He drew up the briefcase he'd been carrying and plonked it on the table for all to see and began to undo the clasps. Matthias had not sat down but was drumming his fingers on the table, eager for the man to get on. Andrew Fitzsimons took the hint.

'There's some paperwork to get through, and some clauses I needed to verify before I brought the news, but the gist of it is this: when the older Wengler died the rights to the Galena Ore Mines were left in trust, him not wanting the mines' disposition to be left to the unreliable notions of his son; and now the younger Wengler has been convicted of a capital crime the rights revert completely and utterly to the named executor of the trust, as do the deeds of the island named Havengore, and that person is Matthias McQuat.'

Matthias could not stay still. He slapped Andrew Fitzsimons on the back, a gesture the lawyer did not appreciate, not that Matthias noticed.

'I told you it was a miracle,' Matthias said, quieter now, as if by speaking of it too loudly he might jinx it away, right at the last moment.

'All we need do to initiate the relevant clause,' Andrew Fitzsimons forged on, 'is for two witnesses to declare that this is indeed Matthias McQuat and he is in a position to undertake the bequest, that all has been explained and understood; and lastly that the case against Gustav Wengler the younger was true and fair.'

'Well, my word,' Sholto said, standing up and flinging an arm around Matthias's shoulders. 'But that is good news, Matthias. The best of news! Tell me where to sign and I'll sign it, for I've never met a person more fit for the purpose than Matthias McQuat.'

Matthias beamed, and then glanced shyly towards Orla.

'And you, Orla,' he asked. 'Will you sign too? Will you be my second witness?'

Matthias looked expectantly at Orla, as did Sholto who noted how well she looked, how straight her back, had a brief worry she might be illiterate, a notion dispelled by her next words.

'I would be delighted,' she said, 'and not to worry, sirs,' she added, 'I know fine well how to read and to write and can put down my name with the best of them.'

Θ

The deed was done, Andrew Fitzsimons keen as a newly sharpened knife to get away, everyone breathing a sigh of relief at his departure for no one spends time with lawyers if they can help it.

'I can hardly tell you how pleased I am, Matthias,' Sholto said, the moment Andrew Fitzsimons was out the door, 'but I'm afraid I can't stay. There's a few errands I must run and I need to speak to Oswald, and maybe Hesketh too. Can we hold off celebrating until I get back?'

Matthias nodded. He was so happy he wasn't quite sure what to do with himself.

'Go,' he said. 'But please don't tell anyone yet what has happened. And if you see Oswald and Hesketh ask them to come back here to do the thing properly, for none of this would have happened without any of you.'

'Shall we say around six?' Sholto asked.

'That would be perfect timing,' Matthias answered, looking suddenly over at Orla. 'If that's all right with you?'

Orla smiled and my Lord, Matthias thought, she looks like an anemone that has just been washed over by the tide and opened up, her expression so exactly reflecting his own frame of mind that he sat down in the chair Sholto had just vacated.

'It will do just fine,' she said. 'Six o'clock it is.'

CHAPTER 43

ANOTHER SHIFT IN THE EQUATION

Sholto caught up with Andrew Fitzsimons as he regained the cart he'd had waiting, flinging himself and his briefcase in with vigour.

'Hold up!' Sholto shouted, just as the cart was about to pull away. 'Hold up!'

The boy in charge of the cart took heed, much to the lawyer's annoyance, Sholto running up beside them, clutching a bundle of letters in one hand, holding the side of the cart with the other to keep it still.

'I'm sorry to intrude,' Sholto said, 'but please, Mr Fitzsimons, if you're away immediately back to the city then I beg that you will take these missives with you. I can't explain now, but rest assured they have to do with Gustav Wengler and that I mean to make sure he doesn't profit from his crimes. These letters will do just that, and the faster they're delivered the better for it. Myself and Brogar Finn, we work for the Pan-European Mining Company. They've an office newly set up in Edinburgh and will take care of any costs.'

'I know of them,' Fitzsimons said, taking Sholto's letters, looking briefly at the persons and places to whom they'd been addressed. His entire professional life was based on carrying out instructions for people and purposes he would never have full knowledge of and had never possessed an iota of curiosity about either. He did what he was told and that for him was the perfect way to live his life.

'Very well, Mr McKay,' Fitzsimons said, unfastening his briefcase, slipping Sholto's messages inside. 'Rest assured I will send these on as soon as I am able.'

'As I said, the Company will bear the costs, and if not I will pay them myself,' Sholto added.

'You will not,' was Fitzsimons curt reply. 'If these letters have to do with the Wengler estate then it is entirely the estate's duty to shoulder any payments due. All I need from you is a signed statement about the contents.'

'That I will do,' Sholto said. 'I will draft it immediately. It may take some time to reach you…'

'This, sir, is the worst backwater I have ever had the misfortune to be sent to,' said the lawyer, 'so I certainly won't hold you to time.'

And with that the man knocked his hand against the boards, the lad whipped up the horses and they were off.

Θ

Brogar went down on his knees for the twenty seventh time that morning. He'd taken his own advice and started looking further up the valley from the central hub of the working mine. He'd caught sight of a small nodule of rock crystal no bigger than his thumbnail, but Brogar was thorough and cautious as always when out in the field and took his eyeglass out to study the sample closely. He looked at it this way and that and then took up a trowel and dug away the surplus peat and soil from around it, and what he saw made him catch his breath. The small portion of the mineral to be seen from above was only a tenth of what lay below, and it was beautiful. It had none of the dendritic spines he'd noted from sketches of the samples already found here, he saw instead white extrusions like solidified bubbles, but the lustre of it, the purity of its colour made him certain. Minerals were like that, turning up in one guise one day in one situation, and quite another the next. He carefully dug the nugget up and held it in his palm. He would need to get a chip of it under a microscope but knew in his bones this was it, the moment geologists like Brogar truly lived for. And such a smile he smiled, knowing that here was something so rare, so precious, it had only been discovered twice before, and only here – in the obscurity of a lead mine on the very edge of Scotland – and nowhere else, the whole world over.

$$\Theta$$

Sholto got to Oswald Harlow's manse only to learn from his sullen and somewhat alarmingly named neighbour, William Gotobed, that Oswald had left a while earlier, gone for Ockle. Frustrated, he went on to Hesketh's, found him sitting on his bench – a long slab of gneiss worn smooth in the centre by all the years of him sitting there looking up and down the Sound, telescope in hand, for signs of flags being raised to summon him into action.

'How do,' Hesketh said amiably as Sholto approached. 'Any news?' he added, Sholto sitting down beside him, taking in the view which was truly wonderful: sea, sky, heathery islands and isthmuses as far as the eye could see. An otter was basking in the meagre sunshine in the loch below, stomach-up, tapping an oyster shell held in one paw with a stone held in the other, employing its exposed belly as a kind of anvil. The snow hadn't gone and the sun was not particularly warm, but the sky was of the deepest blue, and the water lapping a few yards from their feet so clear Sholto could see every stone, every frond of weed, every scuttle of every crab as it made its way from one hiding place to another.

'I need to get over to Havengore,' Sholto said. 'How's the tide running?'

Nobody could have accused Hesketh of being a busybody, but like everyone else he needed to know what the situation was with the mines they were all so reliant on now Wengler had been convicted of the murder of Kurti Griffen and the attempted murder of Simmy McRailty, and also how Hugh was getting on and what the devil Orla Pirie was still doing at Matthias's house. Everyone was gossiping about it, but no one knew anything for certain. And so Hesketh did not answer Sholto directly.

'Any news?' he repeated instead.

Sholto gazed over at the White Cathedral, unfazed by Hesketh's curiosity, understanding.

'A lot,' he said, 'but I can tell you everything once we're underway.'

'Right enough then,' Hesketh said, levering himself up. 'Let's be gone.'

Θ

Oswald was not too far from Ockle. Wengler might have been found by a court of his peers to be of uncertain mind but Oswald knew there was no mind more certain than Gustav Wengler's and was damned well not going to let him get his murdering hands on the sundial. Unknowingly, he'd come up with the same plan Sholto had, namely that if he could get the sundial into the chapel then he could legitimately claim it as church property and therefore subject to canon law. He knew he could count on Harald's strong arms to help with that, Harald having been slipped from the noose by Dunstan's confession, which was Oswald's own miracle of the month. He didn't understand all that had happened, why Dunstan hadn't chosen to drop Harald right in it but Jesus God, he was more pleased for it than he could say.

He was arrested in his task by running into Simmy McRailty, back on her feet after several weeks careful nursing on Aileen's part.

'So you're back in the pink?' Oswald asked.

'I am, Reverend,' Simmy answered brightly. 'All stitched up like a patchwork quilt and hoping someone could take me over the way to Strontian.'

Oswald hesitated and then obliged, hoisting her carefully up on his horse behind him, turning them all around and heading back; his own task could wait another day.

'And what of the croft?' Oswald asked after a while. 'Is the Factor fine with it all?'

'He is, thanks to you!' Simmy answered quickly. 'Don't know what you said in your letter to him and the laird but they've agreed we can work off the debts as we can.'

'Extraordinary circumstances, was what I told them,' Oswald explained. 'And I don't think they'll ever come across any circumstances more extraordinary than yours.'

He smiled, glad that his word had counted with the Riddell family, the same Riddells he'd gone up against with the Floating Chapel.

'So, Harald and Aileen. Have they fixed a date yet?'

Simmy jiggled behind him, her small arms releasing his waist as she answered.

'Oh but yes! In fact that's part of the reason I was coming over to Strontian, to let you know to do it the first Sunday you can.'

'It will be my absolute pleasure,' Oswald said, smiling into the early afternoon. 'And are you to stay with them?'

'Of course!' Simmy replied, happy as the first lark rising in spring. 'They're already over at da's house getting it fixed up so Aileen can move about like she does in her own place. She's pretty good at it already, and she's only been there a few days.'

'She's an extraordinary woman,' Oswald said.

'She is that,' Simmy agreed, tightening her hands about his waist again. 'And she says I'm to carry on with my learning, if that's all right with you.'

'It's more than all right, Simmy,' Oswald said, letting one hand go from the reins, squeezing Simmy's small hand in his own. 'And long overdue.'

He cleared his throat, a little choked, wondering how best to broach the subject bringing him over to Ockle in the first place, a journey now abandoned. Simmy had always been a direct and intuitive child but he waited another few minutes before he got it out.

'How do you think the Ockle folk would feel if I brought the sundial into the confines of the chapel?' he asked.

Simmy bit her lip, considering her reply. She didn't think the Ockle folk would care in the slightest what he did with the sundial, but she liked it where it was. On the other hand she knew Oswald wouldn't contemplate such a removal unless he had good reason, and was not oblivious to what that reason might be.

'They'll not mind much,' she said. 'Mr McKay already said someone's going to take it away from us.'

Oswald nodded.

'They are,' he said. 'But if we have it inside the chapel then it will be so much the harder, and I'll keep hold of it as long as I can, Simmy, because I know how much you value it. If you still do, that is, after what happened.'

'Oh all the more so!' Simmy said almost before Oswald had

finished speaking, and allowed another few minutes to pass before she spoke again.

'Do you know that when I was lying there I saw all the stars scattered above me even though it wasn't night?'

Oswald hadn't known this, but he'd met plenty of folk on their death beds who'd seen similar things: dark tunnels, bright lights of varying descriptions.

'I think,' he told Simmy, as they clopped along their way, 'that God sees fit to give everyone one last glimpse of something beautiful before they die; not to aggravate them but to reassure them, to remind them He knows them through and through and will make their passing good.'

Simmy waited, absorbing the words, before she spoke again.

'I thought other things too,' she said quietly. 'About the sundial, about all the words I'd written down in my notebook when I did that project for you. Do you remember?'

'Of course,' Oswald said, remembering also Sholto's accusation that he'd never given it much mind, which was true, given that it had been around the same time Fraser McRailty stepped in and made any further forwarding of Simmy's intellectual development impossible.

'There's something I never told you,' Simmy went on, unusually subdued. 'I knew Harald was in trouble and I didn't want to get him into any more, and he only did it to help Aileen but Aileen told me she didn't need helping and that I was to do with it whatever I thought best.'

Simmy's sudden rush of words did not bamboozle Oswald.

'You mean the ring,' he stated. 'I know all about it, Simmy, as do the folk down at Matthias's; no need for secrecy any more.'

Simmy blinked behind him, not that Oswald could see it.

'There's more,' she added quietly.

'Tell me,' Oswald said, hoping it wasn't more of Harald's misdeeds that might yet lead to his arrest and condemnation and tip this small family back into destitution, Simmy's next words almost jolting him right off his horse.

'We know where it belongs,' she said simply. 'Aileen figured it out.'

Oswald could not have been more surprised and let out a laugh into the late afternoon, Simmy joining in, the two of them collectively spurring their heels into the horse's flanks and hurrying him on.

CHAPTER 44

THE BAD DYING OF THE ALMOST DEAD

The soldiers from Fort William returned from their fruitless search for the Piries' smuggling accomplices, met by the Provost who was already at the barracks having been informed they were on their way. He welcomed them warmly, singled out the six-strong guard he needed and explained their duties, adding a coda.

'I don't want it made a big deal of,' he said. 'People here know who the Piries are but they've never heard of the man Dunstan murdered. I want them to be made an example of, of course, but I don't want any huge song and dance about it, and I certainly don't want Dunstan attracting some penny balladeer with a witty remark right at the end about how good the smuggling life is. Very bad for business that would be, considering all these new folk coming to visit our town on the steamers coming up the Sound from Glasgow. I want it done quick and fast and without any fuss.'

'We can do that, certainly,' the captain of the guard replied. 'But can we give the men some time to rest? If we leave it another hour or so it will be almost dark, and by the time anyone has come out at the noise it will already be over.'

The Provost of Fort William nodded, making his double chins ripple with the effort.

'All right then. It will be as you say. Everything will be made ready, just give the word.'

Θ

Oswald and Simmy joined the track leading down from the mines to the village, seeing an exuberant Brogar Finn running a few yards over the heather to meet them.

'Well, glad tidings to the travellers!' Brogar said amiably as he fell into step with their nag, Simmy gripping Oswald's waist a little tighter, finding this stranger's presence intimidating and intrusive, given that the light had begun to fade and the scar on his face turned purple in the cold.

'Simmy,' Oswald said jovially, 'meet Brogar Finn, and Brogar Finn, meet Simmy.'

And then the face that Simmy had found so immediately frightening broke into a wondrous grin that had her smiling back because she knew the name and that he'd been instrumental in keeping Harald out of gaol and catching the man who'd almost thrown her into the pit beside her da.

'Aha!' Brogar said warmly. 'The famous Miss Simmy! I've heard much about you from both Oswald here and my assistant Sholto. Both think very highly of you, you know.'

Simmy blushed, and couldn't get out a word.

'We're just over from Ockle, Mr Finn,' Oswald said, 'and if I may say so you seem in unusually high spirits.'

'I have every reason to be,' Brogar replied, 'for I'm pretty damned sure I've found an example of the elusive element that has been named for your village.'

'We've better news, Mr Finn,' Oswald said lightly.

'Brogar,' Brogar interrupted, 'call me Brogar from here on in. But what better news can you possibly have than my own?'

Oswald took a breath. Simmy had told him everything on their journey over, about her bringing out the ring at last, about Aileen taking it in her fingers, about Aileen feeling and recognising the grooves on the ring's inner surface that Simmy had taken to be damage from the long time it had been in the water.

'Simmy's figured out the sundial,' Oswald announced dramatically, 'and the ring Gustav Wengler was so keen to get his hands on,' which statement had Brogar raising his eyebrows.

'Have you now?' he asked, looking curiously up at Oswald's gaunt face and Simmy's, half hidden behind Oswald's back but plainly small and round and blushing, right down to the roots.

'There's no need for sarcasm,' Oswald said sharply, misinterpreting Brogar's words, straightening himself in the saddle, ready to protect Simmy with everything he had available to him. Brogar held up his hands.

'No need to fear me on that score,' he said, 'I'm not the one you'll have to convince. And now I'm off! Keep up with me if you can!'

And then Brogar was leaping away from them, bounding his way down the track towards Matthias's house.

'It's a wonder the man doesn't slip and break his neck,' Oswald commented.

'More of a wonder no one's done it for him, with a face like that,' Simmy said back, smiling broadly, their horse choosing that moment to slip on the ice, almost tumbling the two of them to the ground.

'All right, Simmy?' Oswald asked with concern as he righted himself in the saddle, worried the sudden jolt might have ripped her newly healed wounds, the two of them watching Brogar running on down the track, the two of them watching as Brogar slipped and went down on the ice like a sack of spuds but made no mind of it, got up straightaway and was off again, leaping on as if nothing had happened.

'Well, he's agility if not looks,' Oswald said, as they went on a little slower than before.

'Maybe,' Simmy answered, 'or maybe he's just the kind of man who doesn't care if he falls.'

'Wise, as always,' Oswald said, and Simmy smiled, the start of a long season of smiling, deciding she would be just like Brogar, running full pelt towards her goals, not caring how often or badly she fell as long as she got there. And just like that, Brogar changed another life, the latest in a long line of changing; not that Brogar ever knew, nor would have cared if he did.

Θ

Dunstan Pirie was in a stone-walled cell barely large enough for him to walk two yards before he had to turn himself around and walk the same two yards back again. His bed was a slab of rock, cantilevered on chains from the wall, and a blanket that gave him just enough warmth to keep him from dying but not enough to keep him warm, make him sleep easy, which he would never do again. He was the only prisoner here as far as he could tell. No sign of Wengler, and old Ma taken away to who knew where to serve out the sentence she would never see the end of.

He kept his eyes on the tiny window that was at surface level, watching the sporadic passage of people's feet. It was a while after the trial, but he'd no real notion how long, not being one to scratch lines in the wall as others had done before him, their ragged initials presumably the only scrap of them left in the world. He'd always known it would come to this. He'd harboured dreams of getting out, of getting old, of getting enough money together to tell his ma to shove herself headfirst into the potato cellar and never come out again; but he'd always known, in his deepest down, that it would end like this. He wanted to believe that he was sanguine, that he was of no care one way or the other, but that was not the case, not now it was so near the end. An awful fear had started creeping under his skin like mites that would not stop their burrowing, laying their eggs, breeding more of their kin to plague him, an unspecified panic growing with every passing day. He was even wishing the cleric from the monks – his only visitor – would come back again, just for the chance to speak to another human being, no matter what he said in return, which hadn't gone well the first time round.

'My Lord is your Lord,' the man had said, 'and can forgive you if you will submit to Him. He sits in His heaven and sees everything, far worse than you've ever done. All He needs is an apology for wasting the time you've had on His good earth and then you will be shriven.'

'He can go blow smoke up his arse,' Dunstan had replied tersely, never having had regard for preachers of any ilk.

But Jesus, what if the man was right? What if a simple apology could cancel everything out? Brogar had asked him if he wanted to do good things and he actually had, Harald McRailty able to live on when Dunstan would not. It had to count for something.

Θ

Sholto and Hesketh drew up at the island just as Jed and Gilligan were coming down the track to raise the flag.

'Well, that was good timing,' Sholto said, as he stepped out of the boat, Hesketh nodding his head briefly, for Sholto had been as good as his word and told Hesketh everything as they crossed the water, including his plans to keep the sundial from Gustav Wengler and purloin the Astrolabe book while he was about it. It had been Hesketh's idea to mask the true purpose of Sholto's visit with one of concern and rescue instead.

'I was just coming to get you two lads,' Sholto continued casually. 'We didn't want you stuck here overnight. Have you done what was needed doing?'

'We have,' Jed said.

'Everything's thack'n'raip,' Gilligan put in.

'Clean and tidy,' Hesketh interpreted for the others. 'Haven't heard that expression in a while. You must be from the east coast, Gilligan?'

'I am!' Gilligan said happily as he clambered aboard the boat and began chattering away about Kildonan and Solveig McCleery and all the work he used to do for her there.

'Hop in, Jed,' Sholto said. 'I'm just going to give the place a quick once-over and then we'll be off.'

'I'll come with you,' Jed said, a little nervous that their efforts to clean up the long neglected kitchen and bedrooms were to be scrutinised by a third party. He and Gilligan had done their best but Jed wasn't at all sure their cleaning skills would pass muster, and he didn't want Gustav Wengler coming back to his home to find it wanting.

Sholto managed his own muster and smiled a hopefully convincing smile.

'No need to worry, Jed. You stay here. If I'm honest I just want a couple of minutes alone to look over Gustav's monuments. It will be the only proper chance I ever get.'

That was enough for Jed. He and Gilligan had spent the best part of the day doing just that, which was exactly why he thought their actual appointed task might fall short.

'They really are amazing,' Jed said with enthusiasm. 'Do you want me to show you?'

Sholto held up his hand.

'Please don't take offence, Jed,' he said, 'but where amazement is concerned a person is better off on his own.'

Jed understood completely and subsided, and off Sholto went up the track to the house. He didn't have long. Already the light was dimming, but Hesketh had assured him he couldn't be seen from the pier and he went straight into the kitchen and up the stairs and was in the study in a minute. He was seriously impressed by all the books, could have spent a few weeks going through them; he looked at the blackboards, intrigued by the few words there, especially *Titius/Bedrossian* and the depictions of a spiral, a circle and a long rectangular shape that looked like a pillar. He'd always had his doubts about Chaucer's Riddle, the paucity of it as a reason for creating the sundial, let alone Wengler murdering Griffen and almost murdering Simmy just for a look at it. Griffen had done his best to make it sound exciting and alluring and Jed had jumped in with both feet to confirm it. But the discovery of a couple of new planets just didn't cut it. What would Wengler care about finding some extra rocks out there in the solar system? If there were any more there then they'd be found soon enough, telescope and lens design getting better year on year so, Sholto reasoned, there had to be something more. He went to Wengler's desk. Jed had tidied it all into stacks and helpfully left the Astrolabe on top, but that wasn't what caught Sholto's eye. Further down he could see a slim spine and some gold lettering stamped upon it: Ձռռռ'ս Հահռուկ. It couldn't be a coincidence. Armenian on the sundial, Armenian on this book. He pulled it out and started flicking through its pages. He couldn't read Armenian script, though he wouldn't have put it beyond Wengler. And then he stopped short – the text was illustrated, and those illustrations clearly demonstrated the construction of a sundial, and not just any sundial. He quickly flipped to the start of the book and opened it more carefully, astonished to find a long introduction in Danish. He started to read and, as he did, he began to smile, almost laughed out loud but caught himself, glanced briefly at the blackboards nodding in approval, then tucked the book in his pocket. As an afterthought he also took the Astrolabe, though he was more convinced than ever that all it was fit for was chucking on the fire.

He went quickly back down the stairs with a definite sprightliness to his step and stopped briefly at the top of the track leading down to the jetty. Why not actually take a look, while he was here, at Wengler's White Cathedral? He was undoubtedly intrigued, given their provenance and direct connection to the real Havengore, and so he walked towards them, went from the first of the massive monuments to the second and just as well, for here came Jed.

'So sorry,' Jed apologised. 'I know you wanted to look at them alone, but I couldn't stand that I might never see them again. Hesketh told me not to be so selfish, but they're just so incredible.'

Sholto had stopped by the huge pit blown right down into the bedrock, the central pillar rising from its midpoint like a tree bole with its many radiating spokes at ground level. Jed skipped across them with an alacrity that had Sholto's heart pounding.

'Careful, Jed,' he said. 'It's a long way down.'

'I told you he was a genius,' Jed ignored the warning and ran across them, jumping from one to the other, speaking quietly. 'I don't care what he's done. He only killed Griffen because he thought he was standing in his way.'

Sholto shook his head.

'And what if you had been standing in his way, Jed?' Sholto asked. 'Or someone you cared for? Did you ever think on that? Griffen had family, and what are we supposed to tell them?'

Jed jumped down to the ground beside Sholto and stared at his feet.

'There's always sacrifices,' he murmured, 'when science moves on a leap.'

'Discovering a couple of new planets is no leap, Jed,' Sholto said. 'None at all, and certainly not worth killing for.'

He felt the small book in his pocket and could have said more, could have told Jed there and then what was really going on, but he needed more time to study it, winkle out the whole truth and nothing less. But he didn't need to say more, Sholto's words hitting their mark. Wengler had been Jed's inspiration ever since he'd first stumbled upon an article of his in some obscure mathematical journal, but Jed knew Wengler was a tarnished man. His ideas had impressed Jed greatly, his hypotheses so clear, so uncluttered, his mind so focussed; so focussed he'd beaten a man to death with a rock because of them, and what kind of hero was that?

Θ

Dunstan was standing at his window when they came for him. He didn't comprehend what was happening, didn't protest, believed he was being taken from one holding place to another, from Fort William down to Oban or maybe up to Inverness, his guards indicating nothing to the contrary. He turned the corner of the barracks and was brought into its central yard, catching sight of the Provost standing at its centre, black cap upon his head, and his heart went on the gallop, legs collapsing, held up by his escort, his knees dragging against the ground.

'God's sake, man,' one of the soldiers growled. 'Pull yourself together. You're embarrassing yourself.'

Dunstan was having a hard time breathing but he recognised the truth of what the man had said and got himself to standing, back against the pitted wall, trying to hold himself high, Adam's apple bobbing up and down like some demented toy. But he would go out standing, go out right.

'Ready?' said the Provost.

'Ready,' the captain replied, and Dunstan caught the quick movement of the Provost's hand as it went down, and closed his eyes, breathed deeply, the rock behind his head some kind of comfort. Then five rounds went into his chest in a moment, the Provost tutting at the huge leakage of blood he'd not been expecting, the riflemen uncaring, setting down their guns.

Dunstan still had a twitch or two in his body when the soldiers shoved him in a sack a couple of minutes later like so much chicken offal, dropping him into the hole already dug and filling him over, Dunstan finally snuffed out and gone alone into that darkness, just as he'd feared.

CHAPTER 45

AS ALWAYS, ANOTHER BLOODY BOOK

Those not yet in darkness were gathering at Matthias's house, each one met by Hugh who was up and about, happy as a sand flea with his truncated nose and his one good eye – no rancour about the other, whose pupil had turned a milky white like an unseeing moon. First in was Brogar, brimming with his news, next came Oswald and Simmy, Hugh grabbing at the horse's reins – missing a couple of times because he'd not quite got the hang of having just the one eye working – eager to get it stalled and seen to, eager for everyone else getting back too. He'd not long to wait, Sholto arriving with the others from Havengore and soon everyone, including Hugh, was snugged up in the house.

Outside, the snow had begun to fall in whispers, filling in their many footsteps, covering over their many tracks, hiding the disparate directions from whence they'd come. Everyone was sat about the table, excepting Gilligan and Hugh who made themselves comfortable on the rag rug before the fire whilst Orla stood beside them stirring her pots, leaning down to ruffle Hugh's hair every now and then, reminding him to tell her the instant anything about his face or eyes felt tight or dry and needed re-dousing with one or other of her medications, Gilligan poking Hugh in the ribs as she did so.

'Got a new girlfriend?' he chivvied quietly.

'Not likely!' Hugh whispered back, 'but someone has,' and the two of them giggled to see Orla and Matthias exchanging glances they imagined no one else could see.

'So, everyone gathered at last,' Brogar said loudly. 'Exactly the way every adventure should end, although I suspect that for some the adventure is only just beginning.'

Orla had the grace to blush but it wasn't to her that Brogar turned his gaze.

'I know there's a few of us have things to say but let me ask Simmy to start everything rolling.'

Simmy hadn't expected this, but she responded with all the drama Brogar had injected into the moment and made her pronouncement.

'We've figured out how the ring works,' she said. 'Or rather Aileen did. We showed it her last night and it's got kind of marks on its inner surface and the second Aileen felt them, she knew. Said she'd felt something like them before and you'll never guess, but there's another part of the sundial we'd all missed, 'ceptin her.'

Simmy drew out the ring and laid it on the table. Jed put out a hand but Sholto was quicker, picking it up, studying it with fascination, on it the same words as on the book, undoubtedly what the circle represented upon Wengler's boards.

'So, the ring at last,' he said, 'and see here? Just above the lettering? That's an ouroboros, the snake that eats its tail – the sign for infinity...'

He next examined its inner surface that, just as Simmy had said, had been cut with deliberate and exact geometrical grooves.

'Wengler said something in the shed,' Jed said slowly, 'about how the sundial fits into the search for the universe like the ring fits into the sundial.'

'And it does!' Simmy said excitedly, 'that's exactly what it does! We tried it out this morning – that bit Aileen said? Well it's on the underside of the sundial and like two circles, one inside the other, and right at the middle there's a hump like a half moon – only big enough to fit a thumb and finger either side like a tiny cupboard fixing...'

'And just around it is a circle,' Sholto stated, to general amazement, 'just big enough to take this ring.'

'That's it!' Simmy went on. 'And when we put the ring in – well, it took me about ten minutes because I was all upside down and that, and it was really hard to get it into exactly the right place without it falling on top of my face for the millionth time, but anyway, I finally did it and there was a kind of click...'

'Like a magnet,' Sholto said, 'because this ring isn't made from pure gold at all but has several alloys in it to harden it. I can tell from the colour.'

'Exactly,' Simmy agreed, the revelation of it not being pure gold passing her by. 'But that's not the lot of it,' she went on. 'Once it went in and stuck, I put my fingers to the sticky-outy bit and it turned. Went about a quarter, like round a clock and that sort of locked it in. Went another quarter, like down to six, and the first dial around it moved. Went another click around to nine and the second disc moved too.'

Sholto looked hard at the ring and then released it carefully back down upon the table, Jed immediately snatching it up, a little disturbed when Sholto began a small chuckling noise he didn't seem able to stop.

'What's the what?' Brogar interrupted, unused to such behaviour from Sholto but finding it oddly recognisable, akin to his own reaction when he'd finally found the mineral up in the mines.

'Oh my,' Sholto gasped, wiping his eyes, juddering back into normal speech. 'I do apologise, but there's so much to tell, first of which is that the sundial really was created by Titius and his pupil, and I know that pupil's name and why they did it.'

Jed gasped.

'But how? And who?' he asked, the questions tripping up on his tongue. 'Johannes Bode, was it?'

'Not he,' Sholto shook his head, mirth subsiding, 'but it's all in this. I took it from Wengler's study.'

He pulled out a small book and slapped it down, Jed craning his neck to read the title stamped in small gold letters on spine and cover.

'Always a book,' Brogar sighed and shook his head, Jed already speaking over him.

'But whatever language is that?' Jed frowned. 'It's just a load of squiggles.'

'I think it might be Armenian,' Oswald hazarded a guess. 'The first country to accept Christianity as its national religion.'

'And it's like on the ring,' Simmy added, her blood running fast with excitement, making her newly healed scars tingle.

'That it is,' Sholto beamed, 'it's exactly like on the ring.'

'It could be ancient bloody Greek for all I care,' Brogar said, 'but where's the what of it?'

'The body of the book is written in Armenian, not one of my languages,' Sholto explained, 'but that's not important right now. What's important is the introduction, which is in Danish and signed by one *Johannes Titius, resident of the Round Tower in Denmark*, in praise of the book's author...'

'Titius's pupil!' Jed exclaimed, the thrum of discovery overtaking him.

'His pupil,' Sholto agreed. 'One David Bedrossian, former astronomer to the Danish Authorities who had just resigned his post in favour of being admitted as a teacher in one of the schools of the Tatev Monastery in his native Armenia.'

'And?' Brogar demanded, still not getting it and not alone in that.

'And,' Sholto went on, 'in Titius's lengthy introduction – of which I've read some but not yet all, but enough to get the gist – Titius gives a potted history of this Tatev Monastery that has apparently remained on the same site since the ninth century, and one of its most remarkable and ancient aspects is an octagonal pillar, still standing, erected in AD 904, twenty five foot high, called the Gavazan or staff. An extraordinary feat of engineering, constructed so that even during earthquakes it will tilt and shake before settling back into place. And some posit – as Titius's preface is very keen to point out – that originally it was conceived as the gnomon of a giant sundial.'

'Oh my!' Matthias put his hand to his mouth. 'But… what does it all mean?'

'It means, Matthias,' Sholto carried on, 'that what we have here – the ring, the sundial and this book with them, is priceless! Absolutely priceless!'

'Priceless?' Oswald was the first to ask. 'How so? The sundial is certainly elaborate but…'

'Chaucer's Riddle,' Jed said before he could stop himself, tailing off, glancing at Sholto, recalling his rebuke on the island about what it was worth, which was precisely nothing, or rather nothing worth a man's life and certainly not Sholto's apparent turnaround.

'Ah well,' Sholto said, tapping his fingers lightly against the table.

'In fact you're right, Jed, to a point. But the Riddle is not what we thought it was, not at all, and it's not the sundial that's priceless, but the possible discoveires, and of course the joke.'

'What are you talking about?' Jed asked, completely and utterly confounded.

'I'm talking,' Sholto said, all humour now gone, 'about a man who was spurned in his lifetime, ridiculed by his peers, his theories torn to shreds and then appropriated by his greatest supporter – Johannes Bode – who went on, by the way, as the preface points out, to become the director of the Berlin Observatory and took over Titius's work so completely that, wrong as it was, his Numerical Relationships are now known as Bode's Law, Titius not coming into it. But Titius had another influential friend, his old pupil David Bedrossian, who wangled him into the Round Tower, the greatest astronomical observatory in the world and with a library comparable to none, at least in the field of astronomical mathematics. And, like your Riddle has always posited, Jed, he figured not only where he had gone wrong but that his entire Law of Numerical Relationships Theory was flawed right down to its boots.'

'So Chaucer's Riddle is a nonsense?' Matthias asked. 'But if so why didn't Griffen tell us? And if Wengler's such a genius how come he didn't figure out the same years ago?'

Sholto nodded. 'I think he did. I think he knew it the moment he started looking into it, which explains his lack of interest in why the sundial never appeared, but not why he still was keen on getting hold of the Astrolabe. But wait,' he said, 'I'm getting ahead of myself. Let me continue with Titius, because I think I've almost got it straight.'

He looked around him, everyone eager for him to go on.

'Well,' he continued, 'according to Titius's own narrative this is how it went. He chucked away his useless Law, which makes him a better man than many, but now he was in the Round Tower, working with his old pupil who had risen to the heights, and the two of them began to collaborate, supplying the missing parts of each other's work, spurring each other on, collaborating to the point where they both utterly superseded anything they'd done as individuals. And, if we're to take Titius at his word, then they stumbled across evidence for a theory that is truly mind-shifting, the scientific leap Jed mentioned before. But forget discovering a couple of insignificant planets. That was nothing. Nothing at all. What their joint studies strongly suggested to them was that light, speed and mass are all intricately connected. I can't begin to grasp it, but they were convinced they'd discovered the means to prove that the universe is expanding from a single point of creation, and that it is expanding still, *moving and breathing*, is how Titius puts it.'

'Wengler said something like that in the barn,' Jed said softly, awed, amazed, having difficulty getting his head around what Sholto was saying. 'He was on about time and the universe, how we'd soon be able to look right back to the beginning of it, and the end… I thought he was just rambling…'

'Now hang on a just a minute,' Brogar interrupted, emphatically knocking the front two legs of his chair onto the floor slabs with a hard clack. 'If they'd discovered something so world-shattering why didn't they just publish what they'd found? Why go to the ridiculously complicated lengths of scribbling notes in books and creating sundials? What the hell was the point in that?'

'The point was this,' Sholto replied a little sadly, 'that by then Titius was an old man and very ill, and his greatest friend and colleague about to leave his profession and Titius's life to return to his homeland to become, of all things, a monk.'

Oswald shook his head, remembering his small revelation in the graveyard at Ockle.

'Not such a great change,' he said, 'going from one profession to the other. All that looking up at the stars, all that wondering about how perfectly the universe seems to have been put together, how predictable its hidden parts if only you know where to look. It would make anyone consider the possibility there is a greater hand behind it.'

'And it takes forever to get a paper published,' Jed was more pragmatic. 'I've known people wait years to get anywhere near it, and that's with all our modern communications...'

'So, a hundred years ago, or thereabouts,' Brogar put in, finally getting it, elbows on the table, playing his fingers against his cheeks as if on a hurdy gurdy. 'If I was Titius, given that I've already had a load of intellectuals sneering at my back for decades and that my work has been laughed at from Milan to Minsk, I'd be thinking that even if someone accepted my work for publication - and that's a big if, Bedrossian or no - the likelihood of it is that I'll be dead by the time it's disseminated... So what would I do?'

'He would get David to help him,' Jed put in quickly, getting the drift, 'the same person who'd risen high and got him into the Round Tower in the first place, the only person who'd ever stuck by him...'

'And a person who knew sundials intimately,' Sholto confirmed, glancing over at Brogar, who tilted his head.

Your show, not mine, that tilt said, Sholto appreciating it and going on.

'And so instead of trying to get his *magnum opus* into print,' Sholto said, 'Titius chooses another way, and David - who's no interest anymore in making a name for himself in astronomy or anything else associated with it, given his newly discovered vocation - helps him, and together they take a calculated gamble on the future. They design an instrument – the sundial, to encode all their equations, and the ring that can slot into it, turn a few turns to show how it can all be uncoded again; then they point a path to it by scribbling suggestive notes in Titius's copy of Chaucer's Astrolabe – maybe other books too, for all we know – book or books placed on some anonymous shelf in the Round Tower, waiting for someone to uncover its secrets, make them both stars in the universe, cocking the biggest snook they can at their detractors. Going out with a bang. And it's all here in the preface to this little book, and I've no doubt the Armenian text will give the exact details of the sundial's construction and interpretation, judging by the illustrations, some of which, by the way, are very similar to Simmy's, right down to the lists of words in all their twelve languages, another cocking of the snook, given that the Round Tower is famous for having a plaque prominent on its outer wall about its higher purposes and goals, written in the same twelve languages.'

'So how did Wengler figure all this out?' Oswald asked, brows creased.

'Same way I did,' Sholto said, 'from this book. Places like the Round Tower sell off batches of outdated or unwanted volumes all the time. He maybe even got it when he purchased the sundial, not that we'll ever know for certain, nor if he knew it straightaway for what it was, though that I rather doubt.'

'Not unless Wengler tells us,' Matthias put in. 'And surely he could.'

'But he won't,' Brogar said flatly. 'Doubt he'll say anything to any of us ever again.'

Sholto shrugged his agreement. The man had started speaking ancient Greek at his trial, for God's sake, so there wasn't much chance of him opening up any time soon.

'What I don't understand,' said Matthias, 'is how Titius and Bedrossian could be assured that anyone would ever work any of it out. Where's the benefit to either of them in this? Even if someone found their hints to their work how could they be sure someone wouldn't just pinch it and take it for their own?'

'Because they would have started rumours,' Brogar supplied happily, wishing he'd been in on the plot at its inception, sitting around the table with Titius and Bedrossian, drinking a few glasses of wine while they got the mechanics of it sorted. 'The two of them were done, Titius on his last legs, Bedrossian off to his monastery. All that stuff about Chaucer's Riddle you and Griffen kept banging on about, Jed?' Jed reddened, Brogar went on regardless. 'Sholto always knew it was nonsense.'

Sholto looked at Brogar in surprise, for he'd never said it as such, but Sholto's turn now to nod Brogar on.

'Well,' Brogar did not disappoint, 'this is how I'd've done it. I'd've left a few copies of my little Armenian book scattered randomly about the Round Tower library, and I'd also plant a few letters suggesting that not only had I got over my Numerical Law big style but had moved on to something far more important, discovered a new law that so far eclipsed the old they'd need to get their canters on if the other scholars there wanted anywhere near it. And I'd've dropped in here and there that the lot of them were dullards of the first order to dismiss me because I'd got one tiny thing wrong. I'd've salted the wound by telling them it was all there in the library, if only they could find it, figure out the puzzle. I'd give it a good name - and Chaucer's Riddle is a good one - hint at my great discovery without giving too many details, not all at once, maybe scatter it throughout the letters so it took time to put together; but I'd also make clear that the true origins of the work lay with me and Bedrossian and proof of it in our little book, published and

BURNING SECRETS

dated and not only one copy but several, so that no one could take our claim when they put all the pieces together. At least,' Brogar finished up, grinning broadly, 'that's what I'd've done.'

Sholto's turn to smile and speak.

'I think that's exactly what happened,' he said. 'Bedrossian designs the sundial and ring and gets them made, leaves them with the Round Tower when he goes back to Armenia, organises a small print run of the book that contains all those construction details and workings out; Titius scribbles in the margins of his Astrolabe, writes a few letters, slips them between the pages of various books that might occasionally be consulted, knowing that someday either books or letters will be found, and enough back-ups here and there to make sure it will be he and Bedrossian who are finally vindicated and lauded, and not anyone else who figures out their puzzle first. They throw their conundrum into the mathematical community, set the bait, salt the trail.'

'Speaking of salt,' Brogar said loudly, lifting his head, twitching his nose. 'I'm absolutely starving. Any hope of food any time soon?'

CHAPTER 46

REVELATION, DISAPPOINTMENT, AND GENEROSITY

'Let's get to it, boys,' Orla said, Gilligan and Hugh leaping to their feet, Gilligan's stomach gurgling loudly as he did so. They'd been listening to the conversation but also watching Orla, fascinated by the economy with which she moved: checking on this, doing that; cooking anything more than a few skillet scones an unknown art.

'Righto,' Hugh said merrily, getting the warm bowls from beside the cooking fire, Gilligan snatching cutlery from drawers, Orla opening the door to the stove below the fire, filling the room with smells that had the lot of them salivating.

'My God, Orla,' Brogar growled with content, 'but that smells good.'

Orla allowed herself a small smile. She'd loved cooking for Malcolm and the boys when they'd been home and had forgotten how much she'd missed it – Dunstan and old Ma not much fussed, happy with a piece of fried fish and a drappit egg on top, a couple of boiled spuds at the side. The ease with which her body had fallen back into the rhythms of washing, chopping, separating and seasoning had been for her a simple delight and she beamed with pride as she brought out the large cooking dish and placed it on the table for all to see: at its centre a haunch of venison she'd found curing in Matthias's pantry, sizzling in the herbed butter she lathered over it that was laced through with juniper berries picked from the bushes out the back, the meat surrounded by magnificent heaps of golden roasted potatoes, neeps and onions still in their jackets so they broke open at the touch of a knife and melted into the gravy that was a generous flood about the dish's base.

'Oh, but you've excelled yourself!' Matthias exclaimed with quiet pride, loving this woman, astonished that this loving had come with such gentle ease. He didn't care at that moment about Titius and his sundial, didn't care what else was going to happen because of it, or what Jed was going to do, how long he would stay. For the now at least he had the family he'd so desired sitting right here about his table, Gilligan squashing in with Hugh, Orla standing at the top end, hands clasped in her pinafore before suddenly looking startled and moving away and then back again, this time with a hoggit of heather ale given her by Matthias's old housekeeper Elspeth, who'd been mighty glad to retire from her duties, would have done it years before if Matthias had ever had the sense to find a wife which possibly, maybe, he now had.

Θ

'We've still a bit to talk about,' Brogar said twenty minutes later, heaping the last of the tatties into his bowl without bothering to ask if anyone else wanted them, slicing more venison from the bone with his knife, slopping on the last of the gravy.

'Like what?' Oswald asked, letting out a long breath, leaning back in his chair not really caring, filled to bursting, wanting to glory in the moment.

'Like that I think we should move the sundial into the chapel,' Sholto said.

'I've already thought of that,' Oswald announced, to Sholto's surprise. 'It'll be shifted in tomorrow, with Harald's help, soon as me and Simmy get back to Ockle. And there it will remain.'

'Until someone comes to fetch it back to the Round Tower,' Sholto added, 'takes it home. And it will go home. I'm sorry, Simmy,' he added, but Simmy did not look regretful, nor felt it, was instead brimming full with everything the sundial might now be able to do.

'I've neglected to tell you all,' Sholto went on, 'that I've already sent out a letter to tell them the same, and several others besides, all gone with Andrew Fitzsimons and no way to bring them back.'

'What letters?' Jed asked – Jed accused, still convinced Wengler should have first shot, no matter what he'd done, especially now Chaucer's Riddle had turned into something huge and momentous, something that might change the face of cosmology for years to come.

'Open letters,' Sholto explained, swallowing a burp, for the meal really had been excellent, 'to three of the most widely disseminated scientific journals in Europe, stating all we knew then about the sundial. And I'll be sending off more letters tomorrow, now we've Bedrossian's book and Simmy and Aileen have worked out how the ring fits in to it. The sundial and ring will go back to Denmark, and every last inch of what Titius has been trying to tell the world for the past hundred years will finally come to light.'

'So it's done then,' Matthias stated. 'All done.'

'Done,' Sholto agreed, Jed sagging at the words. Forever a round hole in Wengler's monuments that was never to be filled.

'There is something else,' Brogar said, oblivious to the sad ambience that had descended on the room following Sholto's declaration, a collective feeling that all was at an end, but one that was neither as satisfying nor as tidy as it should have been. 'I almost forgot in all the hullabaloo about the wretched sundial,' he took one of his toothpicks out and ran it quickly between his front teeth before going on. 'I've found another sample of your Strontianite.'

The mood changed instantly, as if someone had clicked their fingers and turned all the lamps to full, a happy expectation replacing the gloom that slinked away into the corners where it belonged.

'Where? Where did you find it?' Jed shouted loudly, leaping to his feet, hardly able to keep still, wanting to see it and see it now, Matthias looking nervous, pushing his fork about his empty plate.

'Followed the moraine passage up from one of the workings,' Brogar said, taking his time, Sholto smiling quietly, aware he'd had his moment and this was Brogar's, all alone.

'Hugh,' Brogar said, 'would you fetch my satchel? It's just over there by the door.'

Such a casual statement, but even Orla was hanging on it, Hugh up like a startled hare, bringing Brogar's battered leather bag back in a moment, holding it out deferentially to its owner.

'No,' Brogar said, holding up his hands. 'Give it to Jed.'

'To me?' Jed was hardly able to think straight, to accept the largesse, everyone staring as Hugh obeyed and gave Jed the satchel, Jed's fingers quick at the buckles, reaching inside, lifting out what Brogar had put there that was barely the size of a small apple and yet responsible, if indirectly, for them all being here. Then he held up Brogar's sample for all to see, the white purity of it, the glisten of its stone, nothing like any of them had seen before.

'It's beautiful,' Jed whispered, 'and so different from what I expected. Are you sure?'

'I'll need to get it under the microscope, and I gather from Matthias you have rather a good one,' Brogar said, smiling broadly, 'but yes, Jed. I'm sure as I can be.'

Jed nodded slowly, studying Brogar's find, examining the soft bubble-like exterior, the strange lustre, feeling the coolness of it sitting on his palm.

'So I was looking for the wrong thing all along,' he said quietly, disappointment so evident he looked as if he was about to cry. 'Even if I'd found it I'd never have known…'

'Remember what I said before,' Brogar said, leaning in towards Jed, putting a hand on the lad's shoulder, 'everything changes depending on its circumstances, what's happened to it, where it has been and where it ends up. Strontia is one form, an oxide, and then there's Strontianite the mineral – and that can present differently too – and all has become Strontium the element, taking its place in the periodic table only formulated this very year by the Russian scientist Mendeleyev. Everything changes, Jed, including me and you and that lump of stone. And in the end that's all it is: a lump of stone. But however it was found and whoever found it, we've a whole lifetime ahead of us to discover what makes it what it is, what properties it possesses, what makes it unique, and you, my young friend, are going to take this sample back to London and discover them for yourself.'

Jed screwed up his eyes, rubbed his cheek with his hand.

'No,' he got the word out with difficulty, shaking his head. 'I've no right to it.'

'You've every right,' Brogar said, 'and I'll brook no argument. Nothing here for the Company. Certainly not enough for them to be concerned with, so we'll go on, Sholto and I, to where we're needed next, and so will you, and that's back home, taking this Strontianite with you.'

CHAPTER 47

DECISIONS

Gustav Wengler, of unsound mind or not, was tipped without ceremony from his cart of soldiers into Hesketh's care. It was late, the afternoon darkening, the soldiers eager to rid themselves of their burden.

'Been talking nonsense all the while we brought him up from Fort William,' said the captain, 'and if truth be told we're all dog tired with the travelling and listening to him jabbering on and on. Here,' he said, taking out a purse of coins and throwing it into Hesketh's boat.

'So why not,' he added, 'do the world a favour and chuck him into the water while you've the chance? No one will think the worse of you if you do. Quite the opposite.'

The captain shuffled his feet. He didn't know the entire ins and outs of the trials of either Dunstan Pirie or Gustav Wengler but knew enough, and thought it a bad hand justice was playing to condemn the one to the firing squad and the other to permanent house arrest, even if that house arrest amounted to solitary confinement on an island out in the middle of the Sunart Sound.

Hesketh Wood said nothing. He took the purse and pocketed it, nodding to the captain as he undid the rope holding the boat to the pier.

'Want a couple of us over with you?' the captain asked. 'Make sure it's all done proper, and no harm to yourself?'

Hesketh did not reply, merely shoved at the pier and steered himself, his ferry and the bundle of Gustav Wengler out into the black water that separated them from the dark island of Havengore.

'No worries,' Hesketh said as he pulled at his oars. 'I'll see him right.'

And then he was away, the only trace a small wake of white water where Hesketh's oars broke the surface as he went on out, the captain taking off his cap and raising his face to the softly falling snow, glad all was done, glad he wouldn't have to witness another departure of the damned into darkness, glad the snow was so clean and pure and white, more glad still that he and his men had done their duty and could now rest. What the ferryman chose to do with Gustav Wengler when he was out of sight and out of mind was no concern of his.

Θ

They were halfway between the shore and Havengore when Gustav began to uncurl himself from the bows of Hesketh's boat, peeking over its sides as if afraid of what he might see.

'Are you taking me home now?' Gustav whispered.

'I am,' Hesketh said, speaking in rhythm with his oars. 'Can you not see your White Cathedral?'

Gustav gazed into the darkness. The snow was falling, but only sporadically, making everything it touched faintly luminous, the white marble of his monuments reflecting the tiny hint of light given by the white flakes as they went.

'Is that what you call it? I'd no idea. But yes,' he said, 'I can,' and uncurled a little more, pushed himself into a sitting position, though still hunkered down in the bows.

'And your home? Can you see that too?' Hesketh asked as he pulled them several more yards towards the island, almost within spitting distance now, Hesketh glancing over his shoulder, making out the hunch of Wengler's house, the black isolation of it, the marble monuments beyond. He'd done this run a hundred times, and in worse conditions than this, knew he didn't have much time and that he'd have to make a decision soon.

'But there it is,' Wengler said. 'I wasn't sure I'd ever see it again.'

Hesketh nodded into the falling darkness, aware of the snowflakes falling on his face, on his hands as he went at the oars going in, going out, like he was breathing with them, at one with the water.

Do the world a favour and chuck him into the Sound; no one will think the worse of you if you do.

'Do you know why you were detained down in Fort William, Mr Wengler?' Hesketh asked. He hadn't meant to, it just spilled out of him like wax from a burning candle.

'They say I killed a man,' Wengler said slowly, 'and tried to kill a girl, and I suppose I did. I can see them both, like boulders in my way.'

'Do you remember why?' Hesketh asked, pulling at his oars, pulling at every fibre of his conscience, trying to find this strange man as innocent as the court had, if only by reason of his insanity, or his genius, or whatever else they wanted to call it. Not much time left to do as the captain had suggested and Hesketh was still thinking about that, his oars twitching beneath his hands. He could feel the water changing, the slack giving way to the inrush of an incoming tide and not long left to make his decision.

'You need to tell me,' Hesketh said, keeping his voice safe and quiet, pulling in his oars, letting the boat ride on the incoming tide.

Now or never, Hesketh thought. *Now or never.*

Θ

'You really are the most remarkable man,' Sholto said to Brogar as they bedded themselves down for the night in Matthias's barn.

'How so?' Brogar asked, not much interested.

'Because you're going to let Jed take the claim for finding that sample of Strontianite for one. So where does that leave us? What am I supposed to put in my report?'

Brogar shrugged, pluffing up the pillow Orla had insisted he take, wondering whether or not to chuck it to the ground and use his battered old satchel instead, as he usually did.

'Because it'll do us no good,' Brogar said, 'but will shove Jed in the right direction and bring the right people here.'

'And the Company are not the right people?' Sholto asked mildly, Brogar shaking his head.

'You know as well as I do that if they find a use for it they'll rip this place pluck from pluck for more of the stuff. Maybe even strong-arm Matthias into shutting down the mines on the chance of it, bring in their own men, hang the rest out to dry. Not if I can bloody help it.'

Sholto smiled. The lamp hanging from the hook above their heads glimmered softly as he looked over at his companion.

'It's just you care so much about people,' Sholto said. 'I don't know how you do it.'

'Pah!' Brogar snorted, deciding against the pillow, shoving it to the floor, settling himself easily on his straw-bale bed, familiar battered satchel comfortable beneath his head. 'Not sure about that, Sholto. Don't think caring comes into it; it's more that I've been in this game a long time, seen what can happen to places unprepared. Remember that tiger I talked about before?'

Sholto closed his eyes because of course he did, wasn't sure how he was ever going to rid himself of the images Brogar had put inside his head.

'Yes,' he said, and nothing more.

'Well it's just like that,' Brogar tried to explain. 'We live pretty well, you and me, and those Company directors live far better. Never have to see what folk really go through when the Company stomp themselves into a place, no idea what it does to people there who are only just getting by, and them with no idea how long the Company's bonanza is going to last. And all this Wengler stuff? It's trimmings. It's what people do when they've time on their hands. Strip all that away and we're nothing more than animals fighting for our patch when sometimes we're not the strongest, nor the best.'

Sholto didn't reply. He wasn't sure he agreed. He thought on all the huge leaps the human animal – to put it in Brogar's terms – had made: all the literature, the philosophy, the science, all the amazing buildings people had been building for thousands of years, the implications of what Titius and Bedrossian might or might not have discovered only hitting him fully now, wondering how those words on the sundial fitted together: velocity, infinity, light and mass… that if the universe truly was expanding then it most likely had come from a single point, a single moment of creation; and, more worryingly, presumably it would either go on until it was so far spaced not a single grain or speck of dust would be within a hundred miles of each other, or maybe it would reach a point when it could go no further and just collapsed back in on itself, when everything, absolutely everything – time, space, books, tigers, forests, seas, this planet and every other planet, would be reduced to nothing. The thought was giving him indigestion.

Brogar wasn't bothered about such wild imaginings, was now asleep, breathing soundly, happy in his world of black and white, of being certain, of taking decisions, of being the kind of man who could look a tiger in the eye and give it a damn good fight, if it ever came down to it. Not so Sholto, and not so Hesketh Wood, who was even now laying out in the Sound, hoping he'd done the right and proper thing.

⊖

The snow was beautiful, the night so absolutely perfect. Hesketh could see a half-penny moon up beyond the snow clouds, and the outlines of the White Cathedral in front of him as he rowed his empty boat back to shore, the water below him swirling, the captain's voice loud in his head.

Dear Christ, he hoped he'd done the right thing.

⊖

'He hasn't changed his mind?' Jed asked Sholto the moment Sholto was up and out from the barn the following morning, sluicing his face with ice cold water from the pump, wondering how long Jed had been standing centurion-like at their door, waiting for one of them to appear.

'Brogar never changes his mind,' Sholto said, shaking his head, enjoying the shock of the freezing water on skin and scalp.

'It's just it seems so generous,' Jed skittered at the edge of Sholto's vision. 'I mean he could make his name by this, it doesn't seem right...'

Sholto rubbed his face with his hands to rid it of the last few drops, stretched his jaw, eased his neck upon his shoulders, thinking back on his conversation with Brogar the night before, only now understanding.

'He's already made his name a hundred times over,' Sholto said, 'but not in the way normal people want or expect. And he'll go on doing it, long as he's breath in his body.'

Jed nodded, sort of understanding.

'But will he show me where he found the Strontianite, and how?'

Sholto poured a little mint and charcoal mix on his finger, rubbing vigorously with it at his teeth before speaking again, aware that Gilligan and Hugh had come out of Matthias's stable, the place they'd chosen to spend their nights, as they'd done at Solveig's.

'He'll teach you as much and as deeply as he's able,' Sholto said. 'But we may not have much time. Soon as the Company gets my report we'll be off again. And now they've an office in Edinburgh that mayn't be long.'

'But you ain't written up any report yet, right?' Gilligan asked, sticking his head under the pump as Hugh pushed down its arm.

'And maybe I'm not fixed enough to travel,' Hugh piped up. 'I'm not sure I should be moved for at least another few weeks.'

'Well you've the right of it there, young man,' said Orla, coming out of the house brandishing her water jug, Matthias at her side as if he never wanted to leave. 'In fact,' she added, with a huge smile on her face, 'I absolutely forbid it, as I will be happy to state in writing if anyone – your Company, Sholto, for example – requires it. Three weeks exactly, that's what you'll need. If three weeks is enough?'

'Three weeks will do just fine,' Brogar's voice was gruff and filled with sleep as he stepped out of the barn, striding towards the merry group, slapping Matthias hard on the shoulder. 'And if Matthias can get himself together then we might even squeeze in another wedding asides from Harald and Aileen's. Gotta love the feasting that goes with them.'

He winked broadly at Orla who blinked but did not blush, instead looked over at Matthias, Matthias giving a slight nod in return because he'd already asked Orla the night before and Orla had agreed, only Malcolm's stamp on the divorce being required and that, Matthias knew, would be the easiest part, given what he'd discovered about Malcolm's doings and the new wife he'd already acquired up at Wick.

'I can't think,' Matthias said softly, recovering his balance after Brogar's hearty greeting, 'of anything I'd like better, nor people I'd rather have around me when we do. Thank you both. Thank you.'

'Oh for Heaven's sake,' Brogar blundered through the crowd and shoved his head under the pump, shaking himself like a bear, water droplets cascading over the lot of them like wet confetti.

'Just doing it to hide his tears,' Sholto said, taking a step backwards, thinking how glorious was the day, and how many more glorious days there would be yet to come; the adventure, he was thinking, only just begun.

CHAPTER 48

NARROW TRACKS, WIDE WORLDS

Hesketh was sitting at that moment on his stone bench gazing over towards Havengore, glad to be home, glad for the decision he'd made the night before, believing his decision had been right. He could imagine Gustav Wengler sitting on his stool in the middle of his room, surrounded by all his books and blackboards, as lonely as he'd always been, no hope of it ever being otherwise. Enough of a sentence for Hesketh. Let other men execute the executioners, but he would not be one of them, not with all he knew, not with what Wengler had said to him out there in the dark night of the Sound after the soldiers had given him their words.

'I know what I did, Mr Wood. And I know you don't believe I'm capable of regret, but I am.'

Wengler had resurrected himself from the bottom of Hesketh's boat, seemingly brought alive again by the snow and the scents of salt and seaweed in the air, after almost a month's close captivity at Fort William.

'And I do regret it,' Wengler went on. 'All of it. From Archie onwards. It's the nature of obsession. It pulls you in and keeps you there, makes everything outside seem irrelevant, as if it isn't real.

But I know what I did was real now I'm back here in the middle of the Sunart, in the middle of the sea, just like my island is. It's my life, Mr Wood, so much a part of me I can't function properly without it. And if you choose to throw me in and have done then I'll not resist, for I'm not so self-serving I don't know it's what I deserve.'

And there it was, all Hesketh needed to hear. Gustav Wengler might not be like other men but neither more was Hesketh. He'd seen inside Wengler that night he'd stayed with him, understanding he was not the soulless, uncaring person others took him to be; just a man trapped within his own world, everything extraneous traded off so he could stay within it; a bargain struck somewhere way back down the line that was not exactly a bargain for Wengler patently had no choice in the matter. Set on the narrowest of paths because he could see no other. No forks in that path, no deviations, just on and on and on, and now on and on and on again, all on his own.

Stars above sky above Hesketh Wood, and how many there had been up there the night before, understanding then as now what it was to be part of something vast and wide and deep that had no care of him or anyone else; just like going out on the Sound every day, knowing that it did what it did and, if he got in its way, that would be the end of him. Him and Wengler not so different after all. He leaned back against the wall of his hut and closed his eyes, felt the breathing of the universe overtake him as he listened to the soft sucking of the waves going up and down the shingle. Only a small movement, not like on vast sandy beaches where the draw of the tide was huge, but enough to pull him in, make him a part of it, everything changing with every breath he took, every grain of sand moving with every small wave, shifting and settling, maybe here, maybe there.

The way of the world, and whatever came next, well, let it come was Hesketh's thinking; the exact same sentiment Brogar Finn had later that morning when he spread his arms wide above the Galena Ore Mines of Strontian after showing Jed where he'd found the mineral they'd both come in search of.

'I love my life!' Brogar shouted exuberantly to anyone or anything in earshot. 'And I want more of it, so come on world! Bring it on!'

And bring it on it did.

HISTORICAL NOTE

The history I've put in about the Galena Ore Mines and the discovery of the mineral Strontianite is based in fact, though later discoveries of the same element – Strontium – have been found since. For more information try this website:

http://www.mindat.org/min-3805.html

The details of the Floating Chapel too are as stated, though I've slightly altered the time-line by a couple of years.

The true dimensions of Ockle, Corran, Strontian and the Ardnamurchan Peninsula have been changed somewhat to allow for the plot to flow and not make travelling times too tediously long, and I hope I will be forgiven such changes and discrepancies by the folk who actually live there.

Titius and Bode are real people, as is the Law of Numerical Relationships; and Chaucer's Astrolabe is as described though the Riddle is a fabrication.

The information about Tycho Brahe and Havengore is correct; and I got the details of the astronomical buildings at Jaipur from a hugely interesting article by Peter Engel: Stairways to Heaven, *Natural History June 1993*. In fact, Jai Singh sent emissaries to centres of learning to bring back the most accurate astronomical instruments of the day, including a nineteen-foot quadrant designed by Brahe, and he studied Brahe's work with great interest. He built five of these massive stone observatories, Jaipur being the largest and containing fourteen instruments to measure time and celestial phenomena. They are regarded as amongst the greatest buildings in the world. The smaller of the two massive stone sundials there can tell the time to an accuracy of twenty seconds, and the larger one, the Samrat Yantra or Great Instrument has, as Engels tells us: 'a stone triangle nearly 90 feet tall and 150 feet long. As the sun arcs across the sky, the giant triangle casts a shadow on one of the two marble quadrants rising from its sides. Because of the instrument's enormous size, the shadow moves at the rapid pace of about two millimetres a second. This means the Samrat Yantra can measure the time of day to within two seconds.'

And that is truly extraordinary.

Legacy of the Lynx

Pbk, £8.99, ISBN 978-1911331445

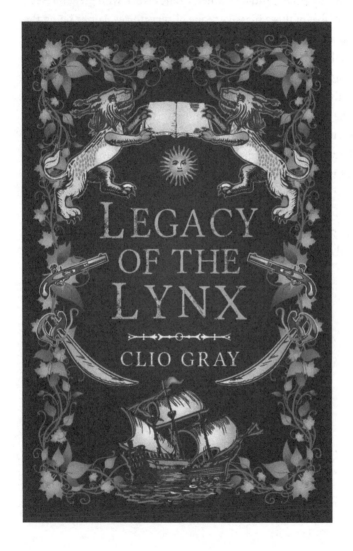

1798. Three people, two brutal murders, and a single promise... Golo Eck is searching for the fabled lost library of The Lynx, Europe's first scientific society, founded in 1603. Fergus, his friend and fellow adventurer, is on the trail of the legend in Ireland when he becomes embroiled in the uprising of the United Irish against English rule. His only hope of escape is Greta, a courageous messenger for the United Irish cause. Following the bloody battles of New Ross and Vinegar Hill, Fergus is missing, and Greta is on the run. Golo meanwhile suspects other forces are on the trail of the Lynx, and he heads to Holland in pursuit. When Golo's ship founders and he disappears, his ward Ruan is left to fend for himself, a stranger in a strange land. Can Ruan pursue the trail to the lost library? Will Golo and Fergus be found? Can Greta escape Ireland with her very life? And will the truth of the Legacy of the Lynx finally be revealed? Award winning writer Clio Gray has written a thrilling adventure story, steeped in historical fact and legend, that will keep readers gripped to the very last page.

Clio was born in Yorkshire, spent her later childhood in Devon before returning to Yorkshire to go to university. For the last twenty-five years she has lived in the Scottish Highlands where she intends to remain. She eschewed the usual route of marriage, mortgage, children, and instead spent her working life in libraries, filling her home with books and sharing that home with dogs. She began writing for personal amusement in the late nineties, then began entering short story competitions, getting short listed and then winning, which led directly to a publication deal with Headline. Her latest book, The Anatomist's Dream, was nominated for the Man Booker 2015 and long listed for the Bailey's Prize in 2016.

'Surprisingly,' Gray says, 'The Anatomist's Dream - although my eighth published novel - was amongst the first few stabs I made at writing a book. Pretty appalling in its first incarnation (not that I thought it at the time!) it was only when I brushed the dust off it a few years ago that I realised there really was something interesting and unusual at its core that I could now, as a more experienced writer, work with. The moral being: don't give up. The more you write, the more self-critical you become and the better your writing will be because of it.'

Clio has always been encouraging towards emergent writers, and founded HISSAC (The Highlands and Islands Short Story Association) in 2004 precisely to further that aim, providing feedback on short listed stories and mentoring first time novelists, not a few of whom have gone on to be published themselves.

'It's been a great privilege to work with aspiring writers, to see them develop and flourish,' Gray says. 'There can never be too many books in the world, and the better the books the better place the world will be.'